LIFE IN STITCHES

Life In Stitches

C.K. Simms

CKS PUBLISHING

A note from the author:

Fifteen years, I have sat on this manuscript, immobilized by fear. A few half attempts to put it out and break free of my insecurities and a quick withdrawal as my anxiety bested me. A lesson learned: If you want to do something, just do it. Don't wait! If it doesn't work, do it again. This book is interlaced with this message: a dream I aspired to in 2008, a belief I live by in 2024. Every chapter you will read has flecks of me dispersed among the characters and the events.

As I read it now, it is a story that is cute, fun, adventurous, and leaves me with that feel-good feeling when you watch someone beat the odds. It's a book that sort of reads like a movie. That's how almost everything plays out in my mind: thoughts, worries, and dreams. Thank you for picking up this book and reading this far. If you choose to continue, you can rest assured you will not find the finest work of literary fiction, but this book intends to elicit a feeling. I am a storyteller, not a writer. There is a distinction! I hope this book conveys inspiration above all else: To carve your own path and settle for nothing less than what you want most. When you finish this novel, I hope it gives you a sense of closure that you, too, can achieve anything you desire.

Best,

C.K.

Dedication

I dedicate this book to anyone who has had a dream and has been told they would never make it or to get their head out of the clouds: Do it anyway! Also, to anyone who has wished they were something different or something more, their hearts burning with a desire to be something better than they are today. It is not too late to start right now!

Prologue

Bonita Smith was a chubby "Plain Jane." She was a poor girl from Bay Roberts, Newfoundland, and all she ever wanted was to be a top New York fashion designer. Living in a small, isolated town and being the daughter of a local Pentecostal preacher was an obstacle that led to fulfilling her dreams.

Growing up, Bonita lived in a less-than-adequate house, attended a run-down school, and lived what she felt was a miserable and hideous life. Although it seemed she would never wiggle away from the hold that life had on her, she believed deep down inside that one day she would break free of her inescapable prison and finally get a chance at owning the high fashion runways.

The only problem was she had to get through today to do it.

1

The sun shone brightly into the room that morning, casting rays of warmth that pierced the never-settling dust. Although picturesque, it prevented the girl from lying lazily in bed to sustain her much-needed sleep. She tossed and turned to avoid the glaring light that blinded her weary eyes, but there was no escape. Finally, a friendly and kind-hearted cloud passed over the sun, weakening its rays and darkening the room to a comfortable shade. With a sigh of relief, she turned on her side and settled back into the nicely worn indentation of her bed. Happy and content, she slowly drifted away, falling into a glorious place, when a loud and consistent beep brought her right back into the land of the living.

"Damn alarm. Give me a fucking break", Bonita yelled, realizing that it was time to get up. It bothered her because she knew what she'd endure in the day ahead.

Today would be considered a milestone in most girls' lives, but not for eighteen-year-old Bonita Smith. It would also be a milestone in her life, except she just wished it would come and go without facing it. It was the final day of school, encompassing the graduation ceremony, the day that teenagers got to hand in their juvenile ways and embrace adulthood. Everyone would gather at the local church and walk up in front of their classmates and the rest of the town to accept their diplomas. She had longed for this day all her life, but the actual event was something she could do without. Bonita was the most brilliant girl in her class — the town geek, as most would put it — and was selected as this year's graduating class valedictorian.

"I could call in sick, pretend to have a rare and contagious virus," she thought as she slowly maneuvered herself out of bed.

The floor felt cold and almost unreal when her feet gently touched the faded ancient hardwood. This made it easier for her to become alive and alert. She had been up all night working on her speech and figuring out what to say. She pondered things like, "Well, I never thought it would happen, but here we are. Finally, I am getting the hell out of this hole," or "It's been great growing up with all you losers." Although it would please her to no end, she knew she would not have the guts to say things like that, and besides, she really couldn't voice any of this stuff; her father would kill her.

No, she had to reach deep down inside herself to find a few phony, heartfelt, and uplifting words that would encourage the rest of the class to go forth and live out their dreams. The truth is, she didn't care about the rest of her class or what their fantasies might be. In fact, she secretly wished they would all die in some freak accident. Although she might seem to be a hateful and heartless girl, Bonita wasn't a mean-hearted person, just a young lady who spent her life being harassed and picked on for being a dirt-poor nerd. She didn't own nice clothes, wear makeup, or do her hair, and she was forced to wear coke-bottle glasses just to see 6 inches in front of her face. Deep down inside, underneath years of emotional scarring and persecution, there lived a great big ball of sugar and love just waiting to get out.

"But not here. Definitely not here," Bonita thought.

So here she was, a few days before she would leave this place behind for good and embark on a new life, career, and identity. She had finished showering and was getting dressed; her mother had already removed her cap and robe and laid it on the chair next to the door. She picked it up and walked out of the room, only to immediately walk back and grab a piece of paper off her dresser.

"Can't forget this. Don't want to be a bumbling idiot on the biggest day of my life," she said with sarcasm. As she walked down the stairs, she stopped and stared into space for a few seconds, and a smile formed from ear to ear.

2

The ceremony was quite lovely and well pulled off. All the students looked magnificent in their robes, and the church pews were filled with ecclesiastical mothers and fathers who were attentive and proud of their children. The students displayed a barrage of facial expressions that colored the church foyer, vexatious and dolorous looks that contrasted their gowns' beautiful reds and whites. The church was warm, and the air was stagnant, as most churches typically are, but today, another smell made most students feel ill. It was the smell of fear, sad realizations, and uncertainty. Together, they create a most unbearable stench that can sometimes make even the strongest hearts fall to its repugnant power.

Bonita was not spared these feelings. Even though she had direction and definitive plans for setting herself into motion, she also exuded the smell of fear, just like everyone else. They were beginning to walk the walk and accept their diplomas, and Bonita wanted to run. It wasn't because of her disdain for the ceremony but from the butterflies in her stomach mutating into angry hawks looking for their next feeding. Her palms had begun to sweat, and her forehead was as if someone poured a bucket of water over her. How could she get up there and deliver a commendable speech when she felt the floor would fall from beneath her?

The music began to play, and the first in line stepped towards the altar. Bonita sensed tension and nervousness in the air. Standing silently, eyes fixed on the floor, she waited until the feet in front of her began to move. She then held her head as high as possible and worked on pulling herself together.

Luckily, she had entirely composed herself when she accepted her diploma and walked to the mic to deliver her speech. She felt tired and worn out and wanted to crawl under the stand and fall asleep, but she could not. Instead, she pulled her notes from under her robe and laid them flat before her. She cleared her throat and began to speak.

"Ladies and gentlemen, mothers, fathers, and fellow students. I stand here today as a memory of years that have passed. It has been a long and eventful journey for all of us, and today symbolizes the first day of the beginning of the rest of our lives. Today, we relinquish our juvenile ways, hang up our caps, and step into the shoes of adulthood. Today is a notch in our ever-changing compass and the beginning of yet another long journey to live out our lives and fulfill our dreams. Some of us have known for a while what our next step in life will be, and for those, we wish greatness and prosperity and that each step may be blessed by the love of your families and friends. Some of us do not know our next steps, and for those, may your decisions be made from your hearts and then your minds. May each choice be prayed upon and carefully selected and may your every step be blessed by the love of your families and friends. Only by the love and support of our closest that we have made it here, and only by the lessons you have taught and the knowledge you have given are we equipped with what is needed to succeed."

The eyes of many people in the church that day had already begun to fill with tears. Students and teachers, mothers and fathers were clinging to tissues, and even the boys in the graduating class were welling up with emotion as Bonita spoke.

"I would like to thank our teachers, who have guided us through academic and educational trials, for we are eternally grateful for your patience and the gifts you used every day when you bestowed upon us your wisdom. I would like to thank the parents for the encouragement and the love you have given. I thank the church for its constant use for school programs and events; our school is small, but your hearts are bigger."

"I conclude by saying it has been my privilege to stand here today and give this speech. I hope that each of you lives a safe and happy life and that you will be blessed in abundance, over and over. Ladies and gentlemen, mothers and fathers, please join me in celebrating the graduating class of 2004!"

The crowd all stood and clapped. The students now had smiles on their faces and excitement in their eyes. It was over. Feeling like she could breathe again, Bonita walked off the altar. She led the graduates down the center walkway toward the foyer in their last march. Conversations could be heard throughout the building; people fussing over their children, and mothers still crying. When they filled the lobby, and Bonita turned around, the class stood looking at her, and they all clapped.

"Amazing speech, Bonita, that was beautiful!" said one girl who had never spoken to Bonita.

"Yeah, that was amazing, Bonita. You did a great job!" said another person, who always picked on her in school.

"Why are all these people acting nicely to me?" she thought. Could they have given up their juvenile ways and embraced her as a peer rather than an outcast? She became overwhelmed by all the attention. She was not used to people congratulating her or even speaking to her, for that matter. One guy even shook her hand and told her she had a very touching speech. He thought it was stellar, and that guy only talked to girls who were sluts. There were plenty of whores in the foyer that day; why would he speak to her? She could not grasp what was happening and needed to remove herself from the situation. She waved at the crowd, turned on her heel, and walked out.

Later that evening, she received a few phone calls from people in her school asking her to come to a couple of parties. She nearly fell to the floor. No one had ever called her house before, and no one had ever asked her to a party. The graduation ceremony was over; school was done now. For the next two weeks, there would be parties galore, and Bonita had no time for them. She would be leaving in a few days and turned down all the requests for her presence that came in over the weekend. She had some work left to do and needed all the time she could get.

3

Bonita had a plan and had already put it into action. Since grade ten, Bonita knew what she wanted to do with her life, and she knew just what she had to do to make it happen. Bonita applied to a top fashion school in New York and had been approved for student financing. She would only have a little money except tuition, books, and supplies. Knowing this, Bonita had to figure out ways of making money over the following two years before leaving for the big city. Bonita took odd jobs whenever she could, babysat for people in the church, and did work at the church for which her father paid her. Over those two years, she saved a colossal amount of money. This would ensure her longevity in New York.

Bonita had been working on this for so long that she had found a place to live in the city almost six months before her moving date. She had every detail worked out and every one of her courses memorized. She even knew the transit system guide from front to back. She had been fully packed for over a month with all her best clothes, which looked like a bargain basket from your local thrift store. Her plane ticket was purchased: a window seat. She felt she should have the best view if she was about to fly for the first time.

Her parents, who had always supported Bonita, were less on board than Bonita would have liked them to be. Her father, the local minister at the Pentecostal church from which she graduated, didn't feel Bonita should go off to live in a city filled with as much sin as the Big Apple. In fact, her parents were totally against her moving there but felt they could not stop her from making this decision. It did not change that neither of them thought New York was a good place for a little Christian girl to live. Her parents didn't know their little girl was not Christian, and she was more than ready for the big city.

4

It was Wednesday morning, and Bonita had been up since before dawn. She had already brought all her luggage down to the front door. She tidied her room and left a note on her pillow for her mother, who she knew would come into her room after she departed to cry. The letter was simple and to the point. It read,

"Mom, I know you are already missing me, but please understand that this is something I have been waiting all my life. I will be careful and check in regularly to let you know I'm okay. I will fly you down as a VIP guest for my first fashion show. Please stop crying, and I love you."

The ride to St. John's was long and uncomfortable; her father was steadily preaching to her since they left the driveway. They pulled into the parking lot at the airport, and as the car pulled to a stop, her father looked at her with a strange look on his face. She thought he was going to really drill her with the *"No matter how far you think you get away from God, honey, you are always just a prayer away"* routine, but what he said she wasn't ready for, and as he spoke she could feel streams of emotion fall down her face.

"I knows you're gonna do grand in New York, and when you're a big shot in the fashion world, don't forget who's got the true love for ya. I'm mighty proud of ya, Bonbon."

Her eyes were turning red by now and streaking her face with tears. She tried hard to keep her composure, but she couldn't stop it. Her father called her "Bonbon"; he hadn't done that for years. The one thing that she was fighting against for the last 6 weeks was her fear. She feared that she would fail in New York, and the only thing that made her get past that fear was her father's constant disapproval of her dreams. It reinforced her sense of rebellion and motivated her to prove him wrong. Now that that was gone, she was feeling terrified, fighting the tears and desperately trying to find the best thing to say, but she could not.

Just when she thought it couldn't get worse, her father did the unthinkable, the most awful thing he could ever do. He put his arm around her and kissed her forehead. That was it. She couldn't take it anymore, and her body began to convulse uncontrollably.

"Aw, me ducky, what's got ya troubled? Why's the water-works? Ya ought to be over the moon and thrilled you're off to New York to chase your dreams." he said.

"I know, Daddy, but I'm scared," she said, looking up at him with big wet green eyes.

"You? Scared? Now, that don't sound like me Bonbon; me Bonbon ain't scared of nothin'; she's tough as nails, on her own two feet, and grins at fear like it's a bit of a joke! Who are ya, and what've ya done with me little one?" He gently chuckled and tugged on her hair as she mumbled through the tears, "I'm not your little one anymore, Daddy, and I am scared. I don't want to fail. I have to succeed."

"You'll always be my little one, and you will succeed," he said, stopping her when she tried to rebut. This was a side of his daughter he hadn't seen in a long time, and although he knew she was hurting, he was glad she was. He was enjoying that he got to have this special moment with his daughter before she went off to become a woman.

They spent another fifteen minutes in the truck, and then after she had dried her eyes and taken a few deep breaths, they grabbed her bags and headed towards the airport. It was hectic that day, and it took them some time to get everything checked in and settled. She heard her flight's boarding call being announced over the intercom. She turned and kissed her father goodbye and gave him a long squeeze with all her might. She told him she loved him and would call when she arrived.

She slowly turned and walked towards her gate, which was already beginning to board passengers. Her father stood there looking after his daughter as she walked quickly through the tiny airport and finally disappeared out of sight. Her father felt a welling up of sadness. He hastily departed the airport; fearing being seen with tears in his eyes. He got into his truck and drove over to an area that sported a wire fence and had a view of the tarmac in the hope of seeing his daughter's plane take off. He sat there for about 20 minutes until the aircraft was no longer in sight, then he let his head drop, and he finally cried.

5

The takeoff was quite bumpy, and Bonita felt a little ill, so she put on her headphones and popped a piece of gum to prevent her ears from popping. This was, in fact, the first time Bonita had ever flown, and up until the point of takeoff, she had not been worried about it at all. Then, she made the mistake of looking out the window. Her stomach did somersaults as the distance between her and the cold, hard pavement got farther away. She closed the slide on the window so she wouldn't have to see outside and focused on the seat in front of her. Thoughts were fluttering through her head. "I only have to do this twice today, and then I'll be back on solid ground, where I will never have to fly again if I don't want to."

It wasn't long before the plane had begun its descent into Toronto's Pearson International Airport and took off again en route to JFK in New York City. She was surprised that the flight from Toronto to New York was quicker than the drive from her house to St. John's. Bonita had to bite the bullet and open the shade to her window. No matter how scared she might get seeing the ground beneath her get closer and closer, she wouldn't miss the view of the big city from way above. It was mesmerizing, intoxicating, and breathtaking simultaneously; Bonita had never seen something so big and beautiful as the island of Manhattan and the beautiful skyline the airplane was flying over. The thought that she would officially live in New York City in just a few minutes flushed her cheeks.

The landing was smooth, and Bonita finally felt she could breathe again as the airplane slowly banked up against the pedestrian portal connecting the plane to the airport. She sat quietly and didn't move as the passengers hustled around, pulling their overhead luggage down from the compartments and trying to get off the plane. Bonita had waited all her life for this, so it wouldn't hurt her to hold on a few minutes longer. Most had already left the plane, and she could comfortably exit her seat and take everything she was about to see at her own pace. She quickly emerged from her seat and grabbed her luggage as the flight attendants, who wanted to exit the plane, hurried her.

As she left the portal and entered the airport, she was overwhelmed by all the different people condensed inside the building. There were people of all other races, ethnic backgrounds, and colors. At first, it scared her, but then she smiled. Bonita now lived where every kind of person could coexist without such boundaries and judgments as she had experienced every day she lived growing up in Newfoundland.

6

Things were a little confusing at first; her eyes began to hurt from shooting in every direction of the airport. She knew she had to find somewhere to transfer her Canadian money to American currency and then go to the luggage claim. She realized she was already in luggage claim but couldn't figure out which conveyor her bags would be on. After a few moments of freaking out, she thought to look for anyone that may have been on the same plane as she was. Their luggage would be where her luggage was. After nearly five minutes, she finally spotted this little old man with a cane; she remembered sitting in first class and walked over to the conveyor he was standing at.

She must have waited nearly 20 minutes to get close enough to the conveyor to pull her things off, but it didn't bother her. Bonita was quite content observing all that was going on around her. People in New York all seemed to be in a hurry to get somewhere. Everyone looked like they were businessmen and women and did important things and met famous people. All of this was somewhat disconcerting to Bonita. Still, she didn't let the fast pace knock her down and continued waiting patiently until she found her luggage and pulled it off the conveyor.

Bonita quickly caught up to the speed of the airport and found herself briskly walking and out of breath; either she matched the flow or got trampled by the hordes of people. While walking, she kept looking up at the signs to find which way she would have to go to get out of the airport. At last, there was the exit sign, and Bonita doubled her speed to the outside. She had thought it was only that busy in the airport because everyone had flights to catch and that maybe outside, she would be less claustrophobic, but that wasn't the case.

Outside, there were half the people but double the number of cars stopping and honking at the sidewalk. People were trying to find a taxi, limo, or their loved ones who were there to pick them up. After roughly 10 minutes, an airport personnel attendant saw she was lost. He pointed her to a small line-up that had stopped cabs, opened the door, and directed her to get in. She smiled and felt great that one person out of everyone on the sidewalk noticed her. As she got into the car, she thanked the airport attendant, and he nodded back at her. She told the driver where she was going, and the taxi quickly jerked into traffic and began making its way toward Manhattan.

7

Bonita was bewitched as the taxi swerved through the busy streets of Manhattan. She found herself staring upward at the large structures that stood before her. Bonita felt like an ant when making its way through a house, intimidated by all the big things that towered above. Although her nerves had taken over, she could not mistake the feeling of wonder and awe growing inside her. It felt as if she were going to explode.

She noticed all the people on the sidewalks hurriedly walking this way and that; she quickly concluded that the airport was, in fact, less busy than the streets of New York. She would use those same streets daily to get to and from school. Her stomach tightened, and a sense of nausea overwhelmed her when she thought that she would indeed be trampled if she couldn't learn to walk fast, like a New Yorker.

Something caught her eye as the car continued to jerk through the sea of traffic. It was a man pulling an odd-looking contraption that had two wheels. She pondered why people would walk on the streets with all the cars and crazy traffic until she saw something stranger: another man pulling the same contraption, and this time, people were sitting in it. Was it some sort of taxi?

With every city block that passed, she became increasingly mystified by the sights she saw. People putting on shows in the street. Businessmen sell things off tables, such as glasses, watches, paintings, and T-shirts. She couldn't understand how they were not afraid that one of the thousands of people walking past wouldn't steal something; it made no sense. She continued trying to take everything in, her head moving back and forth and side to side, checking out different buildings and street names. She wanted to remember where to go and develop familiarity with the city to return and take a better look once settled down.

The taxi eventually pulled to a complete stop, awakening her from her trance. She looked around to see what was going on. The driver noticed the confusion and said, "This is your stop."

Startled and quickly turning to look out her window, she scanned to see the number on the building. There it was, under a posh-looking canopy hanging out over the front door: 361 West 34th Street. Rummaging through her purse, she pulled out 50 American dollars — $45 for the flat fee from JFK to anywhere in Manhattan and a $5 tip. She thought she tipped big and was quite pleased with herself. She thanked the driver as she stepped out of the taxi and saw him nodding at her. She pulled her baggage out of the car and approached the front doors. Her nervous stomach worsened with every step.

8

The doors flung upon as she entered the building. She had never in her life before seen something so beautiful. The decor was beautiful, with black leather couches and marble flooring; she was captivated; nothing back home would ever look like this. Her attention quickly turned to the sexy man sitting behind a desk to her left. The nametag on his jacket read, "Julio." She approached the desk and said, "Excuse me, my name is Bonita Smith, and I am here to see Claude Peters in Suite 1907."

Claude Peters was a man whom Bonita had met in a New York City chat room nearly a year prior. They began chatting through emails and instant messenger, eventually graduating to the telephone. At first, it was only once a week, but it became once a day after some time. Before they knew it, both Bonita and Claude had become exceptionally acquainted. She told him of her plans to attend fashion school in New York City, and he suggested she could live with him in his two-bedroom apartment. Since Bonita didn't know anyone in the city, she gladly accepted and felt quite relieved that that aspect of her arrangements had been taken care of. She would be living with someone she was familiar with and had built rapport with, which made migrating to a strange place a little easier.

Claude was a makeup artist who worked at a prestigious counter in Manhattan; he was also notorious with the local drag queens for his abilities and fine-tuned skills. He would say, "Of course, they need and love me. I'm the only one on this island who can turn their bearded faces into beautiful, flawless swans. Without me, they would be nothing more than mere men in cheap and tasteless lingerie."

Bonita had been dying to meet him since they started talking and loved that he was so funny. Of course, she fell in love with his witty charm and bitchy demeanor. Right from the get-go, she knew they would get along just fine. He told her it would be fabulous to have her stay with him. "You will be my 'fag hag.'" At first, she didn't like to be called a fag hag, so he reinvented the term and told her that she was to be his fag diva.

"Oh, yes, Miss Smith. Mr. Peters informed me that he expects you and said to let you up."

"Thank you," she said as she walked toward the elevator. "Miss Smith," she thought. "No one has ever called me Miss Smith before. I like it."

She stepped on the elevator, and her nerves began to act up again as she moved up the shaft closer and closer to the 19th floor. She exited the elevator and started to walk down the hall. While walking, she noticed windows, so she stopped to look. She was sadly disappointed because it was a view of a courtyard and not of the city. She had never seen a courtyard before — there weren't any in Newfoundland that she knew of — but it wasn't anything to be impressed about. Finally, she was at the door. She stopped before knocking to admire the little gold plate that read "1907." She thought to herself, "This is my new home. This is where I am going to be living."

She knocked on the door and took a step back. She was so excited and hugely anticipated Claude answering the door, and when he did, she froze. Her hands began to sweat, and she could not believe the sight standing before her. Bonita had yet to see a picture of Claude. From all their phone conversations and how he had described himself, she had developed an idea of what he would look like. Still, the man staring at her was nothing like she had imagined.

"I was wrong, very wrong," she thought, as she couldn't help but look at him. He was beautiful. Tall, dark, and handsome with breathtaking green eyes. She thought, "This man looks like what a Greek god would look like if they were to walk this earth. Big arms, flat tummy — and look at those pecs."

"You have amazing pecs," she thought. Oops! She didn't think it; she said it out loud! Immediately, she felt all the blood leave her feet and rush to her face. She felt so embarrassed that she wanted to just turn and run through one of the windows to the courtyard. "It's only 19 floors. I could make it."

"Well, pleased to meet you, too."

Claude chuckled and motioned for her to come inside. Ashamed, she picked up her luggage and entered the apartment.

9

Bonita entered the apartment with her head down, still embarrassed about the uncensored comment she had just made. Then she heard Claude say, "Welcome home," she snapped back to reality and looked around. The apartment was immaculate, unique, and like nothing her eyes had ever seen. She thought she had died and gone to heaven.

The floors were all dark-stained hardwood, with beautiful rugs laid methodically about the central living space. The furniture was all chocolate-brown leather with a barrage of pillows neatly strewn across them and a throw on the back of the couch that looked like it was made of fur. The windows were bright and clean with beautiful treatments, making them look like framed photos, while the color of the walls was rich and earthy, accenting Claude's choice of beiges and tans. The kitchen had a marble countertop and beautifully crafted cabinetry. There were pieces of art hung everywhere and accessories of all kinds strategically laid in every nook and cranny of the house. It was as if each and every item had its perfect place, a home for beauty and splendor.

"How do you afford this?" she asked, absently placing her

things beside the barstools. Walking to the couch, she picked up a pillow and brushed it against her face.

"Many years of bargain shopping. Keeping an ear to the ground for sales in housewares and hardware and much saving and budgeting to ensure I get the most from my dollar," Claude said, "Oh, and rent control," half chuckling at Bonita's reaction, "I am glad you like it, 'cause this is your new home, Miss Smith."

"Why do people keep calling me that?" She turned her attention away from the beauty surrounding her back to the depiction of a God now her roommate. "Do people think that I'm ancient or something?"

He laughed. "No, New York is a very service-orientated city, and they use 'Miss' for respect and to ensure you feel appreciated."

She pondered briefly and then placed the pillow back as neatly as possible. She turned to Claude and began talking about her trip. He listened attentively and informed her that she had not seen her room. She grabbed her bags without hesitation and motioned for him to lead the way. As expected, she loved it; it was perfect, and though the view was not visually elegant, it was stunning, nonetheless. She could see the apartment buildings and the deli across the street. He left the room, thinking that she would like some time to unpack and get settled in, but she followed him right back to the living room with her mouth running a mile a minute. Bonita was excited and had all the time in the world to unpack. She was ready to talk the 'ear off a dead man.'

After sitting for an hour, talking about everything and exchanging what each person thought of the other, Claude suggested they go out and explore the city a bit. The words were no more out of his mouth when Bonita bolted off the couch and was at the door with her shoes on. Claude spun his head around in surprise and said, "Be careful with that rocket up your ass. I don't want you to burn a hole in my sofa." She gave him an apologetic look with a massive smile and said, "Well, I'm sorry, but I'm excited, so let's go, let's go, let's go!"

He chuckled and thought, 'This one is quite the firecracker.'

They spent hours out that day, treading through New York. They went everywhere, and anywhere there was a sight to see. They even went places Claude had never been, and he had lived a long time in this city. She wanted to see all the shops, the places where beauty was made, the designers, the restaurants, the cafés, and, of course, the Empire State Building. Bonita stopped at every street vendor and bought a picture of the NYC skyline, a fancy watch, and an "I Love New York" shirt. She told Claude about the funny contraptions she saw people pulling, and he flagged one down and convinced her to get on. She felt so bad that this poor person was dragging them through the city that she couldn't stop laughing out of nervousness.

The day was nearly over when Claude said, "There is one more place you have to go on your first day in the city." He waved for a cab, and they got in. She asked, "Where are you taking me?" He gave her a little look and said, "You will see!"

They drove for about 10 minutes through heavy traffic and stopped at a sidewalk in front of a low stone wall. There were no buildings in front of them. They both got out, and Bonita gave Claude a confused look. He motioned for her to follow him, and she did. Still perplexed, she kept looking around to get some idea of where she was, and then it hit her.

"Oh, my God! Are we in Central Park?"

She was so excited and worked up that she didn't notice where she was walking and tripped over a raised partition, landing flat on her face. She jumped up, screaming, "I'm okay, I'm okay," and Claude, completely startled and trying not to laugh, asked, "Are you sure?" She laughed so hard that spit flew from her mouth, making her laugh harder. Claude took her to a nearby bench and sat her down. Still laughing hysterically, she was almost to the point of tears.

"I can't believe I fell flat on my face the first day in New York!"

Claude, laughing, said, "I know. Are you okay?"

She looked at him with tears rolling down her face and spit bubbling on her lip. "I hope this isn't a sign of how things will work out here for me!" This pushed her over the deep end, and she laughed even harder. Bonita was now getting all her stress out from the pressure from the flight, from a new city, leaving her family behind, and not knowing whether she would make it.

They sat talking and recuperating on the bench for what felt like only a minute or two, but it was an hour. Claude and Bonita picked up their things and began making their way home. Bonita, fortunately, hadn't hurt anything except for her pride. She was glad it was with Claude rather than someone else.

They arrived home soon after, famished and tired from all the walking. Claude told her to get settled away, and he would take care of dinner. She resigned herself to the idea and went into her room.

10

She stared around at the walls and window in her room and soaked it all up. She unpacked, hung her things in the closet, and placed them in her dresser drawers. She didn't bring too many personal effects. Still, she got a few of the most sentimental items that would keep her from being too homesick. She laid them out, hung them throughout the room, and found something in her suitcase.

It was an envelope with her name on it. She didn't know who it was from or why it was there, but she suspected it was from her parents, and she was right. Enclosed in the envelope was a money order and a letter.

"Bon Bon,

I hope this letter finds you well and that you are all settled in the big city. Your mother and I miss you so very much already. We know you have prepared for this day for quite some time and have saved sufficient money to take care of things, but we are worried. Enclosed in this letter, you will find $3000 in a money order, which we want you to buy yourself something nice and then keep the rest for emergencies.

We sent a money order because we do not know how the banking system works down there, and we didn't want you to be stuck without money. Remember, you will do well; don't let anybody tell you otherwise. If you need anything, and I mean anything, including a one-way ticket home, you call. We will be here to hold you and love you unconditionally, forever.

We love you so very much, and please be safe and careful.

Love, Mom and Dad."

Her eyes were filled with tears, and then it dawned on her it had been seven hours since her plane had landed, and she had yet to call her father. She sprinted to the kitchen to ask Claude if she could use his phone. He laughed at her and said, "It isn't just my phone anymore; call anyone you like, as long as you pay for it."

She took the phone off the counter and ran back to the room. Twenty minutes later, she returned to the kitchen with a smile and looked like she had just had a long cry.

It just so happened that Claude was finished cooking. Dinner was served, and it smelled delicious. In all her excitement, Bonita had forgotten to eat breakfast today, never mind anything else, so when Claude put a beautiful plate of food in front of her, she was ready to chow down, except for one problem.

"What the hell is it?" she thought.

A mound of something resembling shrubs cut from a garden with these weird-looking leaves was on her plate. Also, a slab of meat-like substance had tomato sauce and melted cheese on top. She quivered at first and tried not to look so disgusted, but Claude had already noticed the look on her face.

"Please tell me you have had Parmesan chicken before?" he asked as she shyly hung her head in shame.

"Have I had what?" she said, with a look of fear.

He explained that the meat was chicken, breaded with a tomato sauce and melted cheese on top, and that the greens were a salad with spring mix, and technically, yes, in a way, they were shrubs. Still, they tasted good and were good for you.

Trustingly, she cut off a piece of chicken and put it in her mouth. Her eyes lit up. "This is good!" she mumbled, with her mouth full. She finished her meal, had seconds, and promised Claude never to prejudge anything he made again.

After dinner, they sat down, chatted, and drank wine. Bonita thought, "How wonderful is this? Great food, New York City, and wine after supper — I mean, dinner!" She was in New York now and needed to speak like New Yorkers. It didn't take too long before she could barely keep her eyes open, and they both went to their beds and fell fast asleep.

<h1 style="text-align:center">11</h1>

The following day came too quickly, but she was up and ready to go when the sun broke through her elegantly placed curtains. She had no idea what she wanted to do today. Still, she knew she had so much to do before school started. She tried to complete everything early to concentrate solely on her studies. Over the next few months, she knew she had to get most of the novelty of New York City out of her system, or she would not be able to keep herself in one place once school started.

She heard Claude arise from his slumber and welcomed him with a big, good morning. He laughed and kept walking to the kitchen. Claude needed his coffee and was not used to waking up to someone, period, never mind someone so bubbly. She explained her dilemma, and he took a few minutes to absorb all that was said and only concluded that they better get started, or she might as well drop out of school. "There is no way you will be able to make cute dresses and high fashion couture if you haven't taken in all of the New York City sights," he said.

Therefore, after three cups of coffee and a bagel, Claude

entered his bedroom and quickly emerged fully dressed and looking put together. On the other hand, Bonita was just out of the shower and still in a towel. He hurried her along, and she quickly found something to pull on and made her way to the front door. Claude gave her a once-over and decided to say nothing; this was his new roommate, and he would accept her for who she was.

Day in and day out, they would get up and go out. There were many days when Claude had to work, and then Bonita would have to decide what she wanted to do. She could either go exploring as a solo act and take things in and be adventurous on her own, or she could go hang out at the counter with Claude and watch him do his magic on all sorts of people. She enjoyed watching Claude in action and was enamored with what he could do with a few brushes and makeup. Women and men would come in and sit in his chair, and he would transform them into beautiful people with perfect skin and gorgeous eyes. It was simply magic!

There were days that she would just sit there for his whole shift and watch. She had hit it off with his boss, and it wasn't a problem to just hang around. Although she thoroughly enjoyed watching others having their makeup done, she never once considered having hers done. She was uncomfortable in her own skin; it was what years of persecution had done to her. She never imagined that she could be beautiful, and that Claude would ever care to waste time using his products on her. She was numb to beauty within herself: She had none. That is what she was told her whole life, so she believed it and moved on.

12

The days and the weeks flew by. There were so many things Bonita wanted to do that they had done already, and a million others she would never have thought of if it were not for Claude. After the first month of taking in all the main tourist attractions, he showed her different areas of the city and hidden gems that she never knew existed.

Her favorite place of all that she had visited was Battery Park. She went there on her first day in the city and loved it. She never realized it herself, but it was because she grew up by the water, and Battery Park is right at it. On nights that Claude worked, she would head down there for a walk and just sit on the bench, enjoying the smells, the people, and the cool breeze rolling off the water.

She had been enjoying herself to the fullest and soaking up everything she could that she nearly forgot about her birthday when it rolled around. She didn't expect anyone to know about it and wanted to keep it that way. She never liked being fussed over — not that she was privy to that a lot as a child — but she would rather it be a regular day than any celebration. She didn't know Claude remembered her birthday from that last year of talking and made a few plans. He included the girls at the counter where he worked, who adored her for her silly clothes and innocent demeanor, and a couple of the drag queens she had met at the counter. He set everything up and called her at two in the afternoon, freaking out.

"Bonita! Oh, my god. I am going to lose my job."

"Why?" she asked, with a sense of urgency.

"One of the top New York drag queens I do the makeup for requested that I have a dress made in her size and ready for when she comes to get her face done. I told her that was fine. She gave me all the measurements and a general design, but I forgot to take it to the tailors." Bonita thought that he was going to explode on the phone. She had not heard Claude have a panic attack before and knew that this was serious.

"What can I do to help?" she yelped.

"I need you to go into my room, and a manila envelope is on the desk. Inside is everything the tailor needs. I called ahead and was told they would do what they could to finish it by six, but they needed it soon."

"Okay, what is the address? I will take it to them right away."

He gave her the address and told her he needed her to stay there until it was finished to ensure they stayed focused and completed it in time. She didn't have concrete plans that day and figured, "Why not? It would be interesting to watch a dress being made before I go to school to learn to do it myself." She agreed and offered to pay for it up front since it would take longer to stop by the counter and get the money from Claude.

The day passed as she sat in a cramped space, watching two

Korean women make a dress from a simple sketch on paper. It was unbelievable, and she was learning a lot. She asked many questions but could only understand every second or third word out of their mouths. Then, she felt sad; it was her birthday, and she was sitting in a tiny Korean tailor shop waiting for a dress to be finished for a drag queen. No one had wished her happy birthday. No one even knew it was her birthday. She thought she wouldn't care, but she did.

Once the dress was complete, she used the phone at the shop to call Claude, and he told her to bring it to the house instead. There were some issues at the counter, and he had to do the makeup there. He also informed her that he might be a little late, so if he wasn't at home when she arrived, put the dress by the chaise if she decided to go out. She hailed a cab and headed home, sad and holding an hilarious dress.

She walked in the door of her apartment. All seemed quiet. She went to flick on the lights, and as she did, she was nearly frightened to death. A load of people with hats, drinks, and decorations stood around, shouting, "Surprise!" She was surprised, all right; she started to tear up, and she couldn't believe that Claude had thrown her a party. He gave her a great big hug and shouted, "Let the celebrations begin." She had a great time mingling and talking with everyone and then an even better time opening presents. These people, whom she had only met a short while ago, had taken a chance to come to a party for her and to bring her gifts. She was flabbergasted.

She thought the party was over and decided to wind down, but before she knew it, she was in a cab and on her way to her first gay bar. It was fantastic — flashy lights and beautiful, shirtless men everywhere, and although she knew they were all gay, she couldn't help but think she was in heaven. She danced and drank and danced and drank some more, flirting and even kissing a couple of strange guys. She and Claude hung tight the whole night. He never let her out of sight and loved how much fun she was having.

He gave her one more present when they got home later that evening. She opened it up, and it was a mobile phone. She looked at him funny, and he said, "So I don't have to worry about you anymore when you're alone!" She looked at him softly and said, "Thank you for caring. This is an excellent gift."

13

Only a month remained until Bonita would begin her first year of school. She had been living in New York City for a little over six weeks already, and she had been having so much fun. Things were different here than they were back home; obviously, this was not a surprise to her because the difference in the number of people who lived here made it so very different. She began to learn the New York ways and customs and adapt herself to the fast-paced motion of the city. It wasn't hard because it was all around you, everywhere you looked.

She planned to finish taking in everything to see in the city before her first term started and prepare herself as much as possible. She spent a lot of time with Claude and then a considerable amount of time wandering the streets, looking for shops and fun little places. She began to go to gay bars a bit more frequently. She enjoyed them and always had a ton of fun. Claude was friendly with all of the owners, so getting her in underage wasn't a problem. Most of the boys shot her weird looks when they first saw her; she didn't look like a typical New York City girl but rather like a hillbilly country bumpkin. In the city where fashion counted for a lot, she was at the bottom of the totem pole for what she wore, but people were infatuated with her personality.

She focused on preparing herself for school so well that she wouldn't need anything once school started. Bonita would roll out of bed in the morning, shower, get dressed, eat, and then be out the door like a blur. She walked all over Manhattan, going to different stores to find the best supplies. She had a list that she intended to fill, but only with style. Pencils, pens, scissors, thread, sketchbooks, and more were mulled over, put back, and then reselected. She wanted them to be top-of-the-line — as top-of-the-line as pencils and pens could be.

One morning, she got up to visit her school and map out where all her classes would be. She wanted to be on time once it began. She walked down notorious 7th Avenue, enjoying all the high-end shops and beauty it had to offer. She found her school sitting pretty and magnificent. The buildings intimidated her; she knew it would be big but had no real idea it would be as big as it was. There were so many rooms, studios, and offices. It was overwhelming and disconcerting to Bonita. She knew her work was cut out for her if she wanted to know where all her classes were before the term began.

She spent hours at the school, talking with faculty members, asking for directions, and studying the school maps and class line-ups. She even found a museum. She was enchanted with the different types of fashion shown there — and inspired, simply inspired. Days would pass, and you could always find her there walking the halls, checking the time it took her to get from one room to the next. She had met most of the staff by now, but there were still a few of her teachers that she had yet to meet.

It was a few days before school started, and Bonita was once again walking the halls, finding her classes from all directions to lessen the likelihood of her getting lost. One of her classrooms was always locked, so she could only see what it looked like through a small window in the door with the lights off. Bonita was delighted to see that the door was open, and the lights were on. She stepped up to the doorway and shot her head around the corner.

A middle-aged man sat at the desk. He was probably pushing fifty, at least; he was well dressed, with cropped hair and tiny rectangular glasses that framed his face. He looked like what she thought a male librarian would look like: very straight-backed and with a stiff upper lip.

As she went to walk away, the man at the desk noticed her and said, "May I help you? Are you lost?"

"No, sir. I am a student here — well, I will be in three days — and I was just learning where all my classes were so I wouldn't get lost. I noticed the door was open, so I thought I would take a peek in," Bonita said nervously.

The teacher lowered his glasses and perched them on the tip of his nose.

"And?"

Bonita, puzzled, looked at him blankly. "No, that is it, just trying to find my classes, is all!"

He appeared to be perturbed. "No, Miss. 'And?' As in, 'what do you think?'"

Bonita brayed, trembling from her nerves.

"Oh, I'm sorry! I believe that it looks magnificent, sir, really quite magnificent!"

He turned to his desk by swiveling his chair, removed the glasses from his face, and laid them gently on the book he had been reading.

"Well, I am glad to hear that some students still go the extra mile to ensure punctuality."

He rose from his chair and took a few steps toward her.

"I find these days young people do not have the respect for the institution their predecessors once had. Sometimes, it is challenging for someone who is as 'old school' as I am to deal with their cantankerous behavior!"

Bonita understood what he was trying to say, but she had never heard of the word "cantankerous" or what it could mean. She nodded and said, "I agree!"

"Have you found all your classes, Miss...?" he said, scratching his nose, hoping to catch her name.

Bonita answered quickly. "Smith. Miss Smith, but please, call me Bonita. I find all the times I have been called Miss since I arrived here leaves me feeling senescent, and I am just newly 18. And, yes, sir. I have found all my classes now!"

She had quite the vocabulary herself from being such an honor student in school, and now that she had given him her name, she wanted to know his as well.

"And you, sir? What shall I call you?"

"Well, Bonita, I am glad you have found all your classes, and you can call me Dean! Dean Lalonde is my name, and I believe I will be one of your primary instructors throughout your stay here with us!"

He picked up a book from his desk as if to double-check,

and Bonita seemed thrilled that she had finally met the infamous Dean Lalonde. From what she had heard, he was a hard man but brilliant simultaneously. He did not care for adolescents or boisterous behavior. Still, he had the skills to teach you how to be a great designer.

Bonita left the classroom shortly after that and decided it was time for her to go home. She would have two more days before school started and pondered what she wanted to do with them. Bonita had fully prepared herself, had all the supplies, and had everything packed and ready to bring on the first day. What was she to do for the next 48 hours? She thought of a million possible things the whole way home, but nothing suited what she felt like.

Once she returned home, she stopped and realized what she wanted to do! She would stay home for the next two days, eat junk food, and relax for her first day of school.

14

It had finally arrived! The first day of school was the first day to put her dreams to work. There was no turning back now. Bonita rolled out of bed early and pulled on a dazzling new top that Claude had picked out for her. She spent over two hours in the bathroom trying new things with her hair but realized it wasn't working out. Bonita grabbed breakfast, reviewed her class schedule again, and chatted with Claude. He wished her good luck and reassured her she would be just fine. After what seemed like an eternity passed, it was time for her to go, so she lifted her bag over her shoulder and dashed out the door.

The school was much bigger than her home school, but still not so big that she didn't feel confident about making her way around, especially since she could now walk the halls blindfolded. All the different types of people who walked the halls, who all seemed to have a strong sense of direction, filled her mind with intimidation. She kept her head down and walked to her first class — Draping I: Fundamentals. Her course load would be moderate but high for her because this was a whole new world she was about to enter. She knew nothing about creating fashion except what looked good and what didn't. She looked like a walking fashion disaster, as she could never afford fancy clothes. This would all change, as she would spend the next two years getting an associate degree in fashion. Afterward, she would go for her one-year Bachelor of Fine Arts in Fashion Design with a Special Occasion designation. She wanted to dress the stars for the red carpet, create beautifully crafted haute couture for the filthy rich, and be known worldwide for her radical techniques and latest fashion trends. It all started here with draping.

The classroom was abundant with plenty of stations, as were most classes in the school, and filled with others eagerly awaiting instruction. Bonita found a seat close to the back and sat down. Since the course was fundamentals, she assumed it would be more listening and writing than hands-on fabric handling. Bonita was half-correct; there was a good mixture of both involved, and she walked away from that class in awe and completely enthralled. She had no idea that grain bore any importance on a garment but now understood why, and it made perfect sense.

Her next class was Flat Pattern Design I. She would learn to experiment with slash spread and pivot techniques on basic slopes to develop original designs. She was stoked and ready to absorb all the instructor had to bestow upon her. Her class was as equally whole as the previous one due to the abundance of first-year students who began at the same time she had. Her nerves had slightly lessened in the second class, but she still had yet to meet anyone, so she kept her head down and watched everything happening.

The first day flew by almost too quickly for Bonita. She

felt a little robbed simply because she was thirsty for more. There needed to have been more learned, and there should have been more taught. She quickly collected everything and headed onto Seventh Avenue to return home. Although robbed, she felt cheery and reassured that she could do this and that everything would be okay. She already knew enough to make her think she could make a simple garment. She was wrong, though, and she learned that over her next few days at school.

<h1 style="text-align:center">15</h1>

Bonita and Claude spent countless hours playing with the fabrics and tools she had for school and would imagine all the different clothes they wished they could make. Bonita had yet to go to school long enough to make a complete item, but she understood what it took. They often stayed awake until the wee hours, mock-dressing and prancing around the apartment. They would stand with chenille draped haphazardly around them, saying foolish things, such as, "Look at me, I'm the Queen of England," or, "I have wanted all my life to win an Oscar. Thank you, thank you to everyone, you really like me! They really like me!"

It was fun for both of them, and they had such a riot just messing around. Bonita would occasionally gap out in class due to her lack of sleep, but she never seemed to mind it that much. Claude thought that it was fantastic that Bonita was so open and fun with him. He had lived alone for quite some time now and would never get this much enjoyment from just being home. He and Bonita became close friends, and the relationship between them continued to grow at a rapid rate. Neither stopped thinking about it; they loved spending time together, and nothing else mattered. As time passed, Claude encouraged her to be the best she could, and Bonita encouraged him to do the same.

Bonita had never had a friend like that before, with whom she could be herself. Claude never opened up too much about his life, but he was a great listener, and sometimes, she would just rant about her childhood for hours. Claude would sit beside her, let her talk, and offer her a shoulder to lean on. He hated that she was so mistreated by people growing up. He understood that maybe she wasn't the most alluring girl in the world and that she dressed and looked like a disaster most of the time. Still, once you got to know her, she was such a beautiful person. He thought she was one of the funniest people he knew and often would find himself at work laughing at something she had done a day before. Things were always fresh with her, every day a new adventure, and there was never a dull moment when she was around.

He loved her little quirks and idiosyncrasies. To him, those were what made her perfect and excellent. She was often stubborn and headstrong, and once she set her mind to something, there was no turning back. She didn't seem to care how she looked or what she wore for the most part, and although it took some getting used to for Claude, he now found it refreshing to be around. She was not affected in a city where style, looks, and attitude counted for almost everything. He hoped she would realize how pretty she could be and make a few changes to her appearance.

Laughing and having stitches became their favorite pastime, often leaving them with sore abdomens and tired cheeks. It was something they found that they had in common and utilized for the consumption of their spare time. Bonita felt she had never laughed as much in her entire life, and she was probably right. They would never enter a conversation expecting or hoping it would become a giggle-fest. Still, once it happened, it was impossible to stop. They both possessed infectious laughs, and one would bounce off the other. Often, all hell would break loose.

One night, they had been laughing for hours and talking about everything. Finally, it was early morning, and they both needed to sleep. They went to their own rooms and got into bed. It must have been nearly 15 minutes later when Bonita heard Claude burst out laughing in his room. Neither of them had yet to fall asleep, and her first and uncontrollable reaction was to laugh at him laughing. The next thing anyone knew, they were both in hysterics in their rooms, laughing very loudly. First, Claude would stop for a second, but Bonita was in the middle of a roar, and then he couldn't help but laugh again. Then Bonita would stop laughing momentarily, and Claude would be hysterical, and she would start again. Finally, they both had enough and emerged from their rooms in complete stitches. When they both saw each other buckled over, standing in their doorways, Claude dropped to his knees in total insanity.

Bonita managed to sit in her doorway while trying to nurse her aching sides, still laughing hard. Neither of them was making it any easier on the other. They both sat there laughing and trying to figure out what had made Claude laugh in the first place. He couldn't remember anymore, which they both found even funnier anyway. Bonita grabbed pillows and two blankets off her bed and threw one of each at Claude. She said the unthinkable.

"Well, it looks like us two laughing Nellies are sleeping here tonight!" causing them to roar once more.

After an eternity, they both fell asleep, still laughing! It wasn't long before both of their alarms went off, and they woke up lying in the hallway, curled up in the fetal position and extraordinarily tired. There wasn't any laughing this time. They needed to get up and get ready for their respective days. It didn't take long for them to get ready — not that they had ample time to do so in the first place — and then they were off.

16

When Bonita wasn't laughing her pants off with Claude, she tried to be more social at school. It seemed entirely in vain for a long time but eventually paid off. She met two girls whom she clicked with. The first girl, Lyla Frank, sat behind her in nearly all of her classes, and one day, they finally started talking and shared a laugh when their teacher said something idiotic. After that, they spoke regularly, and Bonita was quite happy that she found at least one person in her school with whom she got along.

Lyla was a taller girl with long flowing blonde hair, a pair of very cool glasses, and a fashion sense best described as modern-day '50s-era. She came from a middle-class family in upstate New York and had loved fashion from as far back as she could remember. This is where Lyla wanted to be, but she didn't seem as serious about it as Bonita did. Lyla liked to party a lot and have mega fun whenever she could. It would often leave her drained and dozing off while in class. Bonita never thought to judge her because she did the same thing, except she stayed at home and irresponsibly spent hours at night making jokes with her roommate. Despite anything else, Lyla was a fun girl and charming to talk to.

The second girl was Bethany Ludemier, Lyla's friend, who sat directly behind her. Bonita met Bethany through Lyla, and they all seemed to click immediately. Bethany was medium height, with jet-black hair that was always well-styled and neatly placed. She looked as if she had fallen off the cover of Vogue, and Bethany might as well have, as she sported all of the top designers. She loved fashion and looking her best, and she felt she would be a gift to the industry because of her cutting-edge eye for hidden gems. Bethany was born here in Manhattan and lived the life of a princess. Her father was a real estate mogul and made plenty of money to pay for the very best for his wife and only child. She was rich, and she made no bones about it. She liked not only to party but also to be the party.

Although each had fascinating personalities that differed from Bonita's, she liked them both. They were her friends in New York City. She hadn't made any friends except for Claude thus far, and they never treated her differently because she was a homely-looking girl. They would spend quite a bit of time together. They were all in the same classes at the same time, and after school, they would often go for a stroll through SoHo and grab a latte or martini. Bonita would often find out about a show happening in the city and convince the girls to go with her, and off they went. They loved just hanging out and shopping at the cutest boutiques. Although Bonita could rarely afford to buy anything, she loved being surrounded by all the beauty.

The three of them became fast friends and eventually

graduated to being referred to as "the girls." Bonita was happy that she had a few female friends to spend time with, Claude fit the bill very well, but sometimes you just needed a complete girls' night to bitch about boys and do girly things. Claude never seemed to mind; Bonita usually planned them around his schedule and only went out with the girls when he was working. Her life had begun in New York: She had friends, fun, and freedom — all of the things she longed for her whole life.

Bonita's primary focus had remained strong since she arrived. School was still her top priority, and her future was always on her mind. She was intensely devoted to learning everything she could in school and conveying it into her work. She wanted nothing else but to master each step her teachers would teach. Bonita attended every possible fashion event, no matter how tired she was. Her core dedication meant being ever-present in the fashion world, not just in school but also in life. It didn't matter what kind of show it was; if she thought it would be anything fashion-related, she went. Bonita couldn't imagine not surrounding herself in her field.

There were ample times that Claude would be working, her friends would be unavailable, and she would go alone. Bonita didn't mind doing things solo; she valued her free time to move about as she wanted, and going alone would help her focus more on meeting people without being concerned about her friends. Getting into some of the higher-profile shows was challenging, so often, she just stuck to events with open doors or tickets that could be purchased for reasonable prices.

She began to network with people, develop relationships, and converse with everyone she could each time she went out. It became a passion for her to network, meet with other fashion-forward individuals, and soak up every word they said. She enjoyed the stories and the wisdom they had to impart to her, and she would listen very attentively. One evening, while she was out, she realized that she had spent over two hours just standing in one spot listening to this flamboyant older man talk about his years designing costumes for movies. There wasn't one word he spoke that she didn't eat up and store in her memory bank for later. He had such different ideas, concepts, and techniques that she wanted to keep them in mind for her own work.

When her friends were with her, they would always try to pull her away after talking to someone too long. They would want to mingle elsewhere. Bonita quickly became a conversationalist that people would remember from prior events and make their way over to. Bethany and Lyla would often feel bored and wander off to find something exciting or sit at the bar, flirting with whatever boys were around. Although the girls were there just to see the show, they never seemed to mind that Bonita would take hours talking to everyone and anyone.

17

The school had picked up, and the workload was piling by the minute. Bonita enjoyed being stretched in different directions regarding schoolwork, which is how she was her whole life. She did better under pressure and loved having multiple tasks to tackle at any given time. Most people were stressed, working hard, and frustrated, but Bonita was as calm as a warm summer day. Her perspective on learning was not laid back but rather the opposite: She felt one could only learn if challenged. She knew she knew nothing about fashion when she came here, and the challenge for her was to learn how to make garments and understand the premise behind color and grain.

It was not unusual to find Bonita sitting at her desk, sketching away, trying to design a dress or garment even if the teachers didn't assign it. She believed that practice made perfect, and she would always practice. Bonita would sketch in her book during her spare time, during dinner, before bed, and at any other time. She still had much to learn, and there were plenty of things, especially with sketching, that she needed to improve and figure out. She could never get the flow of the garment right, and it would often look obscure and abstract.

She and her friends would continue to go out after school, take in shows, laugh, and talk in class when the teacher wasn't listening. Everything was going well for her in school; her grades seemed remarkable, and her assignments were always returned with top marks. All seemed to be perfect, except she had been targeted by a strange boy in school.

There was this guy. No one knew that much about him, or so she thought, and he began to really pick on her. He would make faces and jokes that wouldn't really be a direct insult to her, but he would say things that she would interpret as being attacks on her appearance. He was a real asshole, and she tried her best to ignore him.

His name was Benjamin Ryder, and he was not that popular at her school. He had a group of friends he hung around with, and they all seemed to like him, but other than that, he just tended to make fun of people and taunt them, especially her. She didn't know exactly why, but she figured it had to do with the fact that she was the homeliest girl in her group. She accepted that, but she didn't like him very much. He bugged her, and she wanted him to fall into a vat of deep-fried noodles to teach him a lesson about making fun of people. No one knew how much he bugged her; she never spoke about it. She disliked him very much.

18

It was the Saturday morning that Bonita had been longing for all week. Her stress level was up due to the ever-increasing workload at school, and although she liked it that way, she needed a break. She felt as if she hadn't slept for years; the Friday evening prior, before bed, the alarm was switched off, and a decision to wake up naturally was made. Her inner clock woke her, as usual, at 6:00 am, and it made her feel so good to close her eyes, roll over, and go back to sleep.

Only minutes later, there was a rustling outside her bedroom door. At first, she thought she was dreaming, but then Bonita realized the voice was that of her roommate, Claude. She let out a very muffled "Come in," but there was nothing except more rustling. Finally, she arose from her haven and answered the door with a huffy, "What?" She proclaimed with a raised voice, "What is it that I can help you with this early morning?"

"Early morning?" Claude rebutted. "It is 2:30 in the afternoon!"

Stepping back slowly to avoid an unsightly lashing, he looked at her with weary eyes. Claude had never seen Bonita snap. He was not privy to her temperamental side. All he was exposed to was the meek, funny, easygoing side, and he never even knew that it existed until now.

"What?" Bonita screamed as she swirled around to look at her clock. Sure enough, it was 2:31 pm.

"I'm so sorry, Claude. I didn't mean to snap. I was in the middle of dreaming and didn't realize it was so late." She quickly grabbed her robe off the back of the door and entered the hallway.

"What's up?" she said to Claude.

"Well..." he said, slightly nervously, "I want to ask you something. A request, if you will." He sheepishly lowered his head, only to give her a side-eye shot.

"Yes?" Bonita replied.

"Okay, a huge and significant drag show that one of my favorite drag queens will be competing in is coming up. She has been a client of mine for quite some time, and I really want her to win." His eyes were big, yet his aura was small and meek.

"The drag show isn't an ordinary drag show; it's the Miss Continental Pageant. It is the most exciting pageant for any North American drag queen, next to Miss Gay America."

He stepped forward and made eye contact. "I want her to win, and I was hoping that you might want to design her a dress for the ball gown section of the pageant."

Bonita stepped back with a gasp.

"Claude! I don't know? I don't think I have learned enough to try and pull off a full gown! What about the Korean dressmakers you sent me to? Wouldn't they do a better job?" she said with concern.

"No, they can sew, but this dress has to be perfect and top-of-the-line, and Bonita, you are outstanding. You have designed a few shirts for school. Please? I know you can do it! Please?"

At this point, Bonita was beginning to smile from ear to ear; she couldn't believe that Claude would even want her near this show, never mind designing a dress for it.

"I'll do it!"

She spoke. Claude seemed so happy that she said yes and was still in shock. They started talking about what kind of dress it would be. They would need her measurements, and Bonita suggested meeting her to better understand her persona, and what would complement her. Claude set the appointment, and Bonita rolled up her shirtsleeves and began sketching. She had never made a dress before but was determined to make this one perfect.

19

Over the following few weeks, Bonita would go back and forth between home and school; she took out books from the library to read as much as she could about gown making. She consulted with one of the faculty members, and they offered her a lot of helpful advice. Bonita and Claude spent every moment outside school and work devoted to this dress. Bonita met Claude's favorite drag queen, and she was nothing but a blast. Bonita had it figured out and knew exactly what the dress would look like. They purchased fabrics, cuts of taffeta, jersey, twill, silk, interfacing, and tulle. She sketched a million designs of the same dress until they both agreed it was perfect and then it began. The dress would be a trumpet style with an exaggerated but beautiful bottom, a cinched waistline, a plunging neckline, and intricate placements of sequins.

Claude tried to help as much as he could at this stage, but there was little he could do except step back and allow Bonita to create her first dress. Most students who made their first dress would only show it in class or simply to their teachers, but Bonita's would be aired at a colossal drag queen pageant that many would see. She decided it had to be perfect in every way, and she would stop at nothing until it was exactly as she thought it should be.

Her room looked as if it were ransacked by burglars or a tornado. There were shreds of fabric everywhere, boxes and needles sticking out of everything you could see. The fabric was laid on every surface and hung in the window; books were strewn about with pages and pages of different cuts, styles, and techniques used for dressmaking. Bonita put her heart and soul into every stitch she made and felt good with every piece she snipped. Frustration filled her often. When a wrong cut was made, or an incorrect stitch was placed, she thought she should be better. Still, she would remind herself often that she had yet to make it through her first semester of fashion school.

One of the key elements she desired to get right was the center back. As Ivana was a fit man, she wanted to ensure the fabric's flow helped soften her muscular back. This took up considerable time due to her inexperience with designing overall. Still, the specific need to soften a part of the body felt outside her reach. Ultimately, the winning choice was a carefully tucked and pleated back coming down from the shoulders to the center back on each side at forty-five-degree angles.

Finally, after a few more weeks of countless hours spent stitching, snipping, and cutting and stitching some more, she arose from her room with the most spectacular gown Claude had ever seen. It was the dress you would purchase at a designer store for $6000.00, but it cost at most two hundred for the material and the hours they spent planning and putting it together. Bonita was very impressed with herself, and so was

Claude. He knew Bonita could do it and wanted to force it out of her.

When Ivana Cox, Claude's drag queen friend, saw the dress, she began to cry. "Never before has anyone done something so wonderful for me! Never before has anyone gone through so much trouble to create something so beautiful!" she said, tears falling from her eyes. She may have had a chance at winning the drag pageant, and that meant the world to her. She hugged Bonita so tightly that she nearly broke her, but Bonita was so happy that Ivana loved it that she didn't care.

20

It was the day before the big pageant, and excitement was in the air. Bonita had never known such a huge event happened for female impersonators. She was happy to have met Ivana and had the privilege of creating a dress for her, the first dress Bonita had ever designed.

She had just finished school and was about to enter her door when two hands reached around and covered her eyes. At first, she was alarmed, but when she smelled the expensive cologne that her roommate Claude wore, she smiled.

"Can I help you, Mr. Peters?" she asked.

"How did you know it was me?" he retorted, relinquishing his hold on her. She turned and smiled at him, kissed him on his cheek, turned with a sense of pride, and proceeded to enter the apartment.

She was shocked to see one of her luggage bags next to the door on the floor. She turned to Claude with an alarmed look and question marks emblazoned in her eyes.

"Okay," he said, moving her over to the chair and sitting her down. "I didn't tell you this because I knew you wouldn't think you had the time and couldn't do it, so I left it out and made all the arrangements for you!"

She was staring him down with a perplexed look on her face. "What have you done, Claude?"

"Before you get mad, as I am sure you will, please remember that this is important to Ivana and vital to me. You will have so much fun you will thank me later!"

She did not loosen her pursed lip at all as he continued.

"The Miss Continental Pageant is located in Chicago, Illinois!"

"What?" She screamed, stood immediately up from her chair, and put her hands on her head. "I thought it was right here in the city. I don't have the money or the time to go to Chicago. I have an exam in a couple of weeks that I'm unprepared for."

"I know about the exam, and I know your time is tight, but you have been working hard and need a break. And as for the money, I have paid for the ticket and the accommodations," Claude said with fear. He was afraid that maybe he had gone too far by not telling Bonita, but he stood his ground. "Everything is taken care of. All you have to do is get on the plane!"

He spoke those words assertively and with a sense of urgency. Bonita couldn't understand the pique in his voice at the end when he said: "Get on the plane."

What else is he not telling me? She thought.

"Okay, fine, if it is that important to you, I will go. Why you need me is beyond me, but I will go. I'm sure I will have a lot of fun, but please, for God's sake, the next time there is something important you want me to attend, please, just tell me upfront…. When do we leave?"

Thinking she would have the night to relax and pack accordingly, she was jolted by his response.

"In two hours!"

She nearly fell to the floor in disbelief. "What? Two hours? I'm not ready!"

"I have packed your suitcase with your favorite things to wear, toiletries, and necessities. Everything is done, but you have about 20 minutes before we have to leave for the airport," Claude said with a shaky voice.

Bonita turned sharply to yell and freak out, but since she only had 20 minutes, she huffed, grabbed her suitcase, and fled to her bedroom. Not long after, she emerged looking fresh but rushed. Bonita grabbed her jacket and shoes, threw them on, and she was out the door. She didn't say anything nor look at Claude while he was sitting on the couch, but he got the hint, jumped up, grabbed his things, and ran out after her, nearly forgetting to lock the door.

The ride to the airport was a quiet one; not a lot of tension, just words unsaid. She gazed out the window with a look of fear. She saw the same route when she first arrived in New York: backward. It made her feel as though she had failed and was heading home. She didn't like the feeling but was awakened from her silent misery when Claude gently nudged her arm. He was passing her the ticket, which she took, saying, "Thank you." It was her only words until after the plane had taken off, soaring high above New York State. She turned to him again and said, "Thank you, Claude!"

"You're welcome," he said, with a sense of pride, and

then sheepishly said, "I'm sorry!" She turned her head from the window with a smile and leaned over to kiss him on the cheek. "You're forgiven!"

The plane had landed, and the crowd was thick. Bonita was beginning to think that every airport was jam-packed with people traveling in the United States. They hailed a cab and arrived at the hotel alive. She was happy to see the room was a nice, beautifully appointed room with two double beds and a separate sitting space off the side. All was quiet and surreal when she realized how tired she was. She and Claude sat and talked for a while, ordered room service, and then she curled up in her bed and fell fast asleep.

21

The following day began quite early in the morning and started at a very hectic pace. It was unbelievably noisy; men are men even when you put them in heels and dresses. They are loud, messy, and dirty-minded. They arrived at the lounge a little before two in the afternoon. So many people crammed into each little room that she thought she couldn't move. There were so many nearly naked men running around in stockings, heels, and panties that she would just giggle to herself. She and Claude would keep off to the side when they weren't needed and would talk about all the different competitors. Claude was used to this scene, but Bonita had never seen something as peculiar as this before. All the sights she saw that day transfixed her.

She loved it all and soaked up every moment she could. Ivana was a nervous wreck, running around looking for this and that. Bonita and Claude spent most of their time prepping her for the show — makeup, hair, and wardrobe was the routine. They would joke around with Ivana to keep her calm and keep her glass full of vodka and coke all through the event. It was so much fun that Bonita could hardly contain herself.

The show started, and Bonita felt nervous and sick to her stomach for Ivana. She thought how hard it must be to dress up like that and perform in front of everyone. Bonita had gotten to know Ivana a little more over the day. Ivana told Bonita quite a bit about her life. Ivana was more than just your typical drag queen; she was a successful psychiatrist. Her real name was Marcus Hannigan, and he operated out of New York and catered more towards the gay population. It worked for him. Everyone was on the same page, and most of his clients would rave about him. He helped them through so many parts of their lives that they would have been lost without him. He was calm, funny, and extraordinarily humble. There was no pretense until a few minutes before the shows would start, and then Ivana came out in full force. She would throw on the attitude, which was crucial in these pageants.

The night went well, but unfortunately, Ivana did not win. She was the first runner-up, and to her, that meant just as much. "Next year, I'll get 'em," Ivana said with pride and integrity. Although she did not win the pageant, everyone thought her dress was the most exquisite evening gown, and everyone wanted to know where she got it. Ivana talked up her designer to all of them. Before she knew it, Bonita was being tugged in every direction.

So many of the contestants and other supporting Queens asked if she could make them a dress, one as beautiful as Ivana's. She agreed with everyone and told them they would have to email her the measurements, fabric desires, descriptions of what they wanted, and a money order to cover the cost. The night flew by, and Claude and Bonita were the center of attention. They would exchange funny looks and finally decided it was time to leave. When they arrived back at the hotel, Bonita realized she had been commissioned to design over 40 dresses, including two for the new Miss Continental.

She was thrilled about it, as was Claude, but she knew it would take a lot of work and soak up her free time. After dwelling on it for a while, she concluded that although she would have little free time and a lot of extra work, she would be making a lot of money. It was a blast and a job where she earned her hours and called all the shots. It couldn't have been much better than that. She felt like she was an actual designer so early in her education.

22

The end of the first term was only a mere two weeks away. Bonita was so nervous that she found sleeping increasingly tricky at night and was on edge the rest of the time. Claude tried everything to help alleviate stress and make things easy on her, but nothing would work. Nothing could make her feel at ease or even remotely relaxed for a single second. She had too much work to do. Her most considerable stress was not that she was up to her ears in paperwork and fabric but that the end-of-term exam was coming up. Tomorrow, she would find out what garment to make for 55% of her mark. The rest was easy: paperwork and theories. There would be sketches and questions to answer, but what if she had to make something she knew nothing about? What if she got chosen to make a jacket? She didn't know the first thing about making jackets.

That night, Bonita lay in bed for a very long time. She tossed and turned, changed her pillows, and even listened to soft music to help her fall asleep. Bonita couldn't sleep, and it was beginning to seriously anger her. The angrier she got, the lesser the chance of actually sleeping became. Finally, after nearly five hours, she rolled out of bed and went to the kitchen. Bonita had never been much of a coffee drinker, but in this circumstance, she realized it would have to be her friend for today. She made a cup of coffee and looked in the fridge to get something to eat. She made eggs, bacon, and toast — a big, hearty meal for a stressful day. It was nearly 5 am, and the house was filled with the fragrant aroma of a delicious breakfast. Claude, who had been sleeping all night and didn't have to work that day, woke up to the smell and wandered into the kitchen.

"What are you doing up so early, Bonita?"

"I can't sleep, and if I were to lay in bed another minute, I would have thrown myself through the window!"

Claude had seen her frustrated and stressed before, but not like this. She was so afraid of what the teacher would request of her that it was simply killing her. Claude chose to stay awake with her after asking if company would help her calm down. She had made enough of a hearty breakfast for both of them, and they chatted for quite some time. Bonita then excused herself to go take a shower. It helped a bit, but she became sleepy once she felt clean.

"Fucking figures," she said hopelessly.

She got her things together and went out the door, kissing Claude on the cheek before she left as he wished her good luck. She stepped onto the elevator and relaxed a little. She decided to just take it easy. The worst thing she would have to do would be to design something hard, like a jacket. A month or so ago, she didn't know how to create a dress, but she quickly learned independently. It wasn't as bad as she was making it out to be, but the gnawing in her guts never left no matter how hard she tried to just let it go.

Her class was packed when she walked in from the cold winter weather outside. She sat and put her things underneath her desk at her feet. Everyone noticed her for some reason and was glancing back and forth. They all knew she was under a lot of pressure simply because of the redness of her skin. The massive vein that seemed to take up permanent residence on her forehead didn't help much. She was tense, and everyone knew it. She didn't speak to anyone and just kept her head pointed towards the whiteboard at the front of the room. She only moved when the teacher walked in.

The time had come for the assignments to be handed out. Bonita stopped breathing! No air entered her lungs while the assignments were placed on each student's desk. Finally, the teacher walked past her desk and laid the white sheet of paper right in front of her, face down. She slowly took the paper and slid it towards her, pulling upwards when the bottom of the sheet cleared the edge, still not breathing as she turned it over.

She gasped and then let her head drop a little harder than she intended on her desk, making a loud thud that alerted everyone in the room. Lyla dashed to her side as quickly as she could. Everyone else was convinced that she had died from an aneurysm. "Are you okay, Bon?"

Bonita, covered in beads of sweat, lifted her head and looked at Lyla.

"Yes, I'm fine! Sorry, I'm just really relieved."

Bonita had not been assigned to make a jacket, trousers, or anything requiring a lot of difficulty. Instead, on her paper, eight little black letters took so much weight off her shoulders that she couldn't bear to hold her head up any longer. "Ball gown" was a relief for her; she felt like crying, but she kept herself together long enough to get out of the school and onto the street.

Bonita was sure she would cry once she was back on Seventh Ave., but the tears did not come; just easy thoughts floated through her head. For most, designing and making a dress in only two weeks would leave them absolutely mortified, but not for Bonita. She, in fact, was thrilled because now all she had to do was really focus on the theory for her exam — the rest was already done. She had created five full dresses to fill the requests she received while at the Miss Continental pageant in Chicago. All she had to do was ask to borrow one back until after the exams. It was easy-breezy-beautiful, and she had to decide which dress to use.

23

Later that evening, when Claude arrived home from work, Bonita had made dinner and opened a lovely bottle of wine. He wondered at first what the occasion was, but she informed him just to relax and have a good time. "I need it!"

They sat around the table and ate for over an hour. Bonita even went the extra mile to make a lovely dessert trifle. She told him of her day and how she was assigned to make a dress. He laughed and said, "That won't be hard!"

"Exactly, so I can relax and enjoy the next two weeks!"

She asked his opinion on what to decide and spent the weekend debating which dress to pick. She thought of design, function, draping, and wearability. All her dresses had that, but which one screamed "the best"? She wanted one that would exemplify the best of the best, the best damn dress her teacher had ever seen from a first-year student. Of course, she had no real expectations of that happening, but if she channeled it, it would help her choose.

After much thinking and consideration, she finally decided that the dress she designed for Ivana Cox would be the best choice and the easiest to attain. She was lucky enough to have developed a good rapport with Ivana, so she imagined she wouldn't have too much trouble getting her to let her use it for the exam. She got on the phone and arranged a meeting.

Ivana was happy to lend the dress back for Bonita's exam and felt confident it would earn her more than just a passing score. Ivana had been on the scene for quite a long time and had never met someone with Bonita's skill. The dress she designed for her was off the charts and helped get her the runner-up spot in the pageant.

After that, Bonita had plenty of time to study her theory and ensure she knew the textbooks from cover to cover when the exam came around. The following weeks flew by quickly, but she didn't mind because she felt ready and couldn't wait to get it over with.

24

On the day of the exam, she went in early to pin her dress to a mannequin and get it looking perfect before the exam started. After completing everything, she went to the classroom where the exam was being held, found a desk, sat down, and waited for it to begin. Not long after, the class started to fill up, with her fellow students all looking a mess. Everyone was seated when the teacher came in and began to pass out little booklets for everyone, which he instructed not to turn over until he said so.

The teacher was exact with how the day would play out. They would have three hours to finish the exam, and then they would hand them to his assistant. At that time, they would be free to roam about the school, grab lunch, and make it back for 1:00 pm. At that time, both sections of the tests and the garments would be graded, and the results would be handed out. You could feel the tension building in the whole room. One girl cried when she realized she forgot to add a button to the pocket of her trench coat.

The teacher said, "Turn your tests over and begin!" With that, the sound of an instant rustle filled the air, and pencils were being pressed against the paper aggressively. It didn't take Bonita too long to finish her exam, and she decided she had enough time to go home and make a sandwich. When she got home, she was happy to find the apartment empty and quiet. Not that she would have been disappointed if Claude had been home, but everyone needs a little time to themselves. She sat at the counter, perched on a stool, and ate a tuna sandwich with alfalfa sprouts and pickles, one of her all-time favorite snacks. Long after eating, Bonita just sat there staring off into space. She was daydreaming again. She snapped out of her trance, grabbed her things, and left.

Everyone looked like they would explode when the class reconvened at 1:00 pm. Bonita felt confident for once. She knew she would receive a passing grade and sat back in her chair, relaxed and collected. The teacher entered the classroom and handed the booklets back with the scores on it.

"Some failed, some barely made it, some excelled, and one went above and beyond!" he thundered over the class.

"Miss Bonita Smith had by far the highest grade of anyone!"

Bonita was utterly mortified. She turned so red in the face she could feel the heat rolling off her skin as she sank low in her seat.

"Not only did she score the highest on her written test, but her garment was above and beyond any first-term student's abilities that I have previously seen. The dress is immaculate, Miss Smith. You should be proud of yourself. You show exceptional promise!"

She didn't know what to feel. She was oblivious now to anything going on in the class; she just wanted to disappear and, at the same time, jump for joy. The class was let out, and she bee-lined it to the door. Her friend Bethany sauntered behind her, jealous and upset that she barely made it. Bonita had no idea of her feelings and was so embarrassed that she just wanted to get home and hide in her room.

When Bonita got home, Claude was there with Ivana, and they looked at her with a sense of urgency.

"Well?" Claude said.

"Oh my god, I passed, but hear this."

She continued to tell them about what happened and how she was so embarrassed about what the teacher had to say about her. They both agreed with the teacher: Bonita was gifted; she had a vision and could convey it in sketch form and elegant garments. This was by far one of the happiest days of her life, and she couldn't wait to call her parents and tell them.

25

The snow had begun to fall like giant cotton balls gently on the ground, giving the streets of New York City a clean and beautiful façade. New York was excellent in the winter, and Central Park was so breathtaking that it would even bring tears to the hardest of men. Bonita found herself with ample time to explore the freshly blanketed city. School was out, and she had no plans for Christmas except to stay in the frosty city of New York.

It was rather difficult for her this time of year. It was her first Christmas away from her family, and she missed them more now than she had since she left. Although the snow made her happy and gleeful, it also caused her great sadness. She thought of all the Christmases past. She would reminisce about how her family would decorate the tree together, light a fire in the backyard to roast marshmallows, and spend Christmas Eve and day bundled up in their lovely warm house alone with nothing but fantastic food, good quality time, and many presents. Being the only child, Bonita was often spoiled rotten around Christmas time, as spoiled rotten as a poor girl could be. Bonita could never entirely understand how Christmas was the only time she didn't feel like a poor person. Her father would always have a large number of presents under the tree. They may not have been top-of-the-line or anything, but there were always lots. She would miss that this year, but not as much as she would miss her parents. She thought about going home, but it wasn't in the cards — too much money to fly home for a bit of time.

Claude had noticed that Bonita's spirits were down and knew why. He remembered his first Christmas alone, and how sad it was, so he decided to make as close to a traditional Christmas in New York for Bonita as possible. They had talked so much since she had arrived here that they even spoke about their Christmas and family traditions one night. He couldn't light a fire in the backyard to roast marshmallows, but he could do a lot to make it feel good for her. Claude cared about Bonita so much, and he never regretted asking her to move in. She had been the best possible roommate he could have ever asked for. They lived well together and just simply got along.

Claude surprised Bonita one day with his plans. She was reluctant but still excited. Bonita thought that she should at least make the best of her situation. Her parents had sent her another $3000.00 for Christmas, which she was upset about, and scorned them because they didn't have the money to do that themselves: but much like Christmas, her father seemed to always have a way of bleeding blood from a turnip. They told her to be quiet and let them be worrying parents, and finally, she accepted the offer and told them of her and Claude's plans.

Bonita's parents were never so happy that she had gone

off to New York to live with a gay man. Being Pentecostal preachers, they considered that an abomination and depravity in the eyes of God. They never really voiced their opinions about it but were very happy to know he was taking good care of their little girl. For that, they were eternally grateful.

Over the next few weeks, Claude and Bonita took every chance to shop around the city, looking for cute but classy Christmas trinkets and ornaments. They found some beautiful items perfect for Bonita's first city Christmas. They bought snow globes, ribbons, bows, pre-lit tree boughs, a tree skirt, and everything else they could find. The only thing they had left to get was a tree, which they found at a high-end department store. It was beautiful and looked very close to the real thing. They chose a faux tree because they wanted it to last, and they didn't want to spend their entire Christmas using the dust buster to get the pine needles off the floor.

They spent all their time shopping together except when Claude was at work. Even then, she would shop by herself to buy Claude a few incredible Christmas presents. Bonita wanted him to have a wonderful Christmas, too, since he was so lovely to make this Christmas perfect for her. She found him what she thought was the perfect gift: a pocket watch! He was constantly checking the time, and it would go great with the suit he wore at the counter. Secretly, Bonita believed pocket watches were items every distinguished man should have. It said the man was conscious of himself and others, always ensuring he was on time to make appointments and special occasions. She felt it was sexy and hoped that Claude would love it.

Over the next few days, Bonita found herself in an unusual

place: in the kitchen with Claude, baking cookies and cakes for the holiday festivities. It was so much fun, although she had no idea how to bake since her mother took care of everything back home. They laughed and threw flour at each other. Still, in the end, they created some very delicious cookies and cakes to serve any unexpected visitors over the holidays.

Through it all, Bonita had forgotten the pending sadness looming over her heart. She noticed that she was in great cheer and holiday spirit. She looked forward to Christmas and couldn't wait for it to be here so she and Claude could have some real Christmas fun.

26

It was Christmas Eve, and all through the house, ribbons were a-flying and fluttering about. The sweet smell of turkey arose from the stove; outside, you could see a fresh blanket of snow. Bonita was happy and all aglow; Claude was wrapping and pinning on bows.

It was a joyous time, a happy time, a Christmastime! Bonita had no idea she could feel so good and have such a great Christmas without being home with her family, but she and Claude had proven that wrong. The house was adorned with Christmas lights, garland, and the most beautiful tree she had ever seen. It appeared as what Santa's home would look like if Santa were real. A delectable dinner baking in the oven sent a succulent aroma throughout the house. There were plenty of presents underneath the tree, from friends and each other, that hid the hand-stitched vintage tree skirt they had purchased.

Claude exited his room with a heaping pile of presents in his arms. Much to Bonita's surprise, he had to make a second trip to get the rest, but it didn't make her feel bad because she also bought so many things for Claude. It was to be a fantastic

Christmas for each of them. Both were equally pleased with themselves and as the afternoon went on, they began their festivities with a bit of stiff eggnog.

They sat and chatted for nearly an hour while the turkey finished cooking in the oven. Claude told Bonita of a few of his plans for the evening, and she loved them all. He told her that although he couldn't light a fire in the backyard to roast marshmallows, they would do that over the stovetop. He also told her he wanted to take her down toward Battery Park to see all the beautiful Christmas lights and decorations. She was all for that in every way, and then they were to come back to the apartment and celebrate the rest of Christmas a little more traditionally.

When Bonita was growing up, her family had some solemn traditions that they did every year. First off, Christmas Eve was a day for family. You spent Christmas Eve wrapping presents, sitting around and telling stories, and guessing what your parents had for you, and then the parents would guess what they had for each other. Dinner would always be cooking in the oven, and when dinner time came, only candles were lit around the table and in the kitchen. There had to be candles every Christmas dinner — no artificial light. After dinner, they would get in the car and drive around the community and other little communities to see the lights on the houses.

When they arrived home, they would get chips, chocolate, and pop, or soda if we're speaking New Yorker, out and spread it on the coffee table. She was allowed to open one present on Christmas Eve, typically a pajama set. Although she knew what it was, she wanted to open it every year and wear it to bed that night. They would sit closely on the couch, with Bonita between her parents, and watch a family movie. Halfway through the film, it would be paused so her father could go and make ice cream sundaes, then the movie would resume. After it was done, Bonita would kiss her parents good night and wander to bed. She always found it hard to sleep on Christmas Eve. Even when she got older, Christmas was her favorite time of year, and nothing would change that.

Early the following day, they would all leave bed while it was still dark. That was the rule: Christmas would have been ruined otherwise. They would sit around the tree with all the lights on and soft music playing in the background. After all the presents were open, they would go to the kitchen, where her mother would make a terrific breakfast of home-made waffles, bacon, ham, eggs, and toast. Usually, she and her mother would go back to bed for a few hours, but never her father. He was making baked glazed ham for that night's dinner, and someone had to do it.

27

When Bonita and Claude sat down to dinner that night to enjoy their festive meal, there were no lights on in the house, only candles. They ate until they were stuffed, and she thought the walk would be the best remedy to burn off the big feast. They ventured out into the city for a long walk, and Bonita was awed by what she saw. Unlike a Newfoundland Christmas drive, things were much classier than back home. The buildings were elegantly lit with strategically placed decorations. She could hardly walk straight; her head was turning in many directions. They walked for nearly three hours until they hailed a cab and returned home.

That night, they got chips, chocolate, and pop — and, for the first time, a nice glass of expensive wine — and sat around the living room with a movie to watch and presents to open. It took Claude and Bonita a long time to decide which gift each should open, but it was worth it when they finally did. Bonita got a pair of satin pajamas, much nicer than the flannel ones she would usually get, but pajamas, nonetheless. She hugged him and kissed his cheek, saying, "Thank you." Claude didn't get pajamas because he slept in the nude; that would have been money not well spent. But he did get a robe, a long Egyptian cotton robe for when he had to get up at night to use the bathroom or grab a drink. He loved it and thought it was a very thoughtful present, and then made a wisecrack about how she only bought him the robe in fear of waking up one night and seeing his dangly bits flopping about. They laughed hard for a while and finally relaxed to watch their movie.

It was an hour in when the movie paused. Bonita was startled and looked over to see Claude get up from the couch and walk to the kitchen.

"Getting more wine?" she asked.

"Maybe," he said as he gave her a sly look. She watched him reach up in the cupboard and pull down two bowls, then into the freezer to pull out a box of ice cream. She smiled, and a tear came to her eye. Bonita quickly jumped from the couch and walked toward the kitchen, where she hugged him and told him, "You're the best friend any girl could ask for. I love you, Claude, and thank you so much for everything you have done for me."

Claude turned to her and said, "No, Bonita, you are the best friend anyone could ask for. I cannot tell you how my life has been enriched since you came to live with me. I feel like I am, for once, not alone, and I have someone who gets me. I love you too, Bon Bon," he said with a smirk. They hugged again and went on to make the sundaes together. From that moment on, their bond was more potent than before. They loved each other very much and considered each other their closest friends.

The movie ended, and they both retired to bed. As always,

Bonita couldn't sleep. She tossed and turned, got up, and lay back down again. There was no sleep for her tonight, so she retrieved her finest stationery and pen and began to write her parents a letter. It took her nearly three hours to find what she wanted to say, and she finally dozed off.

Like a kid, she had her alarm clock set so she wouldn't oversleep and miss waking up while it was still dark out. The alarm went off, and she shot out of bed, grabbed her glasses, and swung open the door. The lights on the tree were on, and Claude was already sitting by the chair with warm tea. He motioned for her to hurry up, and she almost skipped to where he was. He also had a cup of tea for her, and they both sat on the floor and began opening presents.

There were many presents. Bonita counted nearly 27 just for her and believed the same for Claude. They spent hours that day opening them up one by one and talking about how much they loved each gift. They spoke of how they would use it or what to use with it.

Then came the last two. Claude beat her to the punch, grabbed hers first, and told her she had to open it. She argued a little bit and then gave in. When she unwrapped it, she nearly fainted. Inside the neat package were two tickets and accommodations to Paris Fashion Week. She couldn't believe it. She was lost for words. She thought, "How can he afford this?" But instead of insulting him on Christmas Day, she gave him the biggest hug she ever gave.

Paris Fashion Week was the biggest fashion event in the world, and anyone who was anyone would try to be there. She had never even thought of it because it was so far-fetched. She could never have pulled it off. Now, here she was, staring at two tickets to the event. She could attend all the shows, the after-parties, the luncheons, and whatever else went on while she was there. Never before had she received something as big as this. She had tears and no words to speak as she kissed Claude's cheek that day.

Now, it was Claude's turn. She was sick to her stomach because she felt her gift was inadequate compared to his. Although it cost a pretty penny, there was no way it would compare to what he had given her. He looked at the box, smiled, and then opened it. When he took the top off, his smile went away. The look on his face was worse than that of disgust — almost pure sadness. She wondered what she had done. The next thing she saw was a single tear drop form on Claude's cheek and fall down onto his lap.

"Claude, I can return it if you don't like it. It isn't a big deal. We can pick something else that you would like."

"Like it?" Claude said strangely, then shifted and glanced up at her, only to return his head toward the package.

"Bonita, this is the best gift anyone has ever given me." He looked up with tear-filled eyes and gave her this expression she had never seen before. It was pure gratitude and thankfulness with a hint of somberness.

"Claude, if that is the case, then why are you crying? Why does it bring sadness to your eyes?" Bonita said softly. She couldn't understand what power this simple pocket watch could have over him.

He let his head drop again and then went on, through sobs, to tell her a story he had never told anyone before:

"When I was a child, my father and I would play a game. It would be a game of time. He wanted me to be able to tell time, so he created this game to help me learn while making it fun."

He sniffled and said, "We would play this game every weekend for years, even after I learned to tell time. I remember the last day we played it, right before my 14th birthday. He would up the ante and hide the pocket watch throughout the house. The point of the game was to find the watch, record the time, and try to make an educated guess on what time he actually hid the watch."

"Two months later, he said we should play the game again. I laughed and said, 'Okay,' for old times' sake. Three days later, my mom received a call. It resulted in her telling me he wouldn't come home for a while. At first, I thought maybe he went on a vacation, but then my mother finally told me he passed away from a massive heart attack. That was the last time I saw my dad or his pocket watch. I asked my mother about it a little while after, and she went looking for it, but we never found it."

"Later, she told me she believed it was misplaced or taken when he took his attack. My heart was broken."

Bonita sat there dumbfounded and entirely without words. She had no idea what to say except the typical cliché.

"I'm so sorry, Claude."

"Don't be," he said. "Whenever I see a pocket watch, I remember all the good times I spent with my dad. I could never bring myself to buy one, but this is different. This is wonderful, heartfelt, and the best gift. You didn't know! That makes it the most perfect gift."

They sat there for a moment in silence, just staring off into space; then Bonita got up, sat by him, and put her arm around him. He cried a little, and she held him close, comforting him.

After all this had passed, and they returned to their Christmas Day, Bonita told him she would go back to bed for a while. He agreed, and they both disappeared into their rooms. Bonita didn't take long before going back to sleep, and a good sleep she had.

She didn't wake again until nearly 3:30 pm. She jumped up and ran into the bathroom to take a shower. She smelled this wonderful yet familiar scent when she got out and dried off. She walked out toward the kitchen, and there was Claude in an apron and oven mitts, taking out a big, glazed ham from the oven. She was so happy.

"How did you make the glaze?" she said. Claude told her what went in it, and she was shocked to know it was exactly as her Daddy made it. She freaked out and told him. He responded with, "I know. He gave it to me."

They laughed, talked about her folks, and then ate a beautiful traditional Christmas Day dinner.

28

Christmas Eve and Day both went very well. They were so stuffed with all their food that they decided to burn calories on Boxing Day. Boxing Day in Newfoundland meant nothing to Bonita; it was an extra day of holiday, and that was it. Boxing Day in New York City was a different story. While the US didn't celebrate Boxing Day like Canada did, New York was a playground, nonetheless.

So off they went, walking the streets of Seventh and Broadway; they visited Greenwich Village and SoHo. None of the major department stores were left unturned. They purchased all sorts of things. Bonita bought so many things she could hardly carry them all. She had already sent home gifts for her folks at Christmas, but she also wanted to find a few more fabulous items to send them.

They spent the whole day out, which meant ten-and-a-half hours for Claude and Bonita. They had had enough when they finally fell back on their couch later that night.

"Phew," said Claude. "I don't know if I could have taken more of that!"

Bonita grunted to agree, as that was all she could muster

up. They both decided that every calorie they ate over the last few days was burnt off. They both hung out for a few more hours, reviewing their purchases. Bonita put together a care package for her parents. Finally, without further ado, she retired to her bed, where she fell fast asleep.

Over the next few days, she did nothing except lounge around the house and cook healthier meals. She had such a fantastic holiday that she felt she should return to normal. It wasn't that hard for her. As she tidied up under the tree and cleaned up around the house, before she knew it, she was feeling a little less holiday and a little more regular. There were still plenty of decorations, and she didn't want to take them down, so she left them for another week.

It was two days before New Year's Eve, and Lyla and Bethany were over to spend some time with Bonita during the holidays. The New Year's Eve plans and activities came up during their visit. Bonita had no agenda and didn't want any. Lyla, Bethany, and Claude disagreed; they thought it would be fantastic for them to go to one of the top parties and have a fabulous time together. Bonita had other things in mind: a quiet night at home, a hot bath, a good book, and a few phone calls to family.

They persisted in persuading Bonita, and she kept up an intense fight. There seemed to be nothing that would budge her on this one. Finally, out of pure desperation, Claude devised a marvelous idea. He offered Bonita the opportunity to have a makeover, a head-to-toe style update. Claude told her she had lived in New York City for a long time and should start looking like it, mainly because she was into fashion. He offered to give her the most luxuriant makeover known to man, a head-to-toe complete change in appearance. Claude wanted to accentuate her natural beauty, hidden so well behind bushy eyebrows, frizzy hair, thick glasses, and un-flattering attire.

At first, Bonita felt slightly offended and excused herself from the room. She made her way to the bathroom and looked in the mirror. She thought she was ugly.

"But am I really that bad?"

After nearly 10 minutes, she took a closer look and realized that Claude wasn't trying to hurt her feelings but rather make her feel better about herself. Also, what could be the harm in trying something new? She had been wearing the same loose-fitting clothes that did nothing for her shape since she arrived here. The New York City walking had helped her lose significant weight and tone up. What is the worst that could happen?

She emerged from the bathroom and looked at Claude, and said, "Just so you know, you're an asshole for telling me I look ratty and worn out, but you got yourself a deal, Mr. Peters!"

She smiled funny, and the girls and Claude jumped for joy. "This is going to be so much fun. You will not regret it!"

29

The following day came early for both Claude and Bonita. It was time to begin creating the new Miss Smith. Over the next three days, Bonita would undergo a complete image transformation that Claude was convinced would change her life forever. He had an excellent idea of what he wanted to create but needed help. Claude needed to call in a few reinforcements and ensure everything went smoothly. He knew Bonita would back out of the agreement if significant hitches occurred. She was not used to being poked and prodded, but it had to be done.

The plan began with Bonita being waxed, plucked, scraped, peeled, frosted, and cut from head to toe. Claude called in an emergency appointment at a local spa to give her a fresh start. She was nervous when she arrived, for she never knew what happened in these little places. A young lady took her into a room and told her to remove her clothes, then before Bonita knew it, she had hot wax spread in places she had never shown anyone before. It hurt like hell, and she cried the entire time.

Next, she was shuffled out to another area, where she got

into a tub of what looked like mud and turned out to be just that. It felt good and made her skin firm and refreshed, but it took nearly a half-hour to get it all off. Following that were the manicure and pedicure stations, where Claude had pulled out all the stops. He gave her the best set of tips they had, and the foot massage was unbelievably delightful.

It was lunchtime, and she figured that her visit was done, but unfortunately, it had only just begun. Next up, they took her to another private area where they started to massage her face, and in a blink of an eye, off went her eyebrows. When she saw the strip leave her face, she gasped and put her hand immediately on her eyebrow.

"Phew," she thought. She was happy that there were still some left. They removed blackheads and blemishes, steamed her face, and then performed microdermabrasion, which felt a little like broken glass being massaged over her skin. Bonita felt like a turkey would feel on Christmas Day, wrapped up and poked with all the trimmings and seasonings. She didn't think it could worsen, but they took her to another room. There, they smothered her in a chocolate body-treatment wrap. The lady said this would give her an all-over tan without streaks and shower fades.

"Finally," she thought, "I'm getting a shower, getting re-dressed, and will be done with this place," so she hurried up to try and get out of there as fast as she could. She was feeling quite hungry by now, and all she wanted to do was eat something. But when she stepped out into the salon section, there were a few more surprises.

Their top hairstylist was waiting for her, along with Claude, who had been talking her up since they arrived. He stressed that it had to be the latest trend: hot and sexy, and the frizz had to go. "I want her with dark hair and soft highlights." He requested it be slightly away from her face, but it was up-to-date and functionally designed. It took Shane three hours to control Bonita's hair, but the result was immaculate. She suggested some insanely priced leave-in hair masks and a couple of tools she could use at home. Bonita stepped off her chair and walked to the back, where the private mirrors were. She pulled back her robe and looked at the woman staring back at her. Bonita loved it. Her hair was long, flowing, and silky, and as she was leaving, she left a very hefty tip.

The next place that Claude had planned on taking Bonita was to shop for the perfect outfit for those hot parties and then for a gown to wear to the New Year's Day ball, which Claude already had tickets for. Claude wanted to give her a fashion one-on-one but was amazed with her chosen items. It took only a short time before they had everything they needed and left. They had found some incredible buys and were ready to return to the apartment and take a moment to breathe. In just a few hours, she transformed from an insecure girl into a confident-looking woman determined to be the next top designer this country would see.

Claude woke Bonita early the following day and took her to an eye doctor. He asked the doctor to help him remove those thick-framed glasses and give her clear contacts. At first, the doctor was reluctant to prescribe her contacts when he found out she had bad eyesight. Still, later, after some convincing and paper signing, he gave her new disposable packets that lasted for one month. Also, during their visit, Claude pushed to see the types of frames they had to offer, so while the guy was working on the contacts, another woman took the prescription. She told them that if they bought one set of frames, their second was free, and the deal was also transferable to contacts.

After several tedious and tiring hours in the shop, she was handed her first pair of contacts and a pair of designer frames much cuter than the Coke bottle glasses she had been sporting. They shaped her face nicely. She was pleased with the purchase but needed to know what else she needed and how to put them in. On the way back, Claude stopped at a Walgreens and picked up eye cases, drops, and a pamphlet with instructions on putting in contacts.

30

The night had arrived, and it was the night everyone came out to party, the most appropriate night of anyone's partying life. It was New Year's Eve, and you could hear the people from the streets below getting ready to ring in another long year. Bonita was feeling a bit nervous and tense and became unsure of going out on such a busy night, but she couldn't let Claude down after all he had done for her over the past few days.

She emerged from the bathroom, all showered and clean. She had practiced the day before, putting her contacts in and then taking them out, so it wasn't so difficult this time. Claude was waiting in the living room with more makeup than she had ever seen, hairbrushes, straighteners, and curling irons. He gave her a welcoming look as she entered the area and asked, "Are you ready to become Cinderella?"

She smiled her quirky smile and then plopped down in the chair before him and let him begin his work. For a girl like Bonita, it was a new experience to allow someone to touch her, never mind prod, poke, and tweeze her, but she trusted Claude with her life and knew she was in good hands. First, he began blow-drying and infusing the spray to tame the frizz. Then came the straightening and, finally, the curling. Claude wouldn't let her see herself, not even a quick glance before everything was finished.

The next part of the evening would be fully dedicated to her face, and there seemed to be a lot of options he had to choose from. He appeared to methodically pick and place each one. She jumped when she saw him take a pencil to her brow. It felt weird and wrong for her. "What the hell is he doing?" she thought.

The cheeks, the contour, the eyes, and the lips all fell into place, and although she knew she was wearing a lot of makeup, it didn't feel as heavy as she expected. Finally, he opened a package of what looked like little hair pieces on a string. She cringed when he put them on her eyes. He noticed her hesitation and assured her that they were just false eyelashes that created a fuller and more dramatic look. She became wary of this because all she saw before was Claude's Drag Queen makeup. He knew what he was doing, but she didn't want to look like a drag queen.

Finally, she was done. Claude told her to stand up, close her eyes, take a deep breath, and hold it. When she did, he sprayed what smelled like hairspray all over her face. She jumped back and coughed, yelling, "That shit is for your hair. How about you get it on my fucking hair, not my face!"

"Oh, be quiet, you volatile Betty! Hairspray sets the makeup and makes it last longer."

She stood for a second and said, "Oh, okay! Well, in that case, spray away."

Claude gave her an excellent twice-over to ensure it lasted

the night, and then he handed her a glass of champagne, and they gulped it down. He then hustled her into her bedroom and gave her the dress. He made her promise that she would only look in the mirror once the dress was on, and when she was ready, she would come out and show him and the girls, who would be arriving shortly.

Bonita kept her promise, even though it was killing her, but she thought, "I can wait another five minutes to see myself." Claude had bought her this sexy little dress, tight and black with Austrian crystals placed around the neckline, which was plunging for Bonita's taste. They also got her a bra and panty set to wear with it, and, well, when she put the bra on, she thought, "Holy fuck. I can rest my chin on these bitches."

Nevertheless, she didn't waver and continued to finish dressing. She then gently pulled the dress over her head, using a shower cap to prevent any damage to the style as Claude had instructed. She was all dressed as she went to her floor-length mirror to take a look when she felt something was missing. Her shoes! She quickly dashed to the closet and opened the cute little box on the bottom. There lay the most beautiful shoes she had ever seen full-on pumps with nearly a 5-inch heel, black with an opened embroidered design on the sides and toe. They fit like a dream, and on the back, they had this simple lace lined with some sort of crystal from the top of the shoe to the bottom of the heel. They were gorgeous. These were the only shoes she considered high fashion and those she never intended to wear. But she had bought these shoes for a night like this and would put them on and walk in style. Try to walk in style; she had never worn heels that high before.

Finally, she took a deep breath and stepped in front of the floor-length mirror. At first, she was shocked. She didn't know who was staring back at her. It wasn't her; it couldn't be her. She never had lovely hair that flowed beautifully, perfect eyebrows, or long, sexy legs. She had never had a figure like a supermodel, but whoever was staring back at her had all these things. "Who is she?" she kept asking herself. After nearly thirty minutes of staring at this woman in the mirror, she decided that whoever it was, for tonight, it would be Miss Bonita Smith, and she intended to have a good time. Her nerves had definitely lessened by this time, most likely due to the glass of bubbly she downed 29 minutes ago. Nevertheless, Lyla and Bethany had arrived, and it was time to grace them with her presence.

The door opened, and she stepped out. She heard the girls and Claude but did not see them. Assuming they were in the kitchen, she stood straight up, glanced back at her mirror, and winked at herself.

"Here's looking at you, kid!" she said, with a gleam in her eye.

As she stepped through the hall, her stilettos made a clicking noise, which Bonita loved because it made her feel like she had power and sex appeal, something she had never felt before. She walked around the opening of the living room with her head held high as if it were just a typical day. It took a lot of energy not to freak out, but it paid off.

As soon as the girls got one look at her, they started screaming and freaking out. They ran to her, telling her she was beautiful, and "Oh my God, how gorgeous do you look?" They pulled on her hair, touched her dress, and one of them smacked her fanny. Claude simply stood there and smiled a big smile. She walked over to him, with her hips swinging wide for effect, and gave him the biggest hug she could give.

He told her that she looked beautiful, and she said, "All thanks to you, my friend!" Then he turned and said, "A carpenter could not make something so beautiful out of bad wood." He winked and said, "Let's go!"

31

Bonita, Claude, Bethany, and Lyla quickly departed the building, hailed a cab, climbed in, and headed for their destination. By this time, Bonita was on cloud nine and floating like a fairy through the night sky. They arrived at the venue and entered. Bonita was frozen in amazement. She had never seen something so elegant before. Bonita often felt that way about many things, but in her heart, each time was as true to her as the last. After she returned to reality, she made a direct line to the bar. Bonita felt warm from the champagne from earlier and didn't want that to end. She grabbed another champagne and met with her friends on the dance floor.

The music was pumping, and everyone seemed to be having a wonderful time. Bonita would find herself stopping and staring once in a while at all the beautiful people and the fun they were having. She busted a move that night but realized she was dancing quite foolishly. Bonita had yet to be introduced to how people danced at clubs and began to observe. She spotted a woman with mocha-colored skin a few feet away from her who seemed to know how to move. She began to mimic her, and the next thing she knew, she was rolling her hips, popping her bottom, and dropping to the floor. Claude took notice and yelled over the music, "Watch it; you don't want to take someone out with that thing." She blushed and kept on working it.

It was one minute from midnight, and everyone was gearing up to find someone to kiss. Bonita was beautiful that night but still very shy on the inside. Claude suggested that they kiss each other. They made a few rules about using no tongue and keeping it to a dry kiss only when the clock struck midnight. Although it was not a romantic kiss, it felt right! He was the only real boy in her life, and she loved him and was so thankful she got to spend the holidays with him exclusively.

The night progressed, and the crowd thinned a little. Bonita figured they were attending other happening parties around town. They found an empty table near the windows, sat down, and ordered more drinks. They laughed and laughed about the year that passed, how Bonita was when she first showed up, and how she was now. It was all so much fun. Bonita was laughing so hard she didn't realize that she needed to use the bathroom, so once the laughter dulled a bit, she quickly flew from her seat and headed toward the ladies' room.

Drink in hand, she walked briskly, paying little attention to her surroundings, for she was on a mission. But then, out of nowhere... CRASH! She bumped into someone, and who could it be? None other than Benjamin Ryder, the asshole from her school. Amidst the collision, she not only spilled her drink all over him but his drink as well. Embarrassed, she bent over to pick up the broken glass from the floor.

Just like in the movies, she lifted her head up, and their eyes met, and they stood still for a moment. She saw a very handsome and alluring man for the first time since the beginning of term. Something changed in her that evening, and the same happened to Benjamin. Something connected. Neither knew what it was, nor did they want to find out right then and there. They quickly said they were sorry and went their separate ways, each looking back at the other multiple times before they were both out of sight.

The night went on, and she often thought about him. In fact, she couldn't get him off of her mind. She felt so bad that she spilled her drink on him that she wished she had offered to buy him a new one. After that, she looked but never saw him at the bar and concluded she ruined his New Year's, and he would never speak to her again. They all left shortly after and arrived home in a drunken stupor. Bonita went to bed. The next day, she would wake up and go to the ball with Claude. Bonita was looking forward to it, but at the same time, she just wanted to stay home. She told herself that it would end the festivities and that there would be nothing else until the summer came.

32

One week into her second term, Bonita felt refreshed and rejuvenated. The holidays were unforgettable, but now she was returning to her routine. Classes were new, but most of the people were the same. She enjoyed her new teachers, and the different things she was learning that complemented her previous courses. Learning theory this year took her most tremendous focus. It was the most enjoyable part of her classes. She found the first year so mundane and unnecessary. This year, it meant more to her than learning simple stitches, and although she worked equally hard on both, she loved learning the stories of how fashion evolved.

Bethany and Lyla were also glad to be back to school. They had enjoyed their holidays as Bonita had. They were still talking about New Year's Eve, telling everyone about Bonita's transformation. It took people a little while to see the change in Bonita. Most actually didn't recognize her at all at first. Although she looked much better, she was still the same little mousy girl.

Bonita had made a decision after her makeover. She would try to maintain her new-found looks and figure and be more conscious about what she wore. Claude had given her some very nice items for Christmas. Still, because Bonita always covered herself up and wore baggy clothes, he bought them too large for her. They had to return most of it for smaller sizes. They repurchased almost everything except a few things that Claude convinced her to return because he found even cuter items for her. She also took some money and bought a new pair of shoes to add to her collection and accessories to dress up some of her dreary attire.

Since Bonita saw how good she looked after Claude did her makeup, she requested his services and took him to the counter. There, she told him to tell her everything she needed to buy to give herself a nice day look and a more dramatic evening look. Hundreds of dollars later, they left the store with almost every shade she liked. When they got home, Claude began giving her makeup lessons. He taught her about contouring, which was the most critical part of his career since many of his clients were men, and they needed to be softened or sharpened at different places around their faces.

Next, he taught her how to do three simple styles of eyes: smoky, soft, and dramatic. He told her she usually had to pick a dark, lighter, and light shade to create most of these looks. It was easy enough to remember. He told her that her lips were full, and the best thing for her to do was to use clear gloss or lightly tinted gloss to keep things natural. Then, the most peculiar part of all, he taught her how to draw in her eyebrows.

With all that new knowledge, she practiced every day, getting up a little earlier than usual just to get it right and give herself time to fix any mistakes she might make. She liked the smoky look the most and chose that as the style she would wear for her first day back at school.

Some people took notice of the new Bonita, especially her familiar classmates from the previous term. A few of her teachers even commented about it discreetly outside the classroom. She felt good and deserved to; she finally felt she was being all she could be.

33

The following few months went by quickly. As Bonita had expected, she spent most of her time studying and designing at home or school. In her free time, she would spend time with her friends and Claude and took every opportunity she could to attend fashion shows in between school and partying every other weekend. Paris Fashion Week was coming up, and Bonita decided there was no better person to take than Claude himself. She figured he would be the one she would have the most fun with. So, she asked him, and he said yes.

It was nearly halfway through the term, and Fashion Week was approaching. She had packed everything she thought was hot to bring with her. She never thought she would ever get to go to Paris, France, but in a week, she would.

It was a frigid afternoon, and her class was relatively quiet. They were all working on a variety of different projects. Lyla asked loudly if Bonita was packed and ready for Paris Fashion Week. Bonita turned and told her she was struggling with what to wear and bring. Amid their conversation, a girl in her class commented very rudely.

"Why don't you just wear your own designs? They would surely laugh you all the way back to America."

Lyla's and Bonita's heads jerked in the direction the comment came from. It was Cassidy Ruthers, the nastiest bitch in the school. She was known for making other girls cry and saying very hurtful things. Bonita went to open her mouth to say something when Lyla beat her to it.

"In case you didn't notice, Cassidy, Bonita got the highest marks in class on both her midterm and her finals; what did you get?"

Lyla's predecessors typically never returned from a battle with Cassidy. If they did, they would never speak another word of it. Lyla was not your everyday person; she was the strong, silent type. You would think nothing more of her than a meek lamb, but if you pissed her off, look out.

Cassidy was an idiot, as most people would say. A pure quim with nothing more than a chip on her shoulder. She was the daughter of a European man who owned several large oil companies. She felt the world should bow to her and demanded they do just that.

"I'm sorry, Miss Lyla, but your words hold no merit with me. You're poor, tasteless, and ugly!"

Bonita was utterly shocked that someone could even say such a thing. She couldn't help but say something. She had had enough.

"Hey, what the fuck is your problem?" she yelled, not knowing what was going to happen next, but no one was going to speak to her friend like that.

"Do you have something to say? If you do, articulate it like a proper young woman, not like a cracked-out, white trash bitch with skinned-out knees. You hear me?" Bonita continued.

"Are you implying that I'm a slut, Bonita?" Cassidy yelled back.

"Well, you're still a member of this school, and it isn't because of your designs. Everyone knows that!" Bonita lashed back without thinking. Everyone in the room was now holding their breath. No one spoke to Cassidy like that without being torn apart in front of anyone who was there to watch. Bonita was new to this game, and for Cassidy, it was her favorite pastime, so when Cassidy rose from her seat, Bonita felt her heart stop.

"Listen here, you illiterate little twat; I was raised in a home with money that taught me proper etiquette. Which forks and spoons to use at dinner. I could speak three languages by age four and have traveled the world. I have seen fashion, I own fashion, I am fashion! What you design is simple, overstated, poorly crafted rags that reek of poverty and ignorance. The next time you open your mouth to me, ensure you have something worth saying!"

Bonita was furious and completely embarrassed. She felt she wanted to cry, but she would not let that show in class.

"Whatever, Cassidy. Quit running your mouth, okay?" she said as she turned in her seat and went back to her work. She was so mad but tried to calm herself down so her skin would return to its standard color. It only worked once the teacher came in and resumed his instruction. The class seemed like it would never end after that, and all she wanted to do was get up and leave.

When the class was dismissed, she turned to Lyla and

roared, "Don't let that stupid bitch ruin your day. Let's go shopping!" She turned again and, while doing so, shot Cassidy a dirty look. It wasn't much, but it gave her great pleasure.

The girls exited the school and laughed at all the tension Cassidy caused. They spoke badly of her all afternoon, and Bethany told Bonita she was her hero for speaking up to her like that.

Later that evening, Bonita told Claude all about what had happened in school that day. Cassidy was now her archnemesis, and she would get her back one day. Bonita didn't know how or when, but she would have her revenge one day. Bonita was never a vengeful girl or one to hold a grudge, but she spent most of her life being picked on and mistreated. There had to be a line drawn sometime.

34

Things went more smoothly the following week, and all seemed well in Bonita's life. She continued seeing Benjamin Ryder throughout the school but had not spoken to him since New Year's Eve. She told no one of her secret crush because she would be mortified if it ever got back to him.

Every time they would see each other, and their eyes would meet, they both looked away quickly in disgust, but the truth was, there wasn't any disgust in Bonita's heart — in fact, there was an ever-growing itch that she just wanted oh-so-very-badly to scratch. Claude knew there was a boy at school she liked, and when he would encourage her to ask him out, she would shut him down. At first, he didn't quite understand. Bonita had been rejected so many times in her life that she would never put herself in that kind of situation again, and it wasn't like Benjamin had ever shown an interest in her.

Benjamin Ryder was an aspiring young student in the Advertising and Marketing Communications Associate degree program that would lead to his BFA in International Trade and Marketing for the Fashion Industries. He loved fashion as much as anyone else but didn't want to design it; he wanted to promote and sell it. His dream was to head up the major fashion houses' sales teams worldwide and then freelance after a few years. That was where the money was. He came from an upper-class family in New Jersey. He was raised right and believed strongly that you should speak your mind. He was your upfront, no-bullshit kind of guy.

His favorite pastime at school was razzing all the fashion students, especially the girls. He didn't have a girlfriend, as he focused mainly on his studies until he bumped into Bonita on New Year's Eve. He didn't know her name or anything about her, for that matter, but what he did know was that she was beautiful. And those eyes — God, he could not forget those eyes. He would often walk through her section of school just to catch a glimpse of her, but if she saw him looking, he would always huff rudely and turn away. He didn't want to be an asshole, but girls were strange creatures to him. He liked them and all but never could quite figure them out. Sometimes, he thought he would be close to figuring out some chick he knew, but then... wham! All bets were off, and she was a crazy bitch.

The two would spend the rest of the term avoiding eye contact but catching sneak peeks on the sly. Neither knew how the other felt, and they never seemed to want to change that. They were comfortable where they were, and who could argue with that?

35

Paris Fashion Week was here, and all her bags were packed. She and Claude had spent the last few days going through everything. He was happy she had invited him along and thrilled they got to go together. He reckoned it to be the best gift he had ever bought anyone. They boarded the plane and fell fast asleep, as they were up the whole night before laughing and planning what they would do and the sights they would see.

The plane landed at nearly quarter-past-six in the evening. They were not awake for long and were not too anxious to leave the aircraft. People grabbed their luggage above them, and Bonita reached over and tugged Claude's jacket. He looked at her, and then she pointed a few seats ahead. This beautiful young man was in his early thirties, wearing a pink shirt and black sweater vest. He had medium-length flowing locks of blonde hair, a chiseled chin, and lips that could shut a door. He was gorgeous, and Bonita and Claude didn't take their eyes off him the whole time. At one point, the young man noticed them gawking and winked at them. Was he straight, or was he gay? Bonita was convinced he was gay because straight men didn't look that good.

They left the plane and entered the airport, where many people fluttered around. They retrieved their luggage and made a quick dash to the outside doors. Once outside, Claude hailed a cab and gave the driver the address. He nodded, said, "Oui, oui," and took off.

They arrived at their hotel, quickly paid the driver, and grabbed their bags. It wasn't the Plaza, but it was still quite lovely. The doorman greeted them.

"Bonsoir Monsieur et Madame, bienvenue à l'Hôtel Belvédère"

They nodded and continued walking. Once inside the door, both of them burst into laughter. They were not sure how to respond.

After they calmed themselves, they walked to the check-in counter and were greeted with "Bonjour." Both Claude and Bonita looked at each other and smiled, and then Bonita did the strangest thing: she spoke. She had been practicing one sentence over and over leading up to this trip.

"Je ne parle pas français, désolé, parlez-vous anglais, s'il vous plaît ? "

The lady behind the counter huffed and muttered something under her breath, then smiled awkwardly and said, "Hello, welcome to the Belvedere! May I have your names, please?"

There was rudeness about how she handled them. Still, Bonita had been forewarned before she came here that they didn't take too kindly to people who didn't speak their language.

They got to their rooms, immediately threw down all their belongings, and ran back out the door. There was so much to do and so little time. Both of them wanted to catch every fashion event involved in Fashion Week. Still, they also wanted to take in all the sights that Paris had to offer. So, they set out to do the impossible: see Paris and Fashion Week in seven days.

36

Their days were up, down, and all around and every-where. If they had a spare moment, they used it to see some-thing new. They always had several copies of the Fashion Week itinerary on them to keep a conscious effort of where they would need to be. They both set their cell phones and watches to go off thirty minutes before each event to remind them to stop what they were doing and grab a cab.

It would be tough for them to have time between going out and attending the shows to change outfits and be pre-sentable, so they would both get up early in the morning and make themselves look as good as they could before leaving. They walked the streets both morning and night, ate at the cutest little cafés they could find, and drank at little bars all over the city.

One thing both Bonita and Claude wanted to do was go to the Louvre. It was their single most important sight to see. They picked a day when there was very little happening in fashion. They decided to skip a few shows on that day and spent it there. Standing mesmerized and wholly intimidated by the power of the artwork. Bonita leaned on the glass of the inverted pyramid and knelt below it, where the two nearly met. It is said that this could indeed be the spot that was the resting place of Christ, and by that simple possibility, she was enraptured. Of course, this ideal was mainly adopted in one of her favorite author's books, who had a way of working supposed facts into his fiction. Bonita always believed in Christ and God, but her beliefs changed as she got older. She thought there was a Christ such as the Bible depicted, but he was just a righteous man instead of a deity.

As they perused through the museum, they often stopped to stare at the art before them. She took the longest at the works of Leonardo da Vinci, by whom she had always been amazed. Bonita's most favored piece by him was the Vitruvian Man. She first saw it in a book she had in school. Since her find, she would often stop and think of what he must have been thinking when he drew it. Time seemed to pass ever-so-quickly in the Louvre, and come closing time, they had hardly taken in a full quarter of it.

Back at the hotel, they would rest and eat, then continue to take in every show they could, enjoying it immensely. The runways were hot, and the designs were phenomenal. Bonita was inspired. Her favorite designer was Vivienne Westwood, and she loved her runway show the most. She saw the latest from Gucci, Prada, Dolce & Gabbana, Valentino, Versace, Vera Wang, Oscar De La Renta, Ralph Lauren and Marc Jacobs. Each show was different but equally unique and breathtaking.

She would sit in her seat clutching her bag, smiling from ear to ear, watching each model traipse down the runway. She imagined it was her show that she watched, and her name was on the moniker. The short-lived trip was over before they knew it, but they left Paris with something they had never had before, having seen it and lived it for one week.

37

They couldn't contain themselves when Bonita and Claude returned to American soil. They decided to throw a little gathering at the apartment for their friends. Everyone who knew they were going wanted to see and hear all about it. Of course, both had loaded up their cameras with pictures galore and made a few beautiful purchases. They brought back little things for each of their friends, and Bonita had made a point of picking out quite a few things to send back home for both her parents.

They were only home for a day when they put on their party. They didn't feel like wasting time because they both had lives to return to. Bonita had taken a week off school, and her teacher, who happened to be Dean Lalonde for the second term in a row, kept any assignments for when she got back. He was happy to hear she was attending Paris Fashion Week, an incredible event to follow when in fashion. She felt a little stressed about what may have been waiting for her when she returned to school, but she didn't let it ruin her time off.

Bethany, Lyla, and a few other people showed up to the

gathering, and as soon as they saw Bonita and Claude, they attacked them with questions. They wanted to hear as many stories as they possibly could. Bonita told them about the different shows that happened, the beautiful fashion, and the upcoming collections of some of their favorite design houses. The girls and everyone else ate up every single word she said.

Claude was getting all the pictures ready on his computer to show them. They had so many, and they wanted to see them all. He wasn't sure if they would have the time to look at every photo, but he tried to get through as many as possible. The night continued with laughs, gasps, and wows from their friends. A few of them were very interested in their trip to the Louvre and seeing what kind of pictures they had taken. It was nearly eleven-thirty when everyone finally left, and Bonita and Claude decided to retire to their beds. It had been a wonderful week, but in two days, Bonita would return to school and try to catch up on what she missed while away.

38

The end of the first year had arrived. Bonita couldn't believe that she made it through. She aced all her final exams and again received the highest marks in the class. No one was really that surprised. Bonita had a true gift and a vision for how things would play out in a garment.

Secretly, it was true! She never told anyone about this except Claude in passing conversation. Still, when she would design a dress or try to find something to create, she would open up her mind and imagine an event. She would envision the woman, whether tiny or robust, tall or petite, and the woman's movements. She would imagine them having martinis at a cocktail lounge, presenting at a business conference, or, her favorite, dancing at a ball. She would play out the scene in her head, from when the handsome prince asked her to dance to the first step she would take following his lead. How he would lift her in the air and how the dress would fall and gather, how the sleeves would dance on her arms, how the bust would envelop her breast, and how the waist would float like a feather. Each angle and view of the dress would be stored in her head before she began choosing colors and fabrics that best matched her vision. If she ever forgot or lost her way, she would play it back in her head and pause where needed.

Bonita was gifted, even more than she ever knew herself to be. She knew she had talent, but her teachers and peers told her often, and her grades resounded it. The gift of imagination came straight from her heart, always wanting to make people beautiful even when she couldn't be as a child, always wanting to make people happy even though she rarely was. The gift was a curse she carried alone from a young age. Now, she had cultivated it into the most acute forward-thinking vision her teachers had ever seen.

At this point, Bonita had created more than 25 dresses, mainly from the requests she received while in Chicago. She had become a legend in the drag world and was often sent emails from other drag queens, hoping she would design a piece for them. She would have loved nothing more than to do them all, but it took a lot of time and energy she never seemed to have enough of.

She wasn't hurting for money when her first year ended. Her dressmaking and ability to save a dollar had put her into a decent financial situation. However, she knew she could make more. Since school impeded her desire to complete all the garments she wanted, the summer vacation would be the best time to do it. Raising her rates, a little since she was becoming known for her talent would allow her to bank a nice penny for the next school year. She knew that the second year would be a little more intense than the last. There would be no trips to Paris due to time restrictions and deadlines, but she was okay with it; she came to New York to study, which was her primary focus.

She quickly contacted all the individuals that had previously requested her work. She informed them that if they were still interested, to let her know and advised them of her new rates. Claude convinced her to double her prices because he felt her work was worth it. At first, she didn't want to, in case people couldn't spend that much. Ultimately, however, she did double her rates, and the queens still ate it up. Before she knew it, she had over 50 dresses to make and a lot of money to bank. It would be a profitable summer; this way, she would keep herself occupied and not go out of her mind with nothing to do.

After days at different fabric retailers around the city and New Jersey, she felt she had enough material to make some seriously kick-ass gowns. She fronted all the money needed to complete the tasks and purchased a state-of-the-art sewing machine and five dress forms to drape her dresses. She threw herself into her work head-on and didn't come up for air for almost two weeks when, finally, her friends came over to hang out.

They talked and laughed for hours, compared notes on school and the people who went there, and pondered what the second year would be like. Sitting on the bed laughing, Lyla mentioned she didn't have anything fun planned for the summer vacation and that she was a bit bummed out about it. Bethany said she, too, was without a getaway during the summer and spent most of her days lounging around her house, bored out of her mind. They both knew that Bonita had a lot of work planned for the summer holidays, so they didn't think to ask if she had anything fun happening. Then, out of nowhere, Bonita spoke up.

"Why don't we rent a car and drive to Los Angeles for a week?"

Recoiled in shock, both the girls were utterly blindsided by her suggestion. Bonita wasn't the super-adventurous kind. Where did that come from? After regaining composure, the three talked about it a little more, and they all decided that was what they would do.

39

They began planning the trip right away. Bonita finished quite a few dresses in a short time and extended her deadlines by two weeks so that she could enjoy her journey out west. The idea just fell out of Bonita's mouth that day, and she didn't realize Bethany and Lyla would be up to going. Now, it was happening, and Bonita was pretty excited. She started packing and working out what she would wear in the City of Angels and purchased a few additional items.

She made an appointment at the spa for the whole package, and this time around, there were no surprises, just primping and getting every part of her body ready for the beach. She had picked out this sexy bikini to wear by the water. She had never worn one before, so she was a little worried. While at the spa, she asked to have her nether regions taken care of and treated accordingly. She was nearly ready to go two days early, and she took those two days to make another three dresses.

She had become quite efficient with sketch-to-garment-making. She could complete a gown in less than a day, provided she had all the suitable materials. The money she made from these dresses was paramount and fattening her wallet. She had more cash than she knew what to do with. She was interested in investing but needed to learn about it. So, she decided to sit on it for now and intended to spend as much as she wanted while in Los Angeles.

They had invited Claude to come, and he was very disappointed to say no — he had some very big appointments at the counter. He was a little worried about Bonita going off to L.A. and made her promise that she would regularly call to check in and let him know she was still alive. Bonita was touched by his concern and assured him she would play safe and check in daily. He helped her pack a little and picked out some steamy outfits.

Bonita had her license but had never driven in New York City before. Lyla had driven in the city, but the highway scared her. And Bethany, well, she never drove a day in her life. So, after careful planning, they decided Lyla would drive until they were out of the city, and Bonita would drive to L.A. Once they arrived, they would share the driving equally, and everyone would be okay. It was to be an enjoyable trip. Just the three of them. Something they would never forget.

40

It was warm and muggy, and an offensive stench filled the air the morning they left for L.A. They had all arranged to meet at Bonita's house. Lyla picked up the car in the morning, grabbed Bethany, and then went to Bonita's. Bethany and Lyla were making another stop before they got Bonita, and they had failed to mention it. It was a last-minute change in plans, but they thought Bonita would be okay if one of Lyla's guy friends came along. They didn't know each other but went to the same school.

The concierge rang from the front desk at nearly 8:30 am, and Bonita had been packed and ready for over an hour. She was so excited to get away and experience something new. When leaving the building, she waved to Julio, told him she would see him in two weeks, and continued walking through the door. The car was compact, which they decided would be the most economical and cheap on gas. It would be easier to navigate in and out of all the cities' crazy streets. Bonita threw her things in the trunk, which was already overly packed and had little room for her, but she managed, and then proceeded to get into the car's back seat.

"Oh my god!" she thought, seeing who was sitting in the back seat with her.

"Hey, Bonita!" Benjamin Ryder said as she sat down.

She had no idea how to react or what to say, so she simply said, "Hi!"

The girls explained that Benjamin was a friend of Lyla's, and when they told him they were going to L.A., he asked if he could come along. They would have mentioned it, but it was a last-minute deal, and they didn't think she would mind. Bonita, wholly floored, managed to muster up, "I don't mind," and then turned her head to look out the window.

Bonita was in pure shock. She never knew that Benjamin was a friend of Lyla's, and she had never told the girls of her crush on him. It would be an interesting trip, but for now, all Bonita could focus on was that when they got outside the city, she would relocate to the front seat and take the wheel for the next three thousand miles.

It was a long trip out. They stopped and saw many sights, stayed in interesting motels, and ate at peculiar restaurants. No one seemed to mind it since it was part of their road trip. Bonita ended up switching it up with Benjamin on the highways. He would sleep, and she would drive, or vice versa. Either way, she planned it; she got to sit in front or behind him the entire time. Luckily, along the trip, she discovered that Benjamin had his own agenda for L.A. and wouldn't join them on most of their plans. This made her very happy since she didn't want the distraction, and she didn't want the girls to sense anything weird.

41

Once they arrived in L.A., they immediately checked into their hotel. An extra star or two makes a big difference over the places they have stayed in on their way. The room had plenty of space; they all chipped in on the cost. There were two beds, one pull-out, and an extra cot for Benjamin to sleep on. Bethany thought the pull-out was quite comfortable and offered the beds to Lyla and Bonita since they did most of the driving. She told Benjamin he was shit out of luck because he was a last-minute addition. He didn't seem to mind at all, and he knew his place among the girls was at the bottom of the totem pole, and he accepted it.

The first thing the girls did was find out where all the fashion shows were happening in the city. One was coming up the next day. It was a Gucci runway show, and, well, Gucci had always been Bonita's second favorite line. So immediately, they tried to get tickets and failed, but they didn't give up. When the show started the next day, they had found three tickets and were very excited to attend.

The show was incredible and nothing like they had ever seen. They walked away from the event so happy and enjoyed their time so much that they made a spectacle of themselves. They didn't mind; three young girls were on vacation, so there were no rules or responsibilities. That was what meant the most to Bonita. At this point in her life away from home, ever since she landed in New York, she had always been predisposed to something or another. This trip meant two weeks of doing what she wanted when she wanted and having nothing stand in her way.

The girls liked shopping the most, and Bonita enjoyed all the high-end stores Los Angeles had. It is similar to New York, except it is warmer, more expansive, and spread out. There was nothing like Manhattan in L.A.; everything required a car or transit. She would have to get in the car and drive where she and everyone else wanted to go. They didn't see much of Benjamin except for late-night arrivals and crashing on the cot in the room with them. Bonita had kept an eye on him and often thought how nice it would be for him to just crawl into bed with her one night, and then that would be that, but no one must know — no one!

Benjamin had been having a lot of fun since he arrived. He knew a lot of people in the city and made an attempt to visit them all. It was challenging since he wanted to avoid bothering the girls by driving him places, so he took transit most of the time. He got the vibe Bonita did not want him there, which made him feel a little out of place. He was not fully aware until the last minute who else was coming on the trip. The girls had neglected to mention that to him, as well. He thought it better that he spent most of his time alone and left the girls to do their own thing. This way, no one would notice that he had it on for Bonita.

She was so beautiful, he thought. No wonder she wouldn't want anything to do with him. He was just an average guy with nothing to offer a girl. She came across bitchy and rude most of the time, but it didn't seem to bother him in the least. He often thought of her and wished he had the balls to make a move, but he was convinced she wasn't interested in having anything to do with him.

42

The following few days clocked by so quickly as they continued to have fun, and just as they thought it couldn't get any better, Bethany received an invitation for her and the girls to attend a who's who party in the Hollywood hills. They all thought it was the coolest thing in the world but started panicking about what they would wear. Bethany, Lyla, and Bonita shopped for hot, sexy outfits on Rodeo Drive, the priciest street in L.A. The girls found what they were looking for. Bonita had seen nothing that she really liked or wanted to show up to a Hollywood party in. In the end, she decided that she would wear one of her own designs.

The dress itself was simple but elegant. Bonita had created it as one of her end-of-term projects and used herself as the pincushion. She brought the dress in case anything came up that would require her to wear more sophisticated attire. This type of party definitely warranted pulling it out and wearing it. This would be the first time she had worn one of her designs, and she felt somewhat nervous about it. She had yet to become fully confident in her own work.

Once she had finished her makeup and her hair, she

slipped into it and was floored. "I did good," she thought as she stared herself down in the mirror. It lay perfectly loose around the breasts, showing off a little cleavage, and then hugged her waist snugly and fit until it fell down in a flowing veil of fabric that lifted in the wind.

They were all stoked and driving across town, laughing and talking about the week thus far. No one knew what to expect of the party, but everyone hoped it'd be like in the movies. When they finally pulled outside the house, they were not entering some second-rate gathering. Their hopes had been fulfilled. Many lovely people wore beautiful garments, all feeling like they fit in. There were tons of complimentary champagne and finger food, music playing, and people prancing. It was marvelous, simply marvelous. They were having a lot of fun — so much fun that none of them even noticed the beautiful man checking Bonita out like she was filet mignon.

A little time had passed, and Bonita was feeling the alcohol. It wasn't a big deal; they had decided to take a taxi back if they were too drunk to drive. If that happened, they would retrieve the car in the morning, no harm done. Bonita was lounging at the bar when she saw the most gorgeous man staring at her.

Then the most amazing thing happened: he spoke.

"Excuse me, miss, would you let me buy you a drink?"

Bonita laughed and said, "At an open bar? I think I could allow that."

The handsome man turned red, and they both laughed at his silly pick-up line. "I'm sorry. I have been standing over there trying to decide what to say to start a conversation with you!"

She was a little thrown off-guard. This guy was gorgeous; what the hell was he doing talking to her?

"How about 'hello,' and we'll take it from there?"

Initially nervous, she let him order her a drink and then decided to make small talk.

They spoke closely right from the start. Bonita had even forgotten to drink after a while. She was stone sober but wouldn't have noticed since her heart was fluttering like a schoolgirl. Bonita couldn't take her eyes off him. He was the most beautiful man she had ever seen, or at least who had ever talked to her. This man was intelligent, funny, and a male model. His profession and demeanor pronounced he had money — not that that would ever decide whether she dated someone, but a man with his own money is always kind of sexy.

The night progressed, and neither of them paid attention to the time. They talked about everything they could think of. After a while, he gave her his number, and when she saw a 212 area code, she realized that this handsome gentleman was actually from New York. They talked about the Big Apple for quite some time and how he moved there 10 years ago when he was 18 to pursue a modeling career. He fell in love with the city, and although he traveled a lot, he would only let a little time pass before he returned to his beloved city. They had both decided that they would like to see each other again and made plans to spend the rest of his and her time together in L.A. sightseeing and taking in certain shows.

It was midnight by now, and they had been there nearly

eight hours, six of which Bonita had spent with Alexander Pierce, the model. Bethany and Lyla found her deeply engrossed in conversation with the beautiful man. They regretted having to break it up, but they really wanted to leave at this point. They had a terrific time but felt a nice late-night snack, and some girl talk was in order.

Being sober, Bonita drove the car back to the hotel, and she was pestered with questions about who he was, what he did, and what happened. Of course, she didn't mind answering the barrage of questions because it meant thinking about Alexander out loud. When they arrived at the room, Benjamin was just hanging out there. He had ordered a ton of pizza for him and the girls to eat and enjoy. Bonita had forgotten about her crush on him due to her new guy, whom she spent the rest of the night talking about.

Benjamin didn't particularly like this Alexander character and voiced his opinion rudely several times throughout the night. He would say how the guy sounded like a tool or make gay innuendos. The girls, especially Bonita, did not take too kindly to his remarks, and soon he was shushed to silence. The rest of the trip was now planned for Bonita, and although it changed many of the other girls' plans, they were happy for her and thought it was awesome that she had found a romance.

43

Over the following week, she and Alexander did as much as possible in the City of Angels but still needed more time. They spent every day together and every night. They did everything except sleep with each other. Bonita returned to the hotel every night to sleep in her bed. This always amazed the girls, and even Benjamin was a little shocked. Bonita was utterly head over heels for this guy, yet she always returned to the hotel. They weren't sleeping together, and Bethany and Lyla thought it strange since they would have tapped that cute little ass a long time ago.

None of them ever mentioned this to Bonita, of course. She was her own woman, and she did what she wanted to do. Neither tried to figure out why they were not sleeping together. Benjamin had summed up that she respected herself and felt it may be too early to go down that road. He highly doubted it, but that was the only conclusion that made sense to him, so, therefore, he stuck with it.

Bonita was so pleased that she had met someone with a head on his shoulders who was also drop-dead gorgeous. She enjoyed herself the last few days they spent together and was excited about returning to New York. They planned to continue dating there in a city they were both familiar with and loved. To her, Alexander was the perfect man of dignity and restraint. They had yet to sleep together, and she felt comfortable with him. He seemed okay with waiting for her, which made her even happier. She felt that when the time came, he would be an excellent person to lose her virginity to.

<h1 style="text-align:center">44</h1>

When they arrived home, Bonita couldn't wait another minute to see Claude to tell him of her new beau, so she quickly threw her things in the room and headed to the counter. He was swamped when she arrived. They were having a lucrative cosmetics and skin care sale, and the place was packed. She had to wait a while but quickly browsed the sale items and made several purchases. Luckily, he hadn't taken his lunch yet, so he quickly finished what he was doing and left with her to grab a bite.

They picked one of Claude's favorite restaurants down the block from his work, and once they had ordered the food, Claude finally said, "Okay, what is it that you want to tell me? " Bonita smiled her quirky smile and said, "Okay!"

She told him about the entire trip, leaving out that she had met a hot model she was now dating. Finally, unable to contain her excitement any longer, she blurted it out. At first, he seemed a little taken aback by it, and then, as if a light bulb went on in his head, he started smiling, congratulating her, and asking her a series of personal questions. Most guys would have had their faces slapped, asking her the questions he asked, but it was Claude. Claude could say pretty much anything he wanted to because he could always play the gay card.

The hour flew by, and the next thing they knew, Claude was back at work, and she was heading home to unpack, take a bath, and settle down. She didn't take long to unpack. Bonita grabbed all the clothes she needed to wash and took them to the laundry room downstairs. While waiting for her clothes to dry, she went upstairs and took a hot bath with bubbles and a glass of wine. She felt on top of the world, something she had never felt. She had just finished her first year of school, she had money in the bank, more money coming over the summer, and a hot boyfriend who absolutely adored her. What else could a girl want?

Alexander had been spending a lot of time with her now that he was back in New York. He actually came back early just to be with her. He was so smitten with how smart and talented she was that he asked her to make him something. She was more than happy to design an outfit for the new man in her life and worked on it immediately. Bonita had been holding off on the sex, and he had never even so much as hinted at it, but Bonita wanted it to happen. So, they planned a romantic evening and set up the perfect night. Bonita even finished making Alexander his new outfit. She was so happy that she called him and said, "I have something for you. I'm sending it over right now! Wear it tonight if you like it!"

They both knew what tonight would actually be: a sex-infused gathering of two bodies who were so drawn to each other it could barely be contained. Bonita was nervous. She had never had sex before, nor had she ever been naked in front of a man. Bonita watched a couple of pornos the night before on the internet just to see what really goes on and to get a few pointers. She paid a visit to the spa, where she had everything waxed. She had picked out her hottest, sexiest cocktail dress and spent hours doing her hair and makeup and priming herself to be perfect for her first time.

45

Later that evening, he picked her up, and they had dinner at a celebrity-owned restaurant in lower Manhattan. It was beautiful and delicious! After dinner, they went for a walk and then returned to Alexander's place to have a glass of wine and let the romance start. Bonita felt her nerves get a little out of hand once back at his place and decided to drink an extra glass of wine to drown them out. He put on soft, sensual music, lit a few candles, and then the romance began.

He was smooth and wonderful and tasted like a sugary treat. He kissed her with such passion she thought for sure she was going to stain his couch. Then Bonita wanted to tell him something. Between gropes and kisses, she said, "I have something I want to tell you!" He straddled her tightly, holding her, and grunted, "Okay, what is it, my beauty?"

She pulled him a little closer and kissed him again. She felt hot, and in the moment, her loins were moist and wet. She could feel beads of sweat trickling down his back and his breath heavy against her skin. She trembled and whispered, "This is my first time."

That moment, as if a loud thunderous bang had shaken

the apartment, the romance stopped, his body seized up, and all was still. Bonita thought at first, he was in shock that she was still a virgin, but she knew something else was up when nothing happened a minute later. It was like he was processing something in his head, and finally, he took her shoulders and held her out from him a little.

"Are you saying that you're a virgin, Bonita?" with a slight grin on his face.

"Yes! Is that a problem, Alexander?" she said, with a little twinge of offense in her voice.

He let his head fall and took the grin off of his face.

"No. I mean... I... I didn't think you were a virgin, that's all."

She was really disturbed by his reaction and shimmied backward on the couch.

"I don't understand why you would think I wasn't. Did I ever lead you to believe otherwise?"

"No, I didn't think you were or weren't. I guess I thought it was a given!" he said, releasing his grip on her shoulders. By now, Bonita was feeling a little rejected and confused. She was trying to grasp what was happening but couldn't.

"So, does that change anything?" she said to Alexander. "Are we finished having sex already, Alexander? Because to be quite honest, that wasn't very satisfying for me!"

"I think we should stop for tonight, yes! We should just get some sleep!" he said in a soft but final tone.

"Why don't I leave, and we can talk about this when it's a better time?" Bonita replied.

"That's not necessary, Bonita. Just let's get some sleep, and we'll talk about it tomorrow!" he proclaimed.

Bonita got up from the couch and started putting her shirt back on.

"That's okay; I understand if it threw you off. I should have told you before tonight!

He had this sincere look and said, "I'm so sorry, honey. I don't know why it caught me off-guard, but it did!" He pointed towards his genitalia. "You don't have to leave; I'd like you to stay," he said.

"I know," Bonita replied, "but I want my first time to be perfect, and perfect just jumped out the window. I would rather sleep in my bed tonight, and we can try this another time. Is everything okay?"

He quickly jumped to her side and pushed the air out of his lips in almost a hiss in response. "Of course, baby. Everything is okay; I'm so sorry. I will call you tomorrow, all right?"

Bonita felt better now that he was simply thrown off by it. "That sounds wonderful; I'll await your call," she said, and he gave her a kiss on the lips and squeezed her tight. Bonita left the apartment disappointed because she didn't get what she wanted. Still, she felt good that Alexander was the type of guy who understood and was at least honest with her.

46

The following day, sunlight abruptly shone into her bedroom window, awakening her from a very heavy sleep. She rose feeling refreshed and energized; she decided to go about her business as usual. She couldn't stop thinking about how good Alexander looked in the suit she made for him. It was like a dream. She also couldn't help thinking of how good he felt the night before. She threw herself into her work and barely left her station except to eat and use the bathroom. It was a busy day because she wanted to take on three different dresses at once to clear up some spare time to spend with Alexander.

The whole day had passed, and she never realized what time it was, except it was dark outside. She finally felt tired and looked at the clock. It was 11:45 pm, and then it hit her; Alexander hadn't called. That wasn't like him at all. She quickly picked up the phone and called him, but there was no answer. She left a sweet voicemail for him and went to bed. She didn't sleep well that night. Something was up, but she didn't know what.

The next day came and went, the day after that, and the

day after that, and not one word from Alexander. She had left numerous messages by this time and was beginning to freak out. Everything was fine the night she last saw him, she thought. They had talked it out, and he was super sweet, as always. What could have happened that he wouldn't call?

Five days later, the phone rang. Julio from downstairs was announcing Alexander's arrival and that he wished to come up. Bonita said yes without hesitation and quickly checked herself in the mirror to ensure she looked presentable. When the knock came at the door, she swung it open and said, "Where have you been? I was worried sick!"

He said, "Something came up that I had to deal with, and now I have to talk to you."

Bonita motioned for him to come in and sit down. He came in but stood at the door and would not remove his shoes or jacket. His following words left her reeling as though she had been stabbed by a knife in the heart.

"Bonita, I don't think it will work with us. We are at two different places in our lives, and I need more than you can offer. I need a woman who has experience who can satisfy me. The other night, I realized you're still a girl yet to discover her body and develop herself. You need someone who can show you the ropes and develop your style. I need a woman who matches me at my level."

"You're a nice girl, Bonita, and beautiful, but I'm sorry. I need someone a little more mature. Experiment and develop yourself before taking on another person. Sorry it couldn't work out, and I wish you the best of luck. Goodbye, Bonita."

He turned and walked through the door. Once he was

halfway down the hall, he turned and said, "Bonita, please stop calling! It's embarrassing!"

When the door closed, Bonita lost it. Everything she had in her — her spirit, her courage, her passion — fell heavily to the floor, and the biggest tears she ever had slipped from her face. It was like the Hoover Dam violently broke into pieces against the massive rush of water tumbling down from it. Bonita was destroyed. Never before in her life had anyone ever hurt her this badly. She couldn't see herself coming back from this one. She ran to her room and sobbed for hours until she finally passed out from exhaustion.

Lyla and Bethany heard about what had happened — not from Bonita, but from people at their school; everyone in the fashion community was connected, both students and veterans alike. Technically, the school year had not yet started and wouldn't for another three weeks. Still, students were allowed on campus to use the facilities. When they heard the story, it was brutal, and what they heard was even more devastating than what actually happened. The rumor was that Alexander found out that she was a virgin, and he tried to have sex with her, but she didn't want to because she was waiting for marriage. He broke up with her because he needed someone a little more mature, and he had to get a restraining order because she wouldn't stop calling or stalking him."

Lyla and Bethany were convinced that that was not what happened. Therefore, they immediately rushed to the apartment and banged on the door until Claude finally let them in. He told them she didn't want to see anyone and begged them to tell him what was happening. When Claude learned of what had happened, he forced himself into Bonita's bedroom and asked her if Alexander had done anything to her. He thought maybe Alexander could have forced himself on her, and that is why she was so upset. Her answer was no. Claude felt better knowing nothing physical had occurred and realized he needed to get her out of the bedroom. Finally, all three convinced her to at least get out of bed and shower. She didn't even have to talk about it, but she had to shower.

After the shower, she entered the living room, where Claude had a cup of her favorite tea on the counter. She said, "Thank you!" and sat on the chair and looked around. Finally, after what seemed to be an eternity, she burst out, "He was such a fucking asshole," and then it all began from there.

She filled them in on exactly what happened, and Bethany and Lyla looked at each other and smiled. They knew that Bonita would never submit herself to that kind of behavior. Being her friends, they decided it was best to tell her about the rumors going around school. This way, she could get used to it and prepare for it when she returned. Bonita was immediately struck down once again by the news. She barricaded herself in her room for yet another two days. Bonita was degrieved and ready to return to the world when she emerged. It didn't take her long to recover, mostly because she threw herself into her work.

47

The new school year had started, and Bonita was finally getting over the devastation of her summer romance. It had damn near destroyed her. Everyone at school knew what happened or what they believed to have occurred. Her two good friends, Lyla and Bethany, tried to tell everyone the real story. Benjamin, who had not seen Bonita since their trip to L.A., also knew what happened — the true story, that is — and felt really bad for her. He never liked this Alexander character and thought it better that it ended when it did.

Bonita had spent the last three weeks preparing for her return to school. Although she did nothing but lay low after the breakup, she was hell-bent on returning to school with her head held high. Nothing was going to stop her from making her dreams come true. No man would stand in her way, no matter how beautiful he was. So, for her first day back, she designed herself a sexy little top and skirt that would make her look and feel good at the same time.

The second year was completely different from the first. The workload was massive, and Bonita could hardly find time. She felt a distance growing between her and her friends due to the lack of time they spent with each other. She believed that everything was fine between them since they had the same amount of work on their shoulders.

Once again, Bonita got the highest grades and was at the top of her class. Bonita's reputation preceded her this year; her teachers were happy to have someone with so much talent and dedication in their class. She was never the type to gloat or brag about anything, but it made her feel good that she seemed to be favored among her teachers. It just meant she was doing it right, and in her world, it was the only way of doing it, period!

The first semester sped by, and she was never sure how much time had passed. She was too engrossed in her work to pay attention to anything else. When she did take note, she was on her final exams for her third term. Still rarely seeing her friends and swamped with work, she took every advantage to fill the gown requests.

The end of the first term arrived, and she planned on having a quiet Christmas with Claude again this year. They had already planned and would spend their second traditional holiday together. They were both excited about this because they had hardly spent time together over the last few months due to her schoolwork. Still, if there was time to socialize, it was spent with him, and he liked it that way. He was just as excited about the holidays this year as he was last. He and Bonita would often talk about how there was no way they could top last year's festivities. Last year, Claude went out of his way to make things perfect for Bonita; this year, everything would be split equally.

Bonita was quite happy that the term was over, and she

decided that she wanted to be able to pay off her student loans and pay for her education herself. Since she began taking and filling dress orders, she had accumulated and saved enough to do it. After carefully analyzing her bank accounts and financial statements, she finally had enough money to live on, pay off her loan, and pay the next term's tuition and fees.

It was a proud moment for Bonita. This meant she succeeded in New York City and was making her dreams come true. She got out her check book and made one to her father for the total amount owed on her student loan. When she was finished, she went shopping, put together a giant care package with presents and treats from the big city, and sent it home. In the package, she included a letter.

Mom and Dad,

Merry Christmas to you both. I miss you so much and think of you daily. I wanted to send home presents early this year so you can enjoy them on Christmas morning. Think of me as I will be thinking of you.

I have enclosed a check for the entire amount of my student loan, and I would like you to pay it off and close it. Over the last eight months, I have been creating dresses nearly full-time. I have made enough money to pay my loan and the rest of my tuition. I also have enough to live comfortably, so please do not worry about me.

Things are going wonderfully here in New York. School is excellent, and I love it very much. I will call you soon, and please do not worry about sending any money this year. I know you worry, but you cannot afford it, and trust me when I say I am doing better than all right.

I love you both so much, and I can't wait to see you some-time soon.

Love and Kisses,

Bon Bon.

She packed everything and sent it off, knowing she would get her father's call when they received it. He would fight with her on this one; she knew it, and he would not back down for a long time. He would try to convince her that she should keep her money until after school, in case anything happened, and that her student loan was okay. She would have to talk a lot to convince him she was better than okay, but she was ready for it.

Her next step was to fill out a check for her school, which made her even happier than paying off her loan in a one-shot deal. Now, she was really paying her own way. She licked that envelope and sent it in the mail with pride. She was an adult, one with responsibilities and one with independence.

48

Although the holidays were magical and lovely, they flew by too quickly. Bonita found it very difficult to just relax, as it seemed she couldn't catch her breath. She received a call from her parents about the package, and as predicted, her father fought with her about everything, but finally, after several phone calls and a heated discussion, she convinced them she was okay. The only problem was that now her parents were asking her to fly home for the holidays. Unfortunately, Bonita had different plans. She felt she could use her money on something other than that while trying to sustain her social life and lifestyle in New York.

Bonita spent most of the holidays shopping for next term's supplies and fabric. Her taste had improved, and she was splurging on expensive materials and tools. She was almost done with her associate degree and wanted to close it out on top, the same way she had started it. Her room was filled with all types of fabrics and school supplies; her closet and drawers were overflowing — she hardly had any space to move around in it. She was focused, prepared for the New Year, and ready to complete her degree.

The only party she planned to attend this holiday season was the New Year's party, which was all the rage. Everybody who was anybody would be there, and she nearly sold her soul to get herself tickets. Lyla and Bethany hadn't been able to get tickets to this event, so they were doing something else. Usually, Bonita would have changed her plans to spend it with them, but there was no way she was missing it, not for anyone.

It had been a year since Bonita had gone through a full-body makeover, and by this time, she could maintain her new look on her own. Claude had given her ample lessons on what to do and what not to do. For her hair, she had been seeing this incredible stylist who had recommended the best anti-frizz conditioners and shampoos money could buy, and they were well worth every penny. Bonita decided to design her dress for the event and spent the month leading up to it doing just that. By the time the night arrived, she was confident that she looked the best she could and was red carpet worthy. She left the building wearing the most elegant gown she had ever worn and was complimented on her beauty by Julio as she walked out.

She felt good and alive and was ready to have an incredible night. She was more excited as to whom she would meet at this party. When she arrived, it was even better than last year — marvelous. The decorations, the dinner, and the entertainment were all incredibly tasteful. She never knew that she could have so much fun. She didn't mind being alone at the table where she was sitting, as it gave her ample time and opportunity to get to know her tablemates. She ate, drank, and danced with many people throughout the night.

She networked and met the Who's Who of New York City's Socialites. She turned out to be somewhat the life of the party. Everyone absolutely adored her in every way. She was fresh and innocent, and people liked that.

The evening was a success, and it seemed as if Bonita had floated the whole way home that night. Nothing could bring her down from her current high. She walked through the door of her home at 3:30 am, still looking as put-together as she had when she had left and feeling inebriated. Claude was there with a couple of his friends, and they all sat around drinking wine and chatting for the rest of the night. It was nearly 5:00 am when she kissed Claude on the cheek and announced she was going to bed.

It took her only a minute or two to wash her face and get undressed, and before she knew it, she was fast asleep, dreaming about the people she had met the night before. She slept that day away with a smile and woke up later with a sense of satisfaction and pride. The holidays were nearly over, and although she was swamped, it was a nice vacation from school.

49

The term ahead brought even more stress and less time than the previous one. Bonita figured it was to be expected, seeing it was the term that decided whether or not she would get her degree. She barely spoke to anyone during the week. She found herself trying desperately to free up time on the weekend for social events, fashion shows, and her friends. Trying to juggle school life and social life seemed damn near impossible for her. She felt most times that everything was just simply going to fall apart.

Her friends Lyla and Bethany still spent time with her, but she noticed a difference in their relationship. She couldn't quite name it, but something was definitely there. Benjamin Ryder was picking on her more than usual, and she couldn't understand why he wouldn't just leave her alone. She still hadn't spoken to him since their trip to L.A. and still had a crush on him, but he was beginning to get on her nerves, making her angry.

Claude was still the stronghold, the never-wavering rock he had always been. They spent more time together than she did with anyone else. It was easier, she guessed; she would finish her work, and it would be 10:00 pm. What was she going to do? Get ready and go out? He was there with her, her roommate, and she found spending it with him more convenient. She loved his company and loved him, so why wouldn't it be him she spent most of her time with?

Benjamin Ryder often thought about Bonita and how much he wanted to kiss her. Still, lately, she had become a little different than the girl he first had a crush on. Bonita seemed to be more edgy and irritable. He figured it was stress from school, but she tended to ignore her friends and not even acknowledge that he was around. He didn't expect much from her. She seemed to be slightly self-centered and uncaring of other people. He didn't want to honestly believe it, but she hadn't given him much choice otherwise.

He continued to pick on her as much as he could. He liked to see her squirm and get all hot in the face. He knew he was probably a pain in her ass, but he didn't care about that; he just liked being near her for some reason. Bethany and Lyla were also feeling the cold shoulder. Lyla was more understanding than Bethany, who couldn't quite grasp it. They had been friends for nearly two years, and Bonita didn't have the time of day for either of them. Bethany thought it was rude and began to think she was more interested in being the class princess. Bonita seemed more interested in sucking up to the teachers than she was in being their friend. It didn't sit well with Bethany, and resentment and dislike began to rise.

Bonita made it through her midterms and well into the second half of the term. She missed her friends and tried really hard to maintain a life with them. Still, she felt her school life was more important to her success than maintaining her friendships, and she believed that if they were really her friends, they would understand.

The end of the term was drawing near, and Bonita felt like she could finally see the light at the end of a very long tunnel. She hoped that with the summer holidays, she could regain her time with her friends, get out, and have some silly fun without too much responsibility.

50

The term ended, and all was well; with perfect scores and an associate degree in fashion, Bonita was so happy she could hardly contain herself. Technically, she could stop school and begin an exciting career in the industry, which is precisely what she wanted. Still, she knew her BFA would open even more doors, which was more important than anything else.

Summer was here, and she was ready to let go and have some serious fun, but only after increasing her design rates and taking on even more requests. When Bonita went to Chicago, she ignited a trend. Drag queens realized that the better the dress, the better the performance, and the better they looked, the more their chances of winning pageants and being asked back to do shows increased. So now, nearly a year-and-a-half later, Bonita Smith was the fashion designer to the drag queens of America — and that didn't bother her. Her clothes were being worn and paid for. She didn't consider it anything less than extraordinary, even though some would perceive it as a joke. Still, the way she saw it was her name was getting out there. People have come to love her work and desire it. It may not be the top fashion gurus in the world, but it was a group of people who could tell a hot dress when they saw it.

The biggest thing that excited Bonita was once again being able to pay for her next term alone. She was doing it, and all by herself. She was never concerned about funds, where her rent would come from, or how she would buy her next meal. Everything in that department of her life seemed effortless, which made her happy because she couldn't handle any more stress.

The summer was filled with fashion shows and other events. Every chance Bonita got, she was at one thing or another that was going on in the city. She had socializing and networking down to a pure art form, keeping numbers and names on her smartphone with little notes about where they met, what they discussed, and interesting facts about each person. When it came time to contact them in the future, Bonita could simply pull up her notes to create a more personal experience. She had become savvy and forthcoming to most; only a few people attended the same events as she did, whom she had yet to talk to.

It was an open market for her. She saw every conversation as a step further in her path to the runways. Not one person was left out of the equation. You could be the coffee guy or mail lady at a company that dealt in fashion, and Bonita would speak with you. The way she saw it, everybody knows somebody, and the more people she met, she would, in turn, know almost everybody, even if not directly but through association. Bonita wasn't a fake person, nor did she care if you were the assistant to a fashion designer or the water boy. She spoke to you with kindness and compassion and honestly tried to talk to you as another human being just trying to make it in the world. People loved her for that, and although half the people she met usually forgot her a few days later, she knew all of them and would make sure she called them if she needed an in.

51

In her spare time, Bonita would focus on making dresses. She truly enjoyed designing gorgeous gowns for others, and it was never a task for her. She was a perfectionist and wouldn't let a dress get shipped out without ensuring every stitch was precise, hung properly, and pressed to perfection. It was what truly made her such a good designer. She took pride in every stage and thought about what was coming next. She didn't like surprises when it came to her designs, so she always over-imagined it in her head, processing everything that could go wrong and making amendments as she went along.

Since school had ended, she made several phone calls and sent many emails to reach out to her friends, Lyla and Bethany. Each went unanswered. She missed her friends quite a bit and wanted a girl's night with them or maybe a weekend getaway. Every attempt she made to contact them was fruitless, and although she left many messages to have them call her back, they never did. She was disappointed they weren't around all summer; she missed their laughs and good times. Ultimately, she figured they were either busy or out of town.

She continued sending emails, hoping one of them would find the time to say hello. If all else failed, she would see them once school started again in September.

It was a balmy Thursday afternoon, and she was out perusing the city alone, looking for great deals. Walking past 52nd down 5th, she noticed Bethany and Lyla standing outside a shop across the street. The walk sign had just turned, so she skipped across the street to say hi. "Hello, you two! Oh my God, it's good to see you." Lyla turned first and began to smile but immediately stopped when Bethany turned and saw Bonita. "Oh, you remember our names, do you?' Bethany said as she repositioned her purse on her shoulder.

A little surprised, Bonita responded, "Of course I do; what are you talking about? I have been trying to contact both of you all summer."

"Oh, you mean, when it is convenient for you?' Bethany retorted. Adjusting her stance to appear more cavalier than she was. Bonita's mind was spinning, unaware of where this was coming from. "I don't know what you are implying, but I messaged as soon as the semester ended, and I had time to breathe," Bonita said calmingly and graciously.

"Bon, listen. We were your friends, and you just cut us out like we were nothing." Lyla spoke up. "Were my friends?" Bonita responded, surprised. "Bon," Bethany said forcefully, "We were there for you; we had your back when the Alexander debacle happened; we used to be thick as thieves, but just like an outgrown cardigan, you tossed us aside." Bonita, visibly frustrated, began to feel defensive, "That's not what happened, and you know that. You know that! School has been insane for all of us. I never wanted to not be your friend. I tried to balance, but school took priority.

"Oh, Bon!" Lyla said, softening her tone towards her, but Bethany stepped in front of her before she could continue. "No, Bon! You couldn't get your head out of your ass long enough to realize the two people who had your back since day one was missing their friend. You were too busy being the uppity, little miss fucking princess, with your holier than though, everything is all about me, whinny bitch persona to realize that we won't be treated that way. You think you are a gift, Bonita! It's gone to your head, and you will get knocked down a notch one day."

Bonita stood there reeling; she couldn't process what was happening. Never in her mind did she think her friends would turn on her like that. She wanted to fight, but she could feel the heat rush to her face, and tears began to form in her eyes. She looked at them one last time before walking away and said, "School is, and has always been, the most important thing to me, and I am sorry you feel that way. It's not my fault you don't care about your future, but I do, and if it means losing two friends because of differences in priorities, then so be it. Take care of yourselves." She turned and hurriedly headed down 5th. She had made several stops already, and her arms were preoccupied with her bags and an Iced latte. The street was slammed; it being summertime and tourist season, there were people for miles, each coming and going off in their own little world. Bonita was to upset to pay attention and had tears in her eyes.

Further down the street, she collided with something hard. She was still unsure of how it all happened, but she fell in the middle of the crowd and landed flat on her face. This was the second time that had happened to her in New York. The people in the city don't typically notice. They were usually in a rush and unable to stop to help. A small woman with a Southern accent bent down to her and cleared a path around her, asking if she was okay. At first, Bonita was in shock and felt fine, just reeling from her incident with Bethany and Lyla. It wasn't until she went to get up that she realized her arm was badly hurt.

The lovely Southern lady helped her, and when she noticed tears in Bonita's eyes, she hailed a cab. She told Bonita that she would take her to the hospital and see that she got some attention for her arm. Bonita was in so much pain she didn't argue and got in the cab with the cute little lady from South Carolina.

They arrived at the hospital shortly after that and entered the emergency room. It was packed and unbelievably busy with sick people in every direction. She went to the front desk and registered, and when asked what was wrong, she said she fell and hurt her arm. The nurse looked down at her paper with a distant look. Bonita glanced around and knew it was going to take forever to get in with just a broken arm. She remembered a story her father told once over dinner. She immediately piped up, "I also have terrible chest pains right now. I don't know why, but it hurts quite a bit. It feels tight! " Those were the magic words. Within a few minutes, she was sitting on a stretcher, getting her blood pressure taken, and being checked out by a doctor.

Her father once told her how a man's wife was deathly ill, and he took her to several hospitals, and they were all busy.

She was vomiting blood and having trouble breathing, but they would not take her in until, finally, he said, "I think she is having a heart attack!" The hospital then admitted his wife and checked her out right away. They realized quickly that she wasn't having a heart attack but had a severe infection in her lungs and dealt with the problem immediately. Bonita didn't want to abuse the system, but she was in so much pain, selfishly, she chose to pull the same scam just to be seen quicker.

The doctors took a good look and also quickly realized that she was not suffering from a heart attack but instead shooting pains from a broken left arm. They sent her to a different part of the hospital. By this time, the Southern lady had said goodbye and left. Bonita didn't even have the chance to thank her for being so kind or pay her for the cab.

When Bonita found out that her arm was broken, her blood pressure went through the roof. "Summer is almost over. How am I going to design with a broken arm?" They put a cast on it and placed it in a sling. Luckily, Bonita's School had an optional benefits plan for its students, which she took advantage of when she first arrived in New York.

She left the hospital devastated and in severe pain. The doctor prescribed her some painkillers and told her to take it easy for six weeks while it healed. She didn't have six weeks. School started in two, and her BFA would be very hands-on. She was ruined. In her mind, she might as well have gone home because it was over for her. She couldn't afford to have a broken arm, not now. Why not at the beginning of the summer?

When she got home, she sat in her living room and cried

until she fell asleep, only to be awakened by Claude a few hours later.

He fixed her a cup of tea and gave her pills for her arm, and then she proceeded to tell him about her day. Breaking her arm overshadowed her exchange with Lyla and Bethany, but she also told him about that. The pain from the break in the arm was front and center, but she could still feel the burn in her chest from the break in friendship. He reassured her that everything would work out and that he would help her with her homework if she couldn't do it with one arm. He told her, "Look on the bright side: at least it wasn't your writing hand, and it could have definitely been worse — you could have broken a leg." At first, she was pretty miffed that he wasn't babying her the way she wanted, and to her, there could be nothing worse, but he was right; it could have been. As for Bethany and Lyla, he said, "They will either come around once the tension breaks, or they weren't really your friends to begin with. Perhaps it is all a big misunderstanding, and feelings got hurt."

That night, she went to bed, still quite upset. Her arm was throbbing with pain. She took hours to fall asleep, only to wake up several times throughout the night to take more painkillers. It was a long and excruciating night, and she didn't think the pain would go away, but the following day, when she woke up, the pain had lessened. Although she still had a broken arm, she decided to be positive and get as much practice with using one hand as possible.

First, she couldn't do anything, so it was difficult. After that, she found that most of her stitching and designing was not wholly impossible, just that it would take a little more time than usual. She could still write and sketch, and although she could only squeeze her fingers a little, it was still enough to hold the fabric up against a mannequin. She figured it would work out at school, and although it would be frustrating, she had no choice but to make the best of it.

52

The start of her last year had begun. Two more terms, and she would be finished with school forever and well-equipped with everything she needed to be a success. It scared her a little. She felt that as long as she was in school, if she made a mistake, then she would be forgiven. Once she finished school, there would be little room to make mistakes in the real world. The fashion industry was cutthroat and fickle. If she made a mistake in her first five years before making her name a sought-after commodity, she would be ruined, and all her work would be stigmatized forever. It was a harsh world to live in and an even tougher world to make a living in.

Millions of great designers wanted to be in the spotlight, but only a few made it there. What did she possess that made her special? What did she have that set her apart? The reality of this year had begun to set in. She knew there was a considerable chance, more than a real chance, that she would succumb to nothing and would be lucky to have her designs featured in a bargain basement shop in Brooklyn. This bothered her because she was hell-pressed for most of her time here to make it famous and be considered one of the world's top designers, but she never dwelled on the negative aspects. One year left, and that was frightening to her now. She had worked hard over the last two years to make a name for herself in her school and amongst the fashionistas of New York. She had done good, but not enough.

The simple reality was that although she had got her name out there, it was with a group that didn't stand out on fashion's radar. It was with a close-knit community that kept very much to themselves. She would always have the opportunity to design for drag queens, but that wasn't enough for her. She wanted to see people walk down the street in her cuts and concepts; she wanted to be immortalized in magazines and flaunted on televisions around the globe. Nothing she had done had firmly planted her foot in that direction, except for school — but even that wasn't enough.

Bonita's next term would be the hardest to date, and she felt she was ready for it, but she really wasn't. There would be so much work and everything else that had to go into it; she wasn't prepared for what would come. All she could do was simply bite the bullet and do what she had to do, as she had since day one. She hoped it would be enough but didn't know what to expect.

Her first class had begun, and she had everything ready. What she didn't expect was an announcement from her teacher. He came in with a crooked smile and laid his things on the desk. He turned to the class and said, "I have an announcement to make, and I think everyone here will be first excited and then frightened by it!" He explained that every student had to design a complete collection for the end of the first term's final exam. That would be the final exam, worth

80% of their grade. Also, four students from that exam would be chosen to present their collections at the school fashion show in late January.

Everyone burst out in chatter. Everyone got excited, and Bonita almost fell off her chair in absolute mortification. She could not complete a whole runway-worthy collection in that little time. On top of that, she realized that this would be worth 80% of her term's marks and the other 20% would be little assignments she would get over the next four months. Then, the icing on the cake was that she still had a broken arm, which would prevent her from finishing such a task in time. This was the worst news she could ever have received on the first day of her last year. She would fail; she couldn't pull this off alone, and what would she do?

She sat there for nearly five minutes, ready to die. She was done for. She might as well end it now before it got worse. Then, the teacher made another announcement: Because the percentage of the collection was to be so high, the teachers had planned it into their classroom schedules. Everyone would be allotted plenty of time to work in class and after. Bonita, who was slowly processing those words, sat there a little longer than usual, and her face relaxed. This relieved a lot of stress from her, and she felt as if there were bricks taken from her shoulders. Now she could finish it. Maybe... if she were granted a miracle from God.

To pile on to the fury of her last year, the requirement of a complete collection worth 80% of her grade, and her broken arm, Bethany and Lyla hadn't even so much as acknowledged her. Bethany, however, did cast the occasional glare. Her classmates' actions indicated that Bethany and Lyla had much to say about Bonita, but not to her face. Bonita wondered how Bethany might have spun whatever story she told to shine Bonita in a negative light. It wasn't like she had the best track record for being the nicest person in her class, but she wasn't mean, either. Her class would believe what they wanted to believe, and Bonita had far more critical things to focus her energy on. She decided her popularity, the two girls she thought were her friends, were inconsequential to the task at hand and reframed her mind to focus on her collection.

First, she would say, "What concept would I like to design?" She had attended every show in New York that she could since she moved here two years ago and had been an avid reader of magazines that featured anything fashion. She thought about different concepts, but she couldn't find one! One day, while walking home from school, it hit her and made total sense. She was to do a metropolitan/country-bumpkin line featuring a mixture of soft, country style with A-line military cut to make it slightly edgy. She had her concept, and now all she had to do was make her collection and make it good.

53

Bonita now had direction and a sense of conviction that drew from her an abundance of energy and imagination. She began to sketch day in and day out. Bonita wanted to create a fully wearable line that would not only provoke a new trend in fashion but also inspire people to want to explore the lines between Southern culture and mainstream life-style. The sketches were complex, developing each concept to fully detail what she was getting at. Designers often made clothes that were over the top and that the most outrageously fashion-forward people wouldn't wear on a typical day. She didn't want to do that at all. From start to finish, she wanted to create a wearable line for every day and evening.

She decided that because this would be worth 80% of her first term, she would go all-out and create a line of clothes, jackets, and ball gowns. She had never tried handbags, but she thought it would make an even bigger statement if she designed a few to accompany her show. She had so much work in front of her and bit off what most would consider more than she could chew, but nothing would stop her, and she was determined to make it in the school fashion show.

She was determined but not delirious; she knew there would be some pretty sick designs for the final exam, and if she even wanted to be considered for the show, she would have to ensure the utmost quality and quantity.

She worked long and hard, day in and day out, and slept less than she ate. Her mind was so focused that she even forgot to pay rent on time two months in a row. Claude didn't mind because he knew she had the money, but she was somewhere else in her own little world, creating. He had grown accustomed to Bonita's one-track mind. Claude had seen firsthand how she got when she decided to focus on something, and to be quite honest, he was impressed with how diligent she could be. He never had that. He chose makeup because it would take him an hour to do one face and move to the next. It would be difficult for him to spend days creating the same thing, going back and revising, adding different colors, and changing shades altogether. Luckily, he never met a woman who wanted to stay in his chair for three days, and he was happy about that.

Claude noticed one day that Bonita's room had become a disaster zone and didn't even know how she had room to move around there. He decided it would be more practical for the next two months if Bonita used the main living area to do her work. This way, she would at least have a lot of room to set things up and lay the fabric out. He was easygoing like that. He knew that if he were in the same boat, she would suggest the same, and although he liked a neat and tidy house, it was beneficial to his best friend, so it wasn't a big deal. He spent the day helping Bonita carefully move all the manne-quins and fabrics out into the living room. They moved the couches and reorganized the living room to create as much floor space as possible. Claude promised he would stay away from her space because he knew that although it looked like a vast, unorganized disaster to him, to Bonita, it was the way she wanted it, and she knew where everything was.

They created a tiny little living space close to the kitchen where they moved the T.V. and one couch to have a place to sit and watch a show. It was more for Claude than for Bonita; she would rarely stop to breathe, never mind watching television. Claude also had a T.V. in his room, so he could leave her be and catch his shows chilling out on his bed when she was working. Everything was finally moved, and Bonita's room was now her room again, so he decided that she needed to take a break and that they should go for dinner. It was initially difficult to convince her, but she felt a bit peckish in the end, and they embarked on a journey through New York.

Although she didn't realize it initially, it was a much-needed break for Bonita. It was nice to smell fresh air and have a little fun. They ate dinner, saw a movie, and ended up at a bar downtown for drinks. They rolled into the house late that night, and instead of resuming her work, she decided that she was going to go to bed in her reclaimed room and catch a good night's sleep.

54

The next few months flew by quickly. Bonita was steadily working and focused on her line. The living room looked like a tornado had hit it head-on and destroyed everything in sight. The only thing that looked different was the barrage of mannequins that lined the walls with fully finished and complete garments. There were 40 mannequins, and 29 were full — and not just with one garment. Most of them had on complete ensembles, including pants, shirts, and jackets, and a bunch were sporting newly designed handbags clutched in their hands.

She created 10 complete ensembles consisting of pants of various colors and cuts and many tops, vests, and sweaters to go with each. For two of them, she created corresponding hats. The other 19 were a mixture of skirts, cocktail dresses, and five complete ensembles for men. She thought that would be her cutting-edge, full design for women and men. She knew that most of her work was for the female audience, but she thought it would show her versatility if she could create at least five pieces for the men. The remaining 11 mannequins were for her ball gowns. She wanted to end her presentation with gorgeous dresses that would make anyone feel like a country princess in New York.

Most of the work she completed with a broken arm. She had a lot of assistance from Claude in his spare time, but she had become quite efficient with only one arm. It took a solid nine weeks for her to have it removed, which had brought her nearly mid-way through her term. Claude took her to the clinic, where she was booked to have it removed. Getting full use of her arm back was the epitome of feeling whole again, and she refocused herself on building its strength and putting it to work right away. There was occasional discomfort, and it throbbed a little when it was damp outside. Ultimately, she was completely healed and ready to take on the world.

Her collection was nearly finished, and she was beginning to get very excited but extremely nervous at the same time. This was to be shown in front of the whole class. Before she would have to be concerned about one item being seen, maybe two depending on the circumstances, but now it was forty full models wearing her clothing and a lot to criticize. She still had a few gowns to make and to go over her other outfits 10 more times, checking for stitching and all the minor details that would be considered during the grading process. Still, she felt she was nearly done until she looked again and realized something was missing.

It took her a while, but she soon knew it was shoes! She needed shoes for her models, and there was no way around it. She had personally taken each mannequin from her school with permission from her teacher. Her school thought it strange that she needed 40 of them, but they had an overabundance for this particular reason. Over the last few months, Bonita had gone back and forth to the school whenever she could to pick them up. The problem she faced was that she would have to return them to her school for her final exam, and she was not looking forward to that. The great thing about these mannequins was that they came with a head and feet, not like the typical ones they used that only had a torso, so this allowed her to properly shoe her faux girls so that the image was complete.

Bonita had to go shopping and find 35 pairs of shoes, and she needed to figure out where to look for discount shoes that were not discount-looking. She went everywhere and couldn't find a thing! Lots of simple high-heeled shoes, but nothing that would match her clothing. She was ready to give up when she got another one of her bright ideas that usually left her stressed to the max and starved for time. She returned to a store where she found simple black leather pumps on sale for $5.00 a pair. She bought 35 of them and lugged them straight back to her apartment. She still had to make a few gowns and check a ton of her work for quality, but she figured she would have more than enough time to design 35 pairs of footwear to go on her girls.

The race was on. Bonita finished her other gowns, and instead of checking quality first, she decided she would begin making her designer shoes. She had purchased glue guns, gems, and jewels from craft shops and everything you could imagine under the sun that she might need to create a sexy line of heels. Bonita had so much fabric and materials she felt she could complete this task without a problem. She began to cut into the leather, taking out pieces here and adding pieces there. She covered any brand names on the shoes with a made-up insignia that she created herself. There were lace and rhinestones, flowers and fabric, and glue everywhere. Still, in less than a week of working around the clock, she had successfully created 35 different shoes, and no one could tell they were all the same pair and that she had designed them herself. They looked stunning, and she was thrilled.

55

The finals were only a week away, and the students and teachers seemed deep in concentration. Bonita knew why the students were stressed but needed help understanding what the teachers were so focused on. That is until she overheard a conversation in the school's textiles lab. A group of girls and a couple of guys were laughing at how their teacher had a massive vein in his head, and lately, it looked like it would explode. They said this was because the school was known for its fashion shows. The event was huge, and many people came to take it in. People from the press would be there. People from fashion houses and this place and that were going to be filling the seats. Her school put on a show where no mistakes could be made.

The teachers and faculty had the total weight of putting together the setups, picking the designers, and ensuring everything went smoothly. They received funding from arts foundations that made generous donations yearly to keep the school up-to-date and ensure it was always equipped with everything it needed. If the show was a disaster, there would be hell to pay, a loss of funding, and significant criticism from the press. They were the top fashion school in the United States. Although they selected their students based on essays on what they believed fashion to be and what they wanted to do in the industry, they were known for producing the highest educated and trained designers. Nothing could go wrong at this fashion show, and every detail had to be planned 20 times over.

The teacher in the class that day hushed the students and directed their attention to the door. The dean of admissions stood at the entrance, a brittle woman with over-drawn eyebrows and fur cascading down her slim figure. She looked like she had seen better days and was ready for the Betty Ford clinic. She staggered in the class on stilettos, and when she opened her mouth, the class fell silent. Bonita had never heard anyone speak so eloquently before in her life. She had a slight touch of an English accent and pronounced every word with a grace that could swoon a hyena. Although Bonita listened to every word the woman said, she couldn't help but fall into a deep trance. She felt like a snake, and the lady in front of the class was a snake charmer. Finally, once the dean stopped speaking, Bonita returned to reality. She had just finished saying how important this event was for everyone and wished everyone in their lines the best of luck.

Deep down, Bonita wanted to be that woman one day. Maybe not looking as strung out as she did, but definitely with that sort of presence. The teacher went on and on for the next hour, explaining the rules, making sure everyone knew what they would be looking for in the grading process, and letting everyone know what would happen if they were chosen to show their line in the fashion show in January.

There would be four spots, ranked from four to one. The number one spot would be the last to show their line and the one who would be allotted the most time. After they were chosen, they would each meet individually with their teacher to discuss how they wanted to present it. Then, they would deal with the lighting and stage crew to organize the music, special effects, and how their names would appear on the backdrop. Then, after a few other details were managed correctly, they would be shown the spaces they would have to house their models and designs.

Everyone would have to pick an assistant or stagehand from the school specializing in that field and teach them exactly how they wanted everything to go. This was because designers were not permitted backstage while their lines were being shown. Frantic outbursts, drama, and emotional breakdowns could not be afforded.

Once all the terms and conditions were discussed, the class was released. Before they left, the teacher announced loudly and proudly that they would get the rest of the week off to finish their lines. There would be no classes, but the schools would be open for them to use. This excited everyone so very much, and Bonita felt now she had more time than ever to make everything work.

56

The following week passed almost as if time had stopped for a second and then restarted a week later. Although she had prepared herself as much as one woman could, Bonita still felt robbed of time. Throughout the week, she had been bringing her mannequins back to school, as many as she could carry. Claude helped as much as he could, and finally, on the day before, they were all standing in her section, one of the rooms the teachers had delegated for them to use. They were not to be displayed in the classroom because that was where the marks would be given, and space was an issue.

She stayed late at school the night before with boxes and bags of her entire collection. There were only a few others that were there. Still, as a precaution, they had a faculty member keep the school open the whole night to ensure everyone was ready for the following day. Claude came with her to help assemble her collection and set everything up. They snuck in a bottle of wine to help pass the time. Every mannequin was decked out with beautiful garments that Claude said made him feel like he was in a high-end department store. Every mannequin was also wearing a pair of Bonita's freshly designed shoes. She had spent a lot of time researching the shoes and creating them. She looked at the types of high-fashion shoes that were modern and streamlined and then coupled them with designs from older, softer shoe fabrics.

Bonita was pleased and thrilled that she was done before 3:00 am. She wanted to go home and get as much sleep as possible to feel semi-awake the following day. That night, Bonita dreamt of her collection. In her dream, they came to life as real people. They walked down the street and danced at clubs and fancy parties. She dreamt that top celebrities wore her gowns on the red carpet, and everyone looked fabulous.

The following day, she woke to her alarm clock and quickly showered. She grabbed what she needed and made her way to school. When she arrived, her classroom was full of wide-eyed dreamers who all wanted their collections picked for the fashion show. Very few people were allowed to see each other's collections before this morning. The teachers felt it best not to damper the designers' imaginations. It was insinuated that in previous years, exposing the other classmates' designs beforehand created a war between the students. With this approach, it's all done; no changes can be made.

The teachers came in and told the class that the collections were now open to viewing by the students, and they would begin grading within the hour. They let everyone out in groups of 10 at a time. Bonita was in the first group to go. She walked through all the rooms — 15 big ones, to be exact. There were three collections in each room; last night, they were all sectioned off so that others couldn't see them. To-day, the curtains were down, the dividers were moved away, and each collection stood presented for all to see. Bonita circled through each one, observing and enjoying each piece. She wanted to make an educated guess on who she believed would be in the top four.

She passed by Lyla's and thought, "Wow! This will be one of them for sure!" She was mesmerized by Lyla's choice of bold colors and period clothes. They were 18th century brought forth to modern times — much like Bonita's concept, but more old than new. She used a lot of leather and lace with heavy fabrics that hung low and stood stiff when worn. She was impressed, to say the least, and couldn't wait to congratulate her.

After a few more, she came to Bethany's, who she immediately decided would also be in the top four. Her collection was incredible and edgy. She used stiff collars and metal to create a very futuristic look, but in a way that was sexy and sleek. It was astonishing. She loved several pieces and even wanted to ask Bethany if she could buy one of her jackets. There were plenty of other amazing collections that Bonita thought would make it to the top four. There was severe competition, and she had decided who they would be until she encountered the unthinkable.

Cassidy Ruthers, the biggest bitch in all the school, had created one of the most excellent collections Bonita had ever seen. It appealed to her because of where she came from: It was inspired by the water. Cassidy's collection consisted hugely of beachwear. But not bikinis and trunks, but rather sundresses and clothes that one would wear during a romantic walk on the beach. Bonita believed that romance was Cassidy's inspiration, and she had pulled it all together with such flair and buoyancy.

Bonita returned to the class, and during the other students' turns, she concluded that Lyla, Bethany, and even Miss Cunty Cassidy would be in the top four. The other spot was a toss-up among three other students in the class. Aminu Andhandi was a quiet girl with a flair for creating clothing shaped for her culture with a Western edge. Josef Imnagren, dressed to kill but mainly like a cowboy, had a sense of Western chic. Last but not least, Emma Fields was a simplistic girl who believed less fabric, and fewer accents made things more classic, which was her style. All of them were great, but Bonita never put herself in with the winning group. She decided that her collection needed to be more runway-worthy, but it would be good to earn her the grades she expected.

Everyone in the class returned, and the teachers announced they would begin grading. They would be viewing each collection individually, and while they were grading, they would ask the designer to stand in the hallway adjacent to the office and wait for them to come and ask them questions. From what she could understand, they were going to ask the basics. "What inspired you?" "Who do you think will wear this?" "What is your market?" "Why do you feel this would be excellent to show in the school fashion show?" She had worked out answers for all of them and was ready for when they called her name.

57

Finally, after nearly four hours, her name was called. Besides the lump in her throat, she was feeling fine. She always found these sorts of things to be the most nerve-wracking. Even in high school, it was never okay when she would have to present. Bonita would become non-verbal if she had to answer questions and speak about anything she hadn't prepared for.

There was nothing more for her to do than just do it. She had prepared as much as possible, and now it was time to seal the deal. She walked to the designated spot and stood still for nearly a half-hour. Looking through the collections, she noticed that no one else had as many items as she did, not even close. This scared her a bit. Maybe the teachers would feel she was trying too hard.

Nonetheless, she stood there and waited patiently until the teachers came to see her. Finally, after nearly an hour, a whole swarm of people came around the corner to greet her. There were teachers, the Dean of admissions, and several other people she had never seen before. They asked her all the questions she had expected them to ask and threw a few more in that she didn't.

The first question they asked was, "When you were living back home in Newfoundland, Canada, did you ever truly see yourself making it to the top New York fashion runways?" Without waiting for her response, the teacher went on to say, "I mean, really, Miss Smith, there are thousands of designers out there from all around the world who want to be famous, but somehow you are going to come here to New York from a little town called Bay Roberts and expect to own the show?"

He looked at her for the first time with this strange eyebrow-lifted expression. She was completely and utterly mortified. She had no idea what to say or why he was so mean.

She took a second and then noticed the impatient look growing on Dean's face and said, "Actually, sir, with all due respect, I believe I feel the same way as any of those thousands of designers. I do not believe it matters where you come from or how you were raised when it comes to making good fashion. Either you have a vision, or you do not. Either you have talent, or you do not. This school is my outlet for making my personal dreams come true. I knew very little about fashion when I came here, but somehow, I have been at the top of the class in grades since I arrived. Can the other designers add that to their C.V.s? My point is that I have just as much chance as anyone else to own the fashion runways, and I will continue to push myself harder to create better to achieve that dream!"

The teacher let his head fall to his book and then threw

out the most impossible question, which she was unprepared to answer. She hated this question more than any other.

"Do you feel your favorite fashion house would be impressed with your collection? And why?"

Bonita paused for another moment and then said, "I believe that the collection I have designed was the best I could do in the time I had with the experience I possessed and the inspiration that was delivered to me. Whether or not my favorite fashion house would look at this collection and be impressed bears no relevance to me, for I did not create it for my favorite fashion house. I created it for two entities, one being myself and the second being the school for my final exam. I cannot speak for anyone other than myself. I believe this collection is fully wearable, trendy, and fashion-forward. I can envision being at a party or event here in the city and seeing people from all walks of life wearing my line. So, to answer your question, sir, I do not know how my favorite fashion house would feel about my collection, but I think it's great."

Once again, he lowered his head to his book. Everyone had a stone face and bared no expression. He looked up at her and said, "Last question! Miss Smith, if you were chosen for the school fashion show, what do you feel people would take away with them after seeing your collection?"

By this time, Bonita had had enough and was annoyed. "Just tell me my collection sucked so I can go on living my life," she thought. Instead, she said, "I believe they would leave feeling as if they saw a fresh take on rural and urban apparel." Bonita was frustrated because the tone and delivery of these questions were dismissive, pointed, and pointless. She could feel her skin get hot and quickly thought she needed to put an end to the banter. "I didn't make the show, that's fine! I just want my marks and to get out of here," she thought.

The gentleman went to ask another question, but this time, Bonita cut him off.

"Ladies and gentlemen, I appreciate the opportunity to audition for your fashion show in January. If I were to win, I would be very excited, but I do not see how these questions relate to my collection and final grade. I am here to learn, be graded, and leave this institution, having absorbed everything I can. Right now, the questions you ask waste valuable time for the others waiting to be graded!"

When she said it, she wasn't thinking correctly, and then right before her eyes was a group of people who didn't seem entirely too impressed with her quick response.

"Well," the teacher said. "Thank you for your time, Miss Smith. We will announce the grades and winners at the end of the day!" They all turned and walked away, and she stood there, ready to cry. She blew it, she thought. "Why would I say something like that?"

She walked back to class, embarrassed and defeated. All her hard work had just gone down the drain because of her big mouth. She had several hours before announcing the grades and winners, so she looked around for Lyla and Bethany in hopes of making amends and inviting them to go for lunch. She hadn't seen them too much lately, especially this term. She was far too busy, as were they, never mind their last interaction being a nasty word brawl in the street. After a few minutes and no luck finding them, she decided to go to lunch alone.

The end of the day came, and she was back in the class, sitting at her station in pure misery. Her lunch made her feel a little better, but fixing what she had done would take much more than that. She sat there waiting for the teachers, looking around and making some eye contact with Bethany and Lyla. They were diverting their looks away and were clearly still upset about the matter. Bonita thought if she perhaps tried harder. Still, she didn't feel very inclined to socialize this late in the day. Another hour passed, and still nothing. She was getting ready to call it quits and go home but then decided she had waited this long; she could stick it out.

58

After what seemed like an eternity, the teachers all returned to class. It was about time, she figured. She thought,
"How hard could it be to say, 'You suck, you smart-mouthed
little bitch who has no sense of censorship.'" She felt the worst
she had felt for a long time, and her stomach was simply in
knots. How could she ruin this for herself? There was no way
the teachers would give her a passing or a reasonable grade
after she mouthed off to them. She was doomed.

The teachers walked in with the rest of the faculty. Everyone was quiet and still. Not one teacher had a pleasant look
on their face. Maybe they were not impressed with any of
the collections. Bonita knew that couldn't be true and figured
they were still miffed at how she handled herself — but he was
being rather rude, and, well, she just doesn't take that kind of
shit from people. They began passing everyone's grades out,
one by one. Still, there was no dialogue; just silence filled the
room. A couple of the students who had received their grades
had made huge sighs of relief and gave themselves a friendly
yet competitive "YES!" She was among the last to get her

grades, and when she flipped it over, she was shocked at the marks they gave her.

100% was written on the bottom of the evaluation, with a comment from her teacher, saying,

"Great answers to our questions. When we have designers who show promise, we do our best to trip them up; it isn't meant to be mean but rather a gauge of how well you can handle yourself in difficult situations. We want to see strong individuals who can represent themselves and their work. You did an incredible job, and we all say, 'Well done!!! As for your work, Bonita, we were quite impressed with the finished products. Your pairing of grains was a genius attempt at leveraging soft country with cosmopolitan vibes. The stitching was exemplary; we looked intentionally for any threads out of place and were surprised we could find none. We all have very keen eyes, Bonita, and our eyes tell us that you have, in fact, absorbed all the teachings we have to offer thus far. You show great promise, and I hope you are as pleased with your work as we are. Continue to stand firm in your delivery. The fashion world can often be nasty, but we think you will do alright."

She could hardly believe it, but now it all made sense. She thought it was strange for her teacher to be as mean as he was. He treated her so well over the last two years and never raised his voice or made a condescending comment to anyone. She was relieved and happy and well ready to go home. It was time to relax. Finals were done, and it was the end of term. Christmas holidays were just around the corner, and she had a big surprise planned for her Mom and Dad.

The next step was to announce who would take the four

spots for the school fashion show. The teacher cleared his throat and gave a little speech.

"Ladies and gentlemen, for most of you, if not all of you, this is the most important part of the day!"

He turned and looked at Bonita when he made the comment, and she could only assume it was because she had made it clear that her grades were most important to her.

"First of all, please let me say that each collection was beautiful in its own right, and none of you failed the assignment. But as you know, only four spots are available for the fashion show in January, and today, those four were chosen."

"Each of you expressed yourselves in different ways and techniques throughout your collections. What we were looking for in deciding who would present at the show was more complex than just grading. We needed four individuals who possessed imagination and a centered knowledge of fashion and where it has come from, even more than what we have taught you here over the last two-and-a-half years. Someone who went the extra mile and didn't design something they were comfortable with but took the steps needed to ensure a collection had as much character as a piece of fabric could have!"

He was scanning the class and cleared his throat once again.

"This is why we have chosen the following four individuals to present in the school fashion show. Lyla Frank will fill the number-four spot for her collection of 18th-century modern designs. Filling the number-three spot will be Bethany Ludemier for her collection of futuristic metal designs.

Filling the number-two spot will be Cassidy Ruthers, for her collection of aqua romance designs."

Bonita was counting down the spots in her head and was so happy to hear that her friends Lyla and Bethany made the cut. She figured they really deserved it. Their pieces were quite catchy and had a lot of character. Although she knew Cassidy would be in the top four, Bonita didn't like it much. However, logically, she felt that if based solely on her collection, she should get it. Now, Bonita couldn't wait to find out who was next. She was hoping for Aminu but wasn't too sure.

The teacher cleared his throat again. Bonita wanted to ask if he needed a glass of water but thought better of it.

"Filling the number-one spot will be..."

Pause for effect.

"...Bonita Smith, for her collection of southern metro design."

Most of the class smiled and nodded when the other three women were named; however, the class went wild this time. No one was surprised that she won. Everyone who had seen her collection this morning thought she had it hands-down. They congratulated and shook her hand, but no one was in Bonita's body. She had drifted off in a state of shock.

"I'm number one? No, that's not possible; so many were better than mine," she thought, still wholly spaced out. She had worked hard but never believed she would be picked in the number-one slot. This was a fantastic accomplishment for her. She finally snapped back to reality and started smiling a little. She looked at the teacher, who was smiling back at her, and started saying thank you to everyone congratulating her. Everyone in the class felt she deserved the number-one spot. She had the most detailed and well-put-together collection, even down to her handbags and shoes. No one else had branched off from making the garments, and no one else had footwear on their mannequins. Her collection was complete from head to toe.

Not everyone in the class was as happy about Bonita's success as the rest. Three people were actually upset about it. Lyla was the least bitter, but she felt that she wasn't aware that creating a line of shoes and handbags would aid in the deciding factor; she could have designed her own, too. She got the number-four spot, better than the rest of her class, but she truly felt her line was extraordinary. Initially, she just shrugged it off and masked her resentment with a smile. Bethany was more upset than Lyla. She felt her designs were the way of the future and exuded forward-thinking and stepping outside the box. Bethany always felt her designs were better than Bonita's. Before, it never bothered her that she consistently scored less. It didn't matter what happened in class; what happened in the real world counted to her. She wanted this show badly, and although she got it, she was unhappy with being placed number three.

The last person was Cassidy Ruthers. It's funny how the only ones who were upset were those who made it into the show. Cassidy was more than just upset — she was livid and raging mad. She didn't feel Bonita's mousy collection held a candle to hers. Hers embodied romance and passion with hues from the sea. How could some country slop mixed with modern bullshit outplace her line in the show, and how could some small-time, small-town redneck bitch outplace her not only in school grades but also in the most significant event of their school career? It didn't sit well with Cassidy, and she was sick and tired of that bitch stealing her spotlight.

59

Cassidy left school that day angrier than she had ever been. She was so frustrated with how things turned out.

"It isn't fair," she thought as she paced the lot behind her school. She stopped and lit a cigarette by a bench, and to calm her nerves, she decided to sit down and take a moment to compose herself. For the last two-and-a-half years, she had been second in line for everything because of that girl, and now, when it really counted, when it really mattered, she finished second once again.

She was tired of being shown up by that goody-two-shoes, and she intended to stop it. The problem was, what could she really do to put an end to this girl once and for all? Her designs today were the best she had to pull out, and nothing she could do now would change the fact that she had the number-two placement in the fashion show. Nothing would change anything right now. She would still have to go to the exhibit, present her collection, and then wait to be outnumbered by little Miss Bonita Smith. It sucked, and she knew it, and it caused her insides to rage.

Cassidy couldn't accept that someone she considered

beneath her could be a better designer than her. Her problem was that she knew Bonita was a better designer. She would never admit it to anyone, not even to herself; she would push it away from her mind and move on.

It was the weekend, and Cassidy wasn't in the mood to do anything with her friends. Instead, she texted everyone and decided she would go home to sulk. A friend had just left the school and noticed her on the bench. He was a business and marketing major at the school. He asked her what was wrong, and she told him, and he said, "Sometimes, in business, things like that happen. You just have to work harder to outsmart the competition and make sure the next time, you make their work look like shit next to yours."

Cassidy sat momentarily, and then her eyes lit up like light bulbs. She jumped from the bench, saying, "Thank you. That is the perfect idea!"

60

Bonita was thrilled when she got home that afternoon, and Claude knew immediately that it must have gone well. They sat down around the table, now back in its rightful place, and she told him of everything that had happened. He was so happy for her and delighted that he would actually get to see her work in a real-life fashion show. They decided to celebrate and go out for a night on the town. It was the weekend, and Bonita hadn't done anything exciting for quite some time.

They dressed in their finest clothes and left the apartment looking like movie stars out for an awards ceremony or something of the sort. They decided to use their feet tonight and take a long stroll to take in all the sights. They went to Pino's, a celebrity-owned restaurant in SoHo, and splurged on a costly and very delicious meal. They purchased a bottle of their finest wine during dinner and made many toasts to each other, their lives, and successes.

It was evident that Claude had some exciting news that he had been holding back all dinner, but he told her he wanted to wait until dessert to share it with her.

Claude, after years of doing makeup in the city for a couple of medium-range celebrities, was requested to do the makeup for a very well-known actress for a spread in a magazine. His work would be featured on a beautiful and famous woman's face and in a magazine that people would read everywhere. It was so significant to Bonita that she let out a burst of excitement over the entire restaurant. Heads were turned and staring, but Bonita didn't care. This was huge and amazing, and she was so excited for him that she could hardly contain herself. Immediately, the topic of discussion went from her show to his big break.

After dinner and another bottle of wine, they left the restaurant in great cheer. They decided to go to a club and get their dance on. They arrived at Posh nearly half past 10. Already, the club was crawling with people. The music was hot, but the temperature was hotter. It didn't take long for both of them to try and cool down with a few more drinks. They had fun and stayed out until nearly 4:00 am, and when they left, they were so wired neither of them wanted to go home, so they decided to walk around town and chat.

They talked, walked for hours that night, and even sat on a Battery Park bench as the sun rose. At one point, Claude put his arm around her, told her he loved her so much and was sad she wouldn't be around this holiday season. Bonita planned to surprise her parents by showing up a few days before Christmas, and she couldn't wait to make it happen. She explained why it was important to her and that she still wanted to do a Christmas when she got back before New Year's.

They arrived back at the apartment at around 10 o'clock

in the morning. By this time, they were both exhausted and ready for bed. Bonita got undressed and crawled in under her sheets. She thought about all the beautiful things happening to her and Claude, how grateful she was that he was her best friend, and how excited she was to see her parents after so long. Bonita fell into a deep sleep with a smile on her face. She dreamed of only beautiful and wonderful things.

61

Cassidy had been made aware of what she had to do to fix this little problem with Bonita Smith. It was her chat with her friend that made it clear to her. Her friend was comparing what happened to Cassidy in school with business transactions. Sometimes, you work hard in business, and the other company wins the sale or bid. If that is the case, all you have to do is make sure the next time you are bidding, make the others' plans look like shit. This was true for Cassidy; she now knew what to do.

Her first step was to get reinforcements, and she knew the two people who would best fit the job. She had overheard them talking at school about Bonita, and they were also quite upset she got placed number one. It took a little convincing, but Cassidy arranged a meeting between the three for dinner at one of her favorite restaurants the following day. She would foot the bill; that alone should get them on her good side.

That following afternoon, she got ready and left her apartment. She had spent the night devising her plan, but now she needed to ensure she had some help pulling it off. She had contacted the girls and told her where they would meet. When she arrived at the restaurant, they were already sitting down. She sat down beside them and said, "Good evening, ladies. Have you ordered drinks yet?"

"No, not yet," Lyla said with a reserved tone.

"We thought that we would wait for you!" Bethany nodded and smiled at Cassidy, waiting to hear what she had to say. For the first half an hour, they made small talk. Cassidy was extra friendly and congratulated them on making the fashion show. Then, Bethany made the first negative comment about Bonita, and Cassidy had them right where she wanted.

At first, she played the victim, claiming she had worked hard and fell short of her collection. She felt that her collection was better, and so did the other girls. Eventually, the whole meal turned into a Bonita-bashing party, and the hate for her grew around the table. Lyla and Bethany used to be her friends, but she hardly paid any attention to them over the last year. Bethany concluded, "She must have thought she was better than us!"

Lyla agreed that it had to be that. She knew she was busy, but Bonita only called a few times during the summer and had other things on the go. She didn't even speak to them in school half the time. Something had changed in her, something for the worse, and they were sick of her Little-Miss-Perfect attitude, always showing off and showing up the rest of the class. They all agreed she should be stopped and knocked down a peg or two.

That is when Cassidy made her move, and before she knew it, she was spewing out a carefully devised plan to teach Bonita a lesson and to make their collections stand out more at the fashion show. It was purely evil and would completely ruin her, but Bethany and Cassidy were on board. Lyla agreed to do it but was feeling guilty and restrained. All she needed was a little more convincing — a little more work — and now that Bethany was in full swing, it wouldn't be too hard for them both to get her where they wanted.

The three girls left the restaurant that night with a sense of purpose for the holidays and a sense of revenge growing in their hearts. They had planned to get together the following day to discuss and lay out each part of their plan methodically and begin carrying it out. They went their separate ways, and Cassidy felt on top of the world. She would get what she wanted. Why wouldn't she? She always did!

62

The airport was busy as usual on December 20th, and she and Claude were trying hard to make it through all the pedestrian traffic with their boxes and suitcases. Bonita had packed heavily because this was her first time going home to see her parents in two-and-a-half years. She was excited and went all out with the presents and different things she could bring home for the holidays. Bonita had paid for her last term a week before and knew that she was doing well enough financially that she could spoil her parents. Bonita was happy that she could surprise them this year.

Claude was a little sad about Bonita's departure. The last two years, he had her very much to himself, and this year, he would have to find alternate plans to keep himself occupied over the holidays. Bonita had felt bad about leaving, so she invited him to come home with her, but Claude refused. He told her that he wouldn't feel comfortable with people he didn't know, and he would feel like he was imposing on some significant family time. Then he mentioned the fact that he was gay and didn't think it would go over well with her father.

She checked in at the flight desk, loaded all her boxes on the conveyor, turned to Claude, and gave him a huge hug and kiss on the cheek.

"I love you, and I will miss you so much," she said with a little tear in her eye. He choked up a little, too.

"Bonita, don't make me cry in public," he chuckled and hugged her. "See you in eight days!"

She grabbed her carry-on and walked toward the security gate, turning and waving as much as she could without getting trampled by oncoming traffic.

Once she boarded the plane, she felt a tingle of nostalgia. She was going back to Newfoundland. Two-and-a-half years ago, if you had asked her if she would go back, she would have said no; she was glad to be rid of that place and didn't want to acknowledge it existed. After growing into a young woman, she realized Newfoundland had a certain charm, a small-town feeling that made her feel safe and snug. New York didn't have that. It was vast and wide open, and she felt the most secure in her shared apartment with Claude and more so in her room with her things and mementos.

The plane was up, the aircraft was down, and she was making a changeover. There wasn't a terrible amount of time between both flights, but she made it all right, and before she knew she was in the air again. This was the last time; the next stop was St. John's International Airport. Not long after they began the descent, she looked out her window at the ground, getting closer. She thought of how her parents would be so surprised to see her. She couldn't wait until she got to see their faces. The plane landed, and they all marched off. She had arranged for a rental car to be at the airport so she could drive herself home.

The airport was so different than New York. It was small, and very few people were in it. She got all her boxes and made her way to the front doors. The gentleman dropping off the car for her helped her load everything in it, and then she got in, started it, and pointed it toward Bay Roberts. She was almost home.

Unlike driving in the City or L.A., driving on the old roads was a breeze for Bonita. It was relaxing for her and made her think about many things. She had the radio on and listened to good old-fashioned country music, bobbing her head and singing aloud. She was lost in space and making plans in her head for her upcoming fashion show, and that was pretty much all she could think about until she rode into Bay Roberts — the biggest shithole the world had to offer. But at this present moment, it was a refreshing blast from the past and made her feel like she was home. Almost to her house, she remembered that her mother and father hadn't seen a picture of her since she had her makeover. They were going to be seriously surprised.

63

There it was, her two-story house with cheap siding and broken front steps. A long way from the posh building and doorman she had become accustomed to while living in the big city. She was feeling somewhat nervous as she shut the car off and saw the curtains move in the kitchen. "What if they didn't want me to come home this year and they made other plans," she thought. After a short pause, she realized she was home now; there was no turning back, and she knew her family would be happy to see her.

She walked quickly toward the front door, which opened before reaching the stairs. It was her father looking all preacher-like, about to greet someone he didn't know. At first, he didn't know who it was coming up the front yard. He looked at this woman like he would a complete stranger, and then she spoke.

"Daddy, surprise! I'm home for Christmas!"

He jumped back a few feet and rubbed his eyes quickly to adjust his vision. This woman wasn't the baby girl he dropped off at the airport two-and-a-half years ago. This was a woman, a real woman.

"Lord love a duck, woman! Come 'ere quick! Bonita's just showed up on the doorstep!" He yelled back into the house, ran from the front stoop, and grabbed her tightly.

"'Me love, what are ya at? Where ya too, me ducky? Let me haves a good look at yah, luh!'"

He began with the questions, but Bonita didn't have time to answer them because the air was filled with screams. High-pitched screams. It was her Mom, running out through the front door.

"Oh my goodness, Bonita, nar bit of weight gone off ya, I know! You looks some beautiful, I tell yah. Gives me a hug now!" She grabbed her so tight that Bonita felt like the wind had been knocked out of her.

"Thanks, Mom. Surprise!" she said, with the bit of breath she had left.

"Well, b'y, come on in out the cold. Pop, grab her bags there luh, and we'll get her yarnin' to us all about the big smoke!"

Her father took her keys and popped the trunk. He unloaded everything in 10 minutes. He didn't understand what, in God's name, his little girl could have in all those boxes. Her mother pulled her into the house, and Bonita took off her shoes; then she sat down at the table and was told by her mother, "Don't ya stir a muscle now, me ducky. Supper's nearly on da table, and der's plenty to go 'round. You park yerself there luh and take a load off, and whatever's botherin' ya can wait 'til we've had a feed!" It was matter-of-fact, and Bonita knew not to make a fuss. This whole trip was mostly for her parents, so she would let them get all the enjoyment they wanted from it.

Bonita's father finished putting her things up in her room and then joined them downstairs just as her mother was dishing out dinner and putting it on the table. Bonita was allowed to get up briefly to wash her hands and face in the kitchen sink and immediately shuffled back to her chair. Finally, when her mother and father sat down with terrific smiles from ear to ear, they turned to her with such pride and said, "So, let's have da whole yarn! We're itching to know every bit!" Bonita was prepared for this, for as much as she tried to keep in touch with her parents when she was away, there were times she couldn't tell them everything. Her phone bill would be thousands of dollars.

"Well, I don't know what to tell you or where to start or what you want to know specifically, so why don't you ask me questions, and I'll answer them," she said, smiling. She was having a fun time, too. She loved that her parents were so happy that she came home.

"Okay," her father said, "Got yerself a steady, have ya?"

Bonita turned a little red in the face. "Dad?" she responded, embarrassed.

"Whas dat now? Can't yer ol' man ask if yer keepin' comp'ny or not?"

"I guess," she said, "and I do not have a boyfriend. I did, but that ended a while back and was short-lived!"

He turned as he blushed a little. "Did he do ya right, me ducky?"

Bonita shook her head and said: "No, but that is why it was short-lived!"

Her mother chimed in and changed the subject. "So, whas

new 'round the school, me ol' bird? Anyting stirrin'? Sure, yer almost tru da door now, wat wit yer final term comin' on!"

Bonita hadn't told them yet what her great news was, so she took the opportunity now to share it with them.

"Well, Mom and Dad, I had to create an entire wearable collection for this term's final exam. Out of the 45 students in our class, only four would be chosen for the big school fashion show. I was chosen for the number one slot!"

Her mother almost fell off her chair, grabbed her, and kissed her forehead 11 times before she sat back in her seat.

"I always knowed you'd make 'er, I did. Sure as the sun rises, I just knowed it." her mother said.

Her father piped up. "We're right proud of ya, Bonita, for carvin' out your own path, fendin' for yourself, and growin' into a fine young maid. 'Tis grand to have ya back in the bay!"

The dinner went on for over three hours. Even though the food was finished after one, the conversation was rich and filling, and nobody wanted to stop. For the first time, she sat and thoroughly enjoyed talking with her parents. They were so interested in her life in New York and soaked up every word she said. Later that night, they sat around the living room and continued talking for another few hours. Before they knew it, it was pretty late, and Bonita was exhausted from her long day.

She walked upstairs that night and first went to the bathroom to brush her teeth. When she finished, she knocked on her parents' door, told them good night, and entered her bedroom. Nothing had changed, not one thing! She noticed that some of the pages from her graduation speech were still in the same spot she left them. Everything was dusted and cleaned, and the sheets were washed, but her mother had kept everything the way it was. She felt as if she was home, safely nestled in familiar territory, territory she had once hated but now seemed to welcome. She decided that when she woke up in the morning, she would go through everything in her room, just for old times' sake.

64

It was a little frosty in Manhattan when Lyla was the last to join the party at an upscale martini bar downtown. Bethany and Cassidy had been there for nearly twenty minutes before she arrived and had already begun working on their drinks. Lyla had been reluctant about attending this gathering for a little while. She disliked Bonita quite a bit but wasn't convinced it was enough to destroy her, or at least not enough right now.

Cassidy called the waiter over and ordered Lyla a drink, and then she pulled out a notebook and pen and laid them on the table.

"Let's get down to business, shall we?"

Bethany and Lyla agreed and then listened to what Cassidy said.

"I have been thinking for quite some time about what we could do to get back at Bonita for stealing our spotlight, and I think I have come up with the perfect plan!"

Lyla was sucking back her drink pretty quickly and waiting to hear what Cassidy had to say. On the other hand,

Bethany was in first gear and ready to go with whatever she had decided.

"Unfortunately, murder is a crime, and, well, I don't care for her that much, so I have come up with something that would hurt her badly but not kill her. So here is my finalized plan!"

Lyla was a little taken aback by her comment about murder. She didn't hate Bonita so much; she wanted her dead, but rather, she just wanted to teach her a lesson.

"Bonita has the number-one spot on the fashion show, correct? And there will be very influential people attending the show who will be looking for junior designers, or at least ideas, so we have to do something to make her segment of the show a disaster. Create some sort of mayhem that will have the crowd laughing!"

Bethany was all down, as she had been from the start. Lyla took a moment and returned with a "That sounds perfect!" This was a no-blood plan, but it would teach Bonita a lesson without anyone getting hurt or in too much trouble.

The night went on, and they began ironing out precisely what they would do. By the time the bar closed that evening, they had figured out start-to-finish what would happen, and they were all in for the go. They needed to talk to a certain someone to get their plan started, but how would they do that without alerting anyone, especially Bonita? They wanted this to be the biggest shock of her life. They passed around a few ideas and finally decided that honesty was best. They would just be up-front and truthful about the whole thing. The person in question would be glad to help.

65

Bonita woke up the following day a little disoriented. She had expected to wake up in her room in New York. Still, when she opened her eyes and saw she was back in her room in Newfoundland, she shook herself, thinking she had dreamt everything that happened and had a sense of fear fall over her. That quickly dissipated when she remembered that she was home for the holidays with her parents, that it wasn't a dream, and that everything was as it should be.

She crawled out of bed, walked into the bathroom, and immediately showered. She wanted to feel fresh for her first day at home with her parents. When she finished, she could smell bacon cooking in the kitchen. She quickly dressed herself and ran down the stairs. Her mother and father made a big, hearty breakfast and smiled like silly kids. Their little girl was home, and they got to spend time with her and spoil her rotten before she returned to New York.

Her mother was Paula Smith, born of Hubert and Nance Rose. She was initially from Bay Roberts and was thrilled when they offered the church there. Her father, Earl Smith, was from a small town out west called Stephenville, and he left home at 17 after he graduated and went to Bible College. His father wasn't a minister but a very religious man who took the kids to church every Sunday. His firm belief and faith was instilled in Earl at a young age, and for as far back as her Dad could remember, he wanted to be a preacher.

They didn't have much and were often, at times, very poor, but somehow, throughout life, they never went without having meals on their table or clothes on their backs. He was a stout man who could have as serious a face as any, but deep down, he was a joker through and through, and everyone loved him because of it.

Paula was originally Roman Catholic and grew up in a strict Catholic home. She believed the house of God to be a place you respected and honored. There were to be no shenanigans in the church, and she would sit so straight on the Pew that her back would never touch it.

They had been in the ministry even before Bonita was born. They were married by the same preacher Earl grew up with, in a beautiful and small wedding. Paula gave her life to the Lord when she met Earl, and she would say to this day, "I had no choice back then. I loved him, and if I wanted to be with him, I would have to be a Christian." She would admit back then that her heart wasn't in it. She missed going out to the bars and having fun with the girls. Still, as time passed and she and Earl made a wonderful home, she decided to leave her past behind and fully embrace the Pentecostal church.

Her Mom didn't become a pastor until Bonita turned 15, and she started taking correspondence. Every day, for as long as she could remember, Bonita would come home from school, dinner would be cooking, and she would find Mom somewhere in the house with a great big book in her face. You could try to talk to her, but there was no answer. She worked so hard to become a pastor, and when she finally got her credentials, they celebrated with a trip to P.E.I. That was a fun summer Bonita would never forget. They did everything the little island had to offer, and it was only a year before Bonita left home for New York.

"Hungry?" her Mom asked over her shoulder as Bonita walked into the kitchen.

"Oh, yes, very hungry, and it smells delicious!"

Her father, who was flipping pancakes at the time, turned and asked, "Sleep well?"

She yawned and stretched. "Very well. Thank you, Daddy!"

The breakfast was just as conversational as the night before, and they found themselves three hours later at lunchtime, and they hadn't left the table yet. They all decided they were too stuffed to eat lunch, and then her mother asked her if she wanted to go to the store with her. She had called her friend Bettie, who owned the store, and told her Bonita was home and looked different. Knowing that it would make her mother happy to show off her daughter, Bonita agreed to go, but only if they could drive around the bay after and visit a couple of spots she liked when she lived there. Her mother had no objection, and her father had to go to the church and take care of a few things, so he left them to themselves.

Bonita ran upstairs, changed into something extra beautiful, and then came back down the stairs to see her mom wearing a top and jacket she had sent for her last year. She loved it so much and was thrilled her mother wore it that she gave her a big squeeze and a kiss on the cheek, and then they set off.

<h1 style="text-align:center">66</h1>

The following day, Bonita woke up in a better state of mind. She decided that today she would do what she had intended to do yesterday: clean her room. She grabbed a shower and had breakfast with her parents. They talked again, but less time than before. She told her mother her plans for the day and returned to her room.

The smell of her room hadn't changed one bit since she left. There was this old, musty scent that lingered in the air. She could never figure out exactly what it was, but she assumed it was because of the age of the house. She remembered where almost everything was but had forgotten where she put a few things, so she planned to tear it apart and clear out the stuff she didn't want anymore. She decided that starting with her closet would make the most sense, as that is where everything was kept.

A couple of spider webs were in the frame when she opened the door. "I guess Mom just kept this one closed!" She cleared them away sheepishly with tissue and then pulled down boxes and books. She needed a box to dispose of the items she chose not to keep. She went down the stairs and then down the stairs again to the basement to find a box. She located a huge box that had been broken down, went back upstairs, and asked her mom for tape. Once she had the box reconstructed, she began to look through the things she had pulled down already.

Every teenage girl had a shoebox of things they kept that held sentimental value to them, and so did Bonita. Bonita's box didn't contain old movie stubs from her first dates, love letters from boys in school, or anything of that nature. It was old report cards with notes from the teachers, assignments she loved the most, and little mementos like rocks and sand from the beach on P.E.I. She was not a popular kid when she was in school, and that was why she hated her existence back then. She read through each report card and assignment that day and thought it best to finally dispose of them. She kept only a few to have something to return to in the future. She kept the rocks, sand, and a few of her favorite pictures, but she threw the rest in a garbage bag.

The next step was to go through all her clothes and throw out what she would never wear again. Still, she had nothing in her closet she would ever think of wearing again, so after remembering each item and laughing about it, she tossed it in the box. After nearly eight hours in her room that day, she had finished going through everything. She had two boxes, three bags of clothes, and two additional garbage bags. Her father, who heard her struggling, came upstairs to see what was up. He then took all the boxes and bags of clothes and brought them to the church. Bonita brought the two garbage bags outside to be picked up in the morning.

After removing all the junk and only keeping what she

wanted, she rearranged her room. She decorated for when she would come home again. She was having so much fun that she knew this wouldn't be the last time she'd be back there — she wanted to see her parents more. So, she told her mom she was running to the hardware store and would return later. Her mother thought it strange that she was going to a hardware store. She couldn't figure out what Bonita would want to buy there.

A few hours later, Bonita came through the door with paint, pieces of wood, all sorts of brushes, and several large bags full of God knows what. She said hi to her mother and then went upstairs. It was dinnertime, so Bonita knew that her plans would have to wait until dinner was finished. She was pretty hungry by this time, so it was welcomed. They finished dinner in 30 minutes. Bonita apologized to her parents for rushing to her bedroom but explained she wanted to do a few things. Usually, her father would be a little more inquisitive about what Bonita was planning to do to the parsonage, but he knew she was more than capable of using common sense and not doing anything that looked bad or caused any damage.

Bonita started by sanding down a few things manually. Bonita tried to keep quiet, knowing it would take her till sun-up to finish everything. Bonita quietly sanded, stained, painted, varnished, and so much more throughout the night, hoping to be completed by morning. After everything was finished, it was nearly 7:00 am, and she was hungry. She knew her mother would already be awake and down in the kitchen, so she went downstairs to see what was for breakfast.

67

She told her parents that her room was almost done, and when they found out she had been up all night, her father said to her that she was crazy. "Is dat how you live in New York?"

Bonita laughed. "Not most nights, but sometimes I pull an all-nighter to get things done."

Her parents shot each other a grin and went on with breakfast. Bonita finished quickly, rinsed her plate, and ran up the stairs to her room. The last thing she had to do was vacuum the floors and wipe everything down. The paint and finish were dry, and she closed her window after leaving it open all night.

Twenty minutes later, she sang out to her parents to tell them to come up. She heard them chatting as they were coming up the stairs about some last-minute Christmas shopping and preparations, and then they turned the corner and stopped dead in their tracks. What they saw took their breath away; they could hardly speak. They remembered what Bonita's room looked like before, which had changed completely overnight.

The walls were this beautiful chocolate color, with

curtains in the freshly white-painted windows that hung low to the ground. They were heavy and looked like they were purchased from a store but were not — Bonita had borrowed her mother's sewing machine the night before and did them herself.

The dresser and nightstands, which used to be an old, worn-out white color and had scrapes, marks, and rusted handles, were now deep-brown, beautiful finished pieces of furniture with fancy handles that were polished and shined ever-so-nicely. Her bed had also been stripped and stained and was now the same color as the nightstands, with fancy little etchings across the headboard. Her schoolgirl floral-decorated bedding was also different, now a mix of chocolate brown and tan colors on either side with lovely shams and a bed skirt. The entire room had a complete makeover. All the trim was painted a fresh white, and the contrast looked terrific.

In one corner of her room, Bonita had taken satin fabric. She attached it to the wall and ceiling in an overlapping droop effect, making it seem like a sea of waves but in another shade of brown, with lighter contrasting colors intertwined within it. In that corner, she had methodically tucked pictures of her family, her friends, New York, and her designs, all lined with thicker fabric to help them blend. Also, there was a ratty old chair that Bonita had always loved; she had sewn it up the night before and placed a thicker fabric over it to make it look brand new, and it did. A floor lamp she had found in the basement was painted tan and cleaned up. It sat beside the chair and tossed a soft glow upon the pictures.

The room looked amazing in every sense of the term.

Bonita had done a fine job transforming the dreary space, which represented her past, by bringing it forth to define who she was and her future. Her parents were floored, and her mother nearly cried with how beautiful it was. She grabbed Bonita.

"Did ya manage all this on your own steam?"

Bonita looked at her. "Of course, mom. Who else could have possibly helped me so late last night?"

Her mother looked around and sat in the chair. She loved the room and didn't want to leave, but she knew her daughter was tired and decided to let her get some sleep. When her parents finally left, Bonita removed her clothes and crawled into her newly made bed. She looked around at the room, now dimly lit due to her heavy curtains, and smiled.

68

It was pouring in New York City, and Claude Peters, who was enjoying his day off, was quietly sitting alone in his apartment, reading the newspaper. He missed Bonita terribly and wished she could be home with him for the holidays, but in his heart, he knew she needed to spend some time with her parents. There were a few times when he would get up in the morning expecting her to be there, and when she wasn't, he would remember she was away, and he would feel a certain sadness. Bonita was his best friend, the one person he was the closest to in his whole life, and he hated to think about the day that she would move out. He knew it wouldn't be too soon, but it bothered him. He would be alone again.

It was quarter-past-two when he heard a buzz from the intercom in his apartment. He paused momentarily and wondered who it could be, then rose from the couch to answer it. When he answered, Julio from downstairs announced three young women would like to see him. A few minutes later, when he opened the door, he saw some familiar faces — Lyla and Bethany — and another girl he didn't know.

"Hi, guys. Bonita's not here; she is back home. I thought you knew," he said, leaning on the door frame.

"We know!" said Bethany. "We are here to see you!"

Claude was a bit perplexed. He had no idea why they would come to see him, but he let them in the apartment anyway.

"Well, then, how can I help you?"

Bethany and Cassidy both smiled and then Bethany spoke up. "Well, I'm sure you know Bonita made the number-one spot for the fashion show in January!"

Claude smiled gleefully. "Yes, I think it is awesome!"

"Well, we are the other three spots. This is Cassidy Ruthers!" She pointed to Cassidy, and Cassidy gave him the warmest smile she could muster. "We are all her friends, and we are all super proud of her, and we want to put together a fun little package for her, telling her how much we care, and we were hoping you would want to help!"

Claude smiled softly and went to speak when Cassidy cut him off.

"She is such an awesome designer, and we love her work. She deserves it, and we just want to say, 'Hey, we love you!'"

Claude got in a word this time. "I would love to help you, girls. However, didn't I hear that you had a falling out?"

Cassidy and Bethany exchanged looks, and then Lyla said, "We did, that's true," as she hung her head a little.

"We were selfish, and maybe Bonita was too, but we handled it all wrong. We reconciled the day we all found out about making the show. It was time; the argument was silly to begin with." Lyla played it sincerely.

Claude seemed to ponder this momentarily, looking at

Lyla and saying, "We all mess up as humans; that's what life is about. Friendship is recognizing that and still caring about each other."

A stillness filled the air as Claude's words hung a little, Bethany and Cassidy getting uncomfortable. Claude finally said, "Well, I am glad you all made up, as I know what a trio you made. What can I do to help?"

Lyla looked as if she were going to cry as she said, "We need stories, embarrassing moments, and fun stuff! We plan on making up a big book with silly pictures, stories, and embarrassing stuff that we will give her on the night of the show!"

Lyla was so convincing the girls almost believed it themselves.

"Claude, you're her closest friend, so we figured you would know things we don't even know."

"And don't worry, nothing will get out. It is a private gift we want to give to her!" Cassidy piped in again.

Claude stood, smiling and tittering, and then he said, "Sounds fucking awesome. Count me in!"

Hook, line, and sinker, they all thought, as they went to sit on the couch, and Claude went to get drinks for everyone. Cassidy was especially pleased because she thought convincing him would be much more complicated. Still, Claude, thinking they were back to being Bonita's friends, was enthralled with the idea and thought it would make Bonita feel awesome. Who wouldn't love a little scrapbook filled with silly things from your closest friends? Claude got the drinks and sat down with the girls, and they began to talk.

Hours must have passed with Claude telling stories about

Bonita: funny ones, silly ones, and embarrassing ones that would make Bonita cringe if she found out. Cassidy could get what she wanted out of people, so she would reel him tighter when she thought there was more dirt. After nearly three hours of chatting, Cassidy felt they had enough to do what they planned and convinced Claude to let them access Bonita's room.

Claude was so convinced that they were planning the ultimate surprise for Bonita and that it would make her so happy that he didn't stop to think when handing over embarrassing pictures of her and letting them take photos of her room. They found photographs of Bonita from when she was younger in her house back home. They found everything that was juicy and dirty that they could use to sabotage her and knock her down a peg or two.

When they left the apartment, they all thanked Claude for his help and told him they would take it from there, and he'd get to see it the night of the fashion show.

"She will probably give you a little hell over telling us the stories, but she will get over it!" Bethany said.

They each kissed him on the cheek and left. Claude closed the door, feeling proud that he could be a part of such a lovely gift to Bonita. He thought that it was sweet for the girls to include him.

He spent the rest of the evening cleaning around the apartment and making food he could eat over the next few days. He chose not to decorate this year or make fancy dinners but to lay low and catch a few shows around town. He still felt very excited about Bonita's surprise later that evening, so he called her. Of course, he wouldn't tell her anything because it would ruin the surprise,' but he just wanted to chat for a bit.

When he called, her father answered.

"Hi, Mister Smith. This is Claude calling. Is Bonita around?"

Her father seemed extremely cheerful and happy when he said, "Oh, hiya, Claude, me son. Merry Christmas to ya, b'y! How's she cuttin' for ya down there in the big smoke?"

Claude chuckled to himself; Bonita's Dad's accent was something he had only heard a bit when Bonita first arrived. She explained that Newfoundlanders have a very different dialect from the rest of Canada. As for her, she had it too, but it was never as thick as she practiced speaking like the Americans on T.V. "Oh, I'm doing well, missing Bonita quite a bit, but I'm glad she's spending Christmas with you and your wife, Mr. Smith. It is going to be very good for her!"

Mr. Smith chuckled then as well. "I figures as much, what with you two being as thick as thieves these last few years. But thanks, me ol' cock, and we're right chuffed she's passin' it with us too. Ya should've come on up! There's more than enough room 'round here, ya know!"

From what Claude could understand, he knew that was an empty gesture but appreciated it anyway.

"Thank you, sir. I appreciate that, but I get homesick when I spend time away from the city!"

"Well, now, Claude, I'll nip off and fetch Bonita for ya. Can ya hang on a tick?"

"Yes sir, of course!" Claude responded, and then he could hear the hold being pushed on the other line. He only waited for a few moments before Bonita picked up the phone. She was nearly yelling in his ear about how happy she was to hear from him and how much she missed him. Then, without a breath, she moved into what she had been doing while home. Immediately, he was at ease, talking to his best friend and loving every minute. He loved her rambunctious personality, and it made her great when she got all fired up over something. He loved her passion and her energy. Claude was much like his, except he had no one who accepted it before. Bonita was the first person he could be himself with, which was better than gold.

They talked all night until the wee morning hours and finally let each other go. He was on cloud nine and finally decided to go to bed. He was lucky to have a friend like her and couldn't imagine a life without her now.

69

It was Christmas Eve morning, and Bonita woke up late. She had been on the phone with Claude until early in the morning and was still tired. She had loved their conversation last night. She was always happy to speak to him; he had a way of making her feel perfect and wonderful. Claude was her best friend in every way. He was always there for her; she trusted him with her life. She felt terrible leaving him in the city by himself this holiday season. Still, she needed time away from the city and wished he would have returned with her, despite her not trusting her parents to behave around him for all of Christmas.

When she finally pulled herself out of bed, it made her think back to a morning nearly three years ago when she was also exhausted. Still, she knew she had to get up: her graduation ceremony, the one she dreaded going to and the one she couldn't wait to get over. She began to regret not trying to enjoy herself that weekend when she was invited to several different parties and wished that she had gone.

"Maybe they didn't like me because I didn't like me?" she thought as she walked towards her closet. "Maybe if I had gone, I would have met someone genuinely sincere. No one ever saw me have fun. I was always so reserved!"

She dressed and decided to wear something stylish but comfortable, so she picked out one of her pantsuits from her closet — the one she designed as part of her winning line for school — and put it on. It was charming and made with a super soft, airy material. It was stylish but casual and charcoal in color. She brought it home just in case her parents made her go to church, which they didn't, and she was eternally grateful for that. She had to be careful not to make a mess of it and would have to have it dry-cleaned when she returned to the city, but she felt it was a fitting outfit for the occasion. Her father and mother would always be nicely dressed on Christmas Eve — not overly dressed, but casually dressed. Her mother would always wear a relaxed dress or skirt that covered her knees and a blouse that matched, and her father would always wear a shirt, dress pants, and a V-neck sweater.

After dressing, Bonita realized that she was feeling very nostalgic about her time at home with her parents and chose to sit in her newly upholstered chair for a moment. While sitting, she couldn't help but remember her high school years, her time living with her family. Bonita never did anything that would help the other students like her. In fact, she was always the perfect student, even now in her adult years. Her parents never understood her and rarely took what she had to say into consideration, but now her parents hung off her every word. She missed being home and dreaming of making it big because living in the city and trying to make it big was hard work and fraught with challenges.

What would life have been like if she had been social in

high school or even had one friend she could talk to? Would things have been different? Would her life have taken a different path? She sat there and dwelled on those questions for nearly an hour, playing out different scenarios, facing her regrets, and feeling slightly confused about why this was weighing so heavily on her. Finally, she concluded that her regrets were not regrets but rather what-ifs. Also, she was pretty happy with who she had become and how her life had turned out. She wouldn't change it for anything. Then another conclusion came to her... that her parents must think she was still asleep. She jumped up from her chair and went downstairs.

"Merry Christmas, sleepyhead!" Her mother chuckled as she looked over her shoulder from the sink where she was peeling potatoes.

"Merry Christmas, Mom, and I have been up since eleven!"

Her mom chuckled again. "Oh, well then, I guess I can't call you sleepyhead!" she said with a coy little grin.

Bonita quickly joined the festivities around the sink and began peeling carrots. She and her Mom started talking about Christmases past and how much fun they used to be. Her mother was always very soft with her; being her only child, she treated Bonita like gold. She had always wished that Bonita had friends, but she was always more interested in being in her room. They talked about her father and what they got him for presents and then guessed what Bonita had for her mother and what her mother had for her. Time slipped by, and before they knew it, they were done everything they had to do and sat down at the table and had a cup of tea.

Paula was so happy to have her daughter at home. She had

grown so much since leaving and blossomed into a beautiful young woman. Her daughter knew all about fashion and what looked good, and she would find herself trying to get tips out of Bonita to help her look more stylish. She wasn't happy when Bonita left, and deep inside, she hoped she would fail in New York City because she just wanted her home. Still, after the first year, she realized Bonita was right where she needed to be and prayed for her every night.

70

Dinner was hot and ready. The steam was rolling off the gravy boat, and the turkey smelled delicious. Her father had come home and sliced up the bird for everyone to enjoy. Turkey was one of Bonita's favorite foods, and well, when it came to Christmas dinner, she would eat more than she could handle. Every year since she was four, she would always feel sick to her stomach on Christmas Eve, so much so that after dinner, there was half an hour with nothing penciled in just so she could do what she had to and get over it. Every year, her parents encouraged her to eat less and have more to-morrow. However, even with the best of intentions, she still over ate.

Twenty minutes after dinner, she had come downstairs to find her mother and father already had dinner put away and all the dishes clean. They also had their coats on and were waiting for Bonita. Now it was time to go around town and look at all the lights up on people's houses. It was a part of family tradition and would always be. Bonita, who once was so mesmerized by the lights, found herself unimpressed by the lights this year. She believed it to be a product of living in the city for too long, but she still looked, and she still watched as the lights would flicker.

The door to the front of their house swung open, and they all piled in from the cold. Heavy conversation and laughter filled the Smiths' residence that night, and the smell of cookies was in the air. Bonita wanted to get into the presents and open some, so they all went in by the tree, sat around holding hands, and said a prayer. Her father always insisted on thanking the Lord each Christmas for providing a house full of love and splendor. Bonita made her mom open the first present, this beautiful teapot with crystal etching and accents around the handle, the base, and the spout. The body was that of brushed steel — very fancy and quite lovely. Her mother absolutely adored it and wanted to make some tea immediately. However, she set it aside and waited until the other gifts were open.

Next up was her father, who was not used to having presents to open on Christmas Eve from his daughter. When he opened the box, he stopped momentarily, looked up at his daughter, and smiled. It was this dinky old fish ornament that he used to own when he was a boy, and one time, during a move as a young adult, it broke into pieces. It was given to him by his grandfather — just a souvenir he picked up at a variety store somewhere in West Newfoundland. He had tried to find it ever since but could not and would always talk about it. Bonita had seen a blurry picture of it once and had heard her father describe it a hundred times, so she considered looking for it while in New York. She would stop into little stores around the city for nearly a year just to take a peek but with no luck. One day, Bonita was walking by a street vendor, and something caught her eye. She believed it was the exact replica of the fish her father once had. Luckily, it was, and it meant everything to her Dad that she had found him one.

Bonita was last to open her present and was thoroughly excited. It was a pair of pajamas. She kissed her parents and told them she would be right back. This was the part she had been waiting for all day. She went upstairs, stripped off her clothes, and got into her snuggly new pajamas. When she returned, her father had the movie loaded up and ready to go, and her mother had already cleaned the pot and made some tea. They sat down together and watched the movie, and like clockwork, her father paused it 45 minutes in to make sundaes. They ate their sundaes and finished the movie. Bonita quickly gave them both a kiss goodnight and went upstairs to go to sleep.

71

The following day, Bonita was still lying awake in bed, just like every other Christmas she had ever had. She fell asleep at the beginning of the night for about an hour and was wide awake ever since. When her clock struck six-thirty, she got up from her bed and went to the bathroom, where she washed her face and went to wake up her parents. Her mother was already awake in her room, and her Dad was just beginning to stir. They descended the stairs and entered the kitchen, where her mother again made tea with her new pot. Her father made a crack about how her mother was going to end up having an affair with her teapot because she loved it more than him. They all laughed.

There were so many presents beneath the tree that they had to move the couches to fit them all. There were plenty of presents for Bonita, but her parents would be the ones who were spoiled this year. Her mother opened presents at each turn, as did her father. They were both so shocked at things that Bonita had given them and how expensive they were. After each present, her father would say, "Thank ya, Bon Bon, but ya didn't need to go spendin' all yer hard-earned money, little bird!" Her mother was so thrown by all the beautiful things that she could barely muster a thank you. She was simply speechless.

Bonita always felt bad for her mother because they never had a lot of money, and most of the time, they would sacrifice to ensure Bonita always had what she wanted. This year was about giving back for her, and no expense would be spared. Paula's gifts were all across the spectrum; every item was well thought out and perfect for her. She never had much growing up, nor did she have much in her adult life, and some of the things she opened cost so much money she could never afford to buy them for herself.

Some of the first gifts she opened were beautiful dresses and pantsuits for her to wear to church. Most were designers, and her daughter made the others. As she opened everything, she realized that her daughter had spent a tremendous amount of money and bought only the finest things. One of the things her mother never had but always wanted was a complete China set and crystal stemware. She would see them in catalogs and cut them out to post them on her fridge, just to keep in mind that she might get them one day, so Bonita knew this was one present she had to get. The most beautiful set of crystal stemware that Paula had ever seen was now in her hands with torn pieces of gift wrap and tape, along with a magnificent selection of the finest China she had ever laid eyes on.

Things he received for Christmas this year also blew her father away: suits made with the finest fabrics, ties, and shirts as sharp as a tac. He also received a new briefcase and a fancy laptop computer, which he had always wanted but could never justify spending that much. He figured it was too much to purchase if it was something he could do for free with his own hand and a pen. He was happy with everything and couldn't fathom how much his daughter must have spent. He wanted to scold her for wasting money but knew he couldn't because she was proud of her gifts, and he knew it meant a lot to her.

Finally, Bonita had opened her last present. It was this beautiful pair of scissors with her name engraved on them. They were like fabric shears with heavy and sharp edges with a stainless steel frame and dense tips for optimum cutting. She had no idea where her parents had purchased them, but they were engraved on the back, "Love, Mom, and Dad." They were perfect, and she loved them so much that when her mother told her she ordered them online from a fabric store, Bonita almost choked. She was shocked to learn that her mother bought something online.

Finally, two presents were left under the tree, one very small and the other large and heavy. The small one was for Bonita's mother, and the larger one was for her father. He struggled as he pulled them out in front of them.

"Tis right hefty, Bonita. What on the go could be in 'er?"

"You will see!" Bonita said, smiling. Her mother picked up her smaller box and couldn't wait to see what Bonita had chosen for her last present. It was a family tradition to keep the best presents for last. Although the scissors were small, they were expensive and Bonita's last present. Her mother had already received such wondrous things; what could she get from her now? Her father felt the same way.

First, her mother was to open her present, so Bonita

adjusted her sitting position and waited until her mother was ready. Then, without further ado, she unwrapped the gift, only to find a black suede jewelry box inside. Her mother took a sharp breath and shot Bonita a look she would never forget. Her mother didn't have much jewelry, and she personally had always wanted diamonds. Her mother nervously opened the case and gasped. She nearly dropped the case as her hands began to shake uncontrollably.

"Oh, Bonita!"

She spoke almost in a whisper as she looked at the case's splendor. Her father also peeked inside and gasped as well. Inside the beautiful case lay a necklace with exquisite diamonds and breathtaking diamond teardrops. Two very stunning diamond teardrop earrings were with the necklace. It was the most beautiful necklace she had ever seen outside a catalog or on T.V.

They marveled over the necklace until Bonita chirped at her father to open his present. He looked back at Bonita as if he were about to explode and then dropped his head to the large box. He unwrapped the paper to find a cardboard box beneath. He looked a bit perplexed when he couldn't see what the box contained written on the outside. She handed him a steak knife to cut the tape off the sides of the box, and he did just that. When he opened the flaps and peered inside, he also gasped.

Right before him were books, but not just any books.

For as long as Bonita could remember, her father wanted two sets of books, a complete encyclopedia and a complete theological encyclopedia. The two full sets were now before him; the sets were new and the finest editions available on the market. He couldn't speak. It seems silly to buy someone encyclopedias when you also bought them a computer. Still, to her Dad, digital copies would never have held the same weight as the books he could put in his study at the church. Those books cost a small fortune, but transporting them back on the plane cost nearly as much.

Both Bonita's parents sat there for quite a long time looking at their last presents, mesmerized and utterly unaware of anything else. Bonita had slipped into the kitchen to begin making breakfast, and they stayed like that for nearly 20 minutes. She would keep peeking in the living room to see what they were doing there. Her mother ran her fingers over the diamonds and repeated this every second. Her father pulled all the books out, opened them to random pages, and read. She had successfully given her parents the ultimate presents and was quite pleased with herself.

Breakfast was ready, and finally, they both snapped back to reality with the smell of bacon wafting through the air. They quickly tidied up around the tree, and, placing a few things back, her mother went upstairs. She returned a few minutes later wearing one of her new outfits and a diamond necklace, her earrings sparkling when the light from the window caught them. She looked incredible, Bonita thought, and her father thought the same thing. Bonita caught him staring at her, checking her out. At first, she was a little disturbed but then realized that her mother looked terrific, and the man she loved gawking at her was the greatest compliment. They sat down and enjoyed their breakfast. Bonita cleaned up the dishes and kissed her mother and father on the cheek; she was going back to bed and thought her mother was, too, but her mother went beneath the tree to look through all her things again. Her father sat down on the couch with books in hand.

Bonita's room had a chill when she closed her door, and she loved it. Chills meant the need to get cozy under the sheets. That was her favorite way to fall asleep. She thought of her mother and father's faces when they opened their presents. Their faces were the only gifts that Bonita wanted on Christmas Day, and she got them tenfold. She felt so good to give her parents the things they had always wanted. Nothing was better than knowing her parents had the best Christmas they had ever had and also knowing that it meant even more to them because it was given by their daughter.

72

December 28th was a day mixed with emotions — ups and downs all around. It was the day that Bonita was to end her family vacation and head back to New York City to continue her life in school. Claude was ecstatic that she was finally coming home. What was only eight days felt like an eternity. Bonita's parents were both ridden with sadness and despair, for their little girl was leaving them again. Although they knew she would be all right and that she could take care of herself, they couldn't help but think how much they would miss her.

They both treasured the time they had all spent together over the holidays and wished it would never end. They got to know their daughter all over again, except there were some significant differences this time. First, their little girl wasn't their little girl anymore; she had grown into an intelligent and talented young woman who had paid her way through school and managed her money well enough to afford every-thing she spent for Christmas. Secondly, her views and per-sonality changed. She was more sociable, warm, confident, and strong — with ease, not pushed as it once was. She had become who she wanted to be since the young age of seven: a fashion designer. Although she hadn't made it in the industry yet, to her parents, she was already a star.

Bonita was torn in so many ways. She hadn't expected to love being home as much as she did. She thought Bay Roberts would still be the same and living at home would still be the same as when she left it, but it wasn't. So much had changed. She felt like a stranger in her own home and town several times. She was at a loss for words and direction while here. She was convinced the town had changed its ways, and the house was different. Bonita pondered this while she was visiting, and it wasn't until that day that she realized the town was the same, and her home hadn't changed; it was her that was different. It was she who had changed, and her personality that had altered. Her views and how she saw things and reacted to situations had developed since she left for New York.

She didn't want to leave her parents and wished she could stay with them. They brought her so much joy over the holidays; she didn't want to let that go. Being home with her Mom and Dad made her feel so wonderful and complete that she feared returning to New York would cause her to be homesick again. Although the first time wasn't that bad, the second time could be horrific and unbearable. She felt that she had grown closer to her parents during her stay and that they had grown closer to her. How could she leave them? How could she let them go again? She loved them so dearly that her heart nearly exploded when she thought of them. So many times when she was young, she took them for granted, but they were so precious to her, so unbelievably priceless.

She experienced separation anxiety, thinking of being so many miles away that it rendered her ill. What was she going to do? How would she get through this?

With all that on her mind, she knew she had to return to New York. Her dreams did not exist in this town, nor did any opportunity, to be exact. Her school and life were there, and she loved New York, her apartment, and her life. Why was her heart telling her to stay? She missed Claude so much that she would feel homesick. Was that her home now? Or did she have two homes in which her heart longed to be? There were so many questions and not enough time to answer them. This pain she was feeling came on very strongly over the last 24 hours. All she knew was that she had to finish school, and then she could consider her options later.

Her parents were sad they couldn't drive her to the airport this time. They wanted to spend every second she was still on the rock with her, but she had rented a car she needed to return. Once her bags were loaded in the car, and her mother and father were outside making sure everything was secure and talking amongst themselves, Bonita looked around the house and cried a little.

"Bye, house," she said aloud, turning on her heels and walking out the door.

"Mom? Dad? I have something to say to you," she said as her parents turned to look at her. "Coming home for the holidays was the best idea I ever had, and I want you to know how much I have enjoyed spending time with you and just being home with you!"

Her mother was already bawling before she ended her sentence, and Bonita took her hands in hers and cupped them.

Her father's eyes filled with water when he saw his wife, and then, before they knew it, they were all crying a little.

"I have realized that I have two of the most amazing parents God has ever created, and I can't even begin to express, tell, or show you how much I love you both. My heart breaks with the thought of leaving you, and I wish you could both move to New York so I could see you whenever I wanted. Thank you both for always being so supportive. You were there for me even when I was a wretched and miserable kid. Thank you for letting me follow my dreams and be myself and for caring for me every step of the way. It means more to me than you will ever know."

She barely got the last few words out of her mouth; she was crying so profoundly. Her parents embraced her with all their might and told her they loved her. Her Dad spoke through his tears.

"Look, Paula, we didn't make such a bad job of it after all."

They all chuckled a bit. It took them nearly twenty minutes to stop crying that day. Finally, they kissed each other goodbye, and Bonita got in her car. She pulled away, waving at them both, and when she was around the corner and out of sight, she stopped the car and cried again.

73

Claude was up bright and early. He could hardly sleep; he was so excited that Bonita was coming home. She would land around three; he wanted to ensure the house was perfect and dinner was made. The eight days she was away seemed long and dreary, but now she'd be back in New York. Although he won't see her much because of her fashion show coming up, he'll know she's there and will be able to talk to her whenever he wants.

The house was clean, but he still retrieved all his cleaning supplies from the hall closet and went to town. He did a complete spring cleaning around the house, starting with the kitchen. He pulled out the oven and the refrigerator and washed down all the walls. Each appliance was washed with hot water and vinegar to remove any grease or oil buildup, especially the fingerprints. Claude had always thought seeing something with fingerprints on it was the most disgusting thing in the world. He was a little anal-retentive at times with certain things that he developed over the years. He would rinse every glass or mug from the cupboard with hot water before pouring his drink into it. He couldn't fathom taking a glass from the cabinet and drinking from it without rinsing it first. The thought made his stomach turn. Claude also would wash his hands a ridiculous number of times throughout the day to ensure sanitation and cleanliness. If he touched something that he felt wasn't the cleanest, he would make his way to the nearest sink to wash before he touched anything else. At both the kitchen and the bathroom sinks, there were automatic pump canisters that he picked up somewhere on sale that deposited antibacterial soap, so he wouldn't have to touch them when washing his hands.

His most prominent and most compulsive thing was with food going bad. He would most often cook chicken or pork straight from frozen to avoid the possibility of bacteria growth. If the milk was left out on the counter for more than five minutes, he wouldn't drink it, and if it weren't for Bonita, who didn't care that much, he would just throw it out. Mayonnaise, salad dressing, sour cream, or any other dairy-type product must be appropriately packaged and stored. Otherwise, he would avoid it like the plague. He was a special kind of guy in that way. He was simply anal-retentive about certain things, and Bonita had grown to love it.

He continued cleaning the entire apartment and finished it at three in the afternoon. He then jumped into the shower to get all the grime off and feel as fresh as his house. When he got out of the shower, he remembered that he had opened all the windows to allow the house to air out and was shivering like a vibrator while trying to close them all. He dressed and threw on an oversized, thick sweater to keep warm while the house heated up again. "Time to make dinner!" he thought aloud and entered the kitchen.

He decided to make a roast with vegetables and do them the way Bonita liked best: steamed! So he began to cook and tidied every crumb or spill he made as he went about it. It was nearly finished when he heard the door. Someone had inserted a key and was turning the handle. His heart stopped, and within a second, Bonita was home!

Bonita enjoyed being home; she, in fact, loved every minute of it. Claude had the house all clean and perfect for her arrival and even made a delicious dinner for them. She missed him so, and when she got through the door the other day, she went straight to him and gave him the biggest hug ever. It was New Year's Eve, and they had decided to stay in instead of going out this year. They hadn't had the opportunity to spend much time together over the holidays, so a night in seemed very fitting.

Of course, they decided that they must eat. So, together, they went shopping and picked up all the fixings for a traditional Christmas dinner. They chose to do that because they hadn't had Christmas dinner together, and Claude didn't have it at all. The turkey roasted in the oven, creating this wonderful scent throughout the house. The stuffing was made, and the carrots, potatoes, and turnips were peeled and ready to be cooked. The cranberries were mashed and made into this beautiful sauce for the turkey, and two bottles of wine were chilling in the cooler.

Bonita had been in and out of her room quite a few times

over the last few days, bringing out pieces to check them over and get Claude's opinion. She checked everything to the last stitch to have less work to do when her last term started. She loved her collection quite a bit and was proud of its winnings. She was really nervous about the show — her first fashion show. What if something went wrong? Claude would sit her down, encourage her, and tell her nothing would go wrong.

Dinnertime had finally come, and they both sat down at the table, relaxed and ready to enjoy a wonderful meal. Everything tasted so delicious, more than usual, and neither knew why. They were hungry because they finished their plates in record time and went for seconds. The table was shaking from how much talking and laughter went on. They were chatting back and forth about when she first moved there. To Bonita, friendship and memories were what it was all about. She and Claude made many memories together and they would never be forgotten. She had experienced life and grown into a woman with him by her side. That was huge to Bonita; nothing could replace that or go anywhere near it.

After dinner, they cleaned the dishes and sat around the coffee table. Typically, they would sit on the couches, but not tonight. Tonight, they were going to play Monopoly. They had never played it together before, and neither of them played it for quite a long time, but it was a game of choice when deciding what to do on New Year's Eve. They played for nearly three hours before Bonita stopped giving Claude breaks and annihilated him. They laughed and had so much fun playing that they almost forgot about their next New Year's Eve bit of fun.

Claude and Bonita, while they were out, bought a karaoke

machine and a bunch of discs to play in it. They would sing badly at each other for fun, do a few duets, and then try silly songs just for laughs. That was the funniest moment they had ever had, for neither of them could carry a tune in a bucket, never mind sing a song along with a track and in key. They played at that until they both noticed it was eleven-forty-seven. They stopped, turned it off, and got a refill of their wine. The clock struck twelve, and they could hear celebrations all around. They hugged and drank their wine in two big gulps simultaneously.

Bonita needed a little time to use the bathroom before they went for their walk — that was their next plan: go out and see what was happening in the streets of New York. They walked and talked, and before they knew it, the sky was getting bright, and the sun was peeking through two office buildings. They had planned to get a movie in tonight as well, but at this point, they figured it was time to go home and go to bed. However, neither wanted to, so they found a restaurant serving breakfast and sat down.

75

The room was slightly aglow from the computer screen. For some reason, they enjoyed working in the dark when planning Bonita's demise. Paper was everywhere, with scissors and cut pieces of fabric strewn across the room. Cassidy typed something out at her computer while Lyla and Bethany cut up strips and shapes of nasty, ugly fabric. They were working on their project and fully engrossed in every detail of what they were doing.

"This is going to be fantastic!" Cassidy yelled out as she looked around her room. "This will go down in history, girls. There will forever be the story of how a young girl destroyed the school fashion show, and we will shine brightly because of it!" Lyla and Bethany just sat there and chuckled under their breath. They were too busy to look up from their work. Planning something of this caliber was challenging and took a lot of work and ironing out of details. They had almost everything except the one pivotal person they needed to aid them on the night of the show. They would get to him; they didn't know when, how, or what it would take to ensure he was in for the entire run.

Cassidy thought this was great and was happy she had convinced the other two to get in on it. They had everything they possibly needed to make it work. She wanted to make it a big fiasco that would ruin Bonita's collection and destroy her reputation with the teachers and the outside world. She was destined to cripple Bonita so that she couldn't get a job designing scarves for a discount bin, even if she wanted to. There was no turning back now. The wheel had been set into motion, and she would see it through, no matter what it took.

The new term had started, and things were back to being as hectic as they ever were. Most of the time, the teachers were hardly in the classes, and the students were handed their assignments and workloads and expected to keep themselves quiet. Bonita was okay with this because she could do her schoolwork whenever it suited her. Her main concern was getting her collection ready.

She decided she wanted to make a few slight changes but needed to know if that was allowed, so she went to see her teacher to ask for permission. He was okay with it and trusted her. She had developed her collection independently, and although he wasn't sure how she could improve it, he knew she would, somehow. She was his prize student; she could do no wrong. She was serious about being a designer, and although he could never quite figure her out, he still thought she would go far in her life, as far as she wanted to.

With permission from her teacher, she went back home. She began making extra stitches in certain areas to reinforce the garments. This would ensure nothing would fall apart during the show. She made a few alterations to the shoes and shortened some hems so that the outfits would fit the models perfectly. She had already met with her models; they were all quite beautiful, and the school's team was taking care of their hair and make-up. On top of all that, she had a stagehand. Jerri Janes was his name, short for Jerremiah, who was also a last-year student. Everyone chosen for the show would have their own stagehand assigned to them by the school administration. Jerri specialized in the setup and overall process of putting off an excellent runway event. Bonita was lucky to have him. He would take care of everything for her. Jerri knew what make-up the girls should have, the hair they needed, and what each model would be wearing. He handled the whole thing.

There were two reasons this was the way it went. The first reason was simple: The girls chosen to show their collections were not allowed backstage before their shows started because of the potential mess they could create. The school wanted to avoid any meltdowns or tantrums altogether, and designers could get very worked up over the slightest detail being out of place. Therefore, that's where the stagehand comes into play. They are detached from the project and have no emotional investment in it. They could see things clearly while making the show look perfect. It was also their time to shine, as the fashion show would be the first notch on their resume for their particular career, and if all went well, they would be recognized for their talent.

Everything was set, and her stagehand knew every detail he needed to know. He called her unexpectedly several times to review a few details he needed clarification on. She felt confident that all would be well and was able to breathe and calm herself without the use of strong drugs and alcohol. It was only a few nights away now, and then it would be over for her. She would show her work to everyone who came and, with a bit of luck, secure herself some sort of job for when she finished school in the summer. Now, all she had left was to review her address book and ensure she invited everyone. This was her chance to really show the world what she could do.

77

Jerri was a little unnerved to have three girls approach him so unexpectedly. He had been a student at this school for nearly three years and had never even so much as spoken to any of them. That being said, Jerri had yet to be privy to talk to any girls, as he wasn't the most desirable guy attending the institution. He was tall, lanky, and had severe acne that had been with him since junior high and usually deterred girls from approaching him.

Now, not one but three girls had shown considerable interest in him and were asking him out for drinks after class. Unnerved was an understatement, and his sweaty palms were the focal point of his consciousness. What could these girls possibly see in him? What could they possibly want with him? He had no answers to these questions and found his nerves worsening as he thought about it.

The truth was, the reason they asked him out wasn't important. He had never been asked out before and wouldn't let his nerves get in the way. He continued to prepare for the fashion show and iron out any of the final details so that it went off without a hitch.

The day ended, and he packed up a few things he needed to work on when he got home and took a quick stroll through the school. He stopped in the bathroom close to the Seventh Avenue exit. He laid his bag down on the counter. He removed deodorant and applied it generously to his underarms; he had been working hard all day and wanted to ensure he didn't smell ripe for his date with three beautiful young women. He tucked in his shirt and pulled it out a little to hide how skinny he was. He spritzed a bit of cologne on his neck and took a comb to his hair. Lastly, he turned on the faucet, splashed his face, and wet his hair to eliminate the frizz. He picked up his bag, slung it over his shoulder, and quickly looked in the mirror. He smiled boyishly and winked at himself before turning and walking out the door.

78

The girls were laughing very loudly as they walked down the busy streets of New York. Cassidy was beside herself as she recounted their conversation with Jerri Janes. This stage-hand was assigned to Bonita for the fashion show. Lyla was shocked at how easy this was for her. She had never been vindictive, but this felt good, and she believed Bonita needed to learn a lesson. They were her friends, but Bonita started cutting them out of her life and appeared to think she was better than they were. Bonita was always getting the best marks in school and outshining everyone, and it had gone to her head. She had to be shown that you don't just turn your back on your friends and start acting like a pretentious bitch.

Bethany was in hysterics. She couldn't believe that this was actually going to work. All they had to do was convince Jerri Janes that he should help them. The question was, how? They pulled themselves together as they only had an hour before meeting him for drinks and needed to figure out a plan of attack. He was the final piece of the puzzle and the most challenging obstacle they would have to overcome. Cassidy felt confident they could crack him, but the other two girls were less convinced. Why would he help them sabotage Bonita and risk his reputation? If this happened, he would receive the full wrath of the dean and faculty and potentially fail his program.

The other pertinent piece of the pie was why he would want to sabotage Bonita's show? What had she ever done to him? How would they convince him she needed a reality check and be on board? Bonita was probably never rude to him, never mistreated him, and most likely, he had heard what a star student she was, so why? Why would he help?

They bounced around ideas about how they would make this happen and convince him to do the unthinkable. Bethany suggested money and that they explain what a bitch Bonita was and that when she makes it in the industry, she would never think of him to help her with a show. She felt that pointing out and even fabricating what Bonita was like would help teeter him to the dark side.

Cassidy already had a plan for what she would do if she had to. She was committed, and nothing would prevent her plan from being followed through. No person would stand in her way. She was mulling over every possible path of bringing him to their team and solidifying their plan, once and for all.

79

Claude was reeling with joy as he got out of bed, as it was the day he would do his first magazine cover shoot. He had gone to bed extra early the night before, as he had heard that these shoots can often go on for hours. Claude had everything he needed ready and waiting by the door. All of his brushes were cleaned, and he had spoken with the photographer and gotten a good idea of what she would be expecting for the make-up aspect of the shoot.

He was getting ready to leave when he heard Bonita awake from her slumber. He hadn't woken her despite his desire; he wanted her to rest as much as possible. She peeked around the corner and said, "Have you had breakfast yet, mister?"

"No, and I don't really have the time. I should get going. I don't want to be late."

Bonita gave him a stern look. "Isn't the call time for 10:00 am?"

"Yeah," he said sheepishly. Bonita looked at the clock and proclaimed, "It's only 7:30, Claude! You have more than enough time to eat something. You have a long day ahead of you and want to ensure you are operating on a full stomach with fuel".

He knew she was right, so he returned his bags by the door and walked to the kitchen counter.

"What are you going to make me, then?" he said as she walked back toward her bedroom.

"Give me a minute to get dressed, and I'll whip you up a breakfast fit for a king," she shouted.

Sure enough, she emerged from her room and started creating a breakfast feast. She made eggs, bacon, hash browns, pancakes, and toast while chit-chatting about how his day would go and the fun he would have. She so badly wanted to go with him, and he would have taken her in a heartbeat, but the contract made it very clear that it was a closed shoot.

He sat there watching this beautiful woman he called his best friend go to all sorts of trouble to ensure he was fed and energized for the most important day of his life. He smiled and thought how lucky he was to have a friend like her. He knew that she loved him as much as he loved her, and although they weren't overly emotional people, they were truly blessed to have found each other in this vast world.

She was flipping pancakes when he remembered the girls coming to his house that day and the surprise he had helped them with. He couldn't wait until the fashion show to see how wonderful it was. She was lucky to have three friends who didn't care much for competition and wanted to show Bonita how much they cared for her. He could have sworn that Bonita had told him about this Cassidy girl before and that she hated her, but he wouldn't dare bring it up to ask about it for fear that he would spoil the surprise. He figured they must have made amends since the last time they spoke about her and didn't overthink it.

Breakfast was delicious, and the conversation helped calm his nerves, which he was grateful for. A nervous make-up artist is a dangerous make-up artist. He needed steady hands to ensure that every application was precise and perfect. He had done make-up for years and was well respected at his counter for being one of the best, but this was different. This time, it would be immortalized in print, and any mistake or slight error would shine through. He knew that there were digital touch-up artists who could fix nearly everything, but he didn't want to be known as a make-up artist who needed touching up. He wanted to give this celebrity a flawless complexion and perfect eyes, lips, and cheeks that required little or no touching from anyone. He wanted this opportunity to be his gateway into the print and film industry, a break for which most make-up artists would die. This was his chance to take his career to the next level, get out from behind the counter, and work behind the scenes for magazines, TV, and film.

He kissed Bonita goodbye, picked up his bags, and walked out the door towards the elevator en route to the job of a lifetime. He was in sheer bliss as the elevator descended to the ground floor. For once, he felt like he had everything: the life, the house, the career, and the best friend; what more could he ever ask for.

80

Jerri had just crossed the street, and the martini bar where he was meeting the girls was in his line of sight. He could see them sitting by the window, laughing and joking around. For a moment, Jerri thought maybe he should just bail and go home. His nerves were getting the best of him again, and he could feel his hands getting moist the closer he got. He stopped momentarily and went to turn and walk away when he paused and said aloud, "You can do this. Don't be such a pussy!" He wiped his palms on the front of his jeans and walked up and into the bar with his head as high as his confidence would let him.

Cassidy noticed him first, waved him over, and then shared a look with the other two girls at the table. She shimmied over and made room on the bench for him to sit down. He sat, and the girls greeted him. He responded nervously, and then Cassidy motioned for the waitress to come over. When she arrived, she said, "Get this handsome man anything he would like." The waitress furrowed her eyebrows a little and nodded. She waited to take his order for a scotch on the rocks and went to get it for him.

Jerri had never had alcohol before and had yet to learn what to order. Still, he remembered watching a movie where the actor had ordered what he called a 'scotch on the rocks.' The actor proclaimed it was a man's drink, so Jerri thought it might make him look suave and earn him some points with the girls. He turned his attention to Bethany and Lyla and then to Cassidy with a look of inquisition on his face. It was time — the girls knew it — and it was now or never, so Bethany took the lead.

"I bet you are wondering why we asked you here today."

He looked at her with an expression that answered her question. "Well," Lyla piped up, "We have something we would like to discuss with you, something you may not be up for at first, but we want you to hear us out before you decide."

"Okay," Jerri said with a puzzled tone. "Let's hear it."

It was Cassidy's turn to take the floor, so she did. She told him that sometimes people get to places they don't deserve. Good things happen to them when they really shouldn't. She talked about how the undeserving ones often get to the top. Then, they become pompous and pretentious, thinking they are better than everyone else. She said she knew someone like this who was so self-centered that she turned her back on the people who helped her get where she was, and she needed to learn that that isn't how you conduct yourself. She went on for what seemed like forever, spewing bullshit line after bull-shit line until she felt that it was time to drop the bomb and see what happened.

"Bonita Smith," she said, looking into Jerri's eyes. "She is the one I am speaking of." Immediately, Jerri recoiled in his seat as it all became clear why these three girls had shown any interest in him. His eyes narrowed as he glanced around the table, his skin red and lips pursed.

"I should have known," he said assertively, "I should have known there was no way three beautiful girls would be interested in me, would ask me out for drinks without there being a damn good reason behind it."

Bethany opened her mouth to speak, but he cut her off.

"Why would you think that I would do something to Bonita Smith? Why would you even imagine that I would so much as consider it?"

Lyla spoke quickly and anxiously.

"Because she thinks you are a useless tool, Jerri. We are her so-called friends and the other day in passing, she mentioned what a fucking idiot you were and how she has no idea why the school would pair such a fucking disaster with their top student."

Cassidy's eyes grew big, "That was perfect," she thought. "Way to go, Lyla."

Jerri, sitting there, looking all introverted, turned to Lyla and asked, "I find that hard to believe. Bonita has been nothing but nice to me. Why would she say those things?'

"Because she feels sorry for you, Jerri," Bethany proclaimed. "She thinks you are a complete nerd who is a useless waste of good space. You are nothing to her, just someone she is stuck with until this show ends."

Jerri was reeling, thoughts racing through his mind, disbelief filling his head, and a sense of anger growing in his belly. Either these girls are being truthful, and Bonita is as mean as they say she is, or they are really upset with her for something and will do whatever they can to convince him to sabotage her show.

He looked up. "Even if your statement is true, why would I do it? Why would I jeopardize my standing with the school as well?"

It was Cassidy's turn, and she took no time to think it through.

"Because we can make it worth your while!"

Jerri was at least intrigued to hear what they had to offer, so he leaned back in his seat and folded his arms to signify that he was listening. Cassidy told him that money was involved, a lot of cash. Then she went over what he had to do, how it would appear that Bonita herself was wholly responsible and that he was simply doing his job. The only people who would know the truth were the four of them and, of course, Bonita. It was a seamless plan that he would have to do very little to execute, and the girls would do the rest.

This went on for nearly two hours, back and forth, back and forth. Jerri seemed convinced, and then a moment later, he would fall undecided. All three girls were weary and thought they couldn't pull it off. Everything rested on his shoulders, and if he wouldn't do it, what other options would they have to make this go down the way they planned? It was the eleventh hour, and they had minimum time to orchestrate anything else — it was now or never. A bead of sweat formed on Cassidy's head as she tried to figure out what else she could offer this idiot to convince him to do what they wanted.

Then it hit her! Power and Sex! What have women offered men throughout history to get what they want, to have control over them, to make them putty in their hands? That was it. It was the Achilles heel and her last hope. She knew what she had to do but couldn't find the strength. She looked at him and imagined them both naked in a bed together. She shuddered. She couldn't do it, couldn't submit herself to him. He was so gross! But she had to! She had no choice; she knew she was the only one at this table who could make the sacrifice to see this through. It was up to her now, as it had been all along. It was time to take one for the team and get what she wanted. First, the power, then, if need be, the sex or at least the promise of sex.

"Oh, Jerri?" she said, bringing her pointer finger to her lips and nibbling on her nail. "Here are the facts, Bonita Smith is a cold-hearted bitch who has let her pseudo-success go to her head. She has mistreated all of us, maybe not to your face, but she has her opinion of you. Getting the number one slot in this show has only made her more full of herself. She thinks she is above everyone and acts as such. Help us teach her a lesson for believing you and us are just tiny pawns in her success, and I will up the ante. I think I have something that can sweeten the deal."

"Really?" he said feeling the effects of his second scotch. "What is that?"

"You know my dad is well-connected, right? He has a lot of connections around the world, and I, being his only daughter, would do anything for me. What if I told you I can have my dad call in a few favors and have you placed as a stage manager at some of the most lucrative venues?" she replied. Bethany and Lyla gasped at her response. "You would have a good chance of success with me on your arm."

Jerry was speechless at this point. He didn't know what to think, and his palms started sweating again.

"You're a virgin, aren't you, Jerri? It's okay. I know how hard it can be when you aren't the most popular boy in school." Cassidy continued.

He couldn't breathe. He was trying to, but nothing was getting into his lungs. Cassidy offered him a lucrative opportunity and a chance to date a beautiful woman. Something he had never had the opportunity to have before. Jerri felt confident that the money, the in from Cassidy's dad, and a chance to date Cassidy would be a once-in-a-lifetime offer. What was he to do? He was a good person and didn't want to hurt anybody, but he wanted to be successful and something more than just a tall, lanky nerd, and this was his chance.

"How much money are we talking Bethany?" Jerri said, "And what lucrative stages are you referring to, Cassidy?"

"10,000.00," Bethany responded.

"20,000.00," Jerri replied quickly.

"Come on, Jerri, I got money, but I got to get it from my dad." Bethany retorted.

"You want this or not? Is it not worth it for you?" Jerry felt a certain liquid confidence and was ready to ensure he had what he needed if he was going to risk anything.

"Fine, I'll get it to you next week," Bethany said.

"No, you will get it to me tomorrow evening or no deal. If I don't have it before the show, I won't go through with it, and you can watch Bonita steal your thunder once more." Jerri said with finality before looking over to Cassidy.

"Only the best. My dad and I have been to them all, and he knows everyone who is anyone. We are talking about top-tier venues. This is a for sure deal, Jerri!" Cassidy responded confidently.

"And you?" Jerri replied. "What about me," Cassidy said.

"About you and me. If I am to know you are serious, you and I will go to dinner tomorrow night at this restaurant in SoHo that always catches my eye." Jerri said matter-of-factly.

Cassidy could feel herself cringe, but Jerri's stance made him a bit appealing to her. He was ruthless, cutthroat, and taking no chances. Perhaps there was something more to him than she initially thought.

He was quiet, and Cassidy was still thinking. Finally, she said, "Okay, you have yourself a date, Jerri."

He heard every second or third word. He wasn't listening to Cassidy anymore but rather having a full-on battle in his head. The good against the bad, and right now, the bad was winning. What could be the worst thing to happen to Bonita? So, she would do poorly at the fashion show and get in trouble with the faculty, but would it really hurt her in the end? Sure, she would be the laughingstock of the school and everyone who would attend. Still, if she changed her designer name and re-emerged a year later, she had skill and talent and would bounce back. His dream was to work in big venues and date beautiful women, and this was it: take it or leave it. Plus, $20,000.00 in cash would help him pay off his loans and set him up a little. He couldn't pass it up. He gave in, surrendered to the bad, and spoke conclusively.

"I'm in."

The morning of the show had come quickly, and the buzzing of her alarm had given Bonita a sense of relief. She didn't have to try and sleep any longer. The night before, she had gone to bed early to be as rested as possible, but she couldn't fall asleep no matter how hard she tried. Her mind was moving too fast with thoughts; all she could think about was the fashion show. Every detail haunted her: every stitch, the models, the lighting, the sound, and any one of the million other things that could potentially go wrong. She kept telling herself that everything was done, all was well, and that at least she had someone in her corner backstage taking care of everything.

She had gone over every last detail with Jerri Janes at least 25 times, each time adding emphasis to a specific aspect of the show. He was a lovely young man, not very personable, but friendly enough, and he seemed competent and knew what he was doing. She didn't know him well and had only met him a few weeks prior, but she felt she could trust him, as his abilities would also be evaluated.

The entire process was ingenious, a real test of skill and

talent. Although the fashion show was the most important event of the year for most students and the school, they used it as the pinnacle evaluation for their most gifted students. It was top or flop time, and everything would depend on each candidate's performance. There were students from every aspect of the school: lighting, sound, props, media, stage production, hair, and make-up artistry... there wasn't a department that wasn't involved in this event.

Bonita rolled out of bed and put her feet on the floor. She was tired but awake, and she knew there was no time to try and catch a few more hours before she had to begin; she had to start right now. "First thing first," she thought. As she approached the kitchen to start the coffeemaker, she bumped into Claude as she took the corner.

"What are you doing up?" she asked as she recoiled from being startled.

"I am making you breakfast, Miss Smith, the way you made me breakfast on my big day," he proclaimed as he maneuvered around her to get something from his room. He quickly returned to the kitchen, where the bacon began to fry, and a scrambled egg concoction was in a bowl beside the sink. She was too tired to argue, which was her first reaction. There was no need for it, but she did appreciate it. She sat down on a stool and said, "Thank you."

"You look like hell, honey. Restless night?" he said as he noticed her sitting at the counter.

"Thanks, you're a real dear," she said sarcastically. "I didn't get much sleep last night; I couldn't shut my brain off."

He looked at her pitifully and said, "That sucks, Bon. I am going to spend another 20 minutes making breakfast. Why don't you take a hot shower to wake yourself up, and I'll have your coffee ready for you when you're done?"

She didn't want to move but knew it would make her feel better and less exhausted. So, she hopped off her stool and made her way to the bathroom.

Claude felt terrible that he was so blunt with her, but he knew she knew he was coming from a place of sincerity. He heard the shower turn on and then smiled. "She will feel better," he thought as he flipped the bacon.

82

Breakfast was delicious, and the shower and coffee did bring her back to a more alert state of mind. She enjoyed hearing all about his big celebrity make-up session. The celebrity he was contracted not to divulge was lovely and down to earth. He didn't even know who it was until he got there and nearly passed out when he saw her sipping coffee in the corner. The day went very smoothly; the photographer and the celebrity were both amazed at his skill. Claude did say that he was nervous when he saw her complexion and shocked at how poor it was. They laughed at how it seems people only see celebrities with their make-up on and how the public would be shocked at how some of them probably look without it.

All in all, everything went very well, and he was pleased with his work. Not long after, Bonita exited the building and walked out on the street. B&H must have had a sale as a line formed halfway around the block. She wasn't going in that direction, so it didn't bother her. She turned on her heel and headed down 34th towards Seventh.

The air was crisp, and she could see her breath as she

walked briskly down the street. It was surprisingly peaceful this cold winter's morning, and it helped with her nerves quite a bit. She decided to redirect her thoughts to the more positive possibilities that could arise from tonight's show. She imagined that there would be several higher-ups in the audience who would all love her line very much and that there would be people fighting to talk to her after the show. People from all the different fashion houses in New York and around the world wanted to hear what inspired her, what drove her, and what her intentions were when she left school.

Bonita dreamt that Vivienne Westwood, her favorite designer, would be there looking to speak to her. She would swing by and take her arm to pull her off to the side and ask her to come to work with her to help design a new line under her name. Bonita thought that she would just die if that were to happen, and she would be completely lost for words, as her eyes would fill with tears of joy and happiness. A honking cab brought her back to reality and jolted the thought from her mind, but she kept walking with a smile. She had hoped to ease her nerves, and the idea that she could meet someone like Vivienne had the opposite effect.

She kept walking steadily, weaving in and out of pedestrian traffic, making her way to school. The day ahead would be very long as she would finalize every detail and wait for the show to begin. She was due to meet with Jerri at four to review the line-up one last time before the big unveil.

83

Jerri had just finished his meeting with Bonita and was going backstage to her line's special area. This is where the models would be getting their hair and make-up done and waiting for the garments they would be wearing to be unveiled and handed to them. He was feeling sick with an ever-growing knot in his stomach. Was he really about to allow something so awful to be done to someone he hardly knew? He thought of the plan and how he would be spared, but Bonita's career would be ruined before it began. Could he really do it?

He was considering the whole picture and how the girls laid it out. It would appear as if it were all Bonita's doing; that the line delivered to Jerri was the one that would be displayed. Jerri knew that if he followed the girls' plan precisely, he would receive little to no backlash from the faculty and that his job was simply to make sure he did what he was told to do.

The $20,000.00 Bethany hand-delivered yesterday afternoon is a potent reminder of his agreement. He could still smell the scent the cash gave off; it was intoxicating. That

$20,000.00 helped him casually pay the bill at the restaurant with Cassidy last night, where he actually had a great time. He felt like a man on top of his game, a bawler with a beautiful woman on his arm. Surprisingly, Cassidy seemed to enjoy herself. He expected it to feel forced, and while awkward initially, she leaned in and conversed throughout the meal. Afterward, he thought they would go their separate ways, but instead, they walked for a few hours, talking about life. She was gorgeous, her eyes sparkling from the champagne he had ordered; he was feeling it, too. When the night eventually did come to an end, he dropped her at her apartment building. It screamed money! He walked her to the door and said, "Good night, Miss Cassidy." She turned, smiling, leaned in, and gave him a light kiss on his lips. It was probably not longer than a second or two, but time stood still a moment. It was his first kiss; he felt like a king.

He couldn't give that up; he wouldn't give that up. Whether it was real or not, the slight chance he could be with Cassidy was enough to make him do anything. No one would know, and he would never let on, that what he was about to do was different than what Bonita had planned and that he was following directions from three of her competitors. Yes, he knew that all he had to do was tell the faculty that he did precisely as Bonita had asked, and they would believe him. They would never think that he would do something to hurt his academic standing with the school. Why would he? He had no reason to do anything to Bonita, and to keep it from being suspicious, the girls and Jerri didn't acknowledge each other at school. He communicated with them through text messaging and emails that would never be discovered by anyone other than the four. Apart from Bethany coming to his place and him spending a glorious time with Cassidy the night before, no one would put it together.

It was coming to the point of no return, for it was time to pick up all the garments and deliver them to Bonita's area for the models to wear. If everything went according to plan, he would go into the storage locker where they were kept and wheel them out, and the switch would have already been made. The plan was simple: He would pick up the garments on schedule to avoid anyone later thinking something was suspicious. He had left the key in a hidden spot only Cassidy knew about. She was to make the switch, lock up, and return the key to the hiding spot for him to pick up just before the show was scheduled to start.

As he walked through the classroom across the hall from the storage locker, he reached under the third desk from the front in the third row and retrieved the key. He spun on his heels and walked towards the door. He stopped abruptly when he saw an attractive young woman across the hall, peering behind a classroom door. It was Cassidy, watching him with a dirty grin and a sparkle in her eye. He wanted to go and take her in his arms and kiss her, for real, this time. This propelled him even further, and it was too late to turn back now. What was done was done, and the knot grew a little bigger in his stomach, making it hard to breathe. He knew what he had to do to get on with it. He felt sicker as the guilt and prospects fought heavily in his mind as he walked to the storage locker and pulled out the garments.

He wasted no time getting them to Bonita's area, fearing that she would see him with them and immediately know they were the wrong ones. He was sure she was in the students' lounge, trying not to hyperventilate as she was so nervous about the outcome of tonight's show. She had no idea of the mayhem that would ensue once the lights went down for her line to appear. He was almost happy that she would be nowhere near backstage. He was protected for as long as the show was on. All doors to the backstage were locked and guarded from any unauthorized entry. It was once the show was done that he feared. How could he look her in the eyes and pretend that this was what she had given him to use? How could he pull it off without letting on that he was involved in her demise? He thought of Cassidy, her eyes, her smile, the kiss, the possibility of her being his first. Bonita would know, but to get through this without academic penalty, he would have to ensure that his performance for the faculty was Oscar-worthy.

84

Claude was pacing the counter, upset and infuriated. He was supposed to be at Bonita's show tonight, but three staff came down with the flu, and he had to cover the counter. He had called Bonita and couldn't get an answer, but he left a message apologizing for his absence. His tone came off as relatively short and disinterested despite his intent, as the counter was busy, and people were trying to get his attention.

He knew that tonight was so important to her. He wanted to be there for her as much as he could. He knew she would understand, but he wished there was a way he could make it. It was impossible, however, as the show started at six and he got off at nine-thirty. The show would be long over by then. He had to suck it up and accept the fact that he would miss it, but that wouldn't stop him from rushing home right after and prying every detail out of her. He had stopped on his way to work to pick up a few bottles of wine, as this would mark the end of her intense stress, and she needed a night of wine and good conversation to unwind.

85

It was nearing six o'clock, and the auditorium was packed with many finely dressed individuals. She had heard that all the big names were in the auditorium, and they were all expecting to see the newest and freshest. If anything, the show was always an excellent outing for designers because when you have student designers, they are more likely to create original pieces. After all, they are so eager to impress the masses. They have an innate desire to make their names known and pull out all the stops to show off their skills. The event could impact their careers and set the standard for how their lives would develop after they left the institution's safety. If they could make it happen under the pressure they experienced as students, they could usually produce high-quality garments that would sell and evoke envy within the public when given creative freedom without grading pressure.

Bonita was sick with butterflies in her stomach. The Hawks she experienced on graduation day were back and hungry for their next meal. She was trying to keep it together but failing miserably. She hated the school policy that prohibited designers from backstage during the show. She understood why it was in place, but she felt she could handle herself better than just being a bumbling temper tantrum waiting to happen.

She was sitting on a chair in a special room just off the auditorium. Each designer had their own, and they were to sit in there until the show was done. Bathroom breaks were the exception, but faculty members stood watch in the hallways even then. Each designer could sit in their rooms and watch the other contestants on a flat screen, but Bonita didn't care. She decided to sit down, put her head between her legs, and focus on breathing.

The house lights went down, and the music began. She could hear Dean Lalonde on the microphone welcoming the audience to this year's show. He proclaimed that this year's contestants showed great promise and then gave the line-up. The music got louder, and the show began. This was it: the time had come, and in a mere forty-five minutes, it would all be over, and what was done was done. She felt as confident about her line as her teachers had. She got the number-one spot for a reason, and it wasn't because they 'sort of' liked it.

The following 25 minutes seemed to take an eternity, and then there was silence. Bonita's ears perked up to listen for her opening song. The other three designers were allotted 7 minutes apiece to show their lines. Bonita, being in the number-one spot, was allotted 20 minutes. She was happy with that because she had a lot of outfits to show off, and 7 minutes seemed to be little time. The chiming began, which marked the beginning of her first song. It was a Celtic piece she had picked out with a metal undertone to wake everyone up before the actual music started playing. She used a mixture of country sounds — fiddles, banjos, and acoustic guitars —

paired with an urban drumbeat to give it a more city feeling. She was proud of her mix and thought it complemented her line.

Each designer could use the big projection screen that sat as the backdrop to the stage to add a more visual element to their show. She took full advantage of this opportunity and was able to piece together a country landscape with two giant skyscrapers plopped in the middle of it. The final image looked quite impressive. At first, the two towers looked like they didn't belong. She had hired someone to create a short clip of the harshness of the steel and the softness of the country landscape becoming blurred to create a pairing that looked natural and fresh.

She had put a lot of work into this show and left no detail overlooked. Much like her dressmaking, she envisioned how she wanted it to look in her head and then referenced that at every turn to create an exact replica of what she imagined. She was proud and knew she didn't have to worry if the show would go off well. She checked everything a million times, and Jerri ensured everything would go according to plan.

Something was wrong; her track sounded off!

86

The chiming had stopped, the metal had geared down, and a faint sound came from the auditorium. It sounded extra country, too country, almost hillbilly honky-tonk country. This wasn't her track, she thought, as she quickly stood straight up. What was going on? That wasn't her music. That sounded nothing like what she had prepared for her line. How could this happen? What was she going to do?

She ran to the door, yanked it open, and entered the hallway. A stout woman looking through a glass window at the entrance to the auditorium had a look of disgust on her face as she noticed Bonita in the hallway.

"You need to return to your space, Miss Smith," she shouted. "You cannot be out here right now."

Bonita stopped and stared at her for a moment. Why did she look so disgusted? "That isn't my track," she said, shocked and disoriented. "This isn't the track I made for the show."

The woman advanced towards Bonita and took her arm. She led her back to the room Bonita had come out of. "You must wait here until the show is over, when I am certain you will be retrieved," the woman growled.

"What does that mean?" Bonita asked frantically. "Why did you say it like that? Is there something wrong?" Bonita was having trouble breathing. She couldn't imagine what would be so bad about her show to have this woman as upset as she was. The woman shoved her back into the room and closed the door.

Bonita was frozen. "What is going on?" she thought. "What could possibly be happening on stage right now?" She was freaking out and pacing the room. She knew the rules and didn't want to break them, but she was struggling with not at least finding out why the track she provided wasn't being used. She turned the television on, hoping to see for herself, but the video was blacked out. She remembered the faculty saying the contestants wouldn't be able to view their own show on the flat screen to prevent any disturbances coming from the hallways. The school was hardcore when it came to keeping 'flare-ups' from their designers at bay. She turned to walk toward the door when it flew open and nearly knocked her down. It was Dean Lalonde, whose face was a shade of red she hadn't seen before. It looked as if steam was rising off his skin as his eyes narrowed in on her.

"Have you lost your fucking mind, young lady?" he shouted at her. She went to say, "What?" but didn't have the time — he had already begun talking again.

"What the fuck are you trying to prove with this bullshit?" He didn't give her time to answer, and she wouldn't have been capable anyway; she was too busy recoiling from the verbal attack. He jolted towards her and put his face right in front of hers. "You have made a mockery of this institution, the faculty, and your fellow students. How could you do this? Do you not care about your last two-and-a-half years here?"

He was so close she could smell the peppermint on his breath, and it was steaming up her glasses.

"Do you not care about anything? The biggest night of the year, and you single-handedly turned it into a fucking circus?" By this time, she was starting to regain a sense of reality and pushed him out of her personal space. This worsened the situation, as he yelled louder than before.

"You dare put your hands on me? You dare touch me? You may think this all fun and games, young lady, but you will see who has the last laugh."

It was time; she had taken all the yelling she could handle and was still completely unaware of what he was yelling about.

"What are you talking about?" she fired back. "What the fuck is going on out there?"

She didn't think his eyes could get any narrower, but she was very wrong.

"Don't play that bullshit with me, young lady. You know very well what is going on out there. 'Oh, Mr. Lalonde, do you mind if I make a few last-minute adjustments?' You are a disgrace, Bonita, to this institution, me, and everyone else who is a part of it. I thought you had so much promise; I was wrong to believe in you and to trust you."

Her head whipped towards the door, and he said assertively, "Don't even think about it. I'm not done with you yet."

It didn't matter. Bonita had had enough of this abuse. It didn't matter now what the rules were or why they were put in place; something was going on with her line that brought a fury down upon her from a teacher she had so much respect for. She would see for herself if it was the last thing she did at this school.

She bolted towards the door, and when he tried to stop her, she shoved him hard out of the way. She ran down the hallway toward the auditorium entrance, where the stout woman stood. She tried her best to stop Bonita, but Bonita overpowered her, too. She crashed through the auditorium doors into a sight she had never expected to see, something that made her stop dead in her tracks. Her heart stopped, her dreams melted away, and her breath disappeared. What stood before her was an embarrassment, an abomination of fashion with her name written all over it.

The backdrop was not the beautiful countryside she designed with the two skyscrapers that flowed perfectly harmoniously. It was something so awful she recoiled in disgust. She couldn't believe her eyes. She squinted, rubbed them, and even pinched herself because this couldn't happen to her on the most important night of her academic career.

87

Cassidy and the girls had everything figured out, the perfect way to destroy Bonita's career before it even started. They had every detail taken care of, and their plan was being executed as they stood at the flat screen in Cassidy's room to watch their masterpiece unfold. In trying to decide what it would take to pull off the most despicable runway show in the history of fashion that would render everyone disgusted, they left no stone unturned.

They designed a backdrop to replace the one that Bonita had made. It was really the focal point of the whole show. They had searched the Internet looking for the most hillbilly naked men and women they could find, and if they found a good head but not a good body, then they would cut and crop so they got it just right. Their criteria were that both men and women had to be missing teeth and look dirty, trashy, and un-groomed. They found pictures of hillbilly men who were in a sexual pose and Photoshopped in a brown paper bag that had "Fashion" written on it. They animated the men to appear as if they were having intercourse with the bag. The women were naked; the scene bordered on being a pornographic image with only trash bags covering their genitalia. It was perfect, they thought. The concept would elicit a repulsive response to the message it conveyed: Fuck Fashion, Fuck The System! Bonita Smith.

Next, they turned it into a clip using presentation software that would pop up words throughout the show that read things like "Fuck Fashion," "Remember a time when fashion didn't matter? Let's get back there!" and "Fashion is a joke." The icing on the cake was the pictures of Bonita back home in Newfoundland, in her ratty clothes and oversized glasses, looking all a mess. They were perfectly placed and timed, popping up with comment bubbles artistically added with quips like "Eat Shit Like Me," "Virgin Diaries" and, "Fashion Can Fuck Me," and "Kiss Me Like A Dog." It was a masterpiece for them; it was a surefire bet to destroy Bonita's perfect little image.

They didn't stop there, of course. They went all-out on this one. They realized Bonita's line wouldn't match the backdrop, and they couldn't leave any opportunity for someone to think it was someone pulling a prank. They had to sell that this backdrop was a part of Bonita's image, that she didn't care about fashion, and that this was all a joke to her. Therefore, they decided to create a line for her that reflected her ideals on fashion. They picked up faux animal skins and made garments out of each.

They replaced all garments with cut-out jagged patterns that were intentionally broad and unfinished. They used yarn dipped in red wax to haphazardly thread them together. It was as if a hunter violently and primally crafted the garments in the wilderness. There was no hint of craftmanship at play anywhere. What was meant to be a blend of country and modern would become a bunch of ugly, putrid, and misshapen smocks. The male models had stuffed paper bags attached to their smocks with Fashion in bold black letters on either side. It was attached where the smock would cover their genitalia. The notes from the stage hand were to gyrate as they walked the catwalk. Models who are paid to wear clothes on the runway never ask questions about what they are wearing. Their opinions don't typically matter to the designers, and they are just there as a frame to present their line. Therefore, when an item is questionable, they may think it is weird or ridiculous, but they put it on and walk the walk. So, here were these female models walking down the runway with meat carcasses on their bodies for the world to see, and the garments were more like shapeless droops of animal skin with bloodstained threading. Primitive, tasteless, mockery.

Once again, no questions were asked; they came, wore, got paid, and then went home. They weren't fashion experts; no one would have listened to their concerns.

It was a complete fiasco that had the audience in revolt and the faculty in an uproar. Cassidy, Lyla, and Bethany stood watching, trying desperately not to laugh. Still, they had one final thing to do before their night ended. Bonita had just crashed through the auditorium doors, and they knew that she would be out soon. They had to position themselves somewhere they would have a private moment with Bonita before she left the school. They looked around and found the best spot they could.

88

Bonita stood in shock, her mind becoming mush, anger welling up from deep within, and a helplessness she hadn't felt for a long time. She felt a tear fall down her cheek as she stood paralyzed and incapable of thinking. She felt a presence beside her, a looming shadow, and a familiar smell of peppermint wafted across her nose.

"You are trash, Bonita. Fashion could have been your future; why did you even come here? Was this your plan all along? It doesn't matter; you are through. Take your things and leave the premises at once. You are no longer welcome here."

Dean Lalonde spoke with a finality that sent a chill up Bonita's spine. She wanted to rebut and plead her case, but there was no point. Bonita didn't know who did this to her or why this happened, but she knew it didn't matter now. It was her name on that disaster; what was seen could not be unseen, and she couldn't prove it wasn't her. She didn't know where to even begin. No, she knew it would be fruitless and, at this point, just make the situation worse. She looked at the man looming over her, turned, and left the auditorium with her head hanging low. She returned to the room to grab her things and made a beeline to the nearest exit.

She was still holding it all in as she passed through the first set of exit doors that led to the loading dock, the one she used to always exit. It helped her to avoid the mad rush of people leaving through the main entrance. She thought she would be safe once she passed through those doors. When the doors opened, she saw three things that didn't quite belong: Lyla, Bethany, and, unbelievably, Cassidy Ruthers. She stopped cold at the sight of them, standing together with their arms folded and heads tilted ever so slightly. They had looks of pure satisfaction written across all three of their faces.

"Great show," Cassidy mocked.

"I don't want to talk about it," Bonita said as she tried to walk around them, but Bethany put her arm out to stop her.

"Oh, you're not expected to talk, Bonita. Just listen. We didn't go through all this trouble just to have you walk out before you knew why," Bethany stated as she looked Bonita in the eyes. Bonita gasped as she stepped backward in disbelief. What was Bethany saying? That she did this. Bethany was her friend. Why would she do something like this to her? Why would she want to hurt her?

"You did this?" Bonita asked, surprised.

"Yes, well, not just me!" Bethany declared. "It was me, Lyla, Cassidy, and Jerri Janes. We all played a part in this magnificent display of your true talent."

Bonita nearly collapsed as her chest drew tighter by the second. What was happening here? What was going on? Her breath caught as the fight or flight descended upon her.

"This is what happens to someone who thinks she's better

than everyone else, someone who turns their back on their friends because they think they are superior," Lyla explained. "You can't go around acting like your shit doesn't stink, always taking the spotlight and stepping on everyone in your way and not thinking that one day, you'll get yours."

Cassidy thought she would be doing all the talking, but the other two girls handled it just fine.

"I never turned my back on you," Bonita cried, "and I don't think I am better than anyone else. I don't understand; why would you do this?"

"Not just us. Bethany forgot another key player in helping make this happen," Cassidy chipped in.

She thought that one last blow would break Bonita completely. It would leave her alienated and alone in this city, and if you are going to destroy someone, you have to go all the way.

"We couldn't have done this without all the help we got from Claude."

Bonita felt as if she was punched in the gut. Her body instinctively fell a step backward, and her knees weakened. There was no way Claude would help them; he wouldn't do this to her.

"Bullshit," Bonita shouted back.

"Oh, yeah?" Cassidy fired. "How do you think we got all those pictures on the screen? How do you think we knew about those embarrassing tidbits of information that appeared with them? How do you think we knew you kissed a dog when you were eight?"

Bonita thought for a second and then knew they weren't lying. Only Claude knew those things; she couldn't believe it.

She had never told anyone but Claude that story; it embarrassed her. The girls had to be right; Claude had to help them; the photos and stories would be attainable nowhere else.

"Why would he do that?"

"Why do you think, Bonita? Because he is sick of your holier-than-thou bullshit routine as well. He's sick of you living there and just wants you gone." Cassidy explained, "He's hoping you will get kicked out of school for this, and you'll just go back home and leave him alone."

Bonita's knees were weak, she couldn't breathe, her eyes were filling up by the second, and she knew there had to be truth to all of it, but she couldn't believe he would do this to her. She had had enough. She gathered her strength, pushed through the girls, and went through the last exit to the loading dock. It was a long, narrow slope that led up to the street. She was in complete tears and walking briskly up the hill. She could barely see two feet in front of her and didn't care. She didn't care if she walked into oncoming traffic and was struck down; she wanted it to end. She had never felt this kind of pain before, and she couldn't bear to think that Claude was involved, but she couldn't deny that he was.

She had nowhere to go, nowhere to turn. She saw the missed call from Claude and called into her voicemail to check it. It was hard for her to believe he would do this to her, but he wasn't there; he didn't show up. Where was he? She listened to the voicemail and heard the tone of his voice; it was callous and cold, and then she knew: It was true. Bonita was alone in a city where she thought she had companions and friends, people who cared about her, people she trusted. She was wrong. She could barely focus a thought, but she knew in her gut what she had to do. If Claude didn't want her there, she wouldn't be there. She couldn't bear to see him anyway. Seeing him treat her like she wasn't welcome would hurt too much.

She hailed a cab and headed straight to her house. She asked the cab if he would wait 20 minutes and handed him fifty dollars in cash. She knew she would need another cab and didn't want to lug a bunch of her things down the street to hail one. She ran to the elevator and quickly advanced to the 19th floor. She let herself in, went straight to her room, and pulled all her suitcases out from underneath her bed. She started packing clothes — only her best and lounge clothes; everything else would have to stay here for now. She packed a few personal effects, makeup, hair products, her toothbrush, and paste. She grabbed jewelry, her wallet, her shoebox of mementos, and an envelope full of cash from her dresser drawer. She had everything she needed.

Tears streaming down her face, she walked off the elevator and back toward the front door. Julio was on duty tonight, saw that she was upset, and asked if everything was okay. She just looked at him with a blank expression and kept on walking. She threw herself into the car with her stuff and told the driver to take her to a hotel. In a city with many hotels, the driver needed more than just "a hotel." They sped off down the street after quickly deciding where she would stay. As she looked out her window at the building that had been her home for the last two-and-a-half years, tears rolled down her cheeks.

89

The auditorium was a mess. Loud chatter filled the air, and disbelief was thick throughout. What had everyone just witnessed, exactly? Clearly, someone was pulling a prank on the fashion community, and they weren't seriously subjected to this disgusting display for actual purposes. Jerri was peeking through the curtains to the seats filled with confused viewers, expecting an explanation of what had just happened.

Jerri was in shock. He had no idea the magnitude the girls had gone to destroy Bonita's image, but when they set out to do something, they did it. The models had commented about the items they were wearing, but it wasn't until they were on the catwalk that they realized something terrible was happening. Jerri felt guilt rolling off him like a tsunami crashing against his conscience. How could he have let this happen? How could this girl deserve this horrible treatment?

He was as much to blame or more so than the three girls. He went through with it; he could have called it off and raised the flag. The money, the opportunities, and Cassidy's lips were so all-consuming; if he had known the extent, he wouldn't have gone through with it. He just wanted to get ahead, to feel in control, to seize life, and to feel like a man with options. He wondered where Bonita was, how she was doing, and what would happen to her. He thought of Cassidy, and the thought of seeing her made him feel ill with guilt.

He knew it didn't matter now. The girls had achieved what they set out to do, and he heard Dean Lalonde speaking with the Dean of admissions, telling her that he had kicked Bonita out of school. Dean Lalonde also came to Jerri shortly after with a "What the hell happened?" look on his face.

Jerri followed the script and gave Dean the what's-what of what happened. He said, "You said this was your top student, and that was all I needed to know. I was under the impression that you knew what her collection was about and, albeit strange, who was I to say anything? I thought it was a part of some revolutionary fashion statement that could change the world forever. I was never shown her original collection. I know nothing about fashion, just how to pull off the perfect show." Dean clearly accepted his response because he gave Jerri a simple nod of acknowledgment, turned, and walked away.

Dean knew that this couldn't be pinned on anyone else but Bonita. Jerri was just going with what he had learned. "I approved her collection, and how was he to know that Bonita had changed it completely?" He took a long, deep breath and stood behind the stage curtains. He had to go out there in front of everybody, who is anybody in the fashion world of New York City and apologize for what had transpired tonight. He took one last deep breath and walked out.

"Ladies and gentlemen, I sincerely apologize for what has transpired on this stage tonight. It leaves our faculty and institution with troubled minds to know that one of our own went to great lengths to try and sabotage our worldwide reputation. I understand that you are all confused, frustrated, and outraged. We all are as well. We cannot express enough how truly sorry we are that you had to witness this here this evening. We assure you that all necessary precautions, measures, and provisions will be made to ensure it never happens again. The young lady whose work you just had the tragedy of witnessing has had her academia stripped and has been removed from this institution. She will never be allowed to set foot on this campus again."

"Once again, ladies and gentlemen, I sincerely apologize. I hope you will stick around for the gala and meet-and-greet with the other three designers featured here tonight." He took a deep breath, nodded toward the crowd, and walked offstage.

90

Claude was putting the key in the door to let himself into the apartment, excited to hear about the fashion show when he got inside. He had been dying all night to listen to how it went and how much she loved the surprise the girls had given her. Claude had the bottles of wine he purchased clutched in his hand and underneath his arm, ready for a little much-needed winding down. He entered the apartment and was surprised the lights were off.

He had expected Bonita to be home and thought she would be just as excited to tell him of her night as he was to hear it, but there was no one home. He turned on the lights and checked his phone for texts or voicemails, but nothing was there. He checked the counter for a note, which also came up empty. Perplexed, he sat down on a stool in the kitchen and called Bonita's cell phone, only to be surprised that it was turned off. He scratched his head and thought she might have gone out to celebrate with her friends after the show. He was a little disappointed she hadn't called him to come and join them. Bonita usually wanted him around wherever she went.

He walked around the kitchen and pondered it until

hunger pangs brought him back to the present. He hadn't eaten for hours, so he decided that the most productive thing he could do now was make himself a sandwich. He finished the sandwich and chased it down with a glass of wine he had brought home for him and Bonita. She still wasn't around and still had yet to call or text. To prevent himself from going crazy, he decided to take a shower and get cleaned up — although he worked at a makeup counter, it could get quite messy after a full day. So, he got up from the stool, walked towards the bathroom, and stopped dead in his tracks.

The door to Bonita's room was left wide open, and it was a mess. He was used to seeing her room chaotic, but this was different. Drawers were opened and empty, articles of clothing spread across her bed, toiletries missing from the top of her dresser. He walked in and flicked on the light, only to find her closet next to empty. Something was up. Where was she? What had happened? He reached for his phone and called her cell again, only to get voicemail, but he left a message this time.

"Bonita, why is all your stuff gone? What has happened? Where are you? Call me as soon as you get this message."

91

Bonita was lying on her hotel bed, tears streaming down her face. By this time, the quiet crying had turned to sobbing and hysterics. What had happened tonight? How could it have happened? Why did everyone she trusted turn their backs on her? What had she done to them that was so wrong it warranted them destroying her life? Her dreams? There were only questions, no answers, and nothing made any sense.

Her life was ruined, her career destroyed before it even started. Everything she had worked so hard for over the last few years had, in one night, gone completely down the drain. She was alone in New York City with no one to turn to, no one she could trust, and no one who wanted her. She had failed; people she thought were her friends had taken her life's dreams from her. She needed to escape. She needed to feel safe, and she didn't. She felt exposed and exploited, and there was nothing she could do to change that. She didn't know how to fix it or even if she could. She was at rock bottom with nowhere to turn. Thoughts of pulling an Evelyn

McHale rushed across her mind; she was hurting so bad; she just wanted it to stop.

She needed something, a refuge, but there was nowhere she could go where she would feel protected and sheltered. Then, her mind drifted back to the Christmas holidays and how she felt at home with her Mom and Dad. She felt warm, welcomed, and safe at home with her parents. She needed that right now. She needed them. She yearned for her Mom's soft looks and smile and the security of her Dad's arms around her. She needed to go home.

She jumped from her bed, logged on to her laptop, pulled up an airline, and checked when the next flight to Newfoundland would be. After a few short minutes, she saw that a connecting flight to Toronto and then to Newfoundland would leave JFK in two hours. She was already packed, so all she had to do was pay for the flight and check out of the hotel.

Twenty minutes later, she was in a cab to the airport. The taxi driver was speeding through traffic and had her banked up against Departures in what she thought was record time. She hopped out, paid him, and bolted into the airport. She was fearful she didn't have enough time to get through security and bag check. Ultimately, she made it to the gate just as the plane boarded the last passengers. She got on the plane and settled in her seat, only to cry again. She felt defeated, bested, and a complete failure. She was running home to her parents because her life fell apart. This isn't the girl she wanted to be.

<h1 style="text-align:center">92</h1>

The plane landed in St. John's at quarter after seven in the morning, and she waited as usual for everyone else to get off before she attempted to get her things from overhead. Bonita wasn't renting a car this time because she knew in her heart she had no intentions of returning to New York City. The things she left behind weren't of high importance to her, so if she never saw them again, she would get over it eventually. No, her father would pick her up at the airport this time. She had called him from Toronto when she had a two-hour stopover.

He was surprised to hear from her, especially so late at night. He didn't know what to expect when he heard the long-distance ring come through the line so late, and then immediately felt ill when he heard his little girl crying on the other end. She told him that she was okay but needed to come home. She had nowhere to go and just had to get out of the city. She told him when she would land at the airport, and without hesitation, he told her he would pick her up. She apologized for how late and out of the blue it was, but he told her not to worry about it; it was his pleasure to come and get her.

Both her Mom and Dad were worried sick after that and got very little sleep because of it. She had claimed her luggage and exited toward the main doors when she noticed both her Mom and Dad waiting for her on the other side. It was then that Bonita fell to her knees and began to cry. It was then she knew she was safe. It was then she knew that she could get through this.

Her father rushed to her side, took her into his arms, squeezing her tight, and told her she was okay now; her Mom and Dad were there for her. He helped her stand and began walking her towards the car. Her Mom looked so worried; neither her father nor her mother knew what had happened and expected the worst. They were hoping to find out when they got in the car, but as they were pulling out, Bonita had fallen fast asleep with her head on her father's arm.

When they got home to Bay Roberts, her father nudged her awake, only for her to go up the stairs and crawl into bed. She slept through the entire day and all through the night. She didn't stir once, not even to use the bathroom. Her parents were so worried that she had been attacked — or worse, raped — in the city and could hardly bear another minute of not knowing but couldn't bring themselves to wake her. If she was still sleeping, it could only mean she needed it badly, and they left her to wake up on her own.

When Bonita woke up the following day, she felt disoriented; it took her a minute to figure out where she was. After a moment or so, she gained her bearings and remembered what she thought was the last 24 hours until she looked at her clock and saw that it was only 8:30.

"That can't be," she thought, because she didn't even land until 7:00 am. It dawned on her that she had slept for nearly 24 hours straight and hadn't even woken up once. She put her feet on the familiar, cold, rugged hardwood floor and breathed a sigh of relief. She was home.

She could smell breakfast cooking downstairs in the kitchen and wanted to run down and embrace her parents, but she knew she had to shower. She could smell how rank she was getting. She quickly grabbed one of her suitcases, which her father must have brought upstairs for her, pulled out a pair of track pants, a tank, and a sweater, and entered the bathroom.

Her parents could hear stirring upstairs, and when they listened to the water in the shower turn on, they let out a breath of frustration. They still didn't know what had happened and had been waiting patiently. They thought she would come down as soon as she was awake. They slept the night before just as poorly as they did when they received the call because they feared she would wake up during the night and need them. They loved her so much and couldn't imagine what had happened to make her rush home like that. Her mother put her hand on her father's shoulder and whispered, "Just a little longer, me ducky, and she'll spill the beans on the whole works." then she returned to preparing breakfast. Now that she knew Bonita was awake, she cut a few more pieces of homemade bread to toast.

93

Bonita finished dressing and made her way down the stairs. She was sick to her stomach and realized that she was a simple look from her mother away from crying again. It was okay; she needed to get it out, and she needed them to know what had happened. She turned the corner to the kitchen, and her parents turned and stared at her. The tears began to flow. Her mother rushed to her side.

"Bonita, what's the story? You got us all worked up with worry."

Her father embraced the two of them and held them very tight. He ushered Bonita to her spot at the table and laid a cup of tea in front of her.

"Bonita, let's have the whole yarn now," he said reassuringly. Bonita looked up at him with pitiful eyes and then looked down again at her tea.

"Dad, it was so awful." She began to lay it out for them. Some parts, like the school fashion show, they had already known about, but most of it came as a complete shock. They had no idea that people could be so cruel to one another.

They had lived sheltered lives, hiding behind their bibles and prayer meetings.

Bonita talked for nearly two hours, expressing her feelings of sadness, anger, and hatred. They sat and listened to every word. Her father habitually went to speak to her about feeling those emotions and how they create darkness in your heart, but out of respect for the situation, he knew she didn't need to hear that. When she finished, she threw her hands up and got another cup of tea and a few more pieces of toast. Her parents looked at each other in bewilderment. What would they say to all of this? What could they say? They had no idea why these people she called friends would do this or why her best friend Claude, who seemed to love and care for her, would do something like that?

Out of frustration, Bonita's father even suggested he call the school and set it straight, but he knew as well as Bonita did that that isn't how the real world worked. She didn't know if she wanted him to, even if he could. The school turned its back on her so quickly that they didn't give her time to explain or prove she had no part in what happened that night. They threw her out on her ass after two-and-a-half years of working her butt off. There was no voice of reason in Dean Lalonde's head that evening — not one that would have listened to her, anyway. He saw one thing and one thing only: She had ruined the fashion show, and that was all there was to it.

No, Bonita didn't know if she even wanted to return to finish her degree, even if she had the chance. She had her associate degree, which would have to be enough to try and make it, but was it? Bonita knew she was a sound designer, but after that night, no one would even consider meeting with her, never mind offering her an internship at his or her design house. If she wanted to work in fashion, she would have to move to another country. Maybe another continent. Even then, she might not find an opportunity outside of designing scarves for a discount store. She was doomed; she knew it, and all she had left to do was accept it.

A few days passed, and she moped around the house, cried, huffed, and moped some more. It was getting to be pretty gloomy around the Smiths' residence. She would walk through town and avoid any potential meeting she would have with the townsfolk. She would even walk to the other side of the street if she saw someone coming her way. She couldn't swallow what had happened even though she knew she had to, but for now, wallowing in self-pity was the best choice. Her father, however, saw things a little differently and had enough of the constant pity party she was giving herself.

94

It had been five days since Bonita had landed in St. John's. She slept away the first, and for the remaining four, she held her head low, feeling sorry for herself. Her father had a very low patience threshold for people who felt sorry for themselves but an even lower one for his daughter. He remembered her thick skin throughout high school, her ambition, drive, and perseverance. She showed none of those characteristics now, and he couldn't accept that.

He knew how badly his daughter was hurting and how terrible it must have been to go through what happened. He knew that a few jealous individuals had taken all her schooling and the hard work she put into it from her, and he knew that she would face significant obstacles if she went back to New York City. The thing was, though, he couldn't let his baby girl give up. After all, it was never his idea for her to go off alone in the first place, but she did it. She did it all by herself and succeeded beyond his wildest imagination. Now she was up in her room, crying again, and he couldn't stand by a minute longer and allow her to waste another day.

He knocked gently on her door and heard her say, "Come

in." He entered her room with a deep breath as he was about to put his little princess in her place.

"Bonita, how long ya plan to park yourself here mopin' around?"

Bonita shot her head up from her pillow in disbelief that her Dad was being insensitive.

"Don't be givin' me that ol' stink eye. Ya knows what I'm gettin' at," he said as he walked towards the window in her room and opened the shades.

"Dad, I just want to be left alone right now, okay? I don't need a lecture or to be told I shouldn't be upset about what happened. It's my right," she said in an assertive tone.

"Ah now, I didn't say ya shouldn't be vexed, Bon Bon. I was wonderin' how long you're plannin' to be down in the mouth."

Bonita looked at him with finality. "Dad, please, not now."

"Yes, b'y, now more than ever, for sure." he proclaimed as he turned around and looked at her. "You've been back in the bay for five days now, and all you've been at is bawlin', grumblin', and sulkin' 'round the house like a wee calf. But that's just it, Bonita. You're no wee calf no more. I've seen ya bloom into a clever young maid with a solid noggin on your shoulders and a fire in your belly like nothin' I've ever seen. So take it from me, now's the time for me to speak my piece."

Bonita turned on her bed with wide eyes. What was happening right now? Her father did not talk like that to anyone, especially his little girl.

"I knows you're hurt and been through the ringer. I can't fathom what's churnin' in your heart. But, I keeps askin' meself, is this me Bonita here in me house, or did she get lost along the way? 'Cause the Bonita I knows would shed a tear for a spell, then turn that hurt into somethin' mighty and flip it on its head for herself. The Bonita I remember would face the school day, beat the bullies, the jeerin', and the meanness, and then come home to buckle down on savin' coin, gettin' ready, makin' choices, and pushin' herself nearer to her dreams. The Bonita I knows wouldn't be cooped up in her room, takin' none of that nonsense bullshit; she'd use it to fuel her dreams, give 'em wings, and learn to soar. The Bonita I knows would be back in New York City by now, piecin' her life back together, just to show them fools she's better, grander, and tougher than they'll ever be, and nothin' they do can really knock her down. I misses that, Bonita. If you finds her, let me know. I'd like to say a big hello."

During his speech, he had made his way through the door. Perhaps he understood the importance of a grand exit after making such a statement. Bonita was reeling from what she just heard. Her father said the word "bullshit." She had never heard her father say a swear word her entire life. He must really mean what he had to say. She sat there with tears in her eyes, feeling a surge of power enter her toes and make its way up to her head. Her Dad was right. What was she doing, playing the victim here? Why was she letting those fucking bitches win when she knew she was better than they were, bigger than they were, and stronger than they were?

She hopped off her bed and grabbed her laptop once again. She opened the airline's website and booked a flight back to New York City for the following week. She then checked a few places for apartments and found one she liked. She picked up her cell and dialed the number immediately.

When she got off the phone, she felt happy. She had spoken to the woman renting the apartment, and they agreed they would meet the day after her plane arrived. The best part was that if they liked each other, the apartment was empty, and she could just pay the first and last month's rent and live the last few days of January without paying a pro-rated fee. The apartment was in a great part of town, and she was super happy; it seemed so easy. She closed her laptop and made her way downstairs.

Her parents were sitting at the kitchen table, and her Mom looked a little worried when she saw Bonita turn the corner. Her father had filled her Mom in on what he had to say to her, and she thought that maybe that would make matters worse for Bonita. She didn't want Bonita to feel un-welcomed here; she knew she was hurting badly and wanted to ensure that this house remained a shelter and refuge for her little girl.

Bonita stood at the table and looked at her parents. "I booked a flight back to New York City for next week. I know it's short notice, but I have so much to do and need to return immediately. Can you take me to the airport on Tuesday morning, Dad?" Her Dad looked at her and nodded. It worked; he didn't think it would work. She walked around the table and kissed her father on the forehead.

"Thanks, Dad. I really needed that."

95

Claude was in complete shock. He had no idea what had happened to Bonita. She had been gone for five days, and he hadn't heard from her. Yesterday, he ran into Julio at the front desk and asked if he had seen Bonita. Julio looked startled at his question.

"I saw her last week. Thursday night, I think. She came through the lobby with many suitcases and tears in her eyes. I asked if she was okay, but she just gave me this look and said nothing."

Claude was beginning to freak out. What had happened to her? Why hadn't she returned any of his calls?

To make matters worse, after Julio had told him about seeing her, he ran upstairs to his apartment, rifled through an address book, and found Bonita's home number back in Newfoundland. He quickly picked up the phone and dialed, hoping she was back in Newfoundland and praying that nothing had happened to her family. The phone rang four times and went to the answering machine, where he left a message. He hung up and walked to the living room, hoping she would get that message and call him back. Before he sat down, the phone rang, and he raced back to the kitchen to pick it up. It was Bonita's home phone number. He answered, "Bonita? Is that you?"

"No, b'y! This is Bonita's father talkin'. Claude, I'm only gonna say this once: Don't be callin' here again. Ya not welcome 'round here, and Bonita don't wanna yarn with ya. Do us a kind one and heed our ask."

The phone went dead. Claude stood there with the phone in his hand, staring at it, speechless and confused. "What is it they think I did?" he thought. "What is going on? I don't understand what is happening. Why won't Bonita return my calls, and why is her father requesting I never contact her again?" Something was up. He didn't know what, but he had to find out.

The next few days went by rather slowly. Claude was consumed with the conversation he had with Bonita's Dad. "They were always so nice when I called before. I can't imagine what would have made them act that way toward me now." He worked a double at the counter and was dead tired. He kept checking his phone for voicemails or messages and would call his home phone to see if there were any there.

He arrived home that evening to find that the rest of Bonita's stuff was cleared out of the apartment. Nothing was left except a note on the bed. He picked it up and read it, but after the first line, he had to sit down, as he thought he was going to vomit.

"Claude,

It has taken me a week to muster up the mental energy to return to this apartment after what happened at the show. Cassidy told me what you did and how you were more than happy to help them out with their plan to ruin me because you were sick of my self-absorbed ways. I didn't want to believe it initially, but you don't have a choice when all signs point to one thing. If you wanted me to move out, all you had to do was ask. I would have been hurt, but I would have gotten over it. I will never understand why you felt you had to go to such great lengths. I thought we were best friends and loved each other dearly, but now I realize I was very wrong.

Despite your role in this, I want you to know something: the last two-and-a-half years until last Thursday were the happiest of my life. I had the most amazing time being your roommate, and it saddens me to know it wasn't mutual. Despite how much you have hurt me, I still love you, and I think a part of me always will. I wish you all the best in your life.

Take care,

Bonita"

His whole body went weak, and the nausea worsened. He didn't understand what Bonita was talking about. He didn't know what had happened that night or what was so bad she felt that she had to move out. But he knew it had to do with that day the three girls came to him for help. They tricked him into helping them hurt Bonita, and he was blind to it. He was only trying to help but inadvertently did something to really hurt her instead. He blamed himself for not seeing through it and for not paying more attention to his instincts and memories of Cassidy. He blamed himself for not being there that night to protect and show her he had nothing to do with what happened.

He fell back on her bed with tears in his eyes. He had lost his best friend, the one person in the world who knew the real him and accepted everything about him. The one person he could talk to about anything and not feel judged in some way. He lost his partner in crime, his Bon Bon and it was his fault. Like so many things in his life, he screwed it up. It was only a matter of time, he knew that, but he was secretly hoping that she would be his best friend forever. Now, it didn't matter. What mattered was finding out what went down that night and how bad it was. If he could do anything to fix it, he would stop at nothing until it was done. He knew he might never get her back after what he did, but if he could help her get her life back somehow, he loved her enough to do it.

96

The drive that brought Bonita to the airport differed from the one she had taken two-and-a-half years ago. Her father was quiet; her mother and Bonita weren't afraid. Bonita was stressed about what was waiting for her back in the big city, about who she might run into, but she was not scared. She figured the worst that could happen to her career had already happened. Despite it destroying the opportunities she felt confident about prior to the show, she was determined to face this head-on and make it work, whatever making it work looked like. The car pulled to the airport, and Bonita kissed and hugged her parent's goodbye. She told them she didn't know when she would be back, but she would check in regularly. Bonita had boarded the plane and was back in the city heading to the hotel where she would only have to stay for a few nights.

The following day, Bonita hailed a cab and headed to the apartment. The lady she had been speaking with was already there awaiting her arrival. They talked for a few moments and then entered the space. For New York City, it was sizable enough, and the rent, a lot for someone unemployed with no prospects was high but manageable. Bonita and the owner hit it off, and after signing the paperwork and handing over the deposits and rent, Bonita had the keys to her apartment. She was ecstatic and couldn't wait to decorate. Bonita had permission to decorate as she saw fit, as long as there was no damage to the structural integrity of the walls, and she agreed to return it to the normal state upon moveout if the owner didn't like the changes.

Bonita was ready to settle into her new apartment. It was a corner suite located in Greenwich Village with many windows. She was excited to have her own place, but she missed Claude and couldn't shake the feeling that there was more to the story than what she already knew, which was very little. She had visited the apartment, collected the rest of her things, and left a note for Claude. She needed closure and, at the very least, a chance to say what had been smothering her for over a week. Bonita set herself up nicely in her new place. Bonita went to a furniture store just around the corner. She knew she had to be frugal, but she also wanted her apartment to reflect her style and who she was without any outside input. Bonita bought herself some new couches, a bedroom set, and accent tables. She liked soft fabrics with industrial lines, and her new furniture had provided just that. She had gone to a paint shop and purchased all the supplies she needed to redecorate her new pad.

She spent nearly five days painting, trimming, building, and designing her apartment. She had made curtains for her windows and a new duvet cover for her bed, and she found a couple of old ratty chairs on the side of the road and brought them home to varnish and reupholster. She had been in her new space for almost a week and was loving it. It was classified as a two-bedroom apartment, but one bedroom was too small to fit a full bed and have room to move around. She converted that into her own personal design studio. She bought a few light fixtures for the ceilings and a couple of pieces of art for the walls, and when she was finished, she flopped down on her new sofa and sighed. She was now home.

She looked around at her new space and felt proud of her work. Every item, decoration, color, and design was hers, methodically placed to give the apartment a loftier, airier feel but grounded and centered at its core. The space felt tranquil, functional, elegant, and welcoming. It was a photo image of her mind's eye. She sat in that spot, feeling grateful to have an apartment with charm and character that matched her own. It was far from finished, she was a new solo-renter and had a lot of things she would need over time. It's the stuff one never thinks about, like cutlery, utensils, and various pots and pans. She had purchased the basics to get her through but wanted to wait to buy her signature pieces until she had a more structured future in which money would flow in.

Since arriving back in New York City, she reached out to Ivana Cox and inquired about the cost of therapy. They talked for hours on the phone, and Bonita spilled her guts and her new situation to her. Ivana listened intentionally and gave some structured advice that could help Bonita get through the loss and the change, tips on navigating her anger and rage, and techniques on helping her get a hold of her thoughts. Ivana advised that the way forward would be challenging and the path to healing is ugly and messy, but once you get closer to the other side, the growth it brings helps put things into perspective. Bonita loved everything Ivana had to say and appreciated that while Claude was a part of Bonita's heartbreak, she never once commented on her beliefs about Claude's character; Ivana stayed neutral throughout the entire conversation. Towards the end of nearly three hours, Bonita realized that Ivana had just counseled her and did so without payment. She asked her how much she owed him and he responded with, "Honey, you are a friend, one who has never asked me of anything before today. You are hurting; you called because you felt lost, and I listened because I care. Today was not a counseling session; it was a conversation about pain, grief, challenges, and navigating all that while trying to reclaim your identity. It was a conversation between friends, one who just happens to be a top New York City psychologist. Besides, as we are friends, I couldn't counsel you because it would be a conflict of interest. The best I could do is recommend you to someone else. I will be happy to do this, but I think you already know what is needed. You need to get out there and start living, be fearless in what comes your way, and use the techniques I taught you today. You got this, Bonita, and I am so happy you chose to return to the city. You are already halfway there. Now, girl, let's get something on the books for a coffee near your new place within the next couple of weeks. I must run, but you will be Okay."

Bonita was simply grateful for the conversation and thanked her for listening and being so kind. They hung up the phone, and she looked around her space. She felt like she had just received another jolt of inspiration and focus. She was so busy over the last week and consumed with her new space that she hadn't thought about what had happened.

Her phone was turned off, her computer was still in a bag in her closet, and she hadn't even checked her messages. Today, while sitting with her thoughts, she knew she needed help getting her head straight. Not thinking a 3 hour phone call with a brilliant clinically trained drag queen could do the trick. She wanted to regain her focus and figure out what she would do next.

She was hoping to avoid that for a while because she didn't know what she would do next. She needed to re-evaluate her goals and lay out a new path for her future. It wouldn't be easy, but she knew she had to do it, and now was as good a time as ever.

"Well, tomorrow," she thought because it was getting late, and she had just opened a bottle of wine and turned on the TV. A little relaxation and a show or two, and she would hit the sack to wake up the following day and get started on her new life.

97

Claude had been calling the school the whole day and getting nowhere. He knew that the answers he was looking for would be there, and after several failed attempts, he decided just to go there. Claude had only been to the school a few times and never explored it; it was only to help Bonita carry things back and forth. He had no idea where to go to try and figure out what had happened that night, but he had a name, the name of one of Bonita's favorite teachers. Dean La-something-or-other. That would be his starting point.

It was late in the day, and there didn't seem to be many students around, but he stopped one and asked where he would find a Mr. Dean La—?

"Dean Lalonde?" the student asked.

"Yes," Claude responded, "that is who I am looking for. Do you know where I could find him?"

The student looked down at his watch and said, "Well, if he is still here, you would probably find him in his office. Down the hall to the end, take a right, and his office is on the left-hand side. A nameplate is on the door, so you can't miss it." Claude looked at the student and said thank you as he began to walk in that direction.

He used the directions the student provided him and found the office with Dean's name on it. He was in luck; the door was open, and the light was on. He knocked lightly and heard a voice from inside tell him to come in.

"Mr. Lalonde?" Claude said as he entered the room.

"Yes, how may I help you?" Dean lowered his glasses and looked at Claude.

"I'm here to ask you about Bonita Smith. She has disappeared, and I think something that happened here two weeks ago that might have caused it."

"Oh," Dean said, with a tired look in his eye. "Have a seat, Mister...?"

"Claude, sir. It's just Claude."

Claude sat down in the chair across from Dean's desk. "Can you give me any idea of what went down that night? I came home to find her personal effects removed from the house. She hasn't returned my calls, and I just need to know what happened that night."

"Claude, why don't I show you instead of telling you?" He took a moment to fiddle with his computer and then turned it around. "See for yourself," as he leaned back in his chair and rubbed his eyes.

Claude watched what was happening on the screen, and a look of horror fell upon his face. What was he watching? This couldn't be right; these weren't Bonita's designs.

"This is a mistake; Bonita didn't do this. She wouldn't do this." Claude pleaded with the weary man. "I was with her until that day, and I never saw her make any of these things. I saw her construct her lines for the final exam and helped her carry them back and forth from home to school. This isn't Bonita's doing, Mr. Lalonde; I can assure you of that."

"I know," Dean said as he plopped his elbows down on his desk, still rubbing his eyes.

"You know? I don't understand!"

"Claude, someone came forward after the fact and explained what happened. It was a cruel trick that was played on her. One that got her kicked out of school, made her the laughingstock of the fashion industry, and ruined her promising career. There is nothing I can do to help her now. What's done is done." Dean gave Claude an exhausted look and leaned back in his chair again.

Claude stood from his chair and peered at the man before him. "What do you mean you can't help her? You know the truth now; how can you just sit there and do nothing?"

"I can't undo what has been done; I can't recreate that night and show everyone what was supposed to happen. I can't change people's impressions of Bonita; no letter or announcement will overshadow what happened that night. The most I can do is reinstate her and try and convince the faculty to grant forgiveness, but as for her career, that is something she will have to face on her own. I can't send a letter of reference for her, as that would make this institution questionable. There would be too many questions, concerns, and roadblocks created if we backed a student who was perceived to have gone out of her way to mock the very fundamentals of this school. It is out of my control," Dean said, standing as well.

"Well, you better do something. At the very least, let

Bonita back into school to finish her BFA so she can get the education she came here for," Claude pleaded as he walked toward the door.

"I will do what I can," said Dean as Claude left the room.

Claude was infuriated and couldn't think straight. Now, it all made sense. Bonita thought he went in on sabotaging her show and had reason to do so. It hurt him to think she could feel that of him, but considering the circumstances, it was understandable. He had to find her, some way, somehow. But how?

98

Bonita spent a few days looking for different jobs throughout the classifieds. She even went to the websites of the other fashion houses and checked for potential internships. She had a sense of blind hope that she could come in under the radar and get through what lay ahead. She knew that everybody who's anybody saw or heard of the catastrophe with her line. She hoped she could prove to them individually that it was all a colossal mistake. She knew that if she went in blaming someone else or trying to convince them that she was set up, it would only make her look petty. She decided to own it and state that it was an experiment that caused her many problems. This way, she would come out looking like a fool who made a terrible choice.

The next part of her plan was to let her actual designs sell themselves. She knew her sketches were good and needed to shop them around. All of that being said, she knew it would be challenging, and she would be met with a lot of hostility in the process.

Her mailbox was full when she finally turned on her phone and per Ivana's instructions, she chose to close that chapter and move. She deleted her voicemails without so much as a listen. She was eating breakfast and perusing the Internet when a mail icon popped up in the bottom right-hand corner of her screen. Her jaw dropped, and so did the mouthful of cereal when she saw who it was from. "Dean Lalonde" was the sender, and her hands began to shake. Bonita seemed okay when she kept it at the back of her mind, but when it came front and center, her world felt like it was crumbling again. Bonita took a towel to quickly clean up the spilled cereal on her pants and clicked on the icon to open the email. She took a deep breath and started to read.

The subject line read, "Let's have a chat," and the body of the email was short and concise.

"Bonita, I hope this email finds you well. I would like to invite you to visit me at school this afternoon. There is something that I would like to discuss with you, and I prefer to do it in person. If you can give me an answer before lunchtime, I will keep a spot for you.

Dean Lalonde"

She looked puzzled at the computer screen and trembled at the idea. She stood up and started pacing the room. "Why does he want to speak with me?" she thought as she stopped and leaned against the kitchen door frame. "What could he say to me that he hasn't said already?"

She was trying to decide if she would go, pacing again and weighing the options in her head. She didn't have anything planned for this afternoon. She wished she had because it would have made this process more manageable. Finally, after nearly five whole minutes, she walked back to her laptop and hit Reply.

"Mr. Lalonde, I will make some room and stop by around three. Bonita Smith."

Now, she had to shower, dress, do her hair and make-up, and ensure she looked her best. She never thought she would step foot in that school again, and now that she was, she was terrified. What if students saw her? What if they made fun of her or gave her trouble? What if Cassidy, Bethany, or Lyla were there? She was beginning to panic and pondered canceling, but she thought better of it. Bonita would walk in there with her head held high and own it. She wasn't about to let anyone make her feel small or uncomfortable, so she hopped in the shower and began getting ready for her 3:00 pm meeting.

It was nearly two-thirty in the afternoon when she was finally done getting ready. She had picked out her outfit and a new pair of shoes she had just purchased from a little boutique around the corner and checked herself in the mirror one last time. She wanted anyone who would see her in that school that day to see a girl who was looking great and doing just fine. Her days of throwing herself pity parties were over, all thanks to her father's strong words and the one-and-only Ivana Cox. She grabbed her bag and went out the door.

99

The school was quiet when she walked in, and instead of using the main entrance, she used the loading dock, where she had done her walk of shame not more than two weeks prior. Dean Lalonde's office was closer to this entrance anyway, and these hallways were less traveled by students during the day, so she felt it was the best option for her to take. She walked around the corner and saw that Dean's office door was open. She stopped dead in her tracks and began to panic.

"What am I doing here?" she thought. "What could Dean Lalonde possibly have to say to me?" She took a few deep breaths and decided that since she had come this far, she had to get it over with.

She knocked on his door as she peered in. Dean was sitting at his desk, rubbing his eyes again. He seemed tired, worn out, and just off a weekend binge, but he still had a sophisticated and poised air about him.

"Come in, Bonita. Have a seat," he said as he looked up at the young girl standing before him. "I'm sure you are wondering why I have asked you here today," he said as she sat down.

"Yes, I am, actually," she answered rather quickly.

"First off, let me take a moment to apologize for my actions the night of the fashion show. I overreacted and took things too far," he said sheepishly. "I simply couldn't process what was happening and the anger, resentment, shock, disgust I felt I knew only to take out on you."

Bonita was in shock; that was the last thing she thought she would hear.

"What I saw that night was a young girl who didn't care about her future, a young girl who went out of her way to mock what we teach here," he continued. "I didn't give you time to explain yourself or even plead your case. I shut you down before you had a chance to defend yourself, and for that, I am deeply sorry."

Bonita wasn't quite sure what was happening. He was alluding to the fact he knew she wasn't behind it, but to make sure everyone was clear, she said, "Sir, I had nothing to do with what happened that night. It sounds ridiculous, but I was just as surprised and devastated as you were."

He leaned back in his chair and ran his fingers through his hair, looking off to the side of his office.

"Bonita, I know you had nothing to do with what happened that night. Someone came forward and explained that a few people sabotaged your line-up. Furthermore, I received a visit from one of your friends the other day, who also informed me that there was no way you were involved with that fiasco. He told me that he was with you right up to the day of the show and helped you bring your supplies to school, watched you make every garment, and listened to you obsess about how perfectly the show must go for your career".

Bonita sat straight up. "Someone came and talked to you about that? A guy? What was his name?"

"Claude, I believe, is what he said his name was. He said he had not heard from you, that you went missing and moved out of your shared apartment. I have never seen anyone so concerned for another human being as much as he was for you. He is worried sick about you, Bonita."

She felt tears welling up in her eyes. She didn't understand why Claude would do that after he helped the girls ruin her...unless he didn't. Unless he was tricked into helping them, and they made her believe that it came from a cruel place. That made more sense to her than anything.

"Sir, did you ask me here today just to tell me you know the truth?" Bonita said, holding back tears.

"No, I asked you here today to apologize and let you know I am reinstating you as a full-time student. Your final grading will overlook the two weeks you have been absent. The faculty and the Dean of admissions all agree that removing you was a misstep without providing due process. I understand if you want nothing to do with us, but I hope you will consider finishing your BFA with our school. Also, the four individuals involved in doing this to you have been stripped of their academic standing and removed from their programs. They will not graduate from their programs at this school. They will find great difficulty graduating from any other design school in the country." He spoke so offhandedly, and factually, it made Bonita feel ill. Still, she could sense something he hadn't yet said, something not as jovial but rather very negative.

"Sir, what else do you need to tell me?"

"Bonita, this school can do nothing to help clear your name. We already took a major hit in the fashion community. We cannot afford to make our school look less competent than it already does. We cannot provide you with a letter of recommendation; we cannot inform everyone who was there that night that you were a victim of all of this. We cannot undo what has been done. I am afraid that the obstacles this has created for you in your career are ones you must overcome on your own. I know it isn't fair, but as I said, we cannot bring more attention to that evening than there already is. I'm so sorry." He let his head drop a little and stared down at his desk.

Bonita stood up from her chair and began walking towards the door. "As much as it sucks, Sir, I can understand where you are coming from. It isn't fair, but life isn't about fairness and equality; it's about being bigger and owning your shortcomings. That night was my shortcoming, and I can assure you, you haven't seen the last of me. I will finish what I came here to do, no matter what it takes. I will consider finishing my BFA with you and this school. I will give you an answer by the end of the week. Thank you for your time and thank you for your apologies. They do mean a lot to me." She turned and walked out the door.

Dean sat at his desk, still looking troubled, but a little smile came to his face as he thought about Bonita's words. It was a grin, a grin that signified that he knew that she would do what she set out to do, and he was proud of her for that.

100

Bonita was walking down the loading dock again, leaving the place she thought she would never return to. She felt a little different. She was happy to hear that Cassidy, Lyla, Bethany, and Jerri Janes were discovered and kicked out of school. It was an outcome that she was delighted with. It scared her a little how much she reveled in them getting caught and having their hopes and aspirations ripped away. It took a bit of bitterness away from the fact that she still had to try to overcome the school fashion show flop. She knew that so many fashion designers and houses were present to see it. She appreciated the apology from Dean Lalonde more than she would ever let on. Knowing he knew the truth was enough to get the closure she needed from the whole ordeal.

It was time to make some monumental decisions that would affect her entire life from this point forward. She was close to finishing her BFA, and the opportunity to do it had just re-presented itself. That being said, she didn't want to deal with all the looks, whispering, and bullshit she would have to endure if she went back now. No! That wasn't an enticing option for her. As she thought about it, she decided to email Dean Lalonde in a couple of days, saying she was interested in returning to finish her education but would begin attending next January. Most of the students involved were third-years and would all move on this May. If she waited until next January, it would be an entirely new group of students whom she didn't know and, more importantly, didn't know her. She had just turned the corner to the adjacent street when she heard someone call her name.

"Bonita." She froze. A familiar voice totally caught her off guard.

"Bonita, wait up!" she heard again. She didn't want to stop and talk; she wanted to keep walking and avoid him — the guy calling out to her — altogether. He picked on her so much in school that she could only imagine what he would have to say to her now.

"Bonita! Jesus Christ, lady, wait up!"

She heard him again, and this time, he was getting closer. She wanted to run but instead walked slower with her head down. It was only a second or two before he was maneuvering around her. Then, there he was, standing right in front of her.

"Jeez, Bonita, didn't you hear me calling you?" Benjamin Ryder said as he was panting and out of breath.

"I heard you. I slowed down," Bonita fired back. "What can I do for you, Mr. Ryder?"

Benjamin gave her a look as if he was put off by her automatic impatience. "Nothing," he said, "I just wanted to talk."

"Talk about what?" She tilted her head with attitude and put her hand on her hip. "What a loser I am? How could I be so stupid to pull a stunt like that? Don't I care about my future? Before you go off making fun and taunting me like you have done since I started here, you should know I didn't do it."

"I know," Benjamin said, dropping his head a little. He didn't realize that his taunting had bothered her that much.

"What? How do you know?"

"Everybody knows, Bonita! Everybody knows that the stagehand and three girls did it, and you had no part in it."

Bonita stepped back in disbelief. "How?" she asked him, a little shocked at how matter-of-fact he was being.

"They weren't very smart about it. They slipped up, and it got out."

This floored Bonita, as she had no idea that they spoke of it, never mind was loose-lipped around other people. Why would they be so stupid?

"What are you doing right now?" Benjamin asked.

"I'm headed home," Bonita replied.

"Can you come with me for a bit? I promise it won't take too long," Benjamin suggested.

Bonita really didn't care much for going off somewhere with Benjamin. They hardly spoke this last year, and what was his sudden interest in her now? He knew she didn't do anything wrong, so what could he want with her?

"I don't think so, Benjamin. I'm not up for anything right now; I just want to go home."

"Come on, Bonita, please!" Benjamin pleaded.

"No, Benjamin, I am going home. Thank you for letting me know that everyone knows, but goodbye." Bonita said assertively this time.

"God, Bonita, can you take the stick out of your ass for five minutes and just come with me?"

Bonita stepped back again. She was going to yell at him, but she saw this look in his eyes like it was imperative. It was real, something burning just beneath his lens, palpable even. She pondered it briefly and said, "Where will you be taking me?"

"It's a surprise!" he responded.

She rolled her eyes and shook her head.

Benjamin pleaded one last time, hoping to convince her to accompany him. "I want to show you something, and when you see it, you can go home. I'll never bother you again."

"Fine," she said, adjusting the bag strap around her shoulder and putting her hand before her. "Let's go."

They were off, walking down the street, not saying too much. Bonita wanted to ask where he was taking her but knew he wouldn't tell her; he was bratty like that. Instead, she kept her head low and walked by his side for less than five minutes. He led her up a walkway toward an old factory converted into loft apartments and put his key in the door.

"What is this place?" she asked.

"My place," he responded as she stopped abruptly. "Will you just give me five minutes?" he asked as she was turning to walk away.

She stopped. "Well, if that's how long it takes you, then I don't have much to worry about, do I?"

"Ha, ha. Funny girl!" He laughed as he walked through the second set of doors. A few flights of stairs, and they were at his apartment door. He turned the key and let her in.

She stepped inside the apartment and felt a bit amazed

that it didn't look at all what she imagined it would look like. She assumed it would be messy, dusty, and smell musty. It had high ceilings and a hallway, and the kitchen, dining room, and living space were open-concept and nicely decorated. Not what she expected at all.

"What I want to show you is through the door on the right."

She gave him this look as if to say, "You're pathetic," and opened the closed door. As the door swung open, she stopped breathing. What was before her was the most incredible sight she had seen in her entire life. It looked like what was usually an empty room apart from a desk, computer, and a few small bookshelves. It was lined with mannequins, typical for a design student's living space, but Benjamin was not a designer. How the tons of mannequins were placed was orderly, in rows of 5, and 8 deep in total. There was only a little space to move around inside; while closely together, the mannequins took up a significant amount of the floor space. Each one was dressed head to toe. She turned to look at him with the most perplexed expression; all he saw was the most enormous and beautiful eyes he had ever seen. He smiled as she walked into the room. Each mannequin was outfitted with garments that made up her entire line that would have been shown at the fashion show. Right down to the last shoe, every item was perfectly dressed on each mannequin precisely as she had imagined. She thought all the hard work and time she spent designing this line was lost forever, but it stood before her here, in Benjamin Ryder's loft apartment.

"Where did you get this?" she stuttered as she began touching the fabric on a mannequin close to her.

"The school dumpster, the day after the fashion show. When they made the swap, they threw it there to be taken out with the trash," Benjamin responded. Bonita turned and looked at him again with tears in her eyes.

"I thought that this was gone forever," she said.

"If I had been another five minutes, it would have. The garbage truck pulled up while I was still inside fishing everything out," Benjamin chimed. Bonita was beside herself with emotions. There was so much going on inside her mind and her heart. How could this day have turned out so great? Her stomach was flip-flopping because her feelings for Benjamin started rushing back, and she remembered how enamored she was with him in her second year. Was this gratitude, or was this a real attraction?

"Bonita, I picked on you so much because I liked you. I thought you knew that," he said. Feeling awful that she thought he was being mean and never knew he had feelings for her.

She gently turned around while allowing the fabric of the nearest dress to caress her fingers, "I didn't know that, but if I am to be honest, I liked you too." A smile formed on Benjamin's face and on Bonita's. Before they knew it, they were both chuckling a little.

"Benjamin, I really don't know what to say." She turned with her arms pointing toward all the mannequins. "I can't articulate what I am feeling right now; there are simply no words to describe it. I was just beginning to accept that these were lost forever, and now here they are in perfect condition."

"You don't have to say anything. These all belong to you,"

Benjamin said softly as he moved slightly toward her. He was watching her expressions, the way her glasses teetered on her nose after rubbing her tears away. In everything he has ever done, this was his proudest moment. Nothing compares to seeing her light up like this, her cheeks flushed, the way she is trying to process. It was a moment he would never forget, one where he returned something lost to someone as passionate and driven as she was. It felt good; it felt right. He realized that he cared for her more than he thought, more than he imagined. Looking at her now, touching the fabric, a tear falling down her face, he felt overwhelmed with happiness because she was overwhelmed with happiness. "God, she is so beautiful!" He thought, desperate to hold her in his arms.

She was looking at all of them, breathing in every detail of every garment as if examining if they were authentic, as if she was dreaming, and that was her only moment to spend with her collection. Her mind drifted back and forth between the garments and Benjamin. He was handsome, that was for sure, but more than that, he was kind. He did this; why did he do this? How did he even know to look in the dumpsters? Then she remembered what Dean Lalonde had said in his office, that someone had come forward and told him the truth. A string of light bulbs began turning on in her mind; she realized that Benjamin would have had to quickly find out what had happened to check the dumpsters for her line. Then, how did everyone else find out? It didn't seem plausible that the three girls would just let it slip that they were responsible. Why would they be so eager to incriminate themselves if they went to such great lengths to get her out of the picture? Then, the realization washed over her, "It was you."

Bonita spun around and looked at him. "It was you who told Mr. Lalonde! It was you who told everyone else! They wouldn't have let it slip or spoken about it to anyone! It was all you, wasn't it?"

Benjamin stood there with a little grin and a nod to acknowledge what Bonita was saying was correct.

"But how? How did you find out?" Bonita asked with intense curiosity.

"Well, when everything was going down, I came to find you but couldn't. I wanted to know what you were up to," Benjamin said as he moved closer to her. "Then, I heard talking in the loading dock corridor, so I checked it out. I could hear familiar voices, and when I listened closely, it was Cassidy, Lyla, and Bethany laughing hysterically at what they had just done. I peeked around the corner, and you weren't there, so I stayed and listened long enough to hear everything I needed to, and then that was that."

He stepped a little closer. "I couldn't believe that they would stoop so low as to do that to the school but, more importantly, you. I immediately felt awful for entertaining for a millisecond that you, Bonita Smith, would present a show like that. I knew that night wasn't the right time to speak to anyone; emotions were high, so I waited until the next day. I figured that if they swapped your collection, it had to be nearby. I thought they wouldn't risk leaving it in the school overnight, so where would you put something, you didn't want anyone to find?"

"The garbage, the dumpster," Bonita replied as she watched

him with a growing attraction as he told the story of how he became her knight in shining sweatpants.

"The dumpster!" Benjamin said, "I went to the dumpster, retrieved everything, and set them up on mannequins. Then, I went to Dean Lalonde's office and asked if I could speak to him briefly. He agreed, and I led him down the hall to where I had set everything up. When he saw it, he was speechless. I told him I had just fished them out of the dumpster and over-heard Lyla, Bethany, and Cassidy laughing about what they had done outside the loading dock corridor the night before. He was furious. He immediately arranged to retrieve them and brought them to the room with the mannequins. The look on their faces when they saw your line and me stand-ing in that room was priceless. The ruse was up. They were busted. They were stripped of their standing in the school, and the three of them and the stagehand were escorted from the premises. For the last two weeks, I have been methodi-cally telling people what happened and that they were kicked out of school. Now, everybody knows you had nothing to do with it."

Bonita looked into his eyes and said, "But you were Lyla's friend."

He looked at her, offering a grimace at the notion.

"Lyla's parents are friends of mine, and that is how we know each other. I care no more for Lyla than I do this mannequin."

This time, he was less than six inches from Bonita, staring down at her staring up at him. His eyes were big and beau-tiful, glittering with emotions held back. He was transfixed with how lovely she looked in the afternoon sun beaming through the windows.

"I care for you, though, Bonita. I have for a while. I have thought about kissing you so many times," he said as his head moved a little closer to hers. She didn't move, she didn't budge, not an inch. She stayed still, looking up at him, praying he would kiss her. He advanced a little more, and before he knew it, he could feel the heat radiating off her skin. It was now or never as he leaned in and caressed her lips.

He pulled away, and their lips seemed fused together. Bonita looked at him and trembled. He looked into her eyes and saw what he hoped to see: a mutual longing for more. This time, he kissed her more passionately, and her arms moved up his sides toward his back as she pulled him in closer to her. There was passion, emotion, and a yearning for closeness between them. They couldn't stop; they didn't want to, and they gave in to their worldly desires and made love underneath her entire collection.

101

Bonita was in bliss when she awoke to her phone ringing the following day. She had made love three times the night before with a man she had had feelings for and who had feelings for her. After they made love the first time, and he was holding her close, she turned and told him that up until then, she had been a virgin. Thinking that he would be taken aback by this, she was caught off guard when he whispered in her ear, and said, "I remember something about this from when you were dating the douchebag model, but to be honest, if I hadn't known, I wouldn't have been able to tell," and kissed her lips gently. "How was it? Were you comfortable? Did I hurt you?"

Bonita smiled and felt tingly on the inside. Alexander couldn't hold a candle to Benjamin; how he kissed her made her feel like she was the only woman in the world. Benjamin was more focused on whether Bonita was okay than his own needs. Her first time was romantic, beautiful, and everything she had hoped for. Benjamin was gentle and patient, showing her a tenderness she didn't think existed. He was sleeping beside her looking incredibly handsome, and she couldn't bring herself to check her phone. Instead, she nestled back into him as he wrapped his arms around her tightly and moaned a little. It was heaven to her. After all, she had never been close like this to a man before. Physically close, that is. She had almost got there with Alexander, but thankfully, that wasn't the time or the man she was meant to give it to.

They spent the entire morning in bed and made love one last time before getting up and showering together. They went for lunch, walked the city, held hands, and talked all day. He would stop and hold her shoulders, just look at her and smile. Each time, he would lean in and kiss her with a passion that made her knees go weak. It was the perfect day, and she was walking through a wishful haze of romance for the entire time. He couldn't believe that he had finally had the chance to kiss her, never mind making love to her. She was a special girl, not like the others. He thought himself lucky to have been her first and decided to cherish this one and care for her. He watched her as they walked together, memorizing every detail, like how her eyes squinted in the sun, the slight furrow in her brow, and how her hair danced in the wind. He was seeing her, all of her, for the first time. He was always on the outside looking in, but walking with her, he felt like she was more than he had ever imagined.

The day bled into evening and the evening into morning. The following morning, however, she needed to get back to work and get her life back on track. He was supportive, and although he would rather spend the entire day with her again, he had school to attend. They kissed one last time on his front stoop and went their separate ways, already having made plans to meet up later that night. She went to her apartment and began looking up fashion houses. She found a couple on the small side that she liked and decided to give them a call. After a few days of placing phone calls and sending emails, she got an interview with a tiny boutique on the Upper East Side. It wasn't much, but it was a start. She got her portfolio together, made some last-minute changes, and texted Benjamin to tell him the news.

102

The morning of the interview came, and she was up at dawn getting ready for her big day. Benjamin had spent the night and thought it best to stay out of her way. He lay in bed and offered encouragement and excitement to get her pumped for her big interview. He loved waking up to her; her energy was intoxicating. She was this quiet force, an undercurrent of persistence, and you could feel the vibrations from her as she methodically solved the problems at hand. Benjamin had spent a lot of time with her since bringing her to his apartment. He didn't think that day would end like it did, but he was drawn in beyond reason when he saw her staring at the mannequins. The fact that now, he was lying in her bed watching her buzz around the apartment, getting ready, was mind-boggling to him. How did he get the most beautiful, most intelligent, most driven woman he had ever met to let him make love to her?

Bonita sharply focused on getting ready, was not oblivious to the cute stare coming from the handsome man in her bed. She was not oblivious to the growing feeling of wanting to forget everything and crawl back in there with him. It wasn't just the sex; it was more than that. Benjamin made her feel safe, like 'home' safe. The turn of events over the last week was so peculiar. She went from feeling alone in the city to having this kind and warm man holding her and making her feel things. She paused just outside her bedroom door and looked over her shoulder, and he was still staring at her with this cute, mysterious look. He looked like he was trying to figure something out. Bonita blew him a kiss and said, "I have to go get my head in the game; my head is with you in that bed. I will call you when it's over and let you know how it went."

The boutique was small, and she hoped there was no way they were present at the school fashion show. It was only the big names that came to that event, as they were the ones who did most of the hiring. She picked out her best outfit and heels, kissed her honey goodbye, and went down the street. It was a cold day in February, and she was stylishly bundled up, looked professional and put together. She was ready for this. She hailed a cab and sped off toward her interview.

On the drive, her mind drifted back to Dean LaLonde's office when he told her how Claude came to see him. Her emotions could not be resolved with this matter. Did he go there because he felt terrible after the fact? Was he actually knowingly involved in the show but now regretted it? She had a yearning to know the truth but a fear of what she may actually find out. After running into Benjamin after the meeting with Dean and having a whirlwind romance with him, she hadn't had any chance to have Claude in her fore-thoughts. She knew that she missed him, that he left a lot of messages that she had never listened to, and that maybe it was time to face it for what it was and find out his side of the story. "Maybe later today," she thought.

When she arrived, a very flamboyant young man greeted her. He was chipper, well-dressed, and very welcoming. She sat in a small lounge and waited for the owner to retrieve her. She didn't wait too long before this beautiful man called her name. They entered the boutique's back office and stopped at a small conference room. They exchanged small talk at first, joked about designing, and then she handed him her portfolio. He looked at all the sketches and made many a groan or moan throughout. Then, he closed the portfolio and placed it on the table before him.

"Miss Smith, you are a talented designer, it seems."

It wasn't a question but rather a statement.

"Your sketches are quite skilled, and your designs are very trendy." After a short pause, "I cannot offer you a space here at my shop."

Bonita was disappointed but confused, as he said he enjoyed her work. What was the problem?

"May I ask why, sir?" she asked.

The man chuckled a little and then gave her a very stern look.

"It came to my attention this morning that you were the designer in question who made a joke of your school's fashion show. My receptionist recognized your name and showed me some videos on Google. I can't imagine what you were thinking when putting that disaster together. Still, I will not have someone work for me who, even though she shows great talent, can at any point misrepresent and embarrass me to my public."

He crossed his legs, folded his arms, and expressed as if to say, "You have to know this." Bonita was lost for words. She had done what she knew was the silliest thing anyone could do: underestimate the reach of an adverse event.

"I can assure you, sir, that behavior would never surface with this job," she pleaded.

"If you could do that to your school, then you could do that to anyone. I want no part of it. You are a disgrace to the fashion industry, and I would very much like it if you would leave my shop," he said with finality.

He was cold, callous, and outright rude. It took every-thing in Bonita to walk out of that shop, maintaining some dignity. She broke down in tears when she made it around the corner.

She wasn't paying attention to where she was going. She couldn't see anything, anyway. She was sobbing in the middle of the street and could do nothing to try and stop it. She wasn't prepared for what happened in that interview or the nastiness people could deliver. She wasn't like that.

Despite not being able to see, she kept walking, secretly hoping she would fall down a manhole and could hide for-ever. She wiped her eyes away when she brought up solid and stumbled backward. Her bag, portfolio, and cell phone fell to the floor.

"I'm sorry," she said to the person she ran into.

"Don't worry about it; let me help you."

It was yet another familiar voice.

"Oh! Hi, dear. Bonita, is it?" the woman said as she was handing Bonita her things. Bonita remembered who owned that voice: a small woman with a Southern accent. She looked up.

"Yes, it's Bonita. I'm so sorry to have bumped into you like that; I need to be more careful."

"Oh, my! What is the matter with you? Why are you crying?"

Bonita, embarrassed, tried to clear her eyes and regain composure.

"I see your arm has healed quite nicely," the woman said.

"Yes, thank you," Bonita said through the tears. "Thank you again for helping me that—"

"Don't mention it, darlin'. I always try to be a good Samaritan." The woman gave a little chuckle. Bonita, still crying, tried smiling, but the woman noticed it was a little forced.

"Here, why don't you sit with me a while over there on that bench, and you could tell me what has made you so sad?" The woman motioned to the bench behind them. Bonita, too emotional to argue, complied and sat beside the familiar woman.

"Oh my, how rude of me, honey. I have yet to tell you my name. I'm Claire Foster. It is a pleasure to meet you again."

The woman sat with her back straight and in perfect posture. She was no more than 5'2" and dressed in this creamy pink suit with matching heels. Her hair was swept up into a French roll and a bouffant. Her nails were perfectly manicured, her make-up just so, and her eyes sparkled.

"Now! You tell me exactly what makes you so sad. Start from the top, and don't skip any details. We will try and figure out if there is a solution to your problem." Her voice was soft, sweet, and poised. She was graceful and strong, assertive but not forceful. She was the kind of woman you would do anything she asked of you out of sheer respect. Bonita wasn't used to strangers talking to her. Even though they had a previous encounter when Bonita had broken her arm, she felt embarrassed that she had met her again in such uncontrollable emotion.

After calming herself a little, Bonita started in on the story from the top. As the woman had asked, she spared no detail, and Claire sat beside her, listening attentively to her every word. As Bonita got deeper and deeper into her story, the woman started smiling a little. Bonita noticed and thought it strange, as her story was rather tragic and not to be laughed about. Bonita wrapped the story up with her most recent experience at the boutique and explained why she was so upset. She didn't think a small design house would have heard about the tragedy of her school fashion show, but they had. She looked at Claire and said, "There you have it, the sadness that is my life."

The woman shifted backward on the bench and rested her back against it. She looked at Bonita with a peculiar look and spoke quickly.

"That was you, dear? You are Bonita Smith?"

Bonita turned 180 degrees on the bench and cried. "You heard about the school fashion show?"

The woman folded her hands on Bonita's and looked at her with the kind of face Bonita's Mom would have. "Everyone has heard about the school fashion show, darling; it was a big deal in the fashion community." Bonita went to recoil, but the woman held her hands even tighter. "May I see your portfolio?"

Bonita was a little surprised by the request but handed it to the woman without reluctance. At least she would see that her designs were different from what was displayed that night. After a few moments of flipping through the pages, she closed the book and sat straight up again.

"Bonita, these are amazing! I love the country/urban blend in your designs. I'm a country girl myself, and I would wear most of the garments, the ball gowns especially!" The woman shifted in her seat a little more, and Bonita was at least pleased that Claire liked her work — not that it meant anything. Bonita leaned forward to take back her portfolio, "Thank You, Claire, I appreciate that."

"Bonita, why didn't you do something to clear your name?" Claire asked.

"Before the show ended, I had been stripped of my academic standing, banned from the school, and lost everyone, even my best friend. What was I to do? How could I have proved without doubt I didn't do it?" Bonita lamented.

"Oh, I suppose it wouldn't have mattered much anyway. You were unknown before that night, and now your name is attached to that awful display," responded Claire.

"I'm ruined," Bonita said to Claire while wiping tears from her eyes. "I came to this city to make it as a fashion designer, and even a little shop like that turns me down. Who will hire me? Who will give me a chance with that looming over my head?"

"Bonita, I sit on the board of directors for Mackie's," Claire said before continuing.

Bonita's head spun so quickly she could feel her brain move. Mackie's was the largest North American department store. They had their flagship store in New York City and a global presence with stores and partnership agreements.

"We are always looking for new lines to add to our already impressive collection, and I think your line would be a good fit for our stores," Claire said, with authority in her voice. Bonita nearly fell off the bench and couldn't believe what she was hearing.

"Now, I don't make the final decisions, but I have a lot of pull within the company. I would like to meet with our head purchaser and have you show him your line."

Bonita was without air. She couldn't breathe; she had no idea what to think and was speechless.

"Well, say something, dear!"

"Are you serious?" was all that Bonita could muster.

Claire laughed a little. "I would never joke about something so important to someone else. I am most certainly serious, young lady."

She pulled out her phone, fiddled with it briefly, and lifted it to her ear. A moment later...

"Charles, darling, it's Claire calling. You will never believe who I am sitting with, but she is the designer of our newest clothing line. I need to schedule an appointment with you and her; what does your schedule look like this coming Thursday?"

Bonita's mouth was on the floor. Was this really happening?

"Good, let's pencil me in at around 2:00 pm, okay, darling? And make sure we have the run-room booked for the meeting, as she will bring models to wear her complete line. You are going to love her work. Okay, darling, ciao for now."

She flipped the phone closed and turned again toward Bonita.

"It's time to stop crying now, Miss Smith. You have three days to get everything together, and wow, my head purchaser. You can do it. Arrive at this address" — she pulled a pen and paper from her purse and wrote it down — "at one-thirty. I will meet you downstairs and show you where you can set up. I will be present for the meeting, so don't worry too much about the talking, as I am in your corner."

She winked at Bonita and smiled. Bonita stood up from the bench and was smiling from ear to ear.

"Oh my God, Claire! Thank you so much. I can't believe this is happening. I have so much to do."

"Yes, yes, you do, and don't mention it. You are talented, I love your designs, and we, you and I, will make it happen. Now run along and get to work, missy." She chuckled. "This old bird has to go get her hair done."

With that, Bonita was off and running, full steam ahead. Claire got up from the bench and patted herself off. She smiled as she began walking away. "She will be great for Mackie's," she thought as she walked down the street.

Bonita was barely through the door of her apartment before she started singing out for Benjamin. He came running out of the bathroom with shaving cream on his face.

"What? Did you get it?" he asked, referring to the interview.

"Hell no, he was a piece of shit asshole and told me I wasn't worth the risk."

He looked perplexed and said, "Then what has you so happy?"

Bonita sat him down on the couch and filled him in. Benjamin's smile grew continuously as Bonita described the event that had transpired during and after her interview. She told him about Claire and that they had met before when Claire had helped her after she fell and broke her arm. By the end of her story, he had her in his arms; they were kissing, laughing, giggling, and celebrating, and before they knew it, they were making love. There was shaving cream, everywhere!

103

The following three days were a complete blur for both Bonita and Benjamin. He loved how driven she was in the week he had spent with her up until now. However, he had never seen someone move so fast in his life. It was like watching a coordinated circus event, and although it was chaotic and challenging to keep pace, no detail was left unplanned and unchecked. He offered himself wholly to her in any capacity she required; he knew how big of a deal this viewing would be and could right course in Bonita's life.

Bonita was all over her apartment the first day. It was a comfortable size for two people, but if you needed to arrange and get a 40-head fashion viewing completed in three days, it was a nightmare. He gently and assertively convinced her to move the command center to his place. That was where most of her garments were, anyway. His home was significantly bigger with floor space and lofty. He came from an upper-class family, and his parents bought him his loft when he started school. Even though he came from money, he wasn't a brat, and he wasn't someone who flaunted it. He was reserved and didn't talk about it often. He wanted people to like him for him and not his wallet.

Bonita enlisted Benjamin's services to round up models from the school. It was a pretty easy task, even though it was unpaid. Most models there hadn't been to this type of viewing and were excited to be a part of the experience.

He held a meeting at his place. All the models attended and was fitted perfectly into each item. Bonita arranged them in the order she wanted them presented. First, she chose the men. Bonita felt the men's line was minimal, but it was an excellent introduction to her versatility. She had an idea and had to convince Benjamin to do it, but she wanted him to be the lead walk-in for the men. "Oh no, I don't model. Bonita, I can't do that," he said as he turned a ripe color of red.

"You don't have to model; you just have to dress up and walk through a room. You will be first to go in and first out," Bonita rebutted.

"Why me? We can easily find five guys from school. Why would you want me to do this, Bonita?" Benjamin proclaimed, flustered and hot in the face.

"I can see this is stressing you, so let's pretend I didn't ask. It's okay, I understand. I was just being silly and thinking that I wanted my boyfriend to be the first face they see representing the male part of the line, the sexiest guy I know," Bonita responded genuinely.

"Boyfriend?" Benjamin paused a moment, "You said boyfriend? Like exclusive, official, I am your man?" He was teasing, but it was as much a question as they hadn't considered it. He knew he wanted to be with her; it was something he felt on a molecular level. It felt right; the energy was right, but he wasn't sure if she thought the same.

"Boyfriend!" Bonita smiled, "Exclusive, Official, I am your woman, you are my man." She leaned in and kissed him slowly. It was then he knew he was in trouble; it was then he knew it was over for him. He couldn't resist her; he was putty in her hands, which meant he couldn't say no. He smiled at the thought and said, "Okay, I'll do it."

Bonita was the woman who had stolen his heart, and she jumped for joy and kissed him again. He knew he would do anything to make her happy! Anything!

After that was settled, she focused on the women: She started with the lighter outfits, moved on to the more business and formal ensembles, and finally, ball gowns would prance their way through.

Hair and make-up would be done by students as well — another unpaid gig, but something perfect for their resume. Everything was set, and she was ecstatic the night before the viewing at Mackie's. She was having trouble sleeping because her nerves were running high. This was a massive deal for Bonita. It would be a huge deal for anyone, but this was her chance to get out from behind her school fashion show and show her work. Even if they didn't choose to buy her line, it would show some higher-ups what she was really about. She figured if they were at a martini bar and her name came up in a negative light, they would send some much-needed attention her way and at least clarify that she was a good designer.

The morning came too fast, and all that was left was to pack everything up and get to her appointment on time. Benjamin left around 11:00 am and said he would return shortly. She missed him when he was gone. Bonita had hoped he would spend the day with her but quickly realized the time to herself was much needed. The sound of a phone ringing brought her to reality, and as she picked it up, she wasn't sure who was calling. A familiar Southern voice answered, and Bonita and Claire spoke briefly. Claire called to ensure everything was in order, that Bonita would be on time, and that there would be no hiccups during the viewing. Bonita assured her all was well, and the call ended with good luck from Claire.

It was 1:05, and Benjamin wasn't back yet. She called his cell but got his voicemail. She knew she had to leave, but the models weren't there yet either. She panicked and thought, "It's happening again, isn't it?" She had no longer considered the words when the door swung open, and Benjamin and all the models walked in. She sighed deeply and said, "We have to hurry, everybody."

Benjamin said, "No rush! We will get there on time," and Bonita turned to him.

"No rush? We still have to get many cabs and uptown in 25 minutes."

Benjamin laughed a little. "Well, not exactly. I think we will be fine with the bus I rented. It will fit all the models and the garments with room to spare."

Bonita couldn't help but grab his butt and kiss him. She was blown away that he had rented a bus for her. "Thank you, babe. Thank you so much." He was walking in the viewing, and he went out and rented her a bus to transport everything; he went above and beyond without prompting. She was beginning to settle on maybe, just maybe, she had found someone genuine and truly caring. She couldn't help but recognize her feelings of attraction, the ease being with him, the bond they were building. It felt right like they were on the same wavelength.

Moments later, they were all piled in the bus and heading uptown, fighting through traffic. Bonita wasn't worried. She decided that she was going to put away the worry and just let what happened happen. The bus banked the curb outside the building with a few minutes to spare, and she herded the models in the front door.

As promised, Claire was waiting for her in the main lobby. She took them back to the elevators, and they advanced to the 18th floor. When they got off, there were a bunch of cubicles, offices, people running around, and phones ringing every-where. It looked hectic and fast-paced. Bonita quickly picked up her speed and followed Claire down a long hallway to a spacious room with mirrors and booths lining the walls.

"This is where you will get ready. You have half an hour to finalize, and I will come and get you when we are ready," Claire said.

Then, they were alone. 20 models, a hair and make-up artist, Benjamin, and Bonita all stood nervously in silence for a moment. It was as if time stood still momentarily as everyone caught their breath and tried to calm down. Bonita instructed them to get dressed and finish the final touches on their hair and make-up. She went to a nearby chair, sat down, and tried to breathe. She was beginning to panic, she was starting to sweat, and her nerves were out of control.

Benjamin noticed and quickly finished dressing and made his way over to her. He knelt in front of her and took both hands in his. "Everything is going to be okay! You are going to go in there, and they will love your designs, and more importantly, they will love you." She looked at him and wanted to believe him, and suddenly her mind caught something else. There he was, this handsome, kind, incredible man knelt down before her wearing the very outfit she picked out for him. "God, you look fantastic," she said.

"You think?" As he stood up and turned around. She grabbed and squeezed his butt while he was turning. "Hey now, you're my boss, and that's sexual harassment. You need to keep your hands to yourself, lady." He was trying too hard to keep a straight face.

"You're lucky you're cute, or you'd be out of here. I'll tell my boyfriend you were making trouble, and he will kick your ass." Bonita said coyishly.

"Oh yeah, your boyfriend? What's he like?" Benjamin asked.

"He's six feet, 9 inches tall, he's a biker, and his name is Billay, bobbbob." Bonita began to laugh. Her description was too funny. Benjamin pulled her from the chair, wrapped his arms around her, and said, "You got it all wrong, little lady; I would destroy Billay bobbbob." He leaned in and kissed her while both of them were giggling.

When they checked the time, there were less than three minutes remaining. They both straightened up their clothes, and the models were nearly done getting dressed, and then, finally, Bonita addressed them all.

"None of you will ever know how much I appreciate you doing this for me! I cannot articulate the gratitude I feel in my heart toward all of you. It doesn't matter if they pick up my line. What matters is that we tried! We saw something and went after it; that is what is most important at the end of the day. If it isn't today, it will be someday, and we should never give up, no matter how hard it can be to push through. I know about obstacles and the hard reality of life; I have lived it over the last few weeks. Thank you all for being a part of this day with me, and I'd like us all to go out after and celebrate, no matter the outcome."

Everyone in the room looked at her with adoring eyes. They saw a woman who had gone through so much but could maintain a positive outlook on life. It was something they all respected. With that, a gentle knock and Claire was in the room.

"It's time," she said to Bonita with a smile.

Benjamin grabbed her hand and kissed her. "Knock 'em dead, honey."

104

She followed Claire into the next room, where she sat with six other people at a table. A man stood as she entered and introduced himself as Charles Preston, the head purchaser for Mackie's. He was refined, with grey in his hair and a pashmina around his neck. They spoke briefly about what they were looking for in a new line and asked her a barrage of questions. Then, it was time to bring in the models. They all swiveled their chairs around, and Claire opened a sliding door to the other room and peeked her head around. With that, Benjamin Ryder walked into the room, eyes pointed forward; he sauntered through the run mat and out the other side. She looked after him, almost missing the other men and the women entering the room. They all walked professionally and hit the minimal poses she gave. The show went on for nearly 40 minutes, as Charles would often ask the models to stop so he could examine each garment closely. He would ask them to pivot, turn, bend over, squat, and lean. Bonita figured he was checking for wearability and how each garment would fall or flow with different movements.

The last model had walked back through the sliding doors,

which were shut. They were instructed to go to the bus and wait until Bonita finished her meeting. She studied the looks on each person's face as the models entered the room. There were no looks of disgust, so that alone made her very happy. She was waiting for someone to speak, but the room was quiet. Charles had his finger pressed against his chin and stared off in thought. She didn't know proper etiquette, so she stayed silent and let him think.

A few moments later, he removed his finger from his chin, folded his hands on the desk, and looked at Claire.

"You were right, Claire. She is brilliant," he said as he glanced from Claire to Bonita. "I love the marriage between the country and urban fabrics. It's fresh, fun, and completely wearable."

"I think we found our new line, ladies and gentlemen," he said with a smile. Bonita mentally stepped out of the room and excitedly screamed her head off. Her face showed how thrilled she was about Charles's statement. His following comment brought her back to reality.

"What will be the name of your new Mackie's line, Miss Smith?"

She thought for a few moments, she thought about the last two-and-a-half years and couldn't help but feel deep in her gut that it had to be something sentimental, something that would mean more to her than anyone in this room, and then gracefully responded, "Bon Bon, Sir! The line's name will be 'Bon Bon.'"

He clapped and shouted, "I love it; it's like fabric fashion candy." Everyone in the room chuckled a little.

"We would like a spring launch, Bonita," said another person at the table. "Is that possible?"

"Spring is only a few months away!" Bonita exclaimed. "I don't even have a manufacturer yet!"

"Well, how about a June launch? Let's make it a summer launch, and let's have the launch on June 21st, the first day of summer," said the lady at the end of the table.

"And I think I can help with the manufacturer, Bonita. My slimy ex-husband owns some textile manufacturers in Florida and Mexico. I will tell him that he has to make your clothing for you, or I'll go after the house in Spain!" Claire laughed maniacally, and the entire table broke out in laughter.

Bonita sat at the table for another half an hour while they worked out all the details and, most importantly, the financials. Because she was a new designer, they gave her a developmental deal that meant she would make less money than an established designer right off the cuff. Still, they would front her the capital required to get the line going and up to spec. The amount of each item she'd need in different sizes was astronomical. They also told her the developmental deal was only for her country/urban line. However, now that she would be a listed designer for Mackie's, it meant that any collection she created going forward would receive exclusive consideration, and, in turn, she was told that whatever she made going forth would be sold at Mackie's around the world.

She shook everyone's hand, picked up her first check at reception, and approached the elevator. Once inside, she was alone and able to react accordingly. She jumped, screamed, and laughed aloud; she had done it. She was now a professional designer with a development contract with Mackie's. How did this happen? How was this possible? She exited the elevator and practically ran through the front doors of the building. The bus was still parked on the corner, and the doors opened as she neared. She ran up inside and started screaming!

"They loved it! My entire collection and possibly all my future collections will be sold at Mackie's! Oh my God!" She could hardly contain herself and turned to everyone on the bus. "Dinner and drinks on me, everybody."

Benjamin pressed up against her, wrapped his arm around the small of her back, and pulled her in tight against his body.

"See, beautiful? I knew you could do it," he said as he kissed her lips.

She touched his face and looked deeply into his eyes. "I think I'm falling in love with you, Benjamin, and that may scare you, but for the first time in my life, I'm not terrified about something."

He smiled and kissed her again. "I'm not terrified, either," as he took her hand and sat her beside him. The bus rolled away, and the celebration began. The night was beautiful, but something was missing, and even when it was all over, she still couldn't finish celebrating until she found it.

Late that night, she told Benjamin she would be away most of the following day. There was something she had to do, and she couldn't put it off any longer.

105

Claude was sitting on his couch, flipping through a magazine he picked up at the stand outside his apartment. It was 10:30 am, and he was off. It was the third Friday of the month, and he was always off because he typically worked most weekends. This would soon change, and he felt giddy about his future. The only thing missing was the one person he wanted to share it with. He had been unsuccessful in tracking Bonita down despite reaching out to everyone under the sun. He knew he messed up, another notch on his perpetual board of screw-ups. He knew his heart was in the right place when he spoke to those girls, but how could he be so stupid to trust them? Because of his stupidity, Bonita's career was thrown down the drain. He lost her, rightfully so, in his life people didn't stay around for too long. It was a pattern he was beginning to understand pointed to him.

He looked around his apartment; he had still not adjusted to living alone again. It was always quiet, too quiet. It was unnerving. When Bonita moved in, it took an adjustment. Still, her energy, laugh, and determination was infectious and filled the apartment with life. Her energy was there even when she was eyeball-deep in schoolwork and nonresponsive. He didn't know where she was; if she was back in the city. He didn't dare try calling her parents again after their last exchange. He felt the universe had his heart in a vice grip and wouldn't let go until he could see or speak to her. He felt the loss strongly, like a part of him was torn away, and more than ever before, he felt alone.

He was sipping coffee and chilling out, hoping for much-needed relaxation, when he heard a knock at the door.

"Who in the world could that be? It's not even lunch yet." He said.

He got up from the couch and made his way to the door. He opened it to the last person he had expected to see: Bonita. She stood there with a bouquet of flowers and a giant balloon, saying, "I'm Sorry."

"Oh my god!" he said as he lunged at her and squeezed her tight. "I have missed you so much. I have missed you so, so much." Bonita hugged him back tighter than she had ever hugged anyone. Tears streaming down his face, a weight lifted from his chest, he held her out and just looked at her face. It was her, it was really her.

Bonita began to cry; she could feel his love in how he looked at her and how those tears fell from his cheek. It was her best friend, whom she hadn't seen for weeks and hadn't spoken to for weeks. They embraced emotionally for quite some time, and neither was in a hurry to let the other go. They both thought they had lost each other forever. Finally, they both relinquished their grips, and Claude motioned for her to enter as he wiped his face with the back of his hand.

"Bonita, I'm so sorry. I had no idea that they were going

to do that to you. I honestly thought it was a good surprise!" he pleaded.

"It's okay, Claude. I know you didn't do anything to intentionally hurt me, and Dean Lalonde told me you stopped by the school to convince him to let me back in. I was wrong to think you would do something like that, so I'm sorry! Please forgive me?"

Claude didn't hesitate and hugged her again. "You are already forgiven, Bon Bon; my sweet, sweet Bon Bon, I thought I really fucking lost you and it hurt so much. I would do anything to go back and turn those girls away that day. I will never, ever, ever trust anyone with anything besides you again. I've ruined your life, your dreams, your work. I can never forgive myself for that. I am just so sorry! I want to make it up to you."

"Claude, I forgive you, it is not your fault. What those girls did was cruel, but you know the worst part?" Bonita asked.

"What," Claude responded.

"The worst part was that they used you and then weaponized you and made me believe that you were in on it. They took you away from me and made me believe you didn't want me here with you anymore. I was foolish to believe that, but I did in the moment. Losing you was the worst part of all of it because I didn't have my best friend to come home to." She explained through tears, and they embraced each other again.

"let's forget about all this between us and be best friends again. Can we do that?" Claude asked.

"Please," Bonita responded, looking up at his tear-stained face.

They sat together on his couch and began to talk. For hours, they talked about everything that happened over the last few weeks. Bonita started from the top. She told him of the night of the fashion show that when they said he was involved, she listened to his voicemail, which sounded callous and cold. How she flew home to Newfoundland and visited her parents for a few days, and how her father had given her a much-needed motivational speech that got her back to New York City. She told him about her apartment and how she had it all decorated. She invited him over for dinner the following day. Bonita continued with how she received the email from Dean Lalonde, went to see him, and how he reinstated her. Then, he informed her that the four involved were stripped of their academic standing.

Then she went on to tell him about Benjamin, and he mentioned he remembered him from previous conversations. She told him he was the one who overheard the three girls talking and brought the information to the faculty. She spoke about how Benjamin had convinced her to go with him to his apartment. Then, she found a room with mannequins throughout with her complete collection. As it turned out, they both had a crush on each other the entire time, which was why he picked on her so much. Then she told him of her first sexual encounter and loved that she could be so candid with him. She talked about how Benjamin treated her and how he made her feel. Claude teased that it sounded a little like a brewing romance. They talked a little more about the last couple of weeks, and then she made a fuss and told him that she hadn't even given him the best part.

She went off about her interview at the small boutique

on the Upper East Side and how the owner was a complete asshole. Then she told him how she bumped into the same woman who helped her when she broke her arm. They both agreed the chances of that happening in New York City were slim, if not impossible, and that it must be fate. Then she told him who she was. He nearly fell off the couch when she told him they had a meeting and a small show in their conference room. They picked up her line, and she now holds a development contract with the biggest high-end department store in the world. Her launch will be on the 21st of this coming June.

He jumped up from the couch and started jumping up and down and screaming. "My best friend is a major fashion designer. Yeah, baby!" He then ran to the kitchen and grabbed the bottle of wine he had purchased on the day of the school fashion show. He poured two glasses, and they sat and laughed together, making up all kinds of weird scenarios about when she was wealthy and successful.

He had huge news to tell her, nearly as big as hers. It turned out that the shoot he did the make-up for was actually for Runway magazine. They loved his work and had an opening for a seasoned make-up artist at the firm. They contacted him just last week and offered him a senior position with a six-figure salary. He would be their head make-up artist and have the opportunity to write small editorials on products and applications. He, of course, took the position and was set to start there in less then a week. Bonita was beside herself with excitement; not only did she make it, but her best friend also made it. This was the most incredible opportunity for him, a high-paying position with a prestigious magazine about fashion.

It was the perfect day. All was right in the world. She had her best friend back, was allowed back in school, landed a dream deal with Mackie's, and fell in love with a fantastic man. There was nothing more in this world she could imagine she wanted, never mind needed. She kissed Claude good-night, left his apartment, and went home to a man who was patiently waiting for her at her place. When she walked in, he whisked her off her feet and brought her to the bedroom, where they made love until the sun came up.

106

Bonita had a lot of work ahead of her. In her typical style, she put her head down and began working meticulously on every detail. Her mind was reeling from the opportunity, and while she was committed to making it perfect, the reality of her redemption hadn't quite hit her.

Benjamin and Claude had finally met when he came by Bonita's apartment for dinner the Sunday prior. They instantaneously hit it off. She watched them talk about their work, life, and aspirations, which seemed natural. Claude was enthralled with Benjamin's take on the fashion industry; while it wasn't a positive one, Benjamin understood the necessity of it, how it worked, and how to play amongst the fakes and the posers. He believed the fashion industry needed to be less about body image and more about inclusiveness. Everyone should be able to walk into a high-end store and find designer names that fit them. This was something that Bonita loved about Benjamin; he just didn't care for the exclusive nature of the industry.

Benjamin instantly took to Claude because of his down-to-earth charm and practicality. Claude showed vulnerability when he spoke about Bonita, which indicated that their reconciliation meant everything to him. During that visit, Claude shared stories and insights into his life that Bonita didn't even know. About the many times, he sabotaged his own life and happiness, a behavior that formed after his father passed away. Claude felt he had done it again when he lost Bonita. He figured it was part and parcel with how things typically played out for him, and while he accepted it was his own doing, he would never forgive himself for it. A few tears were shed over the situation, and many comments were made about the parties involved in that experience. Ultimately, they got their just desserts and were stripped of their academic standing; they all agreed; however, it wasn't enough.

Bonita felt grateful to have her best friend back and a boyfriend who adored her. Bonita cared for Benjamin; he was something unexpected. He was more than just a handsome guy who was easy on the eyes; he had a quiet confidence about him; he knew what to say, when to say it, and went out of his way to make sure Bonita understood how incredible she was. She had never expected that he would be sensitive, kind, and compassionate when she had a crush on him. At the time, it was simply a physical attraction.

Benjamin felt like he had won at life when it came to Bonita. He knew his career would be okay, and he knew that financially, he was okay, but he never expected Bonita to be all she was. Benjamin liked her for a long time and found her personality amusing and cute, but over the last while, she has shown him a considerable softness, a palpable reciprocation to his adoration, and an all-around genuine beauty far beneath her skin that he didn't know was there. He loved her drive, how she thought, solved problems, and planned ahead. She was neurotic and calm, a storm and a warm, breezy summer day. When he spent time with her, he couldn't help but notice that his heart expanded; he could feel it in his chest. He also noticed that when he was with her, the world stopped. She had a way of bringing his mind and body into the present; he focused on her words, her movements, and her energy. He felt a sense of extreme comfort he couldn't quite articulate. It was as if he was home.

Having felt she had been handed a gift from God himself, Bonita regularly took stock of where she was. She made herself pause daily to practice gratitude and be in the moment. Often, it was when Benjamin was distracted or getting ready for school. He made her heart flutter, visceral, authentic, and often overwhelming. It made her want to collapse in his arms and burrow into his chest and stay there. She often thought about Claude and how they found each other despite the external forces trying to split them apart. Now, it felt like they didn't lose time, but they had, and there were remnants of that loss forever scarred on each of their hearts.

As a severe planner, she took the time to carve out the next 5 months. Bonita knew she was lucky and thanked God daily for this opportunity. She also knew that to ensure the perfect launch, she needed to be hyper-organized and have a system in place to routinely check all deliverables and another system to check those. There would be no way that Bonita would miss something when it came to this launch, and there were a lot of elements that needed proper planning and ironing out. So, Bonita got to work with a structured and highly tight planner. One area she decided needed to be accounted for was the time she had to spend with Benjamin and Claude and simply having a little fun.

107

As the following months began to roll by, Bonita was faithful to her plan; everything was scheduled and documented. Before putting her hair in a pony and pulling up her sleeves, she had a night out with Benjamin and Claude for drinks and fun. She pulled out her schedule in true Bonita fashion and presented it to the guys. She told them that the next 5 months would be hectic but that she wanted to prioritize both as much as possible. Benjamin and Claude were onboard; they had already surrendered to the fact that the next five months would be Bonita in the zone. Which meant that interactions would be limited and time would be stolen in passing. They were pleasantly surprised to see that Bonita had made regular room for both of them and fun.

One of the very first details that needed to be dealt with and ironed out was her designs. Bonita had the sketches and garments, but she needed the patterns. Claire had hooked her up with a reputable and efficient patternmaker specializing in tech-packs. This was one critical step out of the five critical steps of pre-production. Bonita was about to learn the steps of garment manufacturing inside and out. Before this,

Bonita was mulling over a few ideas and began thinking that her line needed to be more robust. She scheduled a meeting with Charles and Claire and asked if she could expand the line by sixty items. She aimed to add another fifteen items to the men's line and forty-five to the women's. Bonita wanted to produce a line that had enough items a person could mix and match for a solid month. Remembering that her line also consisted of ball gowns, which Charles considered a high-ticket item, she wanted to create more options in the casual dressy part of her line. It didn't take too much convincing, and Charles was on board. Bonita got to work immediately and, within three weeks, sent over the additional pieces to the team for review and approval. It was almost immediate.

The next stop was cost accounting. Bonita didn't like this component much; it was a lot of math and many variables she didn't think of. When pricing each item, every plausible factor had to come into play. Raw materials, what were the fabrics she intended to use, where would they be sourced, how would her designs be packaged, shipped and what were the labor and operating costs. These were meetings that made her head feel like it would explode. The nitty-gritty of bringing a product to market she hadn't thought of and was ever grateful she wasn't trying to do this alone; she would have been lost.

Then, it was off to the patternmaker and tech-pack design. She met this gentleman in a lofty office in the fashion district. Every item in her line was put on a mannequin, and the work began. First, the initial pattern in the current size had to be produced, and then the tech-pack for each design had to be made. This is where it got very technical, and while Bonita loved every minute of it, she was beginning to find a deeper appreciation for what went into every piece of clothing she had ever worn. The tech-pack was a set of documents to be sent to a manufacturer who could follow the information and turn it into a finished garment. It's a blueprint of a final garment that includes detailed flat sketches of the design, materials to be used like trims and labels, measurement specs, size gradings, colorways, and so much more. The gentleman told her that when he started, this had to be done by hand; now they had CAD software that took a lot of the manual process out. This surprised Bonita as it still looked very manual and tedious, so the thought that it was worse than this when he started made her head spin.

Once this was done, Bonita had a meeting to decide all the sourcing details. Mackie's had a great reputation and excellent affiliations, so sourcing the raw materials needed to make this happen was a relatively easy choice. What was the most cumbersome was checking and negotiating bulk fabric prices. Who had the lowest prices? How low could they go? Claire was the type of woman who could get what she wanted from everyone, and she did it in such a way that it was kind and genuine. Included in this meeting was a design artist who worked with Bonita to ensure her insignia, logo, and brand were finalized, as the labels needed to be produced and sent to manufacturing.

Manufacturing was the next step in this adventure. Bonita met with Claire every other day, who had threatened her ex that if he didn't prioritize Bonita, she would go after the house in Spain. Bonita found this amusing and wondered what was so special about the place in Spain. Luckily,

Claire's ex-husband was on board and assigned her a slot in his Mexico plant. Claire and Bonita flew to Mexico and spent two solid weeks coordinating with the manufacturers. They went through the proto-sampling, fit sampling, pre-production, and gold seal sampling, shipment samples, fabric inspection, spreading, form layout and cutting, embroidery, screen printing, and embellishments, sewing, testing, stitches per inch checks, material composition checks, quality, defects and severity reporting and lastly, packaging. They decided on a CIF, Cost, Insurance, and freight shipping agreement. They clued up their two weeks in Mexico celebrating at a fancy dinner and margaritas.

108

When Bonita returned to New York City, she took a few days off to spend with Benjamin. While she was away, they talked numerous times a day and always said good night before going to bed. Her time away, while hectic and spent covering every possible detail of the manufacturing process, she realized her heart ached for Benjamin. It became apparent to her that she had fallen in love. It was different than she had imagined, and she was careful to ensure it wasn't the high or speed in which her life was moving that made her feel that way.

Bonita knew that the excitement and good fortune played their part, but she found herself often moving beyond all of it when thinking and imagining life with Benjamin after the launch had happened. She fell into daydreams of moving in together; the obvious choice would be his loft as he owned it. Bonita thought about what the future would be like together, what he would be like as a husband, as a father, and as her aging partner. Whatever she imagined, the good and the bad, felt equally right. Bonita had concluded that this life she would live, she wanted to live it with Benjamin. She knew it was still too early to tell for sure, but she knew in her heart that what she had with him she wanted to keep, grow, and nurture.

Benjamin had missed Bonita terribly when she was away. Bonita had this energy that made him feel grounded and in the moment. A look that made his heart stutter and his stomach knot. It was a lot of intense feelings he hadn't had before. As he was close to his mother, he went to spend a day with her. He told his mom of his feelings; she couldn't help but smile the whole time. After he finished unpacking all of his emotions, his mother looked at him and said, "Oh Benji, you're in love! Bonita has stolen your heart, and you are in love with her. She is a wonderful person from everything you have told me, and I think you need to embrace that love instead of trying to explain it away. It reminds me of when I met your father; I knew quickly that he was the one I wanted to spend my life with. We took our time, but if he had asked 6 months after meeting me, I would have said yes to marriage. It was one of the best things I ever did for myself, and I have a lifetime of happy memories, you, and a growing love because I met your dad."

Benjamin left his mom's house knowing she was right; he was in love. He loved Bonita Smith but feared she didn't feel the same way. He struggled to balance his heart and mind, the feeling she felt the same way and the fear she didn't. When she returned from Mexico, he embraced her as soon as she entered the door. They made love and cuddled for hours as he listened to her explain the last two weeks from start to finish. Most of it he had heard before, but he didn't care, watching her get excited about all the details, the way she would pause in the middle of a sentence and make sure she had done everything needed about that item, reassuring herself she hadn't forgotten anything, it was the most perfect way to spend the afternoon.

Bonita, Benjamin, and Claude went to dinner and caught up the following day. Bonita once again recalled every detail as Benjamin sat smiling as she talked. Claude listened intently and was amazed by every piece of information, data, or thought required to go into each design beyond the design itself. They laughed, ate, and drank until they all returned to Bonita's apartment to do it again.

109

The following few months flew by at rapid speed, and Bonita found herself working day and night; she spent her days planning the logistics of the launch, stressing over every detail. She maintained constant contact with the manufacturing company, ensuring no hiccups, issues, or delays. Bonita was on the phone with Claire daily, double-checking that everything was at Mackie's level and liking. Although Claire didn't know the first thing about designing fashion, she knew a lot about fashion. She had been in the business for years and didn't just wake up one day as a chair of the board of directors for Mackie's. Bonita found it increasingly difficult to sleep the closer the launch date became. Benjamin and Claude put in extra duty to keep her calm and offer assistance.

Although her days were filled with work, she was never alone in the process between her beau and her best friend. They were always by her side every step of the way. In fact, they were all quite inseparable. Claude would be with her on his time off from the magazine, and Benjamin would be with her between and after classes.

Her focus had zeroed in on launch day, and it would be

extraordinary. Charles and Claire had advised her that they would throw a Gala for her launch and invite several notable guests to view the unfolding. Now that Bonita had a 100-item line, one of the most robust Charles and Claire had seen for a first launch, they thought it fitting to make it an occasion. They were happy with the added items and had a few ideas about location in their flagship store and window designs.

Knowing that her launch would now be an event and she could invite whomever she wanted, Bonita began to think specifically about who she wanted to attend. It was obvious that Benjamin and Claude would be there, but who else did she want to be present for the unveiling. It didn't take her more than a breath to realize that there were two people, more so than anyone else, she wanted to be in attendance on her launch day. She immediately picked up the phone, dialed a 709 number, and waited for someone to answer. It was her father and, shortly after, her mother on the other end. Bonita had kept her promise and had been checking in regularly; they were thrilled about the events that set her on a track for success. On the call, she told them the news that her launch would be more than just a launch but a gala where she could invite whomever she wanted. Bonita told them it would mean the world to her if they could come, and she would take care of everything; all they had to do was get their passports. They agreed without hesitation, and her mother was beside herself because she would go to New York City to see her daughter's fashion launch.

Bonita picked up Claire's elegant and classy launch invitations and began sending them out the following week. Bonita sent one to her family, Claude and Benjamin. They had previously been invited, but she also wanted them to have the physical invite. Then she wrote a note and posted an invite to Ivana Cox. She couldn't imagine launching this line without having Ivana in attendance, especially since Ivana was her first-ever fashion client. Even more so, Ivana had been pivotal in helping Bonita reframe her experience with the school fashion show debacle and putting herself out there. Then she wrote another note, placed it with the invitation, and posted it to Dean Lalonde.

Bonita would never forget the seething anger from that man on the night she thought her world had ended. It was a level of attack she had never experienced and it was emblazoned in her mind. However, she spent a great deal of time making peace with it; after all, Dean Lalonde is just a human being like anyone else. While he overreacted, misdirected his anger toward her, and didn't allow her to defend herself, sometimes this happens. Was she to hold Dead to an unachievable and unattainable level of infallibility? She took a great deal of time to process the event down to bite-sized pieces, the actions of those who hurt her, the faculty's actions, and her own. Bonita journaled and practiced the techniques that Ivana had taught her until she could look at that event and remain neutral.

It was an event, one she will never forget, one that caused her a great deal of pain and personal grief, but it was also one that opened an opportunity for Benjamin to show his true self, for Dean Lalonde to apologize, one that afforded Bonita a deep perspective on what she took for granted and what she now knew she wanted to prioritize. An event that pushed her into a realm of discomfort and sorrow that led her to bump into Claire Foster. The event still happened; nothing changed except how Bonita began to view it. It was no longer the worst thing ever but a thing that opened her to elements she may never have known. Bonita was a long way from viewing it as a positive thing. Still, she was doing the work, being kind to herself, and practicing forgiveness, not for anyone else but for herself.

110

The show was only two weeks away, and everything was done. The final shipment of garments had left from Mexico and would arrive in a few days to be checked and merchandised. Mackie's had dedicated an entire alcove for Bon Bon the collection on their fifth floor, and two of their world-famous window displays were in the midst of being created specifically for her line. They had mapped out a space just outside the alcove for the gala and the models to walk through, showing off her line. They had hired a DJ to handle the music. Bonita spent several hours talking with her to finalize the songs, style, and essence she wanted to convey. It was strategically arranged to provide an immersive experience in all things Bon Bon. A contracted caterer would provide the guests with champagne, coffee, tea, hors d'oeuvres, pastries, and her favorite, macaroons. The waitstaff would wear royal blue shirts with gold embellishments. It would be a savvy gala thrown in her honor.

The invites had been received and RVSP'd.

Her mother and father had successfully gotten their passports and were thrilled; her mom admitted she always wanted to visit Mackie's. Her father was as proud as anyone could be of his daughter's success, a success she might have thrown away if she hadn't gone back to pursue her dreams. They spent a lot of time talking to the church folk about their upcoming trip to the big city, and her mom took every chance she could get to tell the ladies at the store.

Bonita had an outfit picked out for her dad and a beautiful dress she designed for her mother. She was so excited that they would be there to see what the last three years in New York City were all about. Finally, they would meet Claude, her best friend, and her boyfriend, Benjamin, the man of her dreams. Bonita's parents knew now that Claude had nothing to do with what happened at the school fashion show, and Bonita was lied to by the girls. Her father, a man of integrity and humility, called Claude after finding out and apologized for reacting like he did. Claude didn't feel it was necessary but appreciated it, nonetheless. Her parents also knew about Benjamin; although they didn't know him well, they talked to him a few times on the phone. Her father and mother agreed that he sounded like a lovely young man.

Everything was set. There was nothing else left to do.

"Oh, wait," she thought as she put her finger to her chin. She wanted to do one thing but would need some help with it. She went to see Dean Lalonde and told her what she wanted, and although it went against school policy, he found it impossible to say no to her after what she had been through. Once she got what she wanted, she took a stroll to the Upper East Side to visit Claire Foster and fill her in on her plan. It didn't take any convincing to have her on board, and before Bonita knew it, her plan was in motion.

"Now, everything is set," she thought as she whistled a little tune down Fifth Avenue.

111

The launch day had arrived, and Bonita and her parents had breakfast in her apartment. She considered putting them in a hotel for their stay but wanted to always be close to them. New York City was intimidating; she wanted her parents to stay calm if they decided to venture out independently. Besides, this was Bonita's big moment; she needed them there for support and prayers.

Out of respect, Benjamin hadn't spent the night since they arrived. Although Bonita was a grown woman now, she still thought that having Benjamin spend the night might make her parents uncomfortable. This trip was as much about them as it was about her, so she wanted them to have the experience of a lifetime with zero discomfort.

Bonita had taken her mom to a salon the previous day to give her a fresh look. Her mother couldn't stop staring at herself in the mirror. She had never seen herself look quite so good before in her life. As a pastor's wife, it was considered carnal to dye your hair and wear makeup, but she was in the big city now, and Bonita thought she needed a little pampering. She had a day at the spa planned for her, the same spa

Claude took her to a couple years back, and she was pulling out all the stops. Well, not all the stops — there are services her mother would be mortified if she were submitted to. She wanted her mother to have a manicure, pedicure, facial, and full-body massage. When they left the spa, her mother was floating around like she was a movie star.

Her parents had met Benjamin, and her father spent the morning with him, taking in some sights. They got along quite well, and her father approved of their relationship, which meant a lot for Benjamin. Her parents also met Claude. Her father thought he was a charming young man. However, he still didn't understand that he liked other men and was a little uncomfortable but civil and at ease most of the time. Claude was a good guy, and her dad respected that; he also appreciated the level of care he gave Bonita during her time in New York City. Bonita's mother, on the other hand, was smitten with Claude. She thought he was very handsome and loved how he made her feel. Like most gay men, he knew how to sweet-talk a woman and sweet-talk he did. He could have gotten her to do just about anything he wanted, within reason.

Bonita and her Mom made their way to Claude's apartment. Her hair was styled at the salon, as was her mother's, and now it was time for the makeup. She would trust no one else in the world with her face on this significant day but Claude. He was waiting patiently for them to arrive and was super excited about getting to do her mother's makeup. He was going to turn her into a starlet.

The day progressed, and it was just approaching 2:30 pm, an hour and a half before the launch of her new line at

Mackie's. She had a lot of perfect days lately, but today took the cake. Claude finished Bonita's and her mother's makeup and then turned her mother around to look in the mirror. She gasped and put her hands to her face.

"Who is this woman I am looking at?"

She couldn't believe how beautiful she looked. She hadn't seen that girl in over thirty years. She kissed Claude on the cheek and grabbed his face. "You are my darling boy, and you made this old woman look young again." He kissed her cheek, hugged her, and told her he did very little and that a carpenter couldn't make something beautiful from imperfect wood. Bonita smiled as she remembered that same line used on her a few years back. She loved him for how he made her mother feel. She had never seen her mother so happy and full of life before, and she couldn't wait until her father got a look at her.

Her father and Benjamin showed up around a half hour later. When her father saw his wife, he did something that would typically make Bonita's stomach sick, but instead, she smiled. He took her hand, grabbed her bottom, and planted a very passionate kiss on her lips.

"Honey, you're making a married woman think naughty thoughts." Her mother giggled, and it was almost like they were newly in love again. What a little hair and makeup could do for a person and their significant others was always fascinating. Benjamin looked at his lady and told her she was beautiful, but Bonita noticed he seemed on edge and nervous. His hands were trembling, and he was acting very shifty.

"Did everything go all right with my Dad?" she asked,

wondering why he was wound up. She was the one that was supposed to be a stress case.

"Yes, of course, everything went great," he responded. Bonita would have pried a little more, but it was time — time for them to leave and make their way to Mackie's department store. So, off they went, down the elevator and out the front, where a black stretch limousine was waiting. The driver was holding a placard with her name on it. She gave Benjamin a look, and he said, "It wasn't me."

As she approached the limousine, the driver said, "Compliments of Ms. Claire Foster, Madam Smith," as he opened the door for them to get in. As she climbed in after everyone else, she thought, "A star. That's what I feel like, a star."

The place was packed with people everywhere, typical for Mackie's, except they had a large section cordoned off for her launch party. She recognized many people there that day, some huge names in fashion who were present the night of the school fashion show. The unveiling was top secret; no one knew who this new designer was that got signed by Mackie's, but apparently, many people wanted to find out. Claire Foster made her way through the crowd over to Bonita to stand with her during the big unveiling. Then, out of the corner of her eye, she saw three very familiar faces standing off toward the wall. Cassidy, Lyla, and Bethany all stood there, looking uncomfortable with each other. "I guess they hadn't stayed in touch since they were kicked out of school," Bonita thought. They hadn't seen her yet, and she wanted to keep it that way for now but was very happy that her special invitations made it to them on time and that they showed up.

A refined and distinguished man took to the top of the

room, where he cleared his throat to get everyone's attention. Then, off in the distance, she could see a familiar man standing with a glass of champagne: Dean LaLonde.

"Ladies and gentlemen, thank you all for coming here today to bear witness to our latest collection offered internationally at all our stores. It brings me great pleasure to introduce to you the Bon Bon collection by Bonita Smith," Charles said as he pointed out into the crowd in Bonita's direction. "Without further ado, here it is."

The curtains to her alcove were dropped, and models wearing her line began to walk out into the crowd. There were a lot of different noises and looks happening within the room. People heard her name and gasped. Then, more gasping once they saw the models walk out with beautifully pieced-together ensembles designed by the girl who had smocks of animal skin making a statement at her school fashion show. Her mother, father, best friend, and boyfriend were all cheering, and many others were clapping. She looked in the direction of the three girls she had sent the invitations to, and the looks on their faces were revenge enough for what they did to her. Cassidy was shocked and angry, Bethany mortified, and Lyla cried. Everything was just as it should be. Bonita toyed with the idea of approaching them but felt the invite and shock were harsh enough. Bonita wanted the last laugh, but as much as they hurt her, she didn't hate them; she pitied them. Bonita would never understand their actions but realized it didn't matter anymore; she was at the beginning of her career with a gala thrown in her honor. Bonita felt a squeeze on her arm and looked to see, Marcus Hannigan standing next to her. He leaned in and gave her a kiss on the cheek and said, "Look what we have here, redefined success. Girl, I knew you wouldn't be held down for long."

The launch was a success. Everyone in attendance seemed to love the line; a lot of congratulations and confusion approached Bonita that day. Instead of telling them she was sabotaged, she simply said, "It was a completely avoidable mistake if I had just been more careful." The window displays outside were incredible and awe-inspiring. The artists who styled them captured the very essence of her designs, and it was surreal. Bonita posed for many pictures that day, on her own in front of her line, in front of the window display, and with a barrage of guests and her friends and family.

Benjamin was trying to be present, but he couldn't help but feel sick to his stomach; he couldn't do this; he shouldn't do this; this was her day, and he couldn't ruin it for her. He had been planning this for months, but now that it was here, he couldn't go through with it. Benjamin couldn't watch her fall apart again, not on her day. This whole thing had been such a gamble that he felt like he was on the losing end; how could he have been so foolish to take cues from someone he wasn't sure he could trust.

Claude and Bonita were perusing the room when they happened to stroll upon Cassidy, Lyla, and Bethany, who were still there, much to Bonita's surprise; she assumed it was to save face. Bonita decided to continue walking; however, Claude had other plans.

"It's so good to see you have landed on your feet, girls, but it's too early to pick up the trash. You should head in the back and wait till you're called." He tilted his head ever so slightly and just stared at them as if to say why are you still standing there? Go do your jobs.

"We don't work here asshole, we were invited," Cassidy said.

Lyla mumbled, "Although we are not sure by who."

Bonita, wrestling with her scruples, finally gave in and turned around.

"Good day, girls," Bonita said with the fakest smile she could muster. "It looks as though you got my special invitations."

Cassidy shot her a dirty look and went to say something, but Bonita cut her off.

"I wanted you here today to thank you in person. Thank you for sabotaging my line at the fashion show. You see, if you girls weren't as jealous and insecure about your lines, you may not have done what you did, and that would just be awful. If it wasn't for you, I wouldn't have had the chance to fall in love with an incredible man, I wouldn't have forever solidified my trust and bond with my best friend, and I would never have had the spite and the drive to get out there and reclaim what's mine. This day, this entire collection, wouldn't have been possible without the three of you. So, to that, I say thank you." With a curtsey, she smiled at them one last time and nodded, "Good day!"

She turned on her heels and led Claude away. Benjamin had been close by and heard everything Bonita had said. His fear turned to resolve instantaneously; it was now or never. He walked up to Claude and nudged him. Then Bonita saw Benjamin look at Claude, and Claude gave Benjamin a nod.

"What in the world?" she thought as Benjamin grabbed her arm and pulled her to the middle of the room.

She looked at him with confused eyes. "What are you doing?" she asked as he looked around to get people's attention. When the room quieted slightly, he turned back to Bonita and looked deep into her eyes.

"I know this is the most important day of your life, and it has been perfect. It has been perfect for me, too! You see, selfishly, I want today to be one of my life's most important and perfect days, but what I have realized over the last five months is that every day with you is the perfect day."

She was turning red because now all eyes were on her and Benjamin, and he was acting very strange. However, the words he was saying to her were words she had only dreamt of hearing.

"I know that this may seem like I am rushing things, and you have the right to feel that way, but in life, when you feel you know something, you truly know something, you've got to go with it. I know that I am in love with you, Bonita Smith. I know that I wake up every day and think of how lucky I am to have your heart. Now, I'm wondering if I could have your hand?"

Bonita was confused. "What?" she said as Benjamin took her hand and got down on one knee. He pulled a little blue box from his back pocket and snapped it open. Before her was the most beautiful diamond ring she had ever seen.

"Oh," she said as she lifted her hands to her mouth.

"Bonita Smith, will you be my wife?" Benjamin asked, as he trembled and could feel the heat rolling off his face.

The entire room was silent; everyone looked at the two of them and waited to hear what Bonita would say.

Bonita was in shock; her mind began to race, and her logic tried overtaking her. It was fast, but it did feel right. "This is why he was so on edge this morning. How long has he known? How long have I known? Decide, Bonita, decide, say something," she thought to herself. "You want this; you know you want this! He is your dream."

"Yes. Yes, I will be your wife." she collapsed into his arms. He kissed her in the middle of the floor with many onlookers clapping and celebrating. He slid the ring on her finger, jumped up, and lifted her off her feet into the air. The crowd was roaring, pictures snapping, and her Mom and Claude were crying hysterically. After he laid her down on the floor, she turned towards her father, and with his simple nod, she knew that all was right in the world.

It has been a long couple of years for Bonita. Still, in the end, she overcame every obstacle, from the speech at graduation, the move to New York City, the intense academics, and the restoration of her name. She had set out on this journey a young, awkward, rough-around-the-edges girl. She grew into a poised, beautiful, talented, and elegant woman. In three short years, she achieved her goals despite all odds and landed on top with grace and dignity. She shared a great love with her parents, best friend, and fiancé, a love that filled each day of her life with warmth and inner worth, a love that no one or thing could ever influence. It was rock solid.

Epilogue

March 30th, 2024.

Bonita Ryder

It has been nearly twenty years since Bonita Ryder left high school and ventured to New York City. As she walks out of a bookstore on Fifth Avenue, she checks her phone, tucks a book underneath her shoulder, and walks south toward the Financial District. She is going to meet her best friend, Claude, for lunch.

The last twenty years have been quite the journey for her, not turning out exactly as she once imagined. Her line with Mackie's was a catalyst in shaping her life. She learned that being a designer isn't as glamorous as it sounds but can afford a comfortable life doing what you love.

For the first five years, she worked with Mackie's as a designer and went from a development to an exclusive contract. The contract meant that aside from very specific conditions, Mackie's was the only store with exclusive access to Bon Bon.

It took several years for Bon Bon to earn a spot in the world's fashion shows. While she has enjoyed great success and fortune in doing what she does best, she realized she would never embody her favorite designer, Viviene Westwood. Viviene has something no one else has: an innate ability to make art. Bon Bon was fashion, and VW is art!

Bonita became quite comfortable holding her own on the world's runways and has since enjoyed opening and crafting seven flagship stores around the globe. She has dressed celebrities and models, and her work has been featured in every magazine. She is a success!

If you ask Bonita, that isn't her most significant accomplishment. She would tell you that while, yes, achieving what she set out to achieve has been amazing, it is not something she takes lightly. However, Bonita would tell you that her most amazing accomplishments were not made with scissors, pins, and a sewing machine—her most amazing accomplishments were the relationships she has built and surrounded herself with.

At 37, she is happily married to a man who makes her feel as if she hasn't aged a day, who loves her deeply and laughs at all her silly jokes. This man and the marriage they built were the accomplishments that underpinned everything she had done in her life since meeting him. Their shared children, Tyler, 14, Eloise, 9, and Claude Jr, 6, were the delicate threads that wove through their lives, creating a tapestry of happiness and joy.

When Benjamin had finished school and Bonita had a steady, sustainable income, they decided to move out of Manhattan and find a quiet suburb on Staten Island. They purchased a house and still live there to this day.

Claude Peters

Leaving his apartment and heading towards the financial district to have lunch with Bonita, Claude loved feeling the sun's warmth on his skin. It has been a long, cold winter, and he and his partner chose to stay in the city because of Claude's schedule. Claude married the editor at large at Runway magazine after eight years of shamelessly flirty, sneaking around, and romantic getaways. They started getting friendly the year after Claude joined the magazine. Claude would tell you he didn't see himself as the marrying type, and when he began spending time with his husband, he thought it was just a fun office fling. After fifteen years together, they have settled into life and enjoy their routine.

Claude no longer works for the magazine; he now works freelance as, over the years, he has developed a significant name for himself, doing celebrity faces. His talent gets booked worldwide for the most notable skin you can imagine.

As for Bonita, she is still his best friend, and he spends most of the holidays with her, Benjamin, and his nephews and niece. They have had the most fun imaginable over the last twenty years and countless adventures. He has been able to travel with her, do the make-up for her shows, her magazine shoots, you name it.

He no longer thinks about how he seems to sabotage everything because he hasn't sabotaged anything since Bonita came into his life. Since opening his apartment to a strange, silly girl nearly 20 years ago, his life has been more than he could have ever bargained for, and he wouldn't change one thing.

Lyla Frank

Lyla found it quite challenging to get her life back on track after the debacle at school. While it wasn't advertised, people somehow knew she was involved. A year later, she met her now husband and moved to the Midwest to start a family. It was there that she found God. It was there that she found herself.

In the beginning, her husband worked as an engineer, making decent money; for the first child, Lyla stayed home as the dutiful wife and mother. After a year or two, she started designing again, but her style had changed significantly. Instead of a modern twist on medieval dresses, she focused and honed her skills on creating the most adorable and wearable clothing for babies and children.

Over the years, while she hasn't owned any high fashion runways, she has had her line picked up by the major department stores. She has even seen photos online and in magazines of Bonita with her children and her children wearing her line. One article snippet she cut out was Bonita's comment to a Runway magazine journalist asking about her Kid's style, "Lyla Frank's line is perhaps the most durable clothing I have purchased for my kids. It's comfortable, well crafted, and I am a fan."

Despite everything, this meant the world to Lyla Frank.

Bethany Ludemier

At first, Bethany didn't seem too affected by what happened with the school fashion show. Aside from not completing her education or getting her designs out there, she came from money and was doing alright.

That was until her father got arrested for money laundering, embezzlement, and securities fraud.

The feds froze all their bank accounts and seized all their assets, and Bethany's dad was convicted and sentenced to 18 years in federal prison. While she didn't know about his wrongdoings, the apple didn't fall too far from the tree.

No one would have anything to do with her after that, and her friends and family friends turned their backs on her completely. Her father had swindled millions of dollars away from all of them.

Word around town is that Bethany works at a run-down diner off Canal Street and lives in a studio apartment. Her only companions are the mice and cockroaches that live there with her. Life has been unkind to Bethany, but if you ask her why? She would tell you she has no idea what she did to deserve any of it.

Cassidy Ruthers

Cassidy became a social media influencer and succeeded in doing it. She didn't pursue making fashion, but she did pursue commenting on it. Her style, her bitchy attitude, and her lifestyle made her the one to follow when it came to what's what and who's who.

She received endorsement deals, partnerships, and access to all the latest and best, and for two years, she was the most followed social media influencer on multiple platforms. She was known to poke fun at everyone and anyone; it didn't matter who you were or how significant or insignificant. If you landed in her sights doing something that she deemed ugly, gross, classless, pathetic, stupid, or weird, she would comment on it. Her biggest shtick was making fun of celebrities eating; millions of people followed her to see her reenact and make fun of high-profile people eating. Her most popular reel was making fun of an up-and-coming pop star who had this massive hit on the charts, eating a spaghetti and meatball dinner at a fancy restaurant. It went viral; people couldn't get enough of just how savage she was.

The internet seemed to be split on Cassidy Ruthers; some called her an overrated bully, others praised her for not giving two shits what people thought of her. Due to the nature of her account, it saw a constant turnover of followers. People would follow to see what it was all about but eventually be turned off entirely from her brand. Other people who were devout followers for years, and she ultimately did something they felt went too far. This didn't hurt her numbers; she sat comfortably at seventy-five million followers across two platforms.

She got a lot of free publicity for her antics and was often discussed on talk shows, news broadcasts, magazines, and online blogs. It never mattered in which light the publicity came; she soaked it up and enjoyed every minute.

On July 2nd, 2017, Cassidy Ruthers gave her last and most viral live on social media. She was on vacation with one of her boyfriends at a restaurant in Italy. During her live broadcast, she was sitting on a terrace. As she was telling the world, her boyfriend had just left in a huff over an argument about how he was dressed. She was decked out, full glam, fake tan, looking flawless, and quickly moved to how beautiful Italy was this time of year. She showed the spread of food she and her boyfriend ordered and talked about the oysters. "They are so good; I have never had better oysters in my life," she said as she took one and let it slide from the shell into her mouth.

On July 2nd, 2017, Cassidy Ruthers, a famous influencer, died at a restaurant in Italy while filming a live. She became asphyxiated on an oyster that lodged in her throat. The restaurant staff and onlookers tried everything they could to help. Cassidy was pronounced dead at the scene. Twenty-six million of her faithful followers watched as Cassidy passed away, live, choking on food on social media.

Alexander Pierce

Alexander went on for the next eight years to be one of those most sought-after models in the industry, appearing on covers and walking for the best of the best. In the last two years of his modeling career, he was hit with one of the cruelest diseases life has to offer: genetics.

His hair began to thin, he couldn't keep up his physique so easily, and he required pants and top sizes two to four times his normal. It came to a fever pitch when he arrived for a cover shoot, and the young female photographer refused to shoot him because his body didn't meet the magazine's requirements.

Now, at 46, he spends countless hours at the gym trying to retain some semblance of his former physique and tens of thousands of dollars on hair transplants and liposuction. Turning to alcohol to cope with his misfortune life has taken a toll on his once supple, stunning looks, and he no longer holds the ability to capture the mature sexual nature of women worldwide.

He married and settled down with a woman he knew from college; they have two children. Miraculously overnight, his interest in women changed, and he has since had seven affairs with young women more than half his age. They are enthralled with his knowledge of the modeling industry. He has recently divorced and lives in a trailer on the edge of Huetter, Idaho.

Dean Lalonde

Dean worked for eight years at the fashion school and retired. He decided he had had enough of the city life and moved to Burlington, Vermont. It was the town where he grew up, and it felt fitting to settle down there and enjoy his retirement.

He remained in touch with Bonita until he passed away in 2020 from respiratory failure, but her resilience and work always inspired him. He attended every show he could that she put off and often traversed back down to New York to assist her when needed.

Dean died a single man but a beloved man who had impacted the lives of so many of our fashion icons today. He played a small role in so many avenues of the fashion world, some of which he received accreditation for and some he did not.

His funeral was a loving memorial of his wisdom, sharp eye, and keen fashion sense. People traveled from all over the world to pay their respects to this understated legend, just before the world was shut down.

Marcus Hannigan a.k.a Ivana Cox

Marcus after years working in private practice servicing the gay community of New York turned his attention to opening a youth centre on the lower east side for the displaced and often overlooked 2SLGBTQIA+ children. He used his knowledge, resources and money to help positively impact hundreds of lives.

Marcus' alter ego, Ivana finally won a Miss Continental Pageant after many years of runner ups. A title, she held with pride. All her outfits used to compete were designed by her friend, Bonita Smith. While Bonita's brand was world renowned, she was never too busy to take care of her first client and often used her platform to promote and fundraise for Marcus' youth centre.

Benjamin Ryder

Benjamin has had what he would categorize as the most unexpectedly fulfilling life he could ever have imagined. He married the woman of his dreams, moved out of the city, and became a father and a successful suburban house dad. He handled all the particulars that were not design-related regarding his wife's fashion line, the marketing, and trade worldwide.

He worked for a couple of big players at the beginning of their life together, but after they had their first child, Tyler, he felt that he could contribute more at home because her work took a great degree of energy. After several conversations and working out the details of the way forward, he left the workforce to partner with his wife. His focus would be on the shows and the marketing, but that required minimal hours. His primary focus was on his wife and helping raise their children. This life was not what he had envisioned for himself, but it was a life he loved.

He and Claude became close and considered him a part of the family and an uncle to his children. He enjoyed the variety he experienced daily, and his children had the most opposing personalities possible. It kept things interesting.

As for his wife, Bonita, his heart would still stutter when he looked at her. It was the strangest thing; every time he kissed her, it felt like the first time, but that 'home' feeling still holds true. Over the years, he wondered what would have happened if he hadn't stumble on the three girls in the loading dock that night and hadn't found Bonita's collection. Would he still have ended up with her? Would she still have fallen in love with him?

As he sits waiting for his wife to come home from her day in the city, he leans back in his chair and smiles. It doesn't matter what could have been; it only matters what was. He has built a life so rich with love, friends, and family that he could only believe that it was destined to be her and him. No matter what happened, they would have found each other.

It was almost time to get the kids bathed and ready for the big celebration they had planned for Bonita's latest project.

Claire Foster

Retired now and living in Spain, Claire often enjoys the warm weather with her much younger boyfriend, Julio. She decided she would go after the house in Spain, after all. Her ex didn't want to give it up, but she knew just where to hit to make him give in.

You see, Claire was an intelligent woman and ensured that many of their assets were evenly distributed throughout her marriage. One in particular allowed her to see all of his business dealings. Some of which were not above board. Now, the likelihood that he would do jail time was minimal, but he could lose his reputation, pride, and toys; it would do that.

So, a final phone call after he stated he wouldn't budge on the house left him pleading for her to take it. She reminded him to be nice to her, to keep his nose clean, and never miss one of Bon Bon's orders.

Now retired, living in Spain, with the handsome gentleman Bonita and her friend Claude introduced her to, she couldn't be happier. Her professional life was left on a high; she had brought in the highest-selling line that Mackie's had ever had. The exclusive rights deal was a spark of genius, and it worked well for her, the company, and Bonita.

She keeps in constant contact with Bonita, as they have become quite close throughout the years. She thinks of her as a daughter she never had.

She is currently getting her shoulders rubbed by her lover. He is such an attractive and doting young man, attentive and kind. He is incredibly intelligent and business savvy; he and her spend a few hours consulting for businesses in Spain weekly. It is hard for her to believe he was a doorman at Bonita's old apartment complex. It really goes to show you can't judge a book by its cover. Everyone has to work.

Pastor Earl and Paula Smith

Earl and Paula have since retired from the ministry; they were getting older and decided to be closer to their daughter and grandbabies. Bonita and Benjamin bought a house in Bay Roberts and would come home occasionally to let the kids roam free. After a while, however, that wasn't enough.

They decided to look at houses in New York State, not near the city. It was too much for them, but perhaps an hour or so outside. This way, they could still see their family when they wanted. Bonita was immediately on board with this idea, so she found an immigration lawyer and started looking for the perfect house for her parents.

It took roughly two years, but her parents were now living a fifty-minute drive from their Staten Island home. It took Earl and Paula a long time to settle, find a new church, and get their bearings in a new country and town. Benjamin was quite helpful in that regard and helped them as much as possible.

After a while, they learned to love their new home and couldn't have been more thrilled about being so close to the grandchildren, especially with the last one being on the way. They recognized that they lived a very sheltered life back home in Newfoundland and had a lot of judgments about things they didn't understand. With Bonita moving to the city and finding success, they were forced out of their comfort zones a few times and realized that their judgments were just that.

Her father gave a sermon at the new church. He wasn't the pastor there, just a congregation member, but he helped when he could. His sermon spoke of the closed mind, which doesn't serve the lord. If Christians are to be more like Christ, our minds must be open and tolerant and not judge what we don't understand. Every person we judge is just another woman at the well. Benjamin and Bonita bring their kids to church three or four times a year.

Bonita Ryder

As Bonita rides home on the ferry, she can't help but be overjoyed by the life she has made. This next adventure came about when the pandemic hit, and she found herself at home looking for things to keep her mind busy when she wasn't preoccupied with her family.

She had pulled down a few boxes from the attic and found her old journals, sketches, notes, and sentimentals and began reflecting on the life that she had lived. When she started, all she had was determination; she didn't know a damn thing except that she wanted to be a fashion designer, and nothing was going to stop her.

Reading back through her journals, she realized how lost she was in the first three years after high school and how lucky she was to have had the experiences and the people she got to have them with. What started to formulate was a series of life lessons in her mind, a recap of her life in snippets. One evening, when she couldn't sleep, worried about the state of affairs the world was in, she found herself in front of her computer. An open word document, the cursor flashing.

She began to write anecdotes at first, but as she progressed, she began to realize her story, hopes, dreams, and mistakes. What started as an attempt to cull her weary mind became a manuscript. After twenty-plus rewrites and two years later, she realized that she had a body of work that wasn't fashion but was about fashion. More specifically, it was about the artfulness of experience and how each one was a singular thread in the garment of life. You can't make a garment with one piece of thread, but you can make something extraordinary with fabric that thread can weave.

Every word, thought, action, choice, experience, failure, and win come together to weave a unique fabric only known to you. The more time passes, the more it begins to take shape with each stitch. Unless you are a person who lives life with exact precision, most often, the form it takes is not precisely how you envisioned it. However, it is still beautiful because your hands, skill, mind, and heart created it stitch by stitch.

As Bonita stands at the edge of the railing watching the ferry approach Staten Island, she begins tracing her fingers over the cover of her book. It was released for publication today, March 30th, 2024. The book's title is raised against the glossy stock, and she smiles. She could not think of a better way than to have lived her life but to have lived it as a "Life In Stitches."

Acknowledgements

To my parents, whom I may not see eye-to-eye, and who will never read this book, thank you for loving me the best way you know how. I wouldn't trade you for all the money in the world.

To my sister, Rebecca, my sweet, sweet sister. God knew what he was doing when he paired you with me. We are incredibly different, but our shared uniqueness bonds us together. You are a never-ending inspiration of love and kindness, a beacon of constant hope. Thank you for your blind devotion and support for our entire lives. Thank you for your excellent work on the cover of this book.

To my best friend Cindy, you have been and will always be a guidepost in this dark world. Thank you for teaching me what unconditional love was and for being in my corner through thick and thin. I wouldn't be here today if it weren't for you. Thank you for being present through every iteration of this project for the last fifteen years.

To my best friend, Ludovic, you showed me how it felt to have two individuals who could love and support me endlessly. Your friendship has only come along in the last five years but has made me a better human. Thank you for showing me who you are.

I have been blessed in life to have not one but two best friends, both so uniquely different, both being my favorite extensions of myself. Thank you immeasurably for your love, friendship, support and encouragement.

To Nick, Karen, and Regina, the family card nights, the great food, the ease and comfort are constant reminders that people can accept others for exactly who they are. Thank you for making space at your table.